Baby Momma 2

Baby Momma 2

Ni'chelle Genovese

www.urbanbooks.net

Urban Books, LLC
97 N18th Street
Wyandanch, NY 11798

Baby Momma 2 Copyright © 2013
Ni'chelle Genovese

ISBN 13: 978-1-60162-641-7
ISBN 10: 1-60162-641-X

First Mass Market Printing November 2014
First Trade Paperback Printing March 2013
Printed in the United States of America

10 9 8 7 6 5 4 3 2 1

This is a work of fiction. Any references or similarities to actual events, real people, living or dead, or to real locales are intended to give the novel a sense of reality. Any similarity in other names, characters, places, and incidents is entirely coincidental.

Distributed by Kensington Publishing Corp.
Submit Wholesale Orders to:
Kensington Publishing Corp.
C/O Penguin Group (USA) Inc.
Attention: Order Processing
405 Murray Hill Parkway
East Rutherford, NJ 07073-2316
Phone: 1-800-526-0275
Fax: 1-800-227-9604

Dedicated to Yvetta Tonia.

*All too often we don't recognize the Angels
that have been placed in our lives until
they're gone . . .*

ACKNOWLEDGMENTS

It's funny because I used to complain about never getting any sleep, and now I never complain because it's my dream that keeps me awake. To the Creator of all things including this wonderful talent that I've been blessed with—I give God all the glory.

There was shock and awe the first time around and now I'm just happy knowing I've made you both so very proud—to my parents, Haywood and Cheryl Boyd, you set me loose into the world scared that I wasn't ready . . . and um I think it's safe to finally say it's the world that you should have been more worried about. I love you both so very very much.

My adopted big bro, mentor, manager, coconspirator, spiritual warfare counselor, financial advisor lol! You have too many titles for me to list them all! Maurice Tonia, I love you and thank you for the idea and the foundation that started it all—you made the impossible a possibility and then together we turned it into a reality.

Acknowledgments

My Sunshine Tiffany Wynn and My Smoochie Katey Kocsis I owe you both a world of thank-you's for all the inspiration, patience, and the distractions even when I should've been writing. <3

Author Dahni McPhail, aka Dj Sporty—I've got so much love and respect for you, you are one of the most creative and multifaceted people I know and I'm happy to step aside and watch you take off, it's definitely your time. Iisha, Pk Allday, Christie, Angel—thank you all for accepting me with open arms. I owe all of my Bruncher's a huge thank you for all the warmth and support, oh yeah and the crazy adventures.

Brandy V., Beverly H., Keshara, Stephanie P., Gwennetta aka my Gigi, y'all all kept me from going crazy in between those three walls of my cubicle on more than one occasion. Marie H., thank you all for your friendship and understanding. My literary agent, Joylynn, thank you for keeping me on track.

To my oh so supportive FB fam Lana, Eve, Detra, Velma, Terricka, Jina, Mrs. Stephanie H.L., Leslie H.J., Shatika, Jerrell, Elmyra, Dawnsheika, Marissa, Deirdra, Aray, Lanika, Shannon, Kristine, Anoosha, Brandi, Sonya, Penny, Shauna, Lakesha and the Diamond Divas Book Club, Keyiona and Angie B's Reading Between the Lines book club in Cincinnati. Everyone that's shown their support I <3 you all. Ni'chelle G.

Follow me on Twitter @NichelleG4.

Everything I do is for Jazmyn. Montre. Bryce. Asia. Kailah. Techa aka Westside Carman Ayala and Carol Mackey of Black Expression book club my two BFF for life. To all my sisters & FB friends: To Sissy Tonya Clay. Saran Day. Gwen. Cherly. Erica. LeQuisha. Brooke Taylor. Tia Pic. Mishelle. NiQua. Latoya. Glynnis Tasha Felder. Tracy Jeter. Renay. Mellissa. Latoya. Andrea, aka Miss Sunshine. Mocha. Connie. Helena. QuTasha. Carlene. Anza. Marissa Palmer. Jennifer of NJ. Pansy. Michelle Rawls. Jatoria, aka LuxHair. Adina. Tasha Powell. Renatta. Tara. Rashida Elisha, my Jersey sis. Shanell Red, one of the best songwriters in the world, thank U for all the advice. Darren Hicks & Tish, thank U. To my brothers. Governor. Moosh. Mark. TKO. Shawn Clay. Marysol, aka Ms Latin. Stephanie. Juilia McElligott. Tracey Jenkins. Albert. T-Black Big Mike. Gary. Larry Jr. & Toya Tonia. To my wife, I don't need to say a word just "I Love You."

RIP Yvetta Tonia: When I thought God couldn't hear my voice, she prayed for me. When everyone turned their back, she stayed with me. When I failed, she stood for me. When I felt suffocated, she breathed for me. When I felt like nothing, I was her everything. *She is everything to me.*

An extra special thank you to the cast and crew of Baby Momma The Movie:

Techa Lewis, Malcom L Banks II, Michael Taylor Ross, Renatta Nicole Spann, Lennel Hall, Ben Lane, Nina McAlpin, Michael D. Ballard, Evelynn Danh Makanaakua, Deontae Marico Harris, Tia Cherrice, Essence Allen, and Victorye Pulliam.

PROLOGUE

"I hate this picture, Chelle; it look like I'm cock-eyed or somethin'."

We were sitting in first class, ready to start our flight from Virginia to Fort Lauderdale, Florida. Taking her driver's license from her I glanced at the photo, and handed it back. "You look fine, baby. Stop bein' so dramatic; ain't nothing wrong with that picture."

"Larissa Laurel. I do like our new last name though. It looks like I could be a model or a actress, some kinda shit you would see on the big screen. . . ." Her voice trailed off.

My mind wandered. It had been roughly three months since the day I'd visited Rasheed in prison to tell him what had happened and, after that, we'd packed up all of our shit and we were getting the hell out of Virginia for good. No looking back and no second thoughts. I glanced over to make sure the baby was still asleep, since we'd just taken off. I didn't want to be the woman with the loud-ass kids up in first class. She was unconscious, and Trey was busy with a pile of Goldfish—he'd be quiet until they disappeared.

I stared at my reflection in the window, my hazel eyes becoming part of one of the clouds and staring back at me. *Who am I?* Michelle Roberts—no, Michelle Laurel—a mother, wife, a heroine, or a monster . . .

"You ain't heard nothin' I been sayin', have you?"

I looked up. I couldn't lie; I hadn't heard a single thing. Ris could go on and on about any- and everything, and I zoned out so much it's a wonder she'd even talk to me sometimes.

"I'm sorry, baby, I was thinking about all the stuff we have to do once we get to the new house. You need a car, the kids need new clothes. I've got the new business starting up, and if this first buy goes through it could make it so neither of us has to work for anyone ever again, but then I'd have to start lookin' into staffing and building a client base—"

"Well I was *sayin'* we should decorate the house in Wang Chung." She rolled her eyes at me and popped her tongue.

I was looking at her like she was crazy, trying to interpret whatever the hell it was she'd mis-interpreted, so I could figure out what she was talkin' about. I couldn't help laughing at her faux pas. "You wanna decorate the house in what? Don't you mean feng shui?"

"Ain't that what the hell I said? Anyway, I was lookin' at this show an' they was talkin' 'bout all the shit that it's good for like wealth an'. . ."

She went on like she hadn't heard anything that I'd just said.

I rubbed my eyes; they were feeling tired and dry from the hours of researching and reading I'd been doing over the last few weeks. I'd been busy starting my own real estate company on top of getting our shit packed and making sure everything went through with adopting the baby and having her name changed with our name changes. The prison was telling me the child's name was Paris and, um, I was not having that shit. Lataya Katrice Laurel was a beautiful name for a beautiful little girl and, since I'd always wanted a daughter, she was the perfect fit for our little family. From day one, I'd been treating her as if she were my own.

I couldn't wait to finally get to a place that we could call home that didn't have any bad memories, or a bunch of bad vibes attached to it. Everything in Virginia felt tainted in some way, shape, or form. We couldn't go eat at Rockafeller's because Rah used to take me there and Ris would get all types of jealous. Then, we'd have an issue over something simple and she'd say, "The only reason you ordered that is 'cause he always ordered that shit. Why you can't try somethin' different?"

My answer to that would be, "Maybe it's because I just like this shit and don't want anything different."

My statement would then be followed by Ris slamming down her menu and staring at me. Her eyes would have that "ready to fight" glow and she'd say, "Nah, I jus' think you miss that nigga."

And *bam:* a fight over something as simple as dinner.

We couldn't eat at IHOP because Rah used to take Honey, and Lord knows who else, up in there and then I would start to feel some kind of way, wondering which waitresses knew he was there with which skank. I knew I shouldn't think like that about Lataya's birth mother and call her a skank, God rest her soul. But still, it bothered me knowing some of those people there knew he had a family at home and not only watched him, but *encouraged* him in his bullshit; parading them hoes around town, fuckin' whichever one was the flavor of the moment. Yes, a change was definitely going to do the entire family some good.

I didn't tell Larissa that, as part of the surprise, I'd already had the house decorated but, maybe, we could take everything out of one room and decorate it "Wang Chung" style just for her. I giggled to myself again for that one, besides it was a big-ass house we would grow into. It was way too big for just the four of us right now but when I saw it I knew it was perfect. There was a playroom for the kids with this beautiful jungle mural painted on the walls and ceiling, with monkeys swinging from the trees and a giraffe. The kids would be in awe. I had a library that I couldn't wait to fill up with all kinds of books, and a pool to swim in. It had all that fancy shit that neither of us grew up with. We'd have it all from now on if I could help it and we both deserved it so much. My family wasn't going to want for anything because I planned on doing *everything* in my power to see us all well taken care of.

CHAPTER 1

HOME INVASION

(2 years later . . .)

Glancing down at my iPhone calendar, I checked my itinerary one last time. I could still show the Matthews property, finish up the paperwork, and make the forty-five-minute drive home in time for dinner. I pulled my all-black Lexus ES350 into the large circular driveway, careful not to scratch my rims on the damn rounded curb as I parked. Last time Larissa drove my car she curb-checked the hell out of the left side and I still cringed whenever I thought about what it cost to replace just two of those Lexanis.

The mansion loomed before me, picture perfect, like something straight out of a movie. Sand-colored cobblestone led the path toward the massive oak front doors. I grabbed up my things, deciding, instead, to take the long way around the back of the house. This way I could personally make sure the new landscaping company we were using was on point. It was the minor details that meant everything to the people who bought these types of homes and I had no intention of missing out on a major sale over a fuckery and bullshit minor technicality.

Everything looked in order. The hedges were trimmed into neat, identical squares and the thick carpet of lush green lawn was cut and edged beautifully. Small palms lined both sides of the large backyard overlooking the ginormous pool and Jacuzzi. It was early June and nearly eighty degrees out, and the water looked all too inviting. I didn't think I'd ever adjust to the difference between eighty degrees in Florida and eighty degrees in Virginia. My blouse was already starting to stick to my back from the humidity and the moisture in the air. At least in Virginia we had dry heat; this damp hotness was for the birds. I walked past a flowering bush. Its scent immediately reminded me of the Botanical Garden and instantly I knew why this was one of my favorite estates. It had that *Alice in Wonderland* kind of feeling, like at any moment a little rabbit wearing a Queen of Hearts jacket would come running out from in between the shrubs to offer me a drink. I laughed to myself. I wasn't sure exactly what it was but the place just felt like it could be home.

I let myself in through the back door into the kitchen. I paused mid-step, head tilted to one side. *What the hell?* I knew, too well, what it sounded like when a woman was gettin' the business, and Lord knows I heard what sounded like heavy breathin' and the soft telltale moans of a woman obviously lost in the type of passion that makes you not care who's listenin'. I gently laid my leopard-print Pineider Cavallino briefcase on the granite kitchen counter. My Mace was in a small, light brown leather clip attached to the side that slid off almost effortlessly. I removed it and silently made my way toward the sound.

Here I was, Gretel following a breadcrumb trail of hastily shed clothing. All these fairy tale analogies—whew, I'd definitely been reading way too many bedtime stories to the kids. Red pumps, Michael Kors loafers, black tube top, Rock & Republic jeggings; all items that led me from the kitchen down across the foyer to the double winding staircase. I was in stealth mode, creeping along on my toes, heels never touching the floor for fear of the click-clack alerting the intruders to my presence and ruining my element of surprise. I gripped my Mace tightly in my hand.

I was greeted at the top of the carpeted stair-well by a black and grey Burberry button down and Armani slacks. Somebody had good taste in clothes and by the sounds coming from the cracked door a few feet in front of me, it didn't stop there. My pulse quickened as I edged toward the door. Greedily my eyes took in the display of what a bitch can only describe as masculine perfection. Unconsciously, I licked my lips as I followed a trail of sweat that ran down his spine and pooled in the small of his back. For a moment I was lost in a voyeuristic fantasy. I could hear him accenting each pump with a word.

"Say. You. Want. This. Dick."

The nigga was workin' it. A dull ache started in between my own legs and my hand flew to cover my pussy out of some stupid fear that he'd actually hear it screamin' back, "I want it!" I couldn't see shit but two thin, stork-like legs poking out from either side of his hips, the black down comforter on the bed being so thick and all. I wouldn't have known there was a woman beneath him if it weren't for her pencil legs and loud porn star–sounding moans.

I hadn't been with a man sexually in what seemed like forever, maybe three years; hadn't looked at one, hadn't thought about one. Damn sure hadn't desired one—until now.

Months of faking and falling asleep unsatisfied had brought me to this moment. Ris and I were at that point where the spark was kinda gone out of our situation. My ass was bored. I was tempted to start moving my fingers. Use this as a chance to release all my pent-up frustration. I glanced down at my watch: 2:45 p.m. My three o'clock appointment would be here at any moment and I definitely had no time for this bullshit. I needed to straighten up the mess these fools were making before my client arrived. After one last longing gaze I straightened up my blazer, patted my bun, and stepped into the room, clearing my throat.

I wasn't sure what was more alarming: the fact that I was now no more than an arm's reach away, or that he looked directly at me and didn't even miss a stroke. I bit my lower lip. The nigga had the sexiest almond-shaped brown eyes. They glowed like golden coals against his dark skin. *Damn.* I was not expecting that. His eyes focused in on mine in an almost predatory manner. He visually drank me in and suddenly I was the recipient of each thrust. We were pretty much eye fuckin' right now for lack of anything else to call it. I felt parts of me start to awaken and throb in such a way that my ass was scared to keep watching and too damn fascinated to turn away.

The woman, now more clearly visible, seemed oddly familiar. Her head was thrown back, eyes closed tight in ecstasy. She was so thin and palely light skinned beneath his thick, muscular frame that it looked like he was splitting her in half. *Double damn!* Dazed, my nipples hardened beneath my blouse as he lowered his head and flecked his tongue across her barely there breasts, her physique embarrassingly boyish compared to mine. It was as if my body had a mind of its own and even though my brain was saying, *girl, go,* I was glued to the floor. My nostrils involuntarily flared and I felt myself slowly coming to life as blood rushed to my most sensitive parts. I could smell his sweat and her wetness, all mingling with the woodsy aroma of the $4,000 cherry nightstand in the corner that I'd just had unpacked yesterday, and *him.*

As if splashed with cold water my body jolted back to reality. I only knew *one* mu'fucka who wore Issey Miyake and now the scent alone brought to mind entirely too many bad memories. I snapped out of my daze and cleared my throat again, loudly this time.

"Excuse me, you need to get out of here before I call the police."

Hearing my voice, the woman sprang to an upright position, resting on her elbows, pulling the comforter up to cover herself. I recognized her almost immediately: Yylannia Besore. She was one of the hottest models out right now, half black and French, or something like that—I couldn't remember. But, I'd seen her a hundred times in the latest magazines and commercials. I couldn't believe she'd appear so boyish and lanky in person. She was nothing like the sexual vixen she appeared to be on camera but, lo and behold, I guessed that's what the wonders of makeup and Photoshop could do for a person.

"Where the fuck did *she* come from?" Yylannia was trying to untangle herself from the statuesque man who had her pinned in place.

He sat back on his haunches with a sigh of frustration and obvious resentment at my intrusion, allowing her to scamper off the bed and quickly dart past me to grab her things and get dressed.

My eyes molested him from the neck downward. Huge pecs lightly dusted with soft, straight dark hair that narrowed into a thin line as it ran downward in between tight abs and . . .

"You couldn't have waited jus' li'l bit longer huh?"

I jerked myself back to reality. My head whipped up so fast I was surprised it didn't make the snap noise like in one of those old-school kung fu movies. His voice was deep, unbelievably deep. It sounded like warm honey to my ears.

"No, and you need to put some fire to ya ass an' get outta here before I call the police."

The cologne he wore made me dislike him immediately. But his sex appeal was making my psyche do a double take. He reminded me of a large cat as he fluidly uncoiled himself from the bed. *Sway-backed nigga.* The curve in his lower back was so over-pronounced and the muscles in his ass so tight and high the image of a gorilla came to mind. He was thick as hell and sexy as fuck. Right about now, I could use a good gorilla fuck. I almost laughed out loud at the thought. Lord, I was definitely trippin'. He was a dark chocolate version of Leonidas from that movie *300*. My son, Trey, must have made me watch that movie a million times, and the only reason I could sit through it over and over again was because of all the beautifully built men who'd be on the damn TV screen.

Oh yes, he could've definitely passed for an ancient Spartan warrior. He had straight black hair, a Caesar low cut, long, thick sideburns that tapered beneath his chin into a thick, full beard. It highlighted the fullness of his pink lips and gave him an almost dangerous appeal. He picked his boxers up from beside the bed and slid them on. I tried not to smile because, despite my intrusion and threats, he was still standing at full, and I mean *full,* attention. Damn, it had to be painful for him to try to restrain all that behind nothing but a little tight wall of cotton.

"So, let me take a guess. You must be Michelle right?"

My eyes widened in surprise at the sound of my name flowing from Leonidas's beautiful, made-for-pussy-licking lips. *Whew.* I needed to calm down. *How does this fool know my name?*

"Um, yes. And who might you be?" Suspicion immediately made my tone sharp; I couldn't imagine anyone who looked like him actually knowing me.

"Key! I'ma go wait in the damn car!" Yylannia shrieked from somewhere downstairs.

Suddenly, I didn't need an answer. He was Keyshawn Matthews, the superstar rookie drafted to play for Miami. I hadn't noticed how exceptionally tall he was but I now felt dwarfed standing across from him, and I was close to five feet eleven without heels. I could feel my cheeks starting to get hot; my grown ass actually started blushing.

"Mr. Matthews? I . . . I am so sorry. I had no idea you even had a key to view the property. I guess you, um, you like it?" Here I was talking to one of the richest and probably most famous men in the NBA, and he was standing in nothing but his drawers! Ris was definitely not gonna believe this shit. *Oh hell, best to not even tell Ris; she'd probably get jealous and start trippin' any damn way.* He flashed me a dazzling white smile displaying perfect deep dimples and straight white teeth.

"Yeah, I was testin' the place out. My agent got me the key earlier. I parked in the garage. I'm lovin' all the space but the acoustics in this mu'fucka ain't right."

I raised an eyebrow, immediately puzzled. I had no idea what acoustics meant outside of a home theatre or studio. What did acoustics have to do with . . . "Wait, acoustics?"

I knew this nigga wasn't saying what I thought he was saying. The house we were in was one of the most sought after and high priced on the market. Fridays were my busiest days and I'd turned down two other closings and come out to show the property personally because Key's agent swore up and down he wanted to buy and close today. I owned High Rise Estates, the second-largest real estate agency in Fort Lauderdale, and I *only* came out to do closings. Most of our clients were usually in the market for their third or fourth vacation home and I left the aggravating task of showing property after property to the finicky doctors, starlets, and athletes in the area to my staff.

"Yeah, the acoustics is on some mute 'n' shit. I like to *hear* how good it feels when I'm puttin' in work. Jus' somethin' that's important to me. You wouldn't understand though. So, what's next?"

I stared in disbelief. This was that minor detail fuckery and bullshit I mentioned earlier. This fool done lost his damn mind if he was thinking I was gonna let him run his ass through house after house, fuckin' in staged bedrooms and messing up designer linens! I was on the verge of puttin' him on full blast, potentially losing a client and a sale, but I was saved by my iPhone, which had started ringing downstairs.

"I need to get that. You might wanna go ahead an' put your damn clothes back on in the meantime." Turning with a look of pure disgust, I rushed downstairs to answer my phone.

"Hi, Ris. Everything okay?" I breathed heavily into the phone.

"Hey, bae. E'rething's good. Why you breathin' so hard? What you doin'?"

"Nothing, I'm showing a property. Ran to grab my phone."

"Oh, well, when you comin' home so I know when to have dinner ready?"

I couldn't believe she was calling me during a showing to ask something like this. "Ris. Same time I always get home. Five-ish. Why, do you need me to pick somethin' up?" I was trying to make the convo quick since Keyshawn had just walked into the kitchen to put on his shoes. I didn't want him eavesdropping on my conversation. I pressed the volume down on the side of the phone just as Ris gave away the real reason for her call.

"Chelle, we need to talk when you get here. I jus' got this feelin'. I mean . . ."

Damn, here we go again. I could feel the aggravation creeping up the back of neck, causing my teeth to clench. Every other day Larissa seemed to "have a feelin'."

"Larissa, I will call you when I'm on my way home. I don't have time to talk about this with you again." I softened my tone in an attempt to soothe her. "I'm showin' a property right now, baby. Okay?"

She sighed loudly and was quiet for a moment before speaking. "Okay. I love you—my wife."

Damn it. She *only* did that wife shit when she thought I was talking around someone else. "I luh you too. My wifey." I tried to say it as quickly as possible but I knew he'd heard.

I ended the call and silently cursed. She was really driving me crazy with all her insecurities. Every time I left the house, or needed to run an errand, she was overly paranoid about me cheating on her, or going to meet someone else. Marrying her hadn't changed a thing; if anything it seemed like it'd made things worse.

"Damn, lemme find out yo' fine ass into chicks." Keyshawn was leaning on the kitchen counter with his chin in his hands, like we were best friends hanging out on a summer afternoon, talking over martinis.

I would have been mad at him listening if he weren't flashing the most beautiful smile in my direction, dimples and all. In that moment my heart skipped a beat and my body secretly, against my free will, betrayed my wife. I glanced at my watch and then back at the nigga in front of me, who was unknowingly making me grind my teeth and do my Kegels at the same time.

"An' happily married, Negro. Don't try to change the subject. So you don't want this estate now, huh?" I couldn't help feeling drawn into his playful manner and I leaned on the counter opposite him, mimicking his posture. "If you *really* knew how to make a woman scream, acoustics would be the least of your worries, playboy." I flashed a dazzling smile back in his direction and we shared a laugh.

"Ma, I promise, married or not, no woman can take you where a nigga can. I ain't talkin' 'bout no bullshit-ass plastic dick. I'm talkin' flesh and blood. It ain't the same. An' the acoustics, FYI, is to maximize the sound in the bedroom *without* wakin' up my houseguests or neighbors."

I mentally shook my head at myself. That actually shut my ass up. I didn't even have a comeback. The way Ris would let go and wake up the kids made me think about looking into soundproofing for my damn self. He was both disarming and charismatic. This was dangerous. I had a business to run, and if this fool wasn't making me any money he definitely wasn't worth my time.

"Well, I'll have one of my realtors follow up with you and offer several other properties that may better suit your standards, Mr. Matthews. In the meantime, I would suggest you inspect the properties clothed and in a respectable manner. Oh, and should the issue arise, jus' invest in soundproofing *after* you acquire the property, sir." I grabbed my things and approached the front door, intent on getting away from this man and his magnetic pull as fast as humanly possible. My hand was on the latch but the door wouldn't budge.

"What if I only wanna deal wi'chu?"

I hadn't even heard him come up behind me. His voice cascaded down the back of my neck in heated waves that coursed down my body and crashed into the ocean between my legs. Goosebumps rose on my arms and time seemed to stand still as his question floated between us. His hand was planted firmly on the door just above my head; no wonder I couldn't pull it open. He was so close behind me. I could feel a wall of heat along the back of my body as he leaned over me, waiting for my answer, expecting me to react like every other woman who had probably given in to his good looks and sex appeal.

"My wife is crazy as hell, and I think you've got enough on your plate to keep you occupied. I have police-grade Mace. Move, or I'll use it." I held my breath, silently wishing this were a different time, or I were a different me. He was a ride I couldn't afford to take right now.

Reluctantly, his hand slid from the door. I heard him take a step back.

"Ol' girl out there, she ain' nothin' but arm candy. But you, you naturally beautiful wit' all that real hair. Yeah, I can tell, an' I appreciate it. Your wife got e're right to be crazy, 'cause I honestly don't think you into that dikin' shit a hundred percent. I'll see you soon, Michelle."

CHAPTER 2

HOME GROWN

I was bored outta my damn mind. Chelle was always at work or wherever doin' who- or whatever and I was stuck up in here all day every day with the damn kids. The two of them were runnin' around the house, actin' like they were losin' they damn minds, fighting over every single solitary thing. There was nothing for me to do and I was gettin' restless as hell and the kids were startin' to work my damn nerves. I threw down the magazine I was trying to read, only making it halfway through the article on how to tell if your man was cheating. No, I ain't had no man. I just switched all the "if he's" doing this or that et cetera shit to "if she's," and damn if Michelle wasn't fitting the descriptions to a muthafuckin' T.

Lately she'd been working late with special clients on special closings, or taking longer to get home than usual. When we made love—hell I couldn't even call it that—it was more on some "I serve you until I'm bored, okay switch, now you do me" boring-ass shit. Nothing like when we first got together. Everything that damn magazine said was exactly what was going on in our house. *An' I be givin' her ass every opportunity to just tell me she seeing someone else but, like a muthafuckin' nigga, she refuse an' claims nothin's up.* You know how that shit goes. Deny, deny, deny 'til you die type shit. She could probably get caught in the act, dick or pussy in her mouth, ass, or whatever, and still be like, "Baby, it ain't what you think."

Pain shot through my foot; glancin' down, I got even more pissed off as I pulled one of Trey's Legos from underneath it. "Trey, stop chasin' yo' fuckin' sister an' come pick up these damn toys. I done told you 'bout leavin' these damn things all ova' the fuckin' place. I'ma start throwin' 'em away. Try me, li'l nigga." I stared his li'l lazy ass down while he picked 'em up slow as hell one by fuckin' one.

I did not sign up for this shit. I needed to be doing something with myself, running a business, keeping my mind busy earning myself some damn money. I hated dependin' on Michelle for every damn dime I wanted to spend. If it wasn't for the fact that we were basically in a self-induced witness protection program I could easily go out an' get myself some kind of work, but it was just easier if we kept people out of our shit. Daycares, constant babysitters, they all had questions and needed more info than she or I wanted to give.

I needed to talk to a damn adult. All this kiddy shit was getting to my ass. I pulled my cell out of my back pocket and called my cousin back home in Detroit: the only person I trusted.

"Girl, what da fuck you ova' there doin'?" I asked playfully as soon as she picked up. I was jus' glad she ain't let me go to voice mail. When we left Virginia, Michelle insisted we cut everyone off, but I couldn't let my entire family jus' think I'd off and died or disappeared. My cousin, Shanice, was the only person I trusted enough to still keep in contact with.

"Hey, boobie, I miss yo' li'l crazy ass. You lovin' dat married life yet?" She was being sarcastic as usual. She always was a smart ass.

"I don't even wanna go into the details. I think she seein' that muthafucka again or a new somebody. I ain't figured it out yet, but when I do it's gon' be on."

"Larissa, you ain't marry dat bitch jus' to have her doin' all the same shit. Check her ass, fo' I come out there an' check her for you. Paper or no paper all that extra shit ain't worth it."

I sighed into the phone; she had a point. It wasn't worth it and I knew it. After all of these years of loving Michelle and only Michelle it was finally starting to break me down. It's like how they say a tiny stream of water can eventually wear down a mountain until there's nothing left but a flat piece of land and a river. Well my love at one point was that mountain but all these doubts and fears been wearin' and tearin' away at that mountain for so long that we were on the verge of bein' completely torn apart and wiped away.

"Shanice, you've known me my entire life. I think this the longest my ass eva' been straight-up, flat-out sober. Hell, I don't even drink like that no more. The stress an' these kids, all this shit is startin' to get to me."

"Bitch, a blunt ain't neva' hurt shit. My ass ain't neva' heard of a mu'fucka bitin' nobody face off 'cause they was smokin' on some purp'." She was talkin' 'bout the recent drug shit that'd happened down in Miami. Niggas snortin' bath salts or whatever and eatin' other nigga's faces and brains *while the nigga was still alive* on some for real zombie-type shit.

"Girl, I tried to tell Michelle we need to get our asses the fuck up outta here before da Zombie Apocalypse start, an dat heffa told me stop watchin' da damn horror channel. You an' me bof know—don't *no* black folk do no shit like that, an' especially not off no damn weed. Hell, you don't even do nothin' close to that off a bad crack rock."

"True, bitch, *that is so got-damn true,*" Shanice yelled in my ear in agreement and we both fell out laughin'.

Most of my life I'd had a problem with various drugs from crack to cocaine, you name it. Michelle was on some warden-type shit right now. I could barely sniff a glass of wine without her looking at me sideways, getting all weary and talkin' to me in her "house nigga" voice. I could hear saying, "Look nah, Risi-cup, you done made it dis far now, an' ya knows what dey says 'bout stayin' strong an' takin' one day at a time."

Ugh.

"You ever grow that Chia Pet I sent yo' ass?" Shanice was gigglin' in the phone like a straight-up little girl.

"Girl, what da hell I'ma do wit' a damn . . ." I stopped, realizing what she was saying before I could even finish my sentence. "Shanice, you didn't."

"Yup. Dat last package I sent you. Li'l Mr. Ch-Ch-Ch-Chia had a present inside his ass. I hope yo' ass ain't throw him away."

I didn't think I'd felt this damn happy the entire time I'd been in Florida. I'd gone to the post office one day and set myself up a post office box so I could have things shipped without my "warden" all in my business. I laughed and thought the Chia Pet was cute when I saw it.

"Girl, I go'sta go. Hell naw, I ain't throw it away, it's somewhere in the damn garage. Hell Ch-Ch-Ch-Chyeah!" I rushed my black ass off the phone so fast I ain't even say bye.

"Trey, Taya, go lay y'all's asses down, it's damn naptime," I shouted up toward their playroom, satisfied when I heard the pitter-patter of they bad asses running to get in their beds. I needed to figure out exactly where the hell I'd stuck that damn package because apparently it had some extra shit up in it and I *needed* that in my life right now. It would be easier to figure out how I was going to talk to this woman, aka my so-called wife, about this new shit that popped up in our situation if I was at least a little lifted.

CHAPTER 3

JUST A FRIENDLY REMINDER

Traffic was backed up on the I-95 expressway in both directions. Cursing to myself I dialed the house phone. Something told me I should've just gone straight home after meeting with Key. It was already going on six and Larissa was probably jumping to all kinds of conclusions. Times like this made me miss Virginia; at least there I could hop on the midtown or downtown tunnel and be home in twenty minutes, or get off on any of the side streets and still be there like it was nothing. Not here; I had to cut clear across town to get back home, and this shit this time of year with the tourists and the locals trying to get in and out of town was insane.

"Hey." She picked up and that one word said it all: short and shitty mad.

"Baby, I'm stuck in traffic on the highway. I had to drop the contract off back at the office. You won't believe who—"

"No, Michelle, *you* won't believe what it's like stuck up in this house all damn day wit' two kids waitin' on somebody to bring they ass home when they say they will. What da hell happened to 'five-ish'? You know what, don't even answer dat. I'll just see you when you get here." Silence.

Did she just? Yes, her ass did. Chelle, calm down. Edging through traffic, I gave myself a pep talk. I was on the verge of walking up in that seven-bedroom, $3,000-a-month mortgage house and goin' slam the fuck off. I alone paid that mortgage and upkeep on that house her unappreciative ass was suddenly so upset about being "stuck up in all day." Shit, it's not like she didn't have a car. Larissa had two cars. Why she refused to leave the house without me by her side was just another argument waiting to happen.

Forty-five minutes later I parked in front of our garage and braced myself as I walked in through the front door. Even the short distance from the car to the front door broke me out in a mild sweat and the AC gave me an instant chill when I walked in. Normally when I got home from work my babies' little arms would wrap around my legs. Trey and Lataya, my four-year-old son and two-year-old adopted daughter, would squeal and giggle as I play tugged, dragged, and scuffed up freshly waxed hardwood flooring and let them put runs in my brand new stockings, but the house was dead silent. I walked through the foyer into the living room. The curtains were drawn against the setting sun, casting the room in warm shadows.

"A'ight. So, where was you really at?" Her tone was half asking and half accusatory.

I stopped in the entryway. For a brief moment I was alarmed. Was she using again? Was she high on something right now? No, that wasn't possible. I could clearly hear the shakiness and the tears in her voice. After we'd gotten married and gained legal custody of Lataya, the daughter of her cousin Honey and my ex-fiancé, Ris had managed to stay away from all that shit, just like I'd managed to avoid dick. I erased the negative thought just as soon as it occurred.

"Ris, I told you. I had to show the Matthews property an' drop off the paperwork. You know how traffic is this time of year."

She was sitting off in a darkened corner of the living room with her legs drawn up to her chest, chin resting on her knees. Times like this, I exhaled long and hard. It was the times like this that she reminded me of the old hurt and emotionally worn down me. Except I wasn't intentionally putting her through half the shit I was actually going through back then. I walked toward her slowly with the same cautious, timid approach you'd take with a hurt bird or injured deer, scared to move too quickly out of fear that she'd dart upstairs and lock herself in the bathroom and I'd be stuck outside the door for the rest of the night trying to talk her out.

"C'mon, you. Now, what's the one thing I said I'd never do?" My voice was nothing but a low whisper. My emotions were getting the best of me and my own tears slowly started to trail down my cheeks at the sight of her obvious pain.

"I know wha'chu said, Chelle. But, you're you, an' you're smart an' beautiful an' I jus' don't see you lovin' me forever. Not like you try to say you will. Nothin', not a damn thing, last forever, an' I rather you jus' be honest wit' me an' say you gonna do some shit or dat you *are* doin' some shit than play me for a damn fool."

The sun was setting and tiny slits of light were peeking through the thick chocolate-colored drapes that covered the ceiling-to-floor windows in the living room. It was just enough light for me to briefly see dark shadows underneath my wife's usually bright green eyes. Ris always kept herself up but she was still in her thin pink cotton slip from the night before, her long, shoulder-length red hair was piled up in a messy-ass ponytail on top of her head. It was enough for me to realize that she was seriously worried and all for nothing. God knows I hated when she acted like this. I wasn't cheating on her and hadn't thought about it. *Ugh*. Inwardly I cringed. Okay, until *today* I hadn't actually thought about cheating on her. But, let's be real, that wasn't an actual, tangible thought until I had it swinging in my damn face. Let's be honest, it was more of what I'd consider a fleeting whim. A fantasy. Nothing more, nothing less.

"Risi-cup, you'll never enjoy the moments life has to offer if you stay focused on the ending." I recited some psychobabble I'd read or heard somewhere, and dropped down to my knees in front of her, offering up what I'd hoped would look like a reassuring smile.

"It ain't workin', Chelle. Not this time." She handed me a crumpled piece of paper.

"What's this, baby?" *Did I forget to pay the water bill or something crazy? Is that what has her so upset?* Puzzled, I took the crumpled sheet of paper from her cold hand and started to unfold and smooth it out as best as I could. It was a tattered piece of notebook paper; the words hit me to my core. Chills ran through my body and it took my mind a second longer to process what my heart almost immediately comprehended. The sheet of paper was wrinkled as if it'd been folded and refolded, balled up, thrown away, and found again, but the letters were still there—in what I guessed would have to be the worst handwriting I'd ever seen—but the blotchy red ink spelled it out unmistakably clear:

A FAMILY DIVIDED WILL FALL THE FUCK APART

Out of all the possibilities, I'd rather this shit be the sick joke of one of our neighbors. That would have been much easier to stomach. Ris and I were the only same-sex couple in the neighborhood and I could deal with a pissed-off "Jesus Freak" like it was nothin'. Yet my subconscious was raising flags redder than the words in front of my face. I looked up at Ris, who now had fresh tears welling up in her eyes, and only one name came to my mind.

"Did that nigga come here? Was he here? Who left this note? Did you see who left this?" I had a million and one questions. None of which Ris could answer fast enough. My mind was going a hundred miles an hour. There was no way he could be out of jail. No way he could have possibly known how to get to us. I changed my last name, changed the kids' last names. A sense of despair came over me that I fought with all of my being for the sake of my kids alone. Maybe he paid one of his old dope boys to follow us, but the types of men Rasheed dealt with didn't leave little notes, or calling cards, or any evidence. They handled business, got the fuck out of town, and you'd be lucky if they even left a body for your family to bury when they were done.

"I was takin' out the trash last week, an' it was on the back gate." She broke out into fresh tears.

"Last week? And you're just *now* showin' me this." I smacked the offensive sheet of paper in frustration. "Then, what the hell are you even cryin' for? I'm the one in shock right now, *you've* had a whole week to marinate with this shit."

"I thought that maybe y'all were meetin' up or somethin' since you were comin' home late or whatever blah blah bullshit. I been waitin' for the right time to say somethin'."

I couldn't help rolling my eyes at her dumb-ass logic. "An entire week, Ris? Who knows who's been watchin' us. Watchin' you and the kids, me. Ris, I swear. . . ." My voice trailed off. I'd never put my hands on her in anger, but I swear this one time almost pushed me to my limit. I silently prayed for strength and some kind of restraint to keep from shaking her for being so damn stupid.

Ris was obviously under a ton of stress, but for her to think that I'd be seeing Rasheed again after all this time . . . Well, considering my and

Rah's on-again, off-again history, I couldn't blame her. Her reaction was expected. Hell, I'd be a little suspect about me too if the roles were reversed. Our entire relationship was based on Larissa putting me back together every time Rasheed broke me down. It took years of me dealing with him lying and cheating to finally realize that I loved me too much and Ris loved me all along.

"Ugh, I need to think." Closing my eyes, I rubbed my temples, trying to process exactly what this message might mean. "Have you noticed any cars around the house or any strange people since the day you found this note?"

"No. I mean . . . Well I've noticed strange things about you. But—"

"Larissa, I swear on my life I ain't doing anything wrong. I need you to fuckin' focus right now. Where are the kids?" If there was any time for me to "woosah" or "nam-myoho-renge-kyo" meditate and chant, now was it. Out of all the things we needed to worry about concerning my ex and our past I couldn't believe she was still more worried about whether I was cheating.

Rasheed was supposedly in prison in Virginia, serving at least a full life term with no hope of probation. He'd lost everything: his family, his freedom, his businesses, hundreds of thousands of dollars. All because of the two of us.

"The kids upstairs takin' a nap."

Relief momentarily swept through me. At least my babies were in the house and they were safe. I could feel a migraine coming on. I'd have to get in contact with my attorney; there was no way in hell Rah could have found us on his own. I leaned in and hugged Ris, trying to reassure her as best as I could. She was rigid and didn't return my embrace. Pulling back, I looked at her, praying there was nothing more to go with her story.

"Baby. It'll be okay, I promise. Stop worryin'."

But it wasn't worry that I saw in her eyes, it was anger. Glowing, green anger. I was confused. Her face could have been carved out of stone it was so cold and still. Her eyes narrowed into cold green slits, and it was a wonder she could even see me. But I knew that look entirely too well; it meant hell was coming.

"If you weren't wit' da nigga, why you smell like him, Michelle?"

Fuck. Fuck was the first and only word that came to mind. *Fuck Keyshawn and his damn cologne and his damn advances and Ris's sensitive-ass nose. Fuck and double fuck.* She was staring at me so calmly it was scaring the hell out of me. She was gauging my reaction time, watching my pulse, waiting to see if I stuttered or fucked up my answer. The fucked-up part was

I was more nervous about all the shit I knew she watching for and I didn't even do anything to deserve the interrogation I was getting.

"Ris, I told you I had to show that mansion today. Keyshawn Matthews, he plays basketball for the Miami Legends. I closed the deal. We hugged; his girlfriend was there I hugged her too. I called you on my way home to tell you that we're all goin' out to celebrate this weekend, like celebrities. The estate was ten million; it's a *huge* deal for us. I wanted you to be proud of me. And yes, he wears that same funky-ass cologne as Rah. I noticed it too. But that's it; nothing more, nothing less." I could see the wheels spinning, judging my words as true or false, and I must've said everything the right way because her face started to light up with excitement.

"Wait, the rookie 'Keys to the City Shawn' Matthews?"

I shook my head yes.

"The one who goes everywhere with Yylannia the supermodel?"

Once again all I could do was shake my head in agreement, slightly amazed that Ris, A, knew who they were and, B, actually seemed to be impressed.

"Chelle, they were all ova' all the celebrity blogs las' week. Dat fool be up in clubs throwin' thousands at crowds. Bae, he be goin' in. I ain' partied or had a real night out since . . . Ugh. What am I gonna wear? I gotta go shoppin'. We need a babysitter!" She jumped up off the couch so fast she almost knocked me over.

"Oh an' you need a shower. You think you can ask him not to wear dat stank-ass cologne when we go out? Tell his ass I'm allergic to it or some shit, ount care." She took off upstairs in a flurry, mumbling the names of clubs and drinks, dresses and who knew what else.

Lord, forgive me for the lie I just told. I'll never tell another one, just please let Key be available this weekend. But, something tells me as soon as I say the words "go on a celebration date with me and my wife," that fool's schedule will most likely miraculously clear up.

CHAPTER 4

I'LL SCRATCH YOUR BACK—
IF YOU SCRATCH MINE

I waited until Ris left the house to go shopping, making her take both my Mace and the .22 with her just to be safe. Surprisingly the kids were still down for their nap so the house was nice and quiet. Naptime meant playtime so they probably hadn't actually fallen asleep until just before I'd gotten home. I peeked in just to make sure they were still breathing. I guess it's a momma thing, but as long as I could see their little faces and hear the ever-so-beautiful sound of their even breathing, I knew everything was fine and I could go about my business. I grabbed my iPhone out of my briefcase and walked into our bedroom, which was a complete mess, as usual. Clothes were everywhere, on the floor, all over the king-sized bed. The doors to both walk-in closets were wide open, and Tornado Ris had blown through, leaving shoes and whatnot every damn where. I hated all the clutter and mess. She was so bad when it came to that shit, but I had too much on my mind to start picking up after her as I usually did.

I walked up the winding wooden staircase that was secluded off to the corner. It led up to the third floor, or what I liked to call my personal sanctuary. When I furnished the house I wanted one room that would be no one's but mine. I opted to make the small corner studio my home office instead of using the study downstairs as most of the homes were traditionally set up.

There was one large rectangular window that ran the entire length of the room, overlooking our view of the pool and beach beyond. Thin white drapes hung from either side and with the window open the breeze would carry the smell of the ocean. Every time I looked out at the ocean I couldn't help thinking that I had my very own piece of paradise right in my backyard. This was the only area of the house that I allowed white in. I didn't want to deal with the hassle of keeping little fingerprints off my furniture, so everything else in the house consisted of dark earth tones: chocolates, olives, and tans. Everywhere except my sanctuary. The floor was covered in the softest carpeting I could find, the color was called shaved ice, and that's exactly what it looked like. My desk was made completely out of glass and sat in the center of the window; my executive-edition plush white leather chair was just as I'd left it. Across from that on the other side of the room sat my white microfiber couch and sectional.

Lying back on the sofa, I kicked off my pumps. For a moment I just stared at the little clownfish—or the "Nemo's" as the kids called them—swimming around in the hanging tropical fish tank on the wall. *Oh well,* I thought. *Here goes nothing, or better yet here goes hell to pay if I can't pull this off.* I dialed Key's number. I didn't realize I was holding my breath until his voice mail came on and I was forced to breathe so I could leave a message.

"Um. Hi, Key. This is Michelle, from the house earlier. I need a huge favor. I'd really appreciate it if you'd give me a call back, hopefully tonight. Thanks." *Great, what the hell am I gonna do if this nigga doesn't call me back? Think, girl. Think.* I could feel the stress knots in my neck, and I closed my eyes and tried to come up with some kind of a backup plan just in case. I must have dozed off because the phone rang and scared me so bad I jumped. *About damn time.* "Keyshawn, hey."

"Well, well. You find me anotha house already?"

Damn, he ain't listen to his voice mail. Typical.

"Umm. No, I actually need a huge favor."

"Ha, okay, I'm listenin'."

"Well, remember when I said my wife was crazy? I got home stupid late from our showing an' she was spazzin' so I had to kind of lie about closin' on the house with you. I said we'd be goin' out tomorrow to celebrate."

"So, lemme guess. You want me to get us a table somewhere and chill wit' y'all right?"

"You *and* Yylannia, yes. I can knock maybe twenty percent off of whichever house you decide to close on or maybe throw flat screens in every room, work on that acoustic thing you were so interested in." I was trying to think of any- and everything to get him to commit. Even if he just showed up for an hour, played his part, and left. As long as Ris was happy and my life went back to normal I didn't care.

"How 'bout this? We do a date for a date. I chill wit' you an' wifey, an' say this time nex' week I treat you like you should be treated and take you out for dinner, drinks?" I could hear him smiling through the phone, dimples and all. He had me. There was no way I could say no, *but,* I could always cancel on his ass at the last minute.

"Fine, whatever. I heard LIV in Miami is next to impossible to get into wit' this late of a notice, but do you think you could get a table? I'll cover all the—"

"Woman, I don't need you coverin' nothin'. I'll have my man handle all the details, text me ya info an' I'll send a car to pick y'all up. We gonna do this big, since we celebratin' an' shit." He laughed into the phone. His moods were so contagious. It was nice to have someone else take over things, handle the arrangements and all the details.

"Thank you, Keyshawn. Guess I really do owe you one."

"Chelle? You up there?" Larissa was making her way upstairs. I imagined she'd either exhausted herself trying to find something to wear or maxed out another one of my cards. I made a mental note to check all of my balances and pay them all off at the end of the month.

"Yeah, baby. I'm here. All right, Key. Lemme go. I'll send you what you need. Thanks again." I hung up before I could hear a reply, and dropped my phone into my lap.

"Who were you talkin' to?" She stopped just shy of the edge of the stairs and looked at me suspiciously.

"Keyshawn. I was confirming our arrangements for tomorrow and making sure we have a sitter. Did you find a dress?"

She beamed a smile at me and launched herself into my lap. Her small four-foot-nine frame fit so perfectly with mine. Wrapping my arms around her, I couldn't help but roll my eyes. I already knew what she was going to say.

"Yes, I found us *both* dresses. 'Cause you know you ain't got shit to wear either, not to no damn club anyway."

"Ris, you know good an' well you can't shop for me. It's either gonna be too short, too tight, or too damn bright. I'm sure I already got somethin' in my closet that'll work."

"Nah, you'll like this shit. I promise." She leaned her head back on my shoulder and smiled up at me, making me momentarily forget that somewhere out there my crazy ex-fiancé was stalking us and that in all actuality we really weren't celebrating anything this weekend except for a lie I'd told her—and now I owed a date to man I was entirely too attracted to, to even admit to myself. I planted as fake of a smile on my face as I possibly could, and I leaned down, kissing her smiling lips, pretending as if nothing was wrong.

***

Saturday was a whirlwind of getting the kids ready for their day with the babysitter and trying to get my house back in order from a busy work-week. I'd noticed an older blue Ford Mustang in the neighborhood earlier. It went around the neighborhood once when I was checking the mail, and I was going to let Trey and Lataya play outside when I started to feel uneasy and decided against it.

"Mommy, why?" Trey whined. *My poor babies.* I felt bad keeping them cooped up in the house but it was for their own good. I looked down at Trey, who was getting so tall he was almost up to my waist. He was his father's same exact high-yellow complexion, lighter than me with pretty, curly hair and big, round brown eyes. I couldn't hide my smile as I answered him.

"Because Mommy says no, that's all the why you need."

Lataya stood beside him in a pink shorts set, white sandal on one foot and Lord knows where the other one was, looking like a miniature golden version of her mother if you let Ris tell it. When I looked at my little princess all I saw was Rasheed.

I knelt down to take off her sandal, frowning at a red welt on the back of her chubby little leg. She was in that terrible-twos stage, always stumbling around the house and getting into everything; it was probably nothing. Her front teeth were just starting to come in and she looked just like Trey when he was that age: all cheeks, slobbery chin, grinning all day for no reason whatsoever. She was such a happy little girl. I couldn't imagine the life she'd have had if we'd let her go to a foster home. She was so much better off here with us. This was definitely where she belonged.

"Trey, baby, take your sister upstairs to the playroom. I got you guys a new movie. Ask Mommy to put it on for you. You can have cookies if you keep quiet." I kissed the side of Lataya's chubby neck, and she smiled at me through her long, baby-doll lashes and giggled. She didn't care what was going on; she'd heard the word "cookies" and was ready to go. Trey groaned and huffed, reluctantly taking her hand and leading her upstairs. It amazed me that Larissa and I could call each other Mommy and the kids just assumed if one said it in regard to doing something it automatically meant go ask the other one.

I glanced down at my watch; it was a little after one in the afternoon. I perched in the large bay window in the living room and saw the blue Mustang pull up to one of the houses down the

street. Damn, this shit was making me paranoid.
I needed to relax with a capital R. I shouted up
toward the kids' playroom, "Ris, watch the kids.
I'll be in the pool."

"A'ight, bae."

I walked out to the back of the house and
let my sundress slide down my body. The first
time I did that shit Ris had a flat-out fit, telling
me, "Only white folk go out an' swim in they
pool butt-ass naked. Yo' ass end up wit' some
kinda bacterial infection, ount wanna hear it."
Stripping out of my bra and panties, I laughed
at the memory. Our backyard was perfect. Tall
white privacy fences ran along both sides of the
beach so no one could trespass, and we didn't
have to be bothered with the year-round issue of
vacationers or beachgoers parking and camping
out all over the beach. That was the beauty of
the neighborhood: all of the houses were spaced
out and they all faced the ocean, so there was no
need to worry about nosey-ass neighbors either.

I let the warmth from the sun embrace my
bare skin only for a moment before diving into
the lukewarm water. I swam a few laps as part of
my usual workout routine to keep myself toned,
but I didn't want to wear myself out, so I just
drifted on my back with my eyes closed for a
little while. I sighed; this shit did not help at all.

The stress and anxiety was still there. I was wiping water from my eyes when I saw it. It was the briefest movement in the ocean directly in front of me that caught my eye, causing me to freeze mid-motion. The sun glimmered off the water everywhere except for in this one spot. An object bobbed, it was slightly rounded like . . . like a head. I squinted harder and could barely make out a neck and shoulders. And then nothing. It just bobbed under right at the very second that my eyes decided to clearly focus in on it.

I waited, frozen in place, afraid to look anywhere other than where I saw *him,* or it, go under. It didn't resurface. *Okay, woman. You are definitely getting paranoid and super trippin'. It was probably just a dolphin or a sea lion, manatee—fuck. That nigga would not swim five miles out and seven or eight miles across just to stare at the damn house. Or would he?* Not to mention the fact that I still hadn't figured out how anyone from my past had actually found me, or even alerted him to our whereabouts. I must've stayed there staring intently at that square of ocean for a good fifteen to twenty minutes. When nothing resurfaced I gave up and trod back inside, looking over my shoulder every few steps just in case. I made sure to lock all the windows and doors downstairs just in case.

By the time I'd showered and fed the kids it was time to get ready. I was nervous. I wasn't sure what I'd seen out there in the water, but combined with the note that Ris had found, the last thing I wanted to do was leave the house, leave my kids. I pulled the dress Ris picked out over my head and attempted to pull myself together.

"Larissa, what the hell is this ho-ish-lookin', prostitute-in-training shit you got me wearin'?" I stared at myself in the full-length mirror like the woman looking back was a complete stranger.

"Baby, calm da fuck down. Nobody gonna have on nothin' we got on tonight. You look fuckin' hot, too. Like on some straight-up diva shit."

I gawked at myself. The dress was from some collection I'd never heard of and cost entirely too damn much. It was orange, and not no dull spring orange, but bright-ass traffic-cone orange, with black trim around the edges and tiny crystal accents. The neck hung way too low in the front and the back scooped in a V damn near to my ass crack so there was no way I could get away with a bra. It fit tight in all the right places and flared at the arms. It wasn't an ugly dress; it just wasn't me. I always said Ris could not pick out my clothes, but I was such a mess after what I'd seen earlier, I didn't even care. I was dressed. *Fuck it.*

CHAPTER 5

GOOD FOR THE GOOSE—
GOOD FOR THE GANDER

Sitting on the cool leather of the living room couch I impatiently tapped my foot. I was all kinds of nervous about the night ahead. The kids were upstairs with Darla the babysitter and my mind was preoccupied with thoughts of Rasheed. Where the hell was this nigga, and what the hell did he want? How long was he gonna torture us before he showed his ass and started making demands and shit? I'd tried to call the prison to see if he was there and the clerk placed me on hold so long I had to hang up. This happened at least three times.

Scared and frustrated, I'd looked up a few numbers for security services to call, but it was too late in the evening when I'd remembered to do it. I made a mental note to try again one day during the week. Just then the car pulled up to the front of the house as planned. Ris squealed and flew from upstairs so fast she was damn near out of breath.

"Ooh it's here, baby. How I look? My hair okay?"

I stared at her in amazement. She was wearing a bright pink Escada blouse that dipped low in between her breasts, the color complementing her red complexion perfectly. I stared down into her glowing green eyes; I could tell it was definitely more than the makeup and smoky eye shadow lighting up her face.

"You look beautiful, baby, and damn if the club ain't the last place I'm tryin'a go right now."

She giggled and blushed hard. "We'll have time for dat after. Lemme get a li'l nice first and I'll show you a trick when we get back home."

"A trick? What kinda trick you got that I ain't already seen, woman?"

She leaned in and gave me a long kiss before we headed out the door. For the first time in a long time I felt my chest fill up with pride, because I couldn't lie—my wife was bad. She'd somehow managed to pile all her ass into what I'd call about four inches of black fabric and what she had the nerve to be trying to call a damn skirt. Lord, we was gonna get into some fights tonight.

The ride to the club wasn't as long as I thought it would be. Ris made good use of the fully stocked bar and was a lot more than nice by the time we finished the forty-five-minute drive into Miami. As our limo pulled up to the front of the club I texted Keyshawn to let him know we were outside. I was surprised when Yylannia came out to the car.

"Well hello, *mi* gorgeous ladies. Key is inside holding the table, ordering foods. Come—come." She waved her elegant, li'l skinny hand and started to cat-walk away. She was wearing a short, tight black dress that fit her like a second skin. Her jet-black hair hung down her back in long layers that almost touched her ass. I was in awe. She looked exotic and classy.

"Oh my God. That's her, Chelle. She's beautiful and soooo damn skinny. Um, did her ass jus' say 'foods'?"

Yylannia did have a strange accent and way of saying things sometimes. It wasn't Spanish or French, more of a mixture of the two. Hell I'd just settle for calling it a "Franish"-ass accent. Ris's tipsy ass giggled and mock cat-walked behind her. We completely bypassed the line to get inside. It was wrapped damn near completely around the entire complex but we just followed Ms. Walk Like a Model Everywhere and the bouncers nodded and let us inside. I could literally feel bitches glaring and hatin' on us and I actually enjoyed it for once, mentally reminding myself not to trip or do anything embarrassing trying to be cute in front of all these damn onlookers.

The club was packed with men and women, white, black. Mostly white. Mostly women—let me rephrase—mostly model, gold-digger, video, actress, and party-girl types. On this particular night they were playing house music, and I already knew Ris was gonna have an attitude if we didn't get her semi fucked up before she realized they weren't playing any hip-hop. We walked toward a private entryway with so much security you would have thought President Obama himself was up in there. Yylannia just breezed us past and it was like we'd walked into an entirely different club.

The ambiance was sexier, way more elegant than the estrogen zoo we'd just passed through. The entire floor was made of white glass, and changed colors, going from purple to neon pink to blue. Smoke machines filled the entire area in a cool white mist; I reached out and grabbed Ris's hand to make sure we didn't lose her. She was quiet, which was a good thing; it meant she was in awe. We swept past booth after booth. The entire area was about the size of a large restaurant and all of it was exclusively for members-only VIP. You had to pay a yearly fee just to be able to reserve a booth on any given Friday or Saturday, and that was only if they had availability and even then you still had to run up a tab in the thousands in order to keep your spot. All of the booths had round white leather sofas or chaises longues and tables, and the outsides were covered with white curtains that could remain open or be completely closed for privacy.

We arrived at a booth toward the back where Key was sitting with two other extremely beautiful women. He looked completely edible in a deep grey Gucci button down and dark grey slacks. Yylannia scooted in beside him and patted the seat next to her, directing me to sit down.

"Hello, everyone, this is Larissa, my wife." I didn't want to hesitate in making the introductions lest Ris take offense and start to think something was up, as she was accustomed to doing.

"Don't be so formal. Just call me Lania and him Key, over beside Key you have Chanel and Keisha." Lania smiled, beaming straight, blindingly perfect white teeth and deep dimples that I hadn't noticed before. I nodded to the two women who were paying Ris and me no mind.

Chanel was a gorgeous woman the same dark chocolate tone as Keyshawn, with large, dark, expressive eyes that reminded me of one of those Japanime characters. She'd completely dismissed Ris and me and was whispering something in Key's ear, causing him to chuckle and whisper back. I felt a small twinge of jealousy at their obvious closeness; guessed the joke was on me for thinking his ass wasn't like every other nigga with good looks and money. Why I was letting shit like that bother me I had no idea; it's not like he had a chance with me anyway. I looked away quickly, scared my expression might give away my thoughts, and Keisha, to my surprise, was actually watching me watch them. She smiled at me smugly before kissing Chanel on the neck, glancing at me from the corner of her eye. *Bitch, I was not checking out yo' girl,* I thought.

"Um, Lania, you are soooo beautiful. I'm sorry, I'm just a li'l tipsy. There was free liquor on—I mean in—our limo. And oooh, Keyshawn. I mean Key. If I get me a basketball would you sign it?"

All I could do was look down in horror and roll my eyes, and no, the damn liquor in the limo was not *free;* every drop she chugalugged was comin' out of my pocket. I sighed a long, loud sigh.

"Yeah, I'd be more than happy to, ma. Jus' give it to Michelle over there and it's a done deal. So, how about we start off with a bottle of rosé and some muthafuckin' shots, 'cause I don't know about y'all but my ass is thirsty."

I smiled apologetically at Keyshawn, thankful for the icebreaker.

I wasn't sure how many glasses of champagne or how many shots we were in, but things were definitely starting to get fun. We'd each taken turns talking about strange and random sex facts. Thanks to Lania, I now knew that some female penguins actually engaged in prostitution to get pebbles from "single" guy penguins to build their nests. She kept looking at Chanel the whole time she was telling the story, which had me weak as hell. If I didn't know better I'd have said Chanel was giving Key a hand job under the table; he'd suddenly gotten extremely quiet and they both seemed overly interested in something down there.

There was a bunch of commotion at the entrance, drawing everyone's attention. Two bouncers came in and ordered the people in the booth behind us to leave. I could hear the guy complaining and asking for a manager.

"Damn, what's going on?" I asked, glancing around cautiously. *After everything I've put myself through to plan this shit out, they'd better not ask us to move or my ass is going to raise pure hell.* In the center of the bodyguards there was a smaller guy with piercing crystal-grey eyes carrying a Louis Vuitton briefcase, and a group of women flocked around him. I almost twisted my neck trying to get a better look at who he was.

"Who is he supposed to be?" I had to ask when I couldn't figure it out. He didn't look like anyone I'd seen anywhere before.

"That's Angelo Testa, consider him like a billionaire." Lania waved at him and smiled. Keyshawn nodded in the little man's direction. A few of the girls with him looked familiar. I assumed they were models or actresses. One in particular stayed plastered to his side. She was shorter than the others, thick and light skinned. I couldn't make her face out completely but I thought it was the girl from "Pon de Replay"? Maybe. Every video I'd ever seen ran through my head but I only got to see her for a split second before the curtains were drawn and they were having their own private party, in there doing Lord knows what. Ris was zoned out so I couldn't ask her where the hell I'd seen the girl before. Eight different security guys stood guard outside around the booth and I must admit I was impressed. Lania suggested we all get up and dance, but I realized I needed to pee so bad I couldn't sit still anymore.

"Lania, hold on, where's the restroom?"

"I'll take you; it's hard to explain and I have to go too."

Ris looked like she was on the verge of passing out at the table. She either said she did or didn't have to pee, I couldn't tell. But she didn't get up so I guessed it wasn't a yes. It'd been awhile since we'd drunk together and I was gonna have so much fun reminding her in the morning that she'd lost her touch. There would definitely be no tricks tonight; she was in no position to show me anything.

Chanel and Keisha said they'd wait for us at the table. I followed Lania through a maze of booths and a blur of familiar faces I'd seen on TV. She waved and made small talk and I tapped her on her shoulder, reminding her that this was urgent.

The bathroom was just as luxurious as the VIP area. The lighting was dimmed and the speakers in the ceiling played the club music overhead. There was an actual sitting area with small palm fronds and soft chaises longues. There was even an actual walk-in toilet like you would use in someone's house, not a stall like you'd expect to find. I handled my business and walked out, washing my hands and straightening my dress. I looked toward the chaise longue where I'd left Lania and didn't see her. I had just barely opened my mouth to call out and ask her where she'd disappeared to before her lips were on mine. She wore J'adore Dior perfume and she tasted like rosé and fresh cherries and yes—I noticed all of that before I broke myself out of the spell I was in. Pulling my lips from hers I began shaking my head no. I was in such a complete shock, I couldn't make a sound.

I hadn't realized how beautiful she actually was, completely dismissing my initial judgment of her at the house when I'd first seen her. Her eyes were a light golden brown and in the dim lighting it looked like they were aglow from the inside. Like the reflection you see from a flame in the glass when you burn a candle in a hurricane jar. We had a complete conversation without saying a single word, her eyes boldly telling me, "I want you." I backed up a step, shaking my head again, silently saying, "I'm married—this cannot go down." Biting her lower lip, eyebrow raised, she narrowed her slanted golden cat eyes, soundlessly telling me, "I get what I want—and I want you now." My eyes widened in an utter look of "Oh shit." *I'm such a punk*. I mentally slapped myself for this one, because she had me.

I wasn't used to being challenged or pursued by a woman, not since Ris, and it caught me off guard when she came at me again. *I shouldn't have had so many tequila shots. The liquor is definitely my damn alibi and I'm sticking to it*. My eyes closed in anticipation. I was completely ready for the sensual assault of Dior and cherry rosé to consume me—and it did. My hands had a mind of their own and I let them roam freely until I felt warm, smooth, baby-soft skin.

I slid my hand upward, raising her dress as I went. I gently caressed her left breast in one hand, lightly teasing her nipple until she moaned and playfully bit the corner of my lip. The sound she made was low, sultry—every hair on the back of my neck stood on edge. I explored with my other hand, allowing it to slide down the soft, muscled outline of her stomach to the soft lift of her ass. My eyes opened and I gasped in shocked surprise when I stroked her hairless wonder, amazed at how smooth, soft, and *wet* she was. *Shit*.

Mental note number 543: get a damn Brazilian wax. No matter how much they say that shit hurts it's damn sure worth it. To be so thin and frail looking, Lania was *strong*. She had somehow backed me up against the sink and had lifted me up onto it in one solid movement. She roughly wrapped one of her hands around my neck, gently choking me while lightly digging her nails into my skin at the same time. I couldn't take it; it had to be the sweetest torture I'd ever felt. Ris didn't have nails because she'd bite them off, but damn she needed to grow or buy some.

Lania took complete control over everything: my body and my senses. I could feel her fingers burning a trail of heat up my inner thigh and her mouth left mine to take advantage of the deep, plunging neckline in the front of my dress and the fact that I wasn't wearin' a bra. The pressure building in between my thighs was so much it was becoming damn near painful. She was slowly sliding my panties to one side, teasing me at first, letting her finger trail ever so softly across my already throbbing lips. I was about to be extremely embarrassed because I was entirely too damn wet to just be on some second base–type shit, but I couldn't help it. She shoved two fingers deep inside me and I swear I almost exploded right there on the spot.

"Michelle?"

In my tequila-sex haze I almost responded until I realized it wasn't Lania saying my name. Someone pounded frantically on the bathroom door.

"Michelle? Are you in there? I think I'm gonna be sick." Larissa was knocking on the bathroom door.

"Shit." We both cursed quietly. It was like I was doused with cold water and simultaneously hit over the head. Frustration and disappointment in myself set in all at once. I hopped off the sink and straightened my dress and panties, checking my hair in the mirror. Lania arranged her dress and recomposed herself before walking back over to the chaise longue, looking as if she'd been there all along. I unlocked the door and Ris rushed in, eyeing us both suspiciously.

"What the fuck took you so long? The fuck, Michelle?" She was wobbling back and forth.

I raised my hands as if waiving the white flag. "Larissa, not here—not now. Nothin' was goin' on, baby, calm down."

She pointed over in Lania's direction, staggering toward her. "You bitch, I seen you, prissy, Frenchy bitch—lookin' at my bitch."

Lord, I must have turned five shades of red I was so damn embarrassed. I grabbed Ris by her shoulders and turned her to face me so I could at least lie to her directly in the eyes. "Ris, baby, I promise nothing . . ." Shit, before the words could leave my mouth Larissa did some kinda behind-the-back drunk crossover, goin' around me like fuckin' Jordan back in '93 and was on Lania's ass before I could blink.

"Michelle, get your bitch before I kill her."

Ris went flyin' back across the room, and I just stood there, eyes wide as fuck, staring in stunned silence. I told y'all that skinny heffa was *strong*. She'd pushed Larissa's ass up off of her so damn hard I was in shock.

"Ugh, Chelle, I'm gonna be sick." Larissa was definitely done as she staggered toward the stall in the corner.

I followed her into the bathroom and held her hair back just as she let go. "Damn, Ris, I think you're ready to go, baby." She surprised me by shaking her head no in between frame-racking heaves. I looked over at Lania, who surprised me even further by just shruggin' as if this was a normal thing for her ass.

"Well, Risi-cup, I think it's safe to say you definitely can't handle your liquor anymore. Let's go get yo' ass some water so you can sober the fuck up."

"The hell I can't. I's jus' makin' room fa' more." She chuckled, and I helped her fix her hair and walked her back out to the table. Keyshawn was right where we left him, looking just as handsome with his two concubines, waiting patiently as ever.

"Y'all good?" Keyshawn asked, barely glancing in my direction.

Lania slid back into her place beside him and gave him an awkward smile. They exchanged a look, or I thought they exchanged a look; it was so brief I could have possibly imagined it. I just didn't want to seem like I was imposing, and I definitely didn't want to be labeled as the woman with the wife who gets drunk and acts a complete mess in public.

"So, my mans is comin' to hang out with us if y'all up for it."

Ris flopped down into the booth and answered before I could even open up my mouth and come up with an excuse to get us out of there.

"Our asses is up for it. Is he anotha basketball player? Who is it?" She was pouring herself another glass of champagne, but more of it was ending up on the table than in her champagne flute.

"He's the owner of the team. Cool dude. Here, let me pour that for you, you are my guest." He directed his gaze toward me after filling her glass less than full. "Very good connect to have. You never know when you need to know someone like him."

With that statement the business part of me kicked in and I sat my ass down. "Key, pour me a glass too, please." *Never know when you'll need to know an NBA team owner, especially in the housing industry. That's some super official shit right there.*

It didn't take long for Curtis Daniels to arrive; he was a tall, older man with greying hair at the temples on either side of his head. I can't lie; he looked like money.

Keyshawn got up to greet him when he came over, and introduced him. It was a damn near buzz kill having him at the table and I was honestly happy for it. Key's playful demeanor immediately went out the window and he was acting like a perfect gentleman. If I weren't mistaken I'd say he was actually uncomfortable, but I guessed I would be a bit out of my element too if my boss wanted to come hang out at a damn club when I was tryin' to let loose and drink.

"Excuse me. Sir Angelo extends his graciousness." A waiter had appeared at our booth with a bottle of Château Lafite Rothschild Pauillac. My eyes widened and we all looked back toward the booth, but the curtains were still drawn.

"Send it back. I've already paid for champagne." Keyshawn surprised even me, but Lania said what we were all thinking.

"Key, that's a three thousand dollar bottle of champagne. This isn't a dick-measuring contest; are you trying to offend him on purpose?"

Keyshawn acted like he didn't even hear her.

"Tell Angelo we send our appreciation. Keyshawn, that pride will make you lose more than it will ever earn you if you don't get it under control." Curtis accepted a glass from the waiter and I couldn't help but wonder what Key had against that Angelo guy.

Curtis's sophisticated demeanor was a good balance to the group. It kept Ris from suicide tag-teaming shots and glasses of champagne left and right, giving her a little time to sober up. Once the guys got on the subject of basketball plays and seasons and playoffs, I decided it was a good time to call it a night, and I pulled a reluctant somebody away from the table and out to the limo so we could go home.

Ris pouted the first half of the ride and slept the rest of the way. My phone rang. I didn't recognize the number but figured it must be Keyshawn; I even got excited and dared it to be Curtis.

"Hello?"

"Enjoy your time while you still can, bitch." That's all that was said and the call disconnected. The voice sounded like something out of a horror movie. I knew there were plenty of apps on iPhones and other programs that could mask your voice, make it raspy or deeper, but why would Rasheed want to go through all the trouble? Was scaring me that serious? I dialed the number back and it went to a Google voice service that said the call couldn't be completed. My heart felt like it was doing clumsy flips in my chest. Someone needed to put a stop to this shit. The phone vibrated again, showing yet another number I didn't recognize. I hit answer and didn't say a word. I slid the phone to my ear, my heart beating in my throat, afraid to hear whatever murder, death, kill threat I would get next but ready to cuss someone the fuck out.

"Umm, hello? Michelle?"

A woman? It took me a second to place her voice. "Lania? Hey, I'm sorry I . . . I had the phone on mute." I wasn't in the mood for her cat-and-mouse bullshit right this second, especially not with Ris asleep right here, liable to wake up and ask a million questions.

"So, I honestly don't do this that often and I am in understanding with your situation, but I'd really like to be seeing you again. Soon if that is possible."

I had to shake my head yet again at her "Fran-nish" but that low, sultry voice of hers, it was like warm spiced caramel, and I had an instantaneous flashback of what it sounded like when she . . .

I popped that thought bubble before it could float any higher. I had too much going on to entertain this type of bullshit right now. Ris adjusted her head on my shoulder in her sleep and I stiffened.

"Lania, I can't. I'm sorry about what happened tonight too, but I just can't. I've gotta go okay?" I didn't even wait for her to respond. Suddenly I realized that I'd just hung up on one of *Maxim*'s top one hundred. *Actually I think she was numbered as the twenty-eighth most beautiful woman in the world.* I exhaled loudly. My neck was starting to hurt. I needed to be as rational and real about this situation as possible and with the way things were going, Rasheed was probably going to try to kill me. The key word was try, because there was no way I was giving up my life without a damn good fight. That muthafucka had another thing coming if he thought otherwise.

CHAPTER 6

WHAT'S MINE IS YOURS AND
WHAT'S YOURS IS STILL YOURS

Boy oh boy. I almost went slam the fuck off and gave away the fact that my ass wasn't for real drunk sleeping on Michelle's shoulder. I'd adjusted my head so I could hear her conversation better. The first one was quick and weird. I couldn't really hear it that well but based on the way she tensed up it wasn't good news. But the second one, *whew,* I almost nodded my head right into her lap because I was straining so hard to hear. I just *knew* something was up with that pretty-ass model Frenchy bitch mispronouncing- shit-for-no-damn-reason streetwalking ho. *Oh, I bet Chelle ain't even know all that shit.* Keyshawn was on his phone and Keisha had started talkin' all low to Chanel when they left sayin' some shit 'bout Lania needin' her to escort some nigga somewhere so they needed to ditch our party. An' here I was kissin' her ass thinkin' she on some top model shit and she over here running hoes.

Lania's ass had just hopped up too quick to help out when Michelle needed to go piss at the club. An' when Chanel and Keisha had the nerve to ask if I was okay with them going together, it took everything in my power to keep me at the table for as long as I sat there. It took a helluva lot more for me to embarrass myself and stick my damn finger down my throat when Chelle wasn't paying attention so I could throw up. My ass wasn't gonna be sick. I just needed an excuse to whoop that bitch's ass, and being drunk just seemed like a good enough'a one to me, shit.

My Spidey-muthafuckin'-sense was already on ten; I ain't need Tweedledee and Tweedledum-ass pointin' shit out like my ass stupid. I didn't know if Michelle did or didn't do anything up in that damn bathroom, but just in case, I got my ass whoopin' in just for her or that bitch even thinkin' 'bout doin' that shit. Point blank, that's all the fuck it took. Little Ms. Lania's ass was on my muthafuckin' radar. Period.

I could feel the limo roll to a stop. Michelle kissed me on my forehead and I blinked a few times, trying to adjust my eyes since they'd been closed the entire ride.

"Hey, you lush, we're home." She gave me one of her fake-ass "I'm trying to act like nothing's wrong" smiles. It was damn obvious she was worried about something. I just hoped she wasn't thinking about that bitch.

"Is somethin' wrong, bae?" I acted like I was still a little hazy from all the liquor, but I was super alert, watching everything.

"Nothin' baby. I'm jus' tired, it's close to four in the morning."

We climbed out of the car and made our way up to the darkened house, both of us trying to look normal as fuck while secretly eyeballing every tree, shadow, and bush. Most of the main lights were off in the house but the sitter had left the foyer lit. She was sitting in the living room, doing some shit with these long-ass needles. *I guess that's what the fuck knitting looks like. Boring,* I thought. Darla was an older, maybe late-forties white lady with stringy brown hair. Michelle found her through some kind of nanny referral service. She came with this long list of celebrity clients, a resume, a background check, all that shit. The needles clinked together as she dropped them into her little nanny knapsack and walked over to us.

"Hello, misses." She always called us that like we weren't some damn grown-ass women, always talkin' in her polite little field mouse voice. I bet she had a gazillion cats at home an' shit, or a million of those little white china baby dolls and she be talkin' to 'em and shit like they real kids. That's what the fuck she looked like in her pink and white "Nannies 'R' Us" uniform that the agency made her wear.

"A visitor came by not long after you left. As instructed I did not approach nor open the door. The children are upstairs in bed. They are very well behaved and beautiful little ones. Feel free to reserve my services anytime."

I didn't hear a damn thing after the word "visitor." *Who in the hell came by the house?*

You would've thought the two of us were wanted fugitives the way we suddenly looked at each other. Both of us asked the same question in our heads without needing to speak it out loud in front of this person who didn't need to know our business.

"Darla, I'll see you out. Thank you so, so much for your time this evening." Michelle took over and walked Darla toward the front door. She locked and bolted the double front doors, set the alarm, and together we went down the hall into the study that we never used. It wasn't a large study, I guessed. I ain't never had a house with a study so I wouldn't know. Michelle picked all the books that lined all the walls, most of which she'd said she read. I'd skimmed through a few but they were all, "think about this, grow rich that," a ton of shit I couldn't get into. The only one that I'd actually read was an old voodoo tale that scared the hell out my ass and I ain't touched another one since.

Our entire house minus Chelle's "sanctuary" had hardwood flooring, which I personally hated. Michelle's reasoning was it would not only add value to the house but it'd be easier to keep clean with the kids. When I told her I didn't like hardwood floors because they're cold, *Bam,* she had them install heaters *in the floors.* Nothing, not a single thing, in the house was mine or had my touch. Everything was Michelle's vision or Michelle's idea or customized to Michelle's liking or her idea of comfort. She'd furnished and picked it all out before we moved from Virginia as a "gift." She ain't even bother to think that I'd have liked to at least have some say in what color walls I'd want to stare at every damn day, or what kind of couch I'd want my ass on? Hell, I ain't even like the colors or the design on the sheets on the damn bed. *Ugh.*

We walked up to the oversized mahogany desk in the center. Michelle plopped down in the leather seat in front of the touchscreen HP and I sat in her lap, since it was the only place to sit.

"You ever even learn how to use that damn camera system?" I was being a smartass on purpose. Since the day it was installed I'd never figured out how to use it and I sure as hell wasn't sure if she had.

"The man said it's twenty-four hours and backed up to a main server, all we have to do is enter the password and we can view the footage."

I wasn't sure why I never thought of it before. The cameras were all some state-of–the-art bullshit, teeny as hell and hidden around the outside of the house. We had one at the front door, one overlooking the garage, and I was pretty sure there was another that looked out over the back toward the pool.

"So why don't you just use the li'l touchscreen pad things that's all over the house?"

We had one in every damn room. They looked like mini TVs on the wall beside the light switches and they controlled damn near everything. You could dim the lights, turn the music on or off in each room, and, *duh*, look outside using the cameras.

"Because, Ris, those cameras are real time, we need to access shit that's already passed. So we need to go back a few hours. After a week the files are archived so we can't access them." She sounded irritated. There was no reason for her to talk to me in such a know-it-all tone.

"Well damn you ain't gotta snap at my ass. I was jus' askin'." *Shit, I'll keep my suggestions to myself.* She sure did know a lot about all of this, and my ass just felt more and more alienated as she put in her password and pulled up her site, more shit I was oblivious to. It was a wonder she didn't spy on me when I was home with the kids.

She scrolled her finger along the screen and the footage zoomed forward through the day, and I watched us leave in the limo, and a few minutes later a white flower delivery van pulled up, and we watched as a figure got out and walked up to the house with what had to be the largest bouquet of lilies in history. The sun was setting and it was shadowy, so we honestly couldn't tell if it was a man or a woman. *Damn, why hadn't Darla turned on the front light?* We might have been able to see something if she had. He or she had on a huge gardening hat and the lilies completely blocked the side view of their face so watching the video any further was pointless. Michelle groaned and touched stop on the screen.

"What? It's just a damn florist. Probably from one of your fuckin' side hoes." Jealousy seared through me in an instant, flashed with a mixture of anger and pain. It wasn't anyone sendin' me

flowers, that was for damn sure. Climbing off
her lap I started to make my way upstairs, intent
on thinking my way out of this no-win situation
with her lying ass. The thought of being close
to her and thinking that once again Rasheed or
Lania or whoever the fuck else was touching her
or sharing her with me was tearing me up inside.

"Larissa. It doesn't bother you that this florist
had on a sun hat and was trying to deliver flowers damn near in the middle of the night? Every
house out here has security cameras somewhere.
You don't think whoever it was wasn't trying to
hide their face on purpose?"

Her words fell on deaf ears. She was pleading
her case, trying to cover up her lover's tracks
because the flowers probably should've gone to
her fuckin' office and not to our damn house.

"And they just happened to know you love lilies. Most deliveries for most normal companies
do stop at nine, Michelle." I couldn't hide the
smirk on my face. Oooh my ass was heated. I
stormed out to the garage, intent on rolling me
a fat one and putting some clouds up in the air
because this bitch done straight chased away all
of the buzz I had. She had some nerve having
niggas sending flowers and shit up here, and
then on top of that Lania's ass trying to get at her
with me right there just feet away.

I stomped into the garage, the humidity immediately making me break out into a sweat, pissing me off even further. I looked at the layer of dust gathering on my silver Jag and my candy-red Mercedes coupe, both gifts from Michelle. I needed my own got-damn car that I paid for. Not something that was given to me like I was a spoiled brat or someone's child who needed an allowance and permission to do things. At one point in time I thought this was the life I wanted. To have someone just take care of me and just give. She gave me clothes, gave me money. Michelle gave me everything I had. I realized now that the problem with someone doing all the damn giving is that at any moment they could take it all back. I needed to do something, and I needed to do it fast. If our marriage wasn't legal in Florida and she wanted me gone or if I decided I wanted to leave.

The thought of me putting up with so much and walking away with absolutely nothing made my stomach twist into knots. The main reason Michelle even had the nerve to have half of what she had was because of me and did she ever truly show me any appreciation? *Fuck no*. I helped pull her up from her knees and now she wanted to just walk away. We only had one solid rule between the two of us and to this day as far as I knew neither of us had ever broken it. We'd both sworn to never lock our phones and to respect each other's privacy by not going through each other's shit. Pacing in the garage, I couldn't help feeling like a caged animal. Like one of those damn dwarf leopards I'd seen in Trey's zoo magazines. Yup, my ass was a damn endangered ocelot and my habitat, my cubs, and everything else was on the verge of being wiped out if I didn't start fighting. My lifestyle, my way of living, was in jeopardy and so was Lataya's. My mind was made up.

CHAPTER 7

FRENEMIES

I waited until Michelle's ass was at work before I called her, and I prayed that this bitch would actually be cool and not turn around and tell Michelle about our conversation.

"Larissa? Who? Oh, oh I remember your ass. Little Jackie Chan." She sounded like her ass was half asleep when she'd answered the phone.

"Oh yeah, 'bout that. I'm so sorry I was hammered. I hope you can forgive me."

"It is fine. We've all been there. No harm, no foul. What is it you're wanting?" She yawned loud as hell in my ear. *Well, damn, she sure isn't the sugar-coatin' type.*

"So um, Lania, I heard you be on some shit, an' I need to earn some extra money. Fast." I hadn't slept one bit all damn night thinking about what I would say, and was nervous as fuck about finally callin' her, but decided to go ahead an' go through with it.

"And what exactly is this you think you have heard?"

Well, shit, here goes nothin', I thought. Either I'd heard wrong or I'd heard right.

"I want to be an escort, no sex though. Just go on a few dates, look pretty or whatever, an' then bring my ass home. That's it. I heard you could set that up." I held my breath.

"Ahhh. I see, and what does your wife say about this?"

"She don't know and ain't never gonna know."

"Okay. As far as you know I am the alpha, I am the queen of this shit. You want to run with the wolves—you must earn your place in the pack. You're new so no, you won't get first pick or top choice. You have to work your way up."

"So what does that mean, what do I need to do?"

"You won't make as much, the girls who make the most do . . . how should I say . . . . um, favors, but you aren't bad looking so I can work with you. Fix yourself up, text me a picture, full body. I have a client who needs a girl for an event tonight at ten. If you are up to standard, a car will pick you up and drop you off when it's over. One of my men will follow you all evening."

"So when you say 'special favors,' you mean what?" My hands were gettin' sweaty at the excitement an' possibility of doing something new, dangerous.

"I mean, I pay you to go on a date, they'll offer you extra for *extra shit*. I warn you now, sometimes clients can get a bit testy, especially if they drink or do too much drugs. Don't drink or do anything with them so you don't make any kind of decisions you'll regret. You earn three thou, my cut a thousand of that."

Damn. Three grand to sit and look cute. Fuck yes. "Abso-fuckin-lutely. I'll send you a pic in a minute. Thank you, Lania."

I rushed off the phone to get myself sexified. I threw on a red lacy corset that tied up the sides. I glued on some dramatic strip lashes and brushed on a little light makeup. I stood around in the bathroom and played around with the camera on my phone until I had a few pictures I was happy with. I sent them to Lania and waited anxiously for her to let me know if my ass was gonna be able to escort.

Very very nice. Be ready at 9:15 send me your address. btw dress for a play.

That was the text I got back not more than ten minutes later. *Damn, what the fuck do I have that I can wear to a play, and how the fuck am*

I gonna get around Michelle? The answer came to me when I was taking my shower.

Michelle got home at her usual time and I ain't feel like wearing a damn thing she'd bought me. Until I'd earned some money and bought myself some of my own shit, I'd prefer to just fuckin' walk around naked. *Fuck it.*

I crushed up some valiums that were left over from the time she hurt her back rearranging the living room furniture. Them things always knocked her slam the fuck out. Whenever she got home from work she'd usually go straight to the fridge and get a glass of tea. That was her routine. Well, I'd dumped all the tea outta the pitcher except for like half a glass, and mixed in the crushed pills, adding some extra sugar so it wouldn't taste bitter.

"You been home all day, drank all the damn tea, and didn't think to make any more, Larissa?" were the first words she said when she got home from work. I just looked at her ass and raised my eyebrow.

"So you're still doing that no-talking shit I see. Okay. Okay. Well, I'm not making any more. Y'all can all drink water tomorrow for all I care. "

I watched her ass pour that last little bit of tea into a glass, thinking, *yup, drink up, drink up, sweetie.* Gigglin' to myself, I just carried my ass on upstairs to start getting ready for my night.

***

I waited out front, smoking some of the shit Shanice had sent me to help calm my nerves. At nine-fifteen two black Lincoln Town Cars pulled up into our driveway and Michelle was on the couch, unconscious, just like I knew she'd be. I tiptoed out the front door, wearing one of her wack-ass black skirts and a red button-down Michael Kors top. I couldn't resist throwing on a pair of matching red pumps; conservative was not a word in my vocabulary. I was going to be escorting Darnell Wiggs Jr. to see *Le . . . Miser . . . Misera . . .* Fuck, I couldn't pronounce that shit. It was some kinda French play. All I knew was I didn't know this actor and I didn't know the damn play and they both sounded boring as hell. The three Gs I'd get at the end of the night was the only thing exciting me about the whole damn evening.

When we pulled up in front of the theatre my ass was immediately turned off by all the old, rigid, stuffy-collared folk in suits and ties walking toward the place. Darnell walked up to my car and my frowned disappeared. It was time for my escort acting to begin. He wasn't a bad-looking older man; you know, dudes ain't my thing to begin with any damn way, but he was all right, I guess. He looked around forty-five, brown skin, he was kinda pudgy looking with droopy eyes.

"Well hello to you, gorgeous. I'ma have to tell Ms. Lania she done sent me a million-dolla one this time." He grabbed my hand and helped me out of the car. I smiled, not sure what to say back since I ain't never did this shit before. He extended his arm, and after glancing around nervously I'd seen that some of the other women had their hands on the inside of the guys' arms, so I placed my hand on the inside of his.

"How are you doin', honey?"

I almost tripped over my own damn feet and fell on my face. Out of all the pet names, he couldn't have called me sweetie or baby? I smiled at him weakly, trying to push all thoughts of Rasheed and Michelle's drama out of my head.

"I'm good. Thanks."

We walked into the darkened theatre and up to the top. He'd gotten us these special box seats; I guessed they were more expensive, I didn't know. If I was gonna watch a play or anything I'd rather be in the front row than in a seat far up and off to the side, but hey—these rich folk be having they own warped opinions on luxury. I think they just like sitting over top of muthafuckas personally.

I was half asleep halfway through the play when Darnell leaned over, his breath smelling like he'd gone in on a plate of chitlins with extra shit, all up against the side of my face. I did my best not to turn away completely.

"Baby, you play wit' it an' I'll give you another three grand."

Cringing, I tried to hear the words over the stank comin' out of his mouth. *Play with what?* was the first thought that echoed in my brain, but I already knew what the hell he meant. Lania said the girls who sucked, fucked, and did extras made the extra money, but my ass had never even seen a real dick let alone touched one. I shook my head no and watched the stage, silently kissing the thought of $6,000 good-bye.

Once again, "Yuck-Mouf" was assaultin' the side of my face, whispering loud as hell, about to melt the fake eyelashes off of my damn eyelids.

"C'mon, can't nobody see up here; it's dark."

I heard the zipper of his pants slide down. "Gimme yo' hand, baby. It's three thousand more. Easy money. Make Daddy D happy, baby."

Maybe it's because my ass was high and I just wanted this muthafucka to stop whisperin' air shit all upside my damn head. I closed my eyes and let him take my hand. I was trying to tell myself it was just like one of our straps at home.

But nah, our straps ain't got super nappy taco meat hair all around 'em and fat rolls. It was like trying to grab a hold of a short-ass soggy eggroll. Darnell kept his hand over mind, directin' it up and down until his li'l eggroll firmed up. I tried to watch the actors and shit on stage and think about what I'd cook for dinner tomorrow—anything but what the fuck was going on with my other hand.

I almost gagged when I felt his mouth brush the side of my neck. He was breathin' vapors of shit fumes right into my damn hair. He started to move my hand faster. I felt like either we was gonna start a forest fire or Indian burn the skin off his dick, and then his body jerked like he was having muscle spasms and charley horses at the same time. Snatching my hand back from beneath his I cringed, trying to find some place to wipe away the slimy, hot mass of yuck that was now sliding down my fingers toward my wrist.

"Honey, you are amazing. Hold on a sec, baby. I got a handkerchief for you." He handed me the small piece of white cloth and I wiped my hand, still feeling like I needed to scour that muthafucka in bleach.

When the play ended Darnell walked me to my car and climbed into the back with me to pay me out for the night. He started to hand me six thousand but when I reached for it he pulled it back.

"Ten if we fuck."

What the hell? If this old raggedy stank-breath nigga ain't give me my damn money . . . His ass was looking like he just knew I was about to say yes, too. "Sorry, Darnell, I don't have sex."

His droopy face scrunched up in anger. "Stuck-up bitch. You gon' regret that shit."

Money flew all around the back seat. He'd thrown all $6,000 at my face and slammed out of the car. Lania's driver looked back at me through the rearview mirror.

"You okay back there? Not too many girls tell Darnell no."

"Guess my ass ain't too many girls huh?"

He smiled and handed me a few of the hundreds that had managed to land up in the front with him, and I texted Lania to let her know everything went well, and she replied fast as hell.

> Good I have another one for you tomorrow night if you're up to it?

I stared at the message. She didn't get a cut of any of the money earned from the extra shit I decided to do. So minus her little thousand, I was up $5,000 for just one night's worth of work.

Not bad, even though I had to touch that nigga's nasty-ass li'l sausage dick. *What the fuck, might as well get it while I can.*

I'm up–down whateva lol.

We pulled back up at the house late as hell and I crept my ass inside. Michelle was still asleep on the couch where I'd left her ass, so I went upstairs and showered fast as hell and got my ass in bed like I'd been there all along. *Damn, how the hell am I gonna get outta the house two nights in a row . . .*

CHAPTER 8

SPECIAL DELIVERY—SPECIAL K

Michelle went to work as usual and I had all day to plan a way to get ready for my second official day on the job. I didn't know what time Lania would need me so I needed to figure out a way to get up outta the damn house without comin' off kinda suspicious. The damn pill bottle only had two valiums left in it and if there was only one or none left up in there, who was the first person you think she'd look at? My ass. So the valiums were not an option. I texted Lania.

> Don't think I can do tonight. Put da wife to sleep and now I'm outta pills.

I stared out the kitchen window at the pool. *Damn shame I ain't never learn how to swim.* That water was lookin' nice as fuck and it was hot as hell outside. My phone beeped.

I'll send Key over with somethin jus put a few drops of it on the brim of her glass or in the bottom—night night I promise.

No more than twenty minutes later the door-bell rang.

"Who's at the door, Mommy? Who's that?" Trey's li'l nosey ass was all in the damn way.

"It's ya damn daddy. Li'l nigga, it ain't for you, now get the hell on upstairs before I beat yo' li'l ass."

I was surprised to see that Keyshawn actually brought me a signed ball.

"You remembered. Damn, thanks." I was already tryin' to figure out how much I could sell that shit on eBay for.

"Cute kid. He look jus' like Michelle."

I looked back. Trey was still at the top of the stairs. I frowned up at his ass, which sent him runnin'. "Whateva. Lania said you was bringin' me somethin." I ain' have time to be dawdlin' with this nigga. We walked into the livin' room and he handed me a little brown bottle.

"It's Special K, strong shit. You don't need a lot; just a couple of drops or she could die okay?"

I nodded. "So what else can y'all get?" My weed stash was damn near gone, and if I was gonna be doin' any more of these jobs, I was gonna need to re-up or somethin' quick.

"We can get anything you want. Just say the word."

Damn, I thought, *now that is what the fuck I'm talkin' about.* Florida wasn't looking so bad after all.

I walked in the house at my usual time and all was quiet, surprisingly. There was no sign of Larissa or the kids. I set my briefcase down and walked into the living room, no toys all over the place, no babies, no wife. This was strange. Kicking off my shoes I made my way into the kitchen, thinking everyone must be in there, but no, it was empty. I was shocked to see a plate sitting in the middle of the counter with a lonely tuna salad sandwich on it and a glass of iced tea beside it. There was no way I was eatin' that shit. Larissa put so much sugar and sweet pickle relish in her tuna and chicken salad it's a wonder she ain't have diabetes by now. I would do that glass of tea though; that's the only thing she made perfect. It was all impressive; maybe this was her way of saying sorry.

Sitting at the counter, I flipped through most of the day's mail and drank my tea, wondering where everyone had wandered off to. I was halfway through with my glass when I thought

I heard Lataya laughin' upstairs, and I got up to go see what she was up to. The room swayed and it felt like I had the worst case of vertigo ever. Everything in the kitchen was rocking back and forth, and as hard as I tried I couldn't focus my eyes on anything in the room. I fell down to my knees. My only option was to crawl to the stairs.

"Larissa." Yelling, I waited down there like a damn invalid for her to come help my ass. Listening, I waited a few more minutes. *Shit.* The shower was running. The queen of forty-five-minute showers would not be coming to help my ass anytime soon. My eyes were rolling in my head every time I tried to look in any given direction, and, I mean, I'd had vertigo before, but never to this extreme. I pulled myself up the stairs one at a time, surprised I made it all the way to the bedroom without puking before I collapsed in the middle of the bed. The last thing I remembered was jasmine soap and body oil while Larissa stood over me, naked and wet, looking down at me, drying her hair with a towel. And then there was nothing.

CHAPTER 9

DON'T BE EYEBALLIN' ME, MISTER

Hopefully this date would be more exciting than the last one. It was late, midnight when the car came to get me, and my ass was tired but ready to make this money. Lania said this dude was into some kinda kinky bondage-type shit so I put on an all-black cat suit. She was like he usually just be on some step on his balls or paddle his ass type of craziness that I ain't know people really paid for, but as long as I ain't have to fuck him, it was whatever.

The car let me out in front of nice hotel no more than twenty minutes from the house. This was a little too close to home for my taste, but Nino, this big-ass Italian muscle gorilla–looking muthafucka, one of Lania's bodyguards, would be outside if I needed him and would be followin' me back home, so fuck it, I was all in. Nino escorted me through the lobby up to room 376.

He stood a few feet down the hall away from the door so he wouldn't scare the client. Knockin' on the door, I took a couple breaths 'cause I noticed my hand was shakin'. The door swung open and a tall shirtless white guy was standin' there. He was tan as fuck. I mean so tan he looked brown and all the hair on his chest and on his head looked white.

"How you doin', beautiful?" He had a friendly smile that made me feel comfortable, so I smiled back and walked in. He offered me a drink but I turned it down as I was instructed.

"What would you like to do, um . . ." Embarrassed, I realized I couldn't remember his damn name.

"Call me Leslie."

I stared at him, 'cause I wasn't sure if that was part of his fetish, but I was damn sure Leslie was a woman's name.

"It's a unisex name, darlin'."

Damn can this muthafucka read minds, too? I besta stop thinkin'.

"Well okay then, Leslie, you can call me Trista." I made it up and cringed. I coulda come up with somethin' better than that, but oh well.

"Okay, Trista. That's fine an' dandy but I'ma call you Chocolate Thai. Now, c'mere. Take your clothes off."

Did this bitch . . . I wasn't sure if I was supposed to be offended or if that was a racial thing, and, *naked? I could have sworn Lania said he don't do sex.*

"C'mon now, Chocolate Thai. I ain't got all night."

"But, Leslie, I'm sure they told you I don't have sex, right?" I was still close enough to the door that I could run my ass up outta there if I needed to.

"I'm sure they told you I like *other* things. Now. Naked. Here. Please."

He stripped down to his ugly-ass tighty whities and lay across the bed and, fuck, if I ain't feel stuck between a damn couple thousand and a hard Leslie. I took my shit off, gritting my teeth the whole time all the way down to my damn draws. If this fool tried to slide anything up in anywhere, I swear I was screamin' for Nino so damn fast.

"Now, come over here, beautiful, and lemme see what Chocolate Thai taste like." Ladies and gentlemen, when this fool said he wanted to see what it taste like, I kid you not . . . Climbin' up on the bed, I'm preppin' myself to ask his ass if he got a dental dam or some shit, 'cause he wasn't 'bout to be puttin' his mouth all over my pussy unprotected. Before I could get the words out he scooped my ass up—y'all know I'm small—and had me squattin' over his face so he could rub his eyes, *yes, his eyes,* all up in my stuff. I could feel him blinkin' and shit. His eyelashes were tickling the fuck outta me an' I was tryin' not to laugh while I just *squatted* there. His free hand was in his draws strokin' away and I was just perched up there lookin' around like *what the fuck kinda freak nasty shit is this?*

Easiest $8,000 I've ever made in my entire life.

CHAPTER 10

GIVING ME HEAD . . . ACHES

Wakin' up was hell. It felt like my arms and legs were disconnected from my head and my torso. I was all kinds of groggy and couldn't remember why. Larissa and I hadn't spoken more than a few words to each other since Saturday night and not only was she being an asshole, but she was doing it in the most frustrating ways possible. Aside from her time with the kids she spent almost every day walking around the damn house butt-ass naked. I swear the woman was intentionally boycotting her damn clothing. There were times when I'd have to literally tell myself to close my mouth and stop staring. I was so sexually frustrated, I knew for a fact if you put me on a treadmill hooked up to a generator I could provide enough power to run half of Miami for at least a week. I was also having to either cook or order something because most of the time, aside from some tea or a sandwich, she was refusing to cook or lift a finger and I was starting to get beyond fed up with her bullshit.

Every day I'd been home from work on time and today would be the first day that I'd be late. I'd met with Jim Bartell from Strong Arm Security. Until Rah or whoever decided to show their face it just seemed like the logical thing to do. Jim was a much older white man with a leathery tan face, head full of white hair, and the clearest blue eyes I'd ever seen. He made it a point to come meet me at my office in case I was being followed. He didn't want to raise any suspicion or draw the attention of whoever was harassing us. My meeting with him was a blur of paperwork and certifications, where I pretty much put the protection of my life and those of the Ris and the kids at the mercy of his security team. It cost an arm and a leg but knowing that I'd have someone at the house around the clock in addition to someone trailing me wherever I went was a definite relief.

I'd purposefully been ignoring texts and phone calls from both Keyshawn *and* Lania. Their persistence was damn amazing. If the roles were reversed I'd have given up on myself by Tuesday. I was leaving the office as usual when my phone went off. It was a text from Keyshawn:

It's Thursday, haven't heard from you. Dinner party @ Curtis' place Friday 9. Hope you're a woman of your word. Would be honored if you'd make an appearance. Bring wifey if you're feelin' scary.

Damn. The nigga knew how to get my attention. I drove the rest of the way home silently debating whether I should stay or go, take Ris or leave her. There were just so many variables to consider. Was Lania going to be there? Was his entourage of random hoes going to be there? If I asked Key about any of them would it come across as strange? Would Lania act funny toward me since I'd pretty much shut her down and been brushing her off ever since?

My phone vibrated again but it was Jim calling from the security company. I'd been waiting to hear back from him since setting everything up on Monday.

"Answer call." I rarely used the in-car mobile audio feature but figured I'd might as well since I had it. "This is Michelle."

"Michelle, this is Jim. How are ya?"

I smiled when I heard his heavy Southern accent; he sounded like a straight-up farm-raised country boy. "I'm doing well thank you."

"Good. I've been looking into yer situation. The bad news is Rasheed is no longer in custody in Virginia."

My vision momentarily blacked out. If I weren't sitting in traffic I might have crashed, or run off the highway at the sound of those words.

"Rasheed isn't what? You mean transferred? Right? Jim?" I couldn't even form a complete coherent sentence.

"Well now, Michelle, I mean escaped."

The depth of meaning behind those words alone threatened to swallow me alive.

"Apparently three weeks ago a female CO helped him escape. She's been missing in action ever since. Suspected to either be out on the run with him or paid 'nuff to disappear. Put him in a K-9 trainin' unit cage—pretended he was a sick dog, needed to see a vet. Guards on duty were useless pricks, didn't even bother checkin' the crate as required. She drove him out in the mornin'—they ain' know 'til they did the night count." My mind was reeling. God I felt like I was gonna be sick. I fought the urge to vomit and waited for Jim to continue. My worst nightmare was coming true.

"Now don't panic. I want you to go 'bout yer business an' keep livin' as you normally would. Possum only play possum 'til you walk away. So we don't want him to know we watchin' you or the li'l ones."

Did this muthafucka just say, "don't panic"? I almost hysterically laughed out loud. He obviously didn't know how calculating Rah was when it came to getting his revenge.

"Rasheed is a very dangerous man, Jim. As I told you before he's just tormentin' me right now. His revenge is never a pretty or fair thing."

"I read his file, seen his face, I know what he's done. My boys know exactly who they're lookin' fer an' what kinda man they're dealin' with. We've protected folk from much more dangerous people than yer ordinary street thug, ma'am. All I'ma do is double up on yer security an' there's no extra charge fer that. There's already a wanted bulletin out fer him across all states from Virginia all the way down here. The reward to turn 'im in is bigger than the payout fer helpin' his ass, I can assure you that much."

All the blood had drained from my hands, my grip was so tight on the steering wheel. I removed them and tried flexing my fingers. I took a few deep breaths and tried focusing on the traffic as it began to move ahead.

"Jim? I need somewhere to take my children. He isn't going to want to hurt the kids. It's jus' me an' my wife he's really after. Do you have anywhere, like a safe house?" My voice was shaky from fear and from the tears I was fighting back. I refused to cry. I got myself into this shit, and I'd fight my way the fuck out of it.

"Well yes, ma'am. I've got a few places—quieter than gerbil piss on cotton if ya know what I mean. They're well off the grid, very limited access. Gonna take a li'l time tho'—gotta get y'all all clear. In the meantime please try ta relax. You hired some of *the* best men in the business, I swear on my own life. Summa my boys are retired Seals, Secret Service, and CIA. We ain't lost a client yet and I don't plan on losin' one anytime soon, baby doll."

I tried to find the reassurance that Jim was offering. He sounded like an overprotective older grandfather, talking to me like I'd just skinned my knee. But this was no skinned knee and I wasn't his granddaughter; to him I was just another dollar. Shit, another couple thousand dollars a day, but you get my damn point.

"All right, Jim, I'm not gonna panic. I'm gonna do my best to trust you on this." I was saying it more to convince myself than to convince him.

"That's good, sweetheart. Now if you have any events, attend 'em as usual. We want to draw this summa bitch out. You sittin' up in the house ain' gonna do it."

"Really! You want me to do what?" What he was suggesting went against every molecular instinct in my body. The last thing I wanted to do was leave the safety of my home, not after knowing for a fact Rah was out and most likely out for blood.

"Sweetheart, I been doin' this pro'ly since you were in pigtails. When's all the stuff been happenin' that you told me 'bout—when you were goin' or comin', right?"

I sighed and it felt like the longest, most drawn-out damn sigh I'd ever sighed in my entire life. He did have a point. Everything happened when I wasn't in the house. If this was what they needed in order to draw him out and haul his ass back to prison, all I could do was shake my head.

"All right, Jim. My wife and I have a dinner party to attend tomorrow evening with Keyshawn the basketball player. Unless she decides not to go, then it'll just be me by myself." By this point fear literally had me shaking from head to toe; it was like I'd just jumped out of a tub of ice water. I turned on the seat warmer, hoping it would help me regain some of my composure.

"No problem, ma'am. I believe one my boys said they'd seen him stop by the house one day. But the other miss talked with him so there seemed to be no problem. Just call me with yer itinerary before you leave. Jus' lemme know where yer headed, an' what time, an' the information fer the sitter who'll be keepin' the kids while yer gone. We'll handle the rest."

"Okay, thank you." I disconnected the call and pulled over to the side of the highway, on to the shoulder for vehicle breakdowns. All of this had to be a bad dream. At any minute Ris would kiss me and wake me up and everything would be back to normal. I was momentarily stunned. *And Keyshawn was at the house? He talked to Ris? Why?* The only thing that came to mind was that he was looking for me, since I hadn't been answering any of his messages. I just hoped he'd made something up good enough to convince Ris of why he'd stop by unannounced.

My mind was overloaded. I couldn't fight my tears anymore. Technically this was a breakdown, just not a mechanical one. I was freezing in the middle of summer, scared, and I had no idea if I could go through with this shit. I jumped as something hit the driver-side window hard and loud. It was a younger white guy with dusky blond hair, wearing dark sunglasses. I was afraid to roll down my window and only cracked it slightly.

"Yes?" I barely croaked out the word and tried to find something to wipe my nose with.

"Ma'am, Strong Arm Security. I'm Keith."

I breathed a sigh of relief. Keith pointed at the hood of my car. To anyone watching it would appear as if he were just a Good Samaritan asking if I was having car trouble.

"You need not be stoppin' on the highway like this. Are you okay?"

I sniffled loudly and shook my head yes.

"All right, I'm gonna radio in for a switch in case my vehicle's been compromised. But I'm right here until my relief arrives."

"I'm sorry, okay. Thank you." I pulled myself together and put the car into drive, feeling slightly secure with my paid guardian angel trailing me.

The rest of the drive home I was on auto pilot as I silently debated exactly what Ris needed to know. It wouldn't be fair to hide something like this from her but I had two things to consider. Ris already thought I was doing wrong by her and this would further fuel her bullshit misconceptions. Her track record for dealing with Rasheed stress has always been to use and I definitely didn't want to start her on that path again. It would make the most sense for her to go with me to the party, if I could convince her. With us both out of the house I would at least know my babies were okay. After what happened with Derrick, and Rasheed's oldest son, I could almost bet every dollar to my name that he wouldn't dare touch the kids.

Ris and I were the targets. If we kept ourselves busy and away from the kids then hopefully Rah would surface and everything would play itself out. By the time I pulled into my driveway my mind was completely made up. My hands were shaking so bad I could barely type Key's name into my directory to pull up his information.

Send me Curtis' address. Rsvp +1 thanks Chelle.

I sat there with the car still running, trying to pull myself together while I waited for his reply.

Gotcha Lady. 1610 Medallion Arch Miami see you there ;)

I knew the area very well; some of the wealthiest people in Florida had properties in that area. I called to see if Darla was available and called Jim back with all of the information he'd requested before going into the house. I didn't want Ris listening in on anything that would alarm her.

"So we gotta have private convos in the car now?"

Where the fuck did she come from? I wasn't even a good two steps in the door before Ris was in front of me, splendidly naked and pissed the fuck off, eyes glaring up at me—hands on her hips.

"Damn, so we spy out of windows now? We don't speak for an entire week, and these are the first words we say to someone who gets us an exclusive invite to a party with the owner of Keyshawn's team?" I glared down at her, my own anger fueled by my stress.

"Fuck a party. Who da hell were you out there talkin' to dat you couldn't talk in da damn house?"

Wow, she was fuming. That's the best word for anger that I could think of to accurately describe a Ris who wouldn't get excited over a party. As if on cue, the kids came bursting downstairs as they always did. They were oblivious to Ris's lack of clothing, letting me know she'd most likely been like that all damn day. I knelt down and kissed both my babies on the tops of their heads, wondering why they were still in their PJs. She at least could have washed them up and put clothes on they asses.

"Hey my loves, Mommy and I need to talk, go play upstairs. Are you guys hungry?" They both yelled yes in unison, and I rolled my eyes. She apparently hadn't bothered fixing them anything to eat either.

"Okay, go upstairs and I'll call you when it's ready." I waited until they were both out of sight. I stared down at her and tried to be as understanding as I could, but my patience was wearing thin. "Larissa, are you on something?"

"The fuck kinda . . . No. Um, Michelle, are you on somebody dick when you ain't up in dis house?"

I had to count to ten twice before I could speak. "No, Ris. I didn't wanna scare the kids. I hired a security company to watch all of us. There's a unit that follows me and there's another one that will stay wherever you and the kids are. That's who I was on the phone with. I also called and got Darla for tomorrow because I assumed you'd wanna go with me to Curtis's party."

Her face softened up just slightly even though I could still see the doubt in her eyes. I walked into the living room and sat on the couch, pulling the security contract out of my briefcase. I held it out in one hand and just let it hang there. She was no more than a few steps behind me and it wasn't long before she took it from my extended hand and started reading it over. I knew her entirely too well.

"Damn, bae, this shit is expensive."

Inwardly I rolled my eyes, thinking, *no shit*. "Our lives are worth way more than that, Ris."

She dropped down onto the couch beside me and didn't say a word. Not a "thank you," "I'm sorry," nothing.

"Do we really need someone watchin' us all like this? I think you're overreacting. Why didn't you discuss this with me first? I feel like a prisoner bein' followed an' spied on without my permission."

"Ris, you're lookin' at it for the wrong reasons. It's not personal. It's for protection." I couldn't believe she was actually taking offense to having someone watch out for her. I swore when it came to this woman I could never do anything right no matter how hard I tried.

"So when you say they signed confidentiality agreements, that means that they keep our shit private? They just protect us and go about they business."

"That's exactly what it means. And what's up with this sudden aversion you've taken to wearin' your damn clothes?"

"Huh? Oh, um nothin' I jus' ain' feel like puttin' any on one day or the next. So I didn't. So what time is this party we s'posed to be hittin' up?"

Relief swept over me like a cool breeze hitting the desert sand. I leaned forward and kissed Ris's shoulder, expecting her to pull away, but she didn't. I rested my lips there and closed my eyes, inhaling her warm jasmine-vanilla scent that was so familiar to me. I couldn't help myself; it had been too long and I'd been teased and toyed with too many times over the last couple of days. Something needed to take my mind off of all the drama and craziness. Ris was so petite and easy to maneuver, it was nothing for me to grab her and pull her in closer to me. For her to be walking around completely naked she was still amazingly warm and her body heat ignited me—soothing me at the same time.

You know something? Every woman has a tell. The shit works just like poker. No matter how pissed off she was or how indifferent she tried to act—her tell would give her away every single time. I licked my lips and lightly floated a warm, wet kiss from the base of her neck down all the way down to the small of her back, and instinctively she arched. That was Ris's tell. I smiled a devilish smile. I had her.

"Chelle, let's go upstairs." That small action had her voice in an almost breathless whisper. She ain't have to tell me twice. I kicked off my heels and was off the couch before she could even stand up. We tiptoed past the kids' room; they were playing and wouldn't remember they were hungry for at least another hour or so. When we made it to our bedroom, Ris surprised me by pushing me up against the bedroom door and standing on her toes to kiss me. I closed my eyes, enjoying the fullness of her lips and the giving in her kiss. Ris always kissed as if she were kissing with her very soul. Her naked body pressed tightly against me, she could take my take my breath away just with the earnest genuine love and passion in her kisses. My hands began to frantically remove my clothing, desperate to feel the fire of her skin pressed against mine.

"Bae, I've missed you *so much*. I'm so sorry." Her lips broke from mine and she whispered in between kissing each little area of skin I uncovered, and I couldn't get my blazer, blouse, or my skirt off fast enough. We fell onto the bed in a tangle with Ris landing on top of me. I closed my eyes as the heat of her mouth circled and teased one nipple. Her mouth left my skin just long enough to circle and give the same attention to its twin. I was trying my damnedest not to think about cherries or rosé. I reached down with both hands and roughly cupped her ass, making her moan in response, and I silently cursed. It wasn't the same as that hoarse, deep, sultry sound Lania made. Ris ventured farther down my body, her tongue burning a path that just couldn't seem to melt my icy exterior. I needed to stop her before she found disappointment in the fact that she was putting in all this work and I wasn't wet yet.

I started to reach down and stop her but I was surprised when she stopped on her own.

"Remember when I said I had a trick for you?"

I was half excited and half scared to answer her. She didn't need an answer. I stared at the bounce in her ass as she hopped up and disappeared into her closet. She quickly came back with a black bag and a blindfold. Cautiously I started to sit up.

"I know you better not have a damn snake or no crazy shit." I was dead-ass serious. Ris was unpredictable sometimes and I'd be damned if she thought we were gonna play animal kingdom up in here. She giggled and kissed me, kneeling over me blindfold in hand.

"No, baby, it's nothing like dat. I ain't even gonna tie you up or nothin', so you can stop me at any time. Okay?"

I reluctantly nodded, and let her engulf me in darkness as she placed the blindfold over my eyes and climbed off of me.

"Turn on your stomach, bae."

I did as instructed. Without being able to see, my senses were heightened beyond reason. The heat from Ris's body seemed to magnify as she lay fully on my back and gently nibbled at my tell—my neck. I couldn't help it. Any and all thoughts of Lania suddenly vanished as the scent of jasmine and Ris's body heat took over my senses.

She gently sucked at one side of my neck, letting me enjoy the feel of the heat from her mouth before she slid her lips across the nape of my neck to do the same to the other. She made it a point to only lightly graze me with her teeth. Teasing me. Her hands were liquid heat as they slid underneath me to tug and tease at my nipples, twirling them between her warm fingers. I tilted my head to give her lips better access and damn near screamed when suddenly her teeth sank deep into the sensitive spot between my shoulder and collarbone.

I was lost. I could feel myself starting to throb for attention. Her hands were everywhere as she trailed kisses down my sides and my back. She softly nibbled and kissed my ass and my thighs, making me squirm impatiently. We'd never played this game before so I honestly had no idea what to expect. She left me for a second and I could hear the bag rustling as I waited. Unexpected shivers ran all the up my spine that vibrated behind my eyelids when suddenly her nose parted my ass and her tongue drove deep into my pussy from behind, causing me to nearly arch off the bed.

Larissa had *never* done that before. I buried my face into the comforter and prayed it muffled my moans. The heat from her tongue was driving me crazy. She made lazy circles back and forth up and around my clit, teasing and prodding. Ris moaned, and I melted, soaking the comforter and all the bedding underneath. She was lapping up every drop and thoroughly enjoying it. I was so damn close my legs were starting to shake.

"Mmm somebody been eatin' they pineapples. You ready, bae?"

Damn right, I thought, because my ass couldn't talk. She was mumbling with her mouth full, but I still understood her. I was so far gone I couldn't even answer. But oh yes, I was definitely ready. I wiggled my ass farther back onto her nose and tongue as my reply. I could feel the first throb, the first convulsion. I hadn't cum in so long I'd stopped keeping track. Sparks and flashes were starting to appear behind the blindfold due to me squeezing my eyes closed so tight. The comforter was now gripped between my teeth and I was on a downward spiral straight into—*shock!* My eyes widened behind the blindfold. I gasped as every good feeling suddenly fled from me as quickly as it had approached. *No this heffa did not just jam her muthafuckin finger in my damn ass.*

"What the fuck?" I bucked forward. Pain, anger, and just a tinge of feel good still coursed through my system. Her finger was still jammed firmly in place like that little Dutch girl you see in all those pictures plugging the leak in the dam.

"Bae, come back. I said I had a trick for you, damn. It's s'posed to make you cum harder." She sounded aggravated.

I stared back at her, wide-eyed and in complete shock while I tried to relax around the sudden unexpected intrusion in my damn asshole.

"Damn, Larissa, you could've prepped it first. Licked your finger, lubed it up with some K-Y, I don't know." I mentally analyzed my asshole for a second. Surprisingly, it wasn't as bad as I thought it'd be, it was actually kind of tingly. A little numbness seemed to be spreading around, but it sure wasn't super fantastic either.

"I did. What do you think was in the bag? Now come back."

I tried to relax but there was just something "dirty" feeling about anus play and I couldn't help it. I kept clenching my ass cheeks and making the stank face at her. Ris had officially with a single finger killed the moment, and all the blood rushing from my head back up to my head was starting to make me feel lightheaded.

"Ris, you done killed it. I'm good—I can't."

"Mommmmmy." The sound of our voices obviously reminded the kids of the fact that they hadn't been fed and they both chimed in, screaming from outside the bedroom door. Ris actually surprised me for once.

"I'll go, and I'll bring you somethin' for your head." She gently slid her index finger out of my ass and I cringed. *Damn, she could've at least started with a pinky. Where they do that at?*

"Ris," I called after her when she was halfway out the door. "Please wash that thing before you feed my babies."

She wiggled it at me and I leaned back in horror, frustration at yet again *almost* getting off completely pissing me off. Yeah, I definitely felt a headache coming on.

CHAPTER 11

WORKIN' WOMAN

"Taya, sit yo' li'l yella ass down befo' I sit you down."

She stared at me, her eyes all round and shit like she ain't know what I was saying. I gave her a 3.2-second window to drop back down into her little pink plastic chair; otherwise, I was gonna light her ass up. Dropping peanut butter and jelly sandwiches onto the table in front of the kids, I pulled out my cell.

"Don't neitha of y'all move 'til I come back. Mommy is upstairs sleeping. I don't wanna hear a damn peep. Okay?"

They both nodded at me slowly.

"Now eat." I walked out into the garage, sweat beading up on my forehead instantly. *Shit, Michelle so good for heating up floors and wasting money on security and shit, why we can't put air conditioning in the damn garage? That* seemed to be where I was spending so much of my spare time any damn way.

"Ahhh, hey, you. I just got feedback, a complaint from Darnell, who was not very pleased. You do know that, right?" Lania was talking small shit right now.

I already had Darnell's money so I couldn't care less what he was or wasn't happy 'bout.

"Shit, you didn't tell me I needed to take a case of Tic Tacs with me. I might've made a necklace out of mints or offered that nigga some Binaca first."

"Well, Mr. Leslie loved you and Darnell is always hard to please. Plus, I had to know how you would handle not-so-pleasant or beautiful situations. Darnell was like an initiation, you did well, though."

Well damn, let me find out this heffa got herself a mini sorority and shit. I shuddered, a chill of disgust running through my body at just the thought of Darnell's breath on the side of my face.

"Well I'm callin' you 'cause I got a bigger problem. Michelle ass done went out and hired a security company to fuckin' follow us around and shit. Not regular security. These niggas in unmarked cars doin' hidden surveillance-type shit."

The line was quiet for a minute. I could tell I had Lania stumped with that one. Hell, my ass was stumped too.

"Hmm, security company you say? We will have to think on this little hiccup. I'm sure there are ways around her hired dogs. Enough bullshit, are you guys coming to the party?"

"She mentioned a dinner party or somethin' but I don't know. We got a lot goin' on right now."

"Oh trust me we have the best parties, best coke, best everything. If she's worried about security Curtis has his own. No one's going to come up in there with any shit. I might also have something for you, if you feel like making some *extra money.*"

Her emphasis on the words "extra money" let me know plain and simple this wouldn't be a regular meet-and-greet type situation.

"I know how you are about men, this one would definitely be different."

The thought of making another five or eight grand had my heart going triple time. That would put me at damn near $20,000 in less than a week. At this rate I'd be making so much money I wouldn't even need to worry about Michelle taking care of me, or leaving me anymore. I couldn't resist it. "All right, I'm in. What do you need me to do?"

"I'll fill you in when you get to the party, and then we'll have to find a way to get you away from your wifey. I promise we will have so much fun—even your uptight Michelle will be drunk dancing by the time we're all done."

I almost laughed in Lania's damn ear trying to picture that shit happening. *Never in a million years, no—no way—no how.*

"Lania, you obviously don't know my wife."

CHAPTER 12

DOUBLE TAKE

Darla showed up right on time as expected and I led her upstairs to the playroom where the kids were quietly watching a movie. Ris was still in the bathroom, getting dressed. I smoothed an imaginary wrinkle out of the burgundy and gold comforter on our bed and sat down. I'd decided to keep my attire simple, wearing a black high-waist Cavalli pencil skirt and my favorite silver Yves Saint Laurent blouse that flared at my collarbone. It was sexy, yet classy; with the right pair of glasses I could definitely pull off the naughty librarian image.

I was too antsy and stressed out to worry about fussing over my hair. Instead, I opted to just let it hang loose, falling past my shoulders with the ends bumped under so it curled slightly. I might have looked like a perfectly composed, well put together woman on the outside but, on the inside, I was a complete and absolute mess.

Nothing was adding up. I was so careful when we left Virginia. I'd gone through so much trouble getting us away from there as quickly as possible and as discretely as possible. How on earth had Rah managed to find us? The question rolled over in my head repeatedly along with the image of his face the last time I'd seen him. Years hadn't erased that memory: the day he realized that the misery he'd suffer for the rest of his life was all because of us, because of me. There was so much hate and anger.

My stomach had rumbled very loudly, interrupting my thoughts. I hadn't had much of an appetite since talking to Jim, and Lord knows I couldn't eat anything. My nerves were so bad I constantly felt nauseous. A few strong drinks were exactly what I needed, but just enough to calm my nerves so I could talk business with Curtis if the opportunity presented itself.

"I'm all ready." Ris walked in looking like she was going to either a rap video or porn shoot audition. She was wearing her bright pink "come fuck me" stilettos, the ones we only used for playing dress-up. They were paired with a matching skirt and matching see-through fishnet top with a black and pink zebra-striped bra underneath.

"Um, you know this is a dinner party and not a Nicki Minaj lookalike contest right?" I was agitated and didn't bother hiding it.

"Oh whateva. If you wanna roll up in there lookin' like somebody's damn principal dat's on you. I seen how Key an' his people do on TV, my ass gon' fit right the fuck in. Watch."

And watch was exactly what I'd decided to do. The gated mansion community was nothing like the ones Ris had ever been exposed to. We'd been to mansion parties in Virginia, but trying to compare a million dollar house to a multi-million dollar estate is about the same as trying to compare Section 8 housing to Executive Condos. They ain't even in the same playing field.

When the limo dropped us off in front of the main entrance my own eyes widened; this man's house was the size of a small strip mall. There had to be at least five levels to it on the inside. A butler greeted us, carrying a tray of champagne, and we each took glasses. It was nine o'clock on the dot and I imagined we must have been the first to arrive, seeing as how there were no other cars in front, unless he had a damn parking garage somewhere that I just hadn't seen. It was highly fucking possible.

We were led inside through the main foyer by another suited-up butler. It reminded me of the

Roman Colosseum in Italy where the gladiators fought. Huge pillars lined both sides and Ris and I both stopped and looked up in awe. The ceiling was hundreds of feet up, but instead of the typical chandelier the ceiling was a constellation of glittering stars and planets, and every so often a shooting star would fly from one end of the ceiling across to the other.

"The guests are all in the evening ballroom. Follow me please."

I was so busy staring at the place, I'd completely forgotten about the butler.

Ris giggled and downed her glass of champagne. "Follow Alfred."

I rolled my eyes at her immature comment. We walked past statues of Hercules, Apollo, and other Greek gods. Curtis seemed to have a serious thing for power figures. We were led down several long hallways before finally stopping in front of an elevator.

"You are going to the fourth floor, enjoy."

We stepped inside and Ris and I both looked at each other, eyes as wide as saucers. "This nigga got a muthafuckin' elevator *in his house*," we said in unison, giggling on the way up. I immediately felt transported into another world. The doors opened up and before us was what I'm just going to call "Club Curtis." This fool had a disco ball and everything. The entire fourth floor was Curtis's own private club, DJ booth and all. The area was darkened with multicolored strobe lights flashing overhead. I squinted and looked through the crowd of people blocking the elevator entrance, trying to find Keyshawn's ass. Ris nudged me in my ribs when a topless waitress walked by with a tray of syringe-shaped shooters and multicolored Jell-O shots.

"I told yo' ass I'd fit the fuck in, Ms. Know-it-fuckin'-all."

I just ignored her.

"Hey hey hey, *mi* gorgeous, momma's glad you both could make it." Lania swirled out of thin air, pulling me into a hug that lasted a little too long for my taste, which ended with her air-kissing me on either side of my face. She was obviously already a few shots or champagne glasses ahead of us. She then turned and pulled Ris into the same embrace.

"I just love, love, love you in these color. Perfect pink like pussy is, yes?"

"Well fuck yes," Ris chimed back, obviously happy someone else agreed with the outfit that my ass so openly disapproved of.

Oh well isn't this just wonderful. Here I was looking like the Nutty Professor's assistant and everyone—including Lania, in her see-through, barely there, all-white body suit—was in straight-up hoochie wear. Keyshawn approached us, his smile already preparing me for the damn jokes.

"Hmm, now did I say come to a party or come defend me in court?"

I glared and he laughed, making me blush. We hugged and I couldn't help but notice he was wearing Vera Wang for Men cologne, and damn it if that shit didn't smell good. I bit my bottom lip. He escorted us over to the bar and I tried to get the attention of the topless bartender.

"I know this heffa sees me standing here." I blamed my damn outfit.

Key walked up behind me and ordered us all shots of Patrón Platinum and mojitos as chasers from a man who looked like one of the statues I'd seen in the hallway who was also tending the bar.

"Curtis. You remember Michelle and Larissa right?"

I turned and extended my hand but was instead pulled into a tight bear hug that damn near took my breath away.

"Sure as hell do. Beautiful women I never forget."

We exchanged minor small talk over our drinks.

"What the fuck is this?" Key's comment was directed toward the elevator as Curtis walked over to meet the new arrivals. They exchanged hugs before walking back over to our little gathering.

"I'd like to introduce you all to Angelo Testa. This is Michelle and her wife."

It was the same man from the club earlier with his entourage of women. I'd seen them disperse to different parts of the room as Curtis brought him over to meet us. He was a beautiful, younger-looking Italian man to say the least, with piercing grey eyes that looked like they could see straight through you. I reached out to shake his hand and he grabbed mine, turning it over in his and softly kissing the inside of my wrist instead.

"Absolutely beautiful. Such a shame."

"Why, because I'm married or because I like women?" I stared back at him, waiting for his answer. His gaze was making me nervous as he stared up at me. I thought it was the intensity in those grey eyes of his that made me uneasy. He opened his mouth as if he were about to answer me and was distracted as Keyshawn slammed his glass down. The glass shattered as it hit the bar and Keyshawn walked toward the elevator with disgust written all over his face.

Angelo turned to Lania, who'd come up to give him a hug.

"You should tell your people ova' there to be more respectful, need I remind him of his place on the totem pole?"

"Please don't mind Keyshawn, he's been drinking. The champagne you sent over at LIV was wonderful, by the way."

I listened to Lania and Angelo, but I was still looking in the direction Keyshawn had gone. I couldn't help but feel like there was something more to Key's behavior than just the liquor.

"Is he going to be playing at his best or should I be concerned? I have a great deal of assets in play right now—I don't want his dick getting in the way of his focus." Angelo motioned for one of his girls to come over while waiting for Lania to answer his question.

Lania looked anxiously in the direction that Keyshawn had just walked in and gave me a nervous, apologetic smile that I tried to return. *I guess basketball is that serious of a business in these parts.*

"He'll play, Angelo, don't you worry about him. I'll handle it, I always do. You have my word." There was sadness in Lania's voice and I couldn't help but wonder what the hell was going on with these three.

By the end of the night my ass was done. The room was completely spinning and all I could do was sit my ass down and watch everyone else.

Drinking on an empty stomach was such a fucking bad idea. The crowd had started thinning out and I could only see a few people scattered here and there throughout the huge area. Ris was laughing and dancing with Lania and Chanel. I dizzily scanned the room for Keyshawn, but he was nowhere to be found. I only closed my eyes for what felt like a split second. When I opened them, Lania was lying in the floor, covered in what appeared to be blood. My head throbbed as I tried to get up. Curtis and several others were hovering over here. Ris, to no surprise, had vanished.

"Curtis. What . . . what happened?" Fear sobered me up quick as fuck. *Did Ris do this shit?* I was scared to even speak the words out of my mouth. She had a jealous streak, mean, and a crazy streak. Ignite all three and hell would certainly break loose. I kneeled beside Lania looking for a puncture wound, squinting at her face for signs of a fight, but saw none.

"Don't stand y'all asses there. Somebody get a towel. Did anybody call nine-one-one?" I was frantic. At least if she survived it wouldn't be considered manslaughter. There were too many witnesses to keep this one under wraps. Frustrated, I look around. Nobody was moving fast enough to make me happy and I hopped up, sending the room reeling around me.

"Nah. Think she just fainted. That ain't blood; she was drinkin' her umpteenth Bloody Mary. My guess is she done did too much of that shit and not enough water. Got a doc on the way. He said don't move her." It was Curtis who answered and he was so calm, like this kind of shit happened all the time. I looked around again and still saw no sign of Ris.

"Did too much of what shit, Curtis?"

"Oh hell pills, coke, new shit, who knows."

Immediately I started worrying. If Lania had access to anything, Ris did too. The last time I'd seen her they were together. Clumsily I made my way to the elevator and pushed three, two, and one. When it stopped on the third floor I got off in a dimly lit hallway. The first door I came to was a large sauna. Head spinning, I heard faint laughter coming from the other end of the hallway. It sounded like Keyshawn, but I wasn't sure. *If Ris is off somewhere fuckin' this muthafucka, I swear on my life and everything I own and have ever had I will kill them both without a second thought, right on the muthafuckin' spot.*

As I neared the door toward the end of the hall I could now clearly hear Ris and Keyshawn. I instantly saw, for the first time in my life, what I've heard people call "white rage." I tested the doorknob and my heart damn near beat out of my chest when I found that it was unlocked. Twisting the knob ever so slowly, I tried to open it without making a sound. My blood ran cold at the sound of Ris's voice.

"Oh my God, Key, I didn't know I was missin' all this!" Breathless and excited, her voice was a high-pitched squeal of delight. That was a Ris I hadn't heard in forever and it hurt that I wasn't the reason for her excitement.

"Yeah, baby! I know, I know. It take a *real nigga* to show you how this shit get done!" Keyshawn's conceited ass was just as out of breath.

That was it; I saw pure blood red. Bursting through the door like a bull blindly charging a matador I ran into the room. Tears were already starting to run down my face from the pain, and anger, but mostly from Ris's disloyalty. I cursed myself for not having a fucking pistol or a knife or anything with me. In my rage I decided to just beat their asses to death with my bare hands if I had to. I saw Keyshawn first and blindly lunged toward him.

"What the fuck, Key? This is how you do huh? You come at me an' talk all that shit an'. . ." I launched, my body set on full-all-out attack mode.

I was on him before the fact that he was fully clothed and standing in front of the TV beside

Ris, who was also fully clothed, registered. All of that filtered through long after I'd already embarrassed myself.

"Michelle? You on something, ma? You good?" He'd grabbed both of my wrists, restraining me like I was nothing but a rag doll, looking me in my eyes as if he were trying to see if my pupils were dilated.

"I'm fuckin' fine. Let me go, damn."

Ris was beside him, staring at me wide-eyed. I couldn't help standing there feeling like a complete fucking idiot.

"Baby, we was just playin' this dance game on Curtis's Xbox. You were asleep upstairs an' I didn't wanna wake you up. Curtis said it was okay to jus' leave you be 'til e'rebody left."

Deflated, I dragged myself over to the humongous bed off to the side, suddenly feeling like I'd just poured all of my energy out in that fit of idiocy. I sat on the edge, my head down and my shoulders slumped in embarrassment.

"I'm jus' kin'a wasted, a li'l maybe. I think." Damn, and I was slurring. I could hear them laughing as I fell back exhausted from not sleeping, not eating, worrying about way too much, and taking way too many shots.

It must have been close to 3:00 A.M. when I was awakened from my liquor/exhaustion-induced coma to the feeling of warm lips running laps around my nipples. I tried to open my eyes but the room spun like crazy so I closed them and let myself relax. Fresh Jasmine caressed my senses and immediately I knew it was Ris. I moaned when she did that thing I love so much: lightly grazing the sensitive skin around my breast with her teeth. I was still too damn drunk to do much more than just lie there.

The combination of liquor and grogginess were working to her advantage. She was talking to me but I couldn't make out the words. I tried to focus. Cool air hit my skin and I realized I was completely naked. The bedroom was dim and I couldn't tell if it was from candlelight or light dimmers. Ris hovered over me, all of her clothing gone, leaving her completely naked, completely beautiful. Her eyes reflected the lighting as she looked down at me. They also reflected something else. I wasn't quite sure what it was, but it was sexy. She leaned down and kissed me softly before whispering in my ear.

"Baby, I told them they could watch us."

I didn't know what "them" she was talking about. I gazed around as best as I could without making the room move again. I wasn't able to focus. Ris climbed up, straddling me; she was already hot, soaking wet. I could feel the heat and her moisture pressing against my stomach. Suddenly the thought of someone somewhere watching was the last thing on my mind. I blinked, trying to regain my bearings, hoping it would stop the spinning in my head.

In one fluid motion I had Ris off of me and on her back. I could hear one of whomever this "them" was inhale sharply as my ass arched up in the air and I licked and savored every inch of skin I could reach without going exactly where Ris wanted me to.

I sucked and teased every inch of her body from her neck to her toes, never going anywhere near her pussy. I let my fingers wander there, but I wouldn't slide them in. I'd run my lips and tongue around it but never across. The thought of Ris with *any* man gave me such a feeling of anger and rage. I wanted her to beg, but most importantly I wanted her to beg *me*. I parted her legs and pressed myself up against her. Our wetness intermingling, I gently ground my hips into her, not enough to give her what she wanted but just enough to make her want more. Ris closed her eyes and threw her head back, trying to press herself back into me but I wouldn't allow it. She moaned in frustration.

"Say it," I whispered, getting tired of playing this game with her. I twisted, grinding my clit into hers just a little harder this time. We both gasped at the sensation, but I wasn't giving in. Still she refused. I got back on my knees and licked my way down her stomach. I circled her clit with my tongue and smiled to myself when her legs started to shake. I'd get her right to the edge and then . . .

"Okay, please. Now. Michelle, I'm sorry."

I had no idea what the hell she meant about being sorry until it hit me. And I mean it really did hit me. Before I could figure out what was going on I was damn near about to explode. He hit me with long deep strokes, grabbing me roughly by the back of my neck and pressing my face down into Ris so I could continue to savor her while I was being fucked hard from behind. I don't know how I did it, but I was able to concentrate just enough to get Ris back to the point where her legs were starting to shake and tighten around my face, her back arching off the bed. It was all sensory overload. The combination of wet pussy in my face and on my lips and the noises Ris was making only fueled the fire that Keyshawn was stroking up behind me.

One hand still had me by the back of my neck and the other had me by my ass, forcefully pulling me back into each stroke every time he drove forward. The sensations were driving me right over the edge. I couldn't fight it anymore. I pressed my lips hard against Ris's clit, knowing exactly how and where I'd send her. Right at that very moment Keyshawn drove one long, deep thrust that hit my "G, H, and damn I didn't even know that was a spot" and I went into my own free fall. I moaned, cried out, hell I'm pretty sure I spelled the nigga's name too as I fell forward—my legs, suddenly traitors to my body, no longer offered to support my weight. Waves of pleasure crashed over my body, so intense they were damn near painful.

I couldn't believe I'd turned down a lifetime of this feeling, a lifetime of dick downs, by marrying a woman. All I could do was lie there temporarily "dickmatized." That's when a nigga strokes it so good you suffer from temporary paralysis; all you can do is lie there paralyzed. The room could have burst into flames and the devil himself could've jumped out at my ass and it wouldn't have gotten me up off that bed. Ris was stiff beneath me, still breathing heavy. I lifted my head long enough to offer her a weak smile before letting my face sink back into the warm softness of her stomach.

"Guess I did a damn good job huh?"

Okay, scratch everything I said before. If it weren't for the fact that my legs felt like Jell-O, I definitely would've jumped completely the fuck off the damn bed, ninja style. I looked back in complete and utter shock to see Lania crouching on her knees behind me. She was proudly stroking the head of her strap like it was a real dick. She smiled smugly at my expression. I looked down at Larissa, confusion written all over my face.

"Ris, what the fuck?"

She gave me an awkward smile, wrapping her arms around my neck and pulling me up toward her into an even more awkward hug.

"I'm sorry baby, I kind of lost a damn bet. But I figured, what da hell, you'd enjoy a li'l threesome."

"Shit, I definitely enjoyed the show."

My head swiveled toward Keyshawn and Curtis, who were sitting over on a sofa in front of the TV. The back of the sofa faced the bed so now it made sense why I didn't see them before. Keyshawn's head was tilted slightly and he wasn't smiling or looking anything close to his usual self. I hoped I hadn't embarrassed him by calling out his name. I just chalked up the way he was acting to the fact that he was probably ready to go stroke one out right quick, if he hadn't already.

"But, Lania, I saw you, I . . . I thought they were takin' you to a hospital?" *What the hell kind of game is this? Is this some sort of bullshit swingers dinner party?*

"Oh, that? It was nothing, just too many shots early in the day and really good coke. It happens. I'm fine as you can see."

Somewhere an alarm was going off. Realizing it was my phone, a special ringtone I'd set for Jim, a sudden chill came over me as all the blood seemed to drain from my body.

"Oh God, where are my clothes? That's my phone where is it?" I crawled off the bed in a panic, my legs still wobbly and my head pounding. I found my phone and pressed answer.

"Michelle, it's Jim. There's been an incident at the house. The children are fine and I'm on my way there now. I don't want you to be too alarmed but someone tried to break in and we're holdin' 'til you get here. Ain't callin' no cops yet. Gonna let you talk to 'em first."

"Oh God, are you sure the kids are okay? Is it Rasheed?"

"Rasheed?" Larissa sat up in the bed with the comforter pulled up to her chest.

I cursed to myself. I'd forgotten about keeping her out of the loop. Oh well it was too late; so much for that plan.

"What da fuck you mean? Is who Rasheed, Michelle?"

There was entirely too much going on with Jim trying to give me details and Ris on the verge of a spastic panic attack.

"Jim, I'm on my way. Larissa, just put your shit on, we have to go *now*. I'll explain in the damn car."

I could see the questioning looks on both Key's and Lania's faces but I ain't have time to explain. Shit, after what just went down we were way past the formalities stage. They'd just have to fuckin' understand. My hands were shaking so bad I could barely put my clothes on and bright spots kept flashing before my eyes. I'd bet everything on the fact that Rah wouldn't try to go after my kids and I was dead-ass wrong. *What kind of monster had prison turned him into that he'd try to hurt his own children?*

CHAPTER 13

BLOOD MOON . . . BLOODY MONEY

"So when exactly was you gonna tell me you knew for sure Rah was back?" Ris didn't wait five seconds for the limo to start moving before she started in with the questions.

"Damn, Larissa, I just found out my damn self."

"You ain't think I needed to know dat shit? What was you tryin'a do, make friends wit' his ass or somethin' before you told me?"

I was not in the mood. I just wanted to hold my babies, make sure they were okay, and get past this new chapter of bullshit as quickly as possible.

"Look, I handled the shit okay? What the fuck good would it have done if I did tell you, aside from have your ass worried too?" I'd started grinding my teeth so hard my jaw hurt. I stared out the window, content with watching what little traffic there was on the road at 4:00 A.M. whiz by, anything to keep me calm until we got to the house, anything to keep Ris from bringing up all of her insecure-ass doubts about Rasheed. I let my eyes wander and focus on the moon glowing a bright reddish orange in the distance. It was so big it looked like I could reach right out and touch it.

"Do you miss him? I mean y'all was togetha for a long-ass time. Ain't nothin' wrong wit' missin' the nigga."

She was pushing my damn buttons.

"If I was wit' a nigga for that long, I'd pro'ly miss his ass. Even after bein' wi'chu all this time. I can't even lie. But unlike how you do me I probably wouldn't lie to yo' ass 'bout it, Michelle."

"How many times do I have to tell you I don't miss that nigga? Stop fuckin' askin' me. Stop bringin' it up. Just fuckin' stop! And why you ain't tell me Keyshawn came by the damn house?" I was so pissed my voice cracked.

"He just came by to bring me my autographed ball. Said you weren't answerin' his calls. Why you gettin' so mad if you ain't got nothin' to be mad for?"

Her question made absolutely no fucking sense. I didn't know where it came from but it was there. I felt outright rage. Maybe it was because I was under too much stress, I wasn't sure. My hand went across Ris's face so fast her head snapped to the side and still it didn't feel like enough. All the shit I did for her, everything I bought for her, everything I did, I did to make her ass happy and I didn't get anything in return for it but bullshit.

My entire world revolved around Larissa and the kids and making sure they had everything they needed. Suddenly it was all too much for me. Ris was staring at me, holding her cheek, disbelief written all over her face at the fact that I'd even dared to hit her. In that moment I didn't see her as a wife, or a partner, lover, or a friend. She was a possession. I clothed, fed, watered, provided, and she'd take, took, and keep taking.

My rationale was nothing like anything I'd ever thought of before but the fact that she'd dare to question me relentlessly and challenge me and then tonight she would be so bold as to offer *my body* to another *woman* as consolation for a bet *she lost!* Growling like a mad woman I lunged across the limo. There was nothing that I wanted more in that single moment than to just choke the living fuck out of her dumb ass.

"Michelle, what da fuck is wrong wi'chu?" she shrieked, drawing her knees into her chest. Larissa kicked at me but I just grabbed her legs, digging my fingers into her thighs, purposefully bruising her, trying to hurt her.

"Whoa now! There's no need fer all that."

I was grabbed by my shoulders and pulled backward out of the limo. I was so caught up in my anger I hadn't even noticed that we'd stopped. I gave Larissa one last glare before straightening myself up and turning to Jim. Damn I was gettin' out of shape. It took me a few deep breaths before I could speak.

"Sorry about that, Jim. Please tell me what's going on."

He looked shyly toward Ris, who was now starting to climb out of the car. Her hair was a bird's nest on top of her head and I'd torn her fishnet top and broken one of her heels. I was so glad Jim already knew who she was, because I'd hate trying to explain why I was but really wasn't just trying to beat a stripper's or a call girl's ass in my limo.

"Well, like I said on the phone I didn't want to alarm ya. Jackson, over there, works for the Miami PD. He's already started the forensics so we won't have any issues."

"Wait, forensics? I thought you said the kids were fine." *No, I know I heard him say that there was nothing wrong with my babies. I know I wasn't that damn out of it when we talked*. I was shaking my head back and forth, my eyes filling with tears and my heart splitting in half because I was already thinking the words that no mother wants to hear.

"Right. Right. The kids were taken to get somethin' to eat. We had to get 'em away from here. Didn't want 'em seein' too much more than they might already have."

Jim needed to hurry the fuck up and explain to me what was going on, because if he hadn't noticed I was in an ass-whooping mood, and not only did I not see my babies but I had no clue where Rasheed was at or if he was dead or alive.

"Okay, Jim, I need the CliffsNotes version. I can't take this long, drawn-out shit."

"Ahhh, well. Blood on the moon tonight. Reckon we should have known somethin' would be afoot somewhere. Darla was stabbed in the livin' room on the couch. We have her over there in the truck if you'd like to see her." He started to walk toward the truck and Ris and I followed him. Hearing that Darla didn't make it and knowing it could have been me or Ris made me immediately regret how I'd treated her on the ride home. I put my arm around her in an attempt to comfort her.

"I'm so sorry I got that mad at you," I whispered to her as we followed Jim. It suddenly dawned on me that the "her" he was referring to wasn't Darla. There was someone sitting in the back of one of the cars Jim approached. I recognized Keith from the highway and exchanged a polite smile with him.

"See now from what we can tell, she swam in from the ocean and climbed up to that third-story window that was left open 'round back. Keith was the first one inside after hearin' Darla scream, an' apprehended her. The li'l ones were asleep, didn't see it happen." Jim swung open the driver's side door and the interior light beamed on. Ris and I both stared at the younger black woman in the back seat but neither one of us recognized her. I shook my head at Jim.

"She ain't got no ID. Won't talk either. I was hoping maybe y'all would know who she might be."

I stared harder at the girl in the back of the car. Rah was good for conning young women; that's what he did for a living at the strip club. He conned women out of their bodies, their youth, their money, and eventually their minds. She couldn't have been any older than nineteen, maybe twenty, very slender and dark skinned, her hair cut into a edgy, curly Mohawk; nothing like the princess-dancer types Rah messed with back home. She refused to make eye contact with any of us, content with staring down at the floor in the car. I didn't place her face and couldn't figure out how or when I would have ever run into her in Florida or Virginia. I'd turned to walk toward Jackson, who was now calling the scene into the police, when I heard a whisper.

"Blood for blood money."

"What ye' say there, young lady?" Jim approached her, his head tilted to the side.

I didn't need her to repeat it. I'd heard her loud and clear and I knew exactly what it meant, but this was so unlike Rah to send a woman to do his dirty work. There had to be a reason why he wouldn't have come himself.

"Jim, where exactly did you send my kids?"

"Just down the street with David and Jacob. There was a little twenty-four-hour diner where they could get pancakes an' cocoa while we cleaned up and got the nanny's body outta the house."

Panic was coursing through my system. *Did Rasheed send that girl here as a decoy? Was she supposed to distract us, or do something to flush us out on purpose so he could get to the kids?* I didn't think anymore, I just took off running.

"Baby? Where you goin'?"

I didn't answer Ris. There wasn't any time. I'd explain after I had my kids in my arms. Until I saw that they were okay there was no room for anything else.

My car was blocked in on one side of the driveway by Jim and the other guys' vehicles. I ran into the house and grabbed Ris's car keys from the ring beside the front door. I didn't dare look into the living room. I was too scared to see Darla and all the blood. I ran out into the garage and climbed into the red convertible. It was the only car on the side of the garage that I could get out so the kids would just have to sit in each other's laps when I picked them up. I'd risk a ticket, fuck it.

I pressed the garage door opener and sped out. Jim and Ris both called after me but I didn't stop. I had to get to Trey and Lataya before Rasheed did, or at least if he was already there maybe, just maybe, I could talk him out of whatever he was planning on doing. The diner Jim mentioned was no more than a few blocks away and the sun was just starting to come up, illuminating the layer of dust on Ris's car. I made a note to get all of the cars washed later.

I could see the sign for the diner and signaled, braking to turn into the parking lot. The kids were coming out with two big guys on either side of them. They looked fine, smiling and laughing, and I smiled for the briefest moment before realizing that the digital gauge on the Benz was accelerating on its own. I stomped the brake pedal with everything I had but the car kept speeding up.

The sun was back in my eyes again and I pulled down the visor. That's when I noticed the slender, small, feminine handprint in the dust on the hood and I realized what that girl was doing in our house. She hadn't come for the kids. Darla must have seen her, or caught her off guard when she was trying to get out of the house. I threw up the parking brake.

"Shit." It didn't do a damn thing. *She must have disengaged it.*

Fortunately it was early enough that there were barely any cars on the road on a Saturday morning and I was praying like I'd never prayed before as the car hit eighty, eighty-five, and ninety. I could see Jim's men in the rearview speeding to catch up with me. My heart felt like a runaway train in my chest; it was thudding so painfully I could barely breathe. At 145 miles per hour I could barely keep the car on the road, and I was coming to an area where I knew I wasn't going to make it. The turn was too sharp and I was going too fast to jump out.

Squeezing my eyes shut as tightly as possible I turned the steering wheel, praying that maybe, just maybe, I could Tokyo drift or do some kind of donut and keep-it-moving shit I'd seen in movies. For that split second the only sound I heard was my breath as I inhaled what I thought would be my last one. Piña colada air freshener and new car leather would be the last smells I'd ever smell. The tires screamed and the best way to describe the body-jarring effects of slamming into a concrete wall is that it sounded and felt like God Himself put His foot down in the form of an underpass and I'd run right into it. Glass shattered as the passenger side crumpled, the car frame bending around me like a tin can tomb.

My life didn't flash before my eyes. I didn't relive all my happiest moments. In the blink of an eye I went from scared shitless to pitch black.

CHAPTER 14

I SAID—LOVE IS A HELLUVA DRUG

"Michelle? Try to squeeze my finger if you can hear me."

Ugh. Who is this squawking-ass woman in my ear? My head was killing me and my mouth felt like straight yuck. Like I hadn't brushed my teeth or drunk anything since who knew when. I felt so tired. I didn't even bother trying to open my eyes. All I wanted to do was drift back into the dark silence that I'd somehow slipped out of.

"I need you to squeeze, Michelle."

"Scream." My voice sounded crackly and froggish to my own ears. I could barely speak above a groggy, funky whisper. I tried and, damn it, I couldn't squeeze shit. But if she didn't shut the fuck up . . .

"What? Say it again. Use your words, Michelle. Say it to us again."

Oh my God, I groaned to myself, *will she ever stop?* I just wanted some ice water and lots of sleep.

"Shut. Fuck. Up. Scream." It took all the energy I had to get those words out, but whoever the fuck she was left me no choice; she'd refused to let up.

"Well, you are definitely a gutsy one. I think everything will be just fine, Larissa. You can come and talk to her if you'd like; she can definitely hear you."

"Hey, Chelle."

God, if I weren't so tired . . . I tried to say "hey" back to my baby but I was just so damn weak. It felt like the life had somehow been drained out of me and all I was left with was this darkness. Ris sounded so pitiful. I could her sniffling and blowing her nose, and all I could recall was me hitting her and being so nasty to her.

"I love you so much, bae, an' I hope you can forgive me."

I didn't know what I was supposed to forgive her for when I was the one who acted like a complete fool, hittin' her and shit. Maybe she just meant she was sorry for her being an all-around bitch for the last few weeks. I smiled in my mind and let myself drift back into that quiet, dark place, praying that Bird Bitch wouldn't come back for at least a few hours so I could get some rest.

***

When I'd finally come to my senses I found out I was in Memorial Hospital. The car wreck put me in a coma for a week and I slept off and on for a good week afterward. Ris and the kids came to see me every day and I could remember vague bits and pieces of hearing Trey's or Lataya's little voices saying they loved me or asking me to wake up. Ris said tears would roll down my face when the kids would talk to me but aside from that I was pretty much unresponsive. I even thought I'd heard Keyshawn's voice a few times, but I could have been dreaming. Thankfully, even though the car was totaled, I didn't suffer any serious injuries. Still, no one could believe I'd survived the crash. They'd been doing all types of blood work and screenings, trying to make sure I was at 100 percent and clear to be released, when Dr. Traverson came in. As soon as she spoke I immediately knew who she was.

"Michelle, I'd like to ask you a few questions." She glanced at Ris. "Alone please."

I nodded for Ris to wait outside so Bird Bitch and I could have this private convo.

"Okay, what seems to be the problem?"

"The toxicology reports came back from the lab. Now, initially we asked you several times, upon waking, if you were a user of any types of recreational substances, legal or illegal."

I stared blankly at her, waiting for further explanation, not completely understanding where this was going. "I don't use drugs, Dr. Traverson. Never have. I did leave a party and did have a few drinks. I told you that, and my wife told you that also." I was now frowning at her, confused as to why she would insist on asking me these same questions damn all over again.

"I understand your dilemma. You have young children in a same-sex household. A drug-related automobile accident and investigation would not bode well for you or your children, I'm sure."

"What the fuck does my sexuality or how I raise my children have to do with any of this? I don't use drugs. Someone did something to my Benz. I was almost murdered and you have the nerve to come after me? Jim Bartell can vouch for all of this, any mechanic can look at my car and tell you it was tampered with." My head was starting to pound and the IV in my hand was itching, aggravating me. For a second, I debated on snatching the thing out of my skin and just marching my ass right out of that damn hospital.

"The toxicology report shows you had pretty high levels of cocaine and ketamine in your system, Michelle. We kept you sedated initially as a means of rehabilitation, to ease the withdrawal symptoms. Would you like to tell me, on average, about how often you use?" She waited and I stared at her like she was a complete idiot.

"Michelle, we have several very highly recommended and very confidential programs I'd like to recommend to keep you from relapsing once we release you."

"Oh hell no, there has got to be some kind of mix up. I . . . I barely touch a glass of wine here and there but I would never do that kind of shit to my body. What the hell is ketamine?"

The thought of possibly losing my children over some dumb shit like this was making me want to slide right back into another damn coma. *What the fuck really happened at that party with Keyshawn?* I tried to remember every single little detail because that was the absolute last time I could remember even being under the same roof as any kind of drugs. My body shook uncontrollably as tears fell down my face. My life was falling apart and there seemed to be nothing I could do to pull it back together.

"Dr. Traverson? I'm sorry, did you say we was gonna lose our kids?" Ris had poked her head into the room. She'd obviously been listening the entire time.

I lay back and rolled onto my side on the hospital bed facing the wall. For the moment, I was content with just hugging myself and crying quietly. I didn't care to look at Ris or Bird Bitch right that second.

"Yes, Larissa, it is possible. If the mother has an ongoing issue with a controlled substance and refuses assistance, I may have to suggest that we get the state involved before we can release her back into the household. She was in a life-threatening accident under the influence and next time the children could very well be in it with her. It is highly possible that the children will be taken into Child Protective Services. Doctor-patient confidentiality prevents me from discussing this any further with you, however."

Fuck that shit, I'll just get myself a damn good lawyer. These types of things get fought all the time and won. I just ignored Bird Bitch.

"Well, Dr. Traverson, um . . . what if she ain' know she was um . . . actually doin' cocaine or anything else? I mean like voluntarily?"

That one simple little question made all the blood rush to my head. The vein in my forehead suddenly throbbed and probably swelled to the point that I looked like Frankenstein.

"And how on earth would she *not know* she was consuming an illegal narcotic, Larissa? Several *illegal* narcotics?"

I couldn't move, suddenly thinking, *Yeah, Larissa, how the fuck would I not know?* I was scared that if I made eye contact with her the look on my face would suck the life from her body, killing her on the spot and the truth would never be known. Then I'd still be right here, stuck in the same dumb-ass situation. So I didn't dare move a single, solitary muscle or make a sound.

"Um, it . . . it wasn't meant to be like for her to have no habit or nothin'. I jus' did it 'cause I read somethin' in this book we have in our library. You see, there was this voodoo priestess and she wanted her chieftain to come to her bed every night and not sleep with his other wives or ho around. *So,* every day she gave him a slow-acting poison and every time he chose her for sex she'd give him the antidote."

I was pretty sure Bird Bitch and I had the same exact "bitch, is you crazy?" look on our faces while Ris was talking.

"Well what happened is, eventually the chieftain got rid of all the other women and picked priestess 'cause he realized he always felt the best when he was with her and only her."

She paused, taking a deep breath the same way Trey did whenever I caught him in a lie and he was forced to tell me the truth; the rest of her words came out in rushed detail.

"So I got some coke—not no street shit. They cut that wit' who knows what and that could fuck somebody up somethin' serious and I ain't want that to happen. I put it on my finger and stuck it in her ass one day durin' sex. She ain't even like that shit, Doctor, and I swear she ain't know. I jus' figured if she got a high from sex wit' me she wouldn't want anyone but me, an' the only way I could give her the coke without her knowin' was anally—so that might be why she tested positive, 'cause it was pharmaceutical grade. I mean like really good shit." Larissa had started crying by the end of her fucking confession and I was two seconds away from tryin' to figure out if I could press charges on some shit like that or just whoop her ass. I still couldn't believe this shit.

"You did what to me?! All that li'l 'lemme show you a trick, play wit' ya ass' bullshit? Ris! My ass was numb for like two days! Did Lania have it on her strap too? Did y'all give me anything that night?"

Ris shrugged and I immediately regretted my outburst, lying back down, out of breath, my head feeling like it was splitting in half. I couldn't believe it. I was just flabber-fuckin'-gasted at this one. Bird Bitch was standing there, shaking her head back and forth in disbelief with her mouth opening and closing. She obviously wasn't used to lesbian sex, foreplay, or any of the toys, and we'd just given her a crash course.

"I . . . I . . . I'll l . . . leave you t . . . two alone for a m . . . moment." She spun her tight-faced self around and marched out of the room so fast I was surprised the tiles didn't fly up off the damn floor.

There was nothing for me to say to Ris. All I could do was lie there staring at her in utter disbelief. She stood there crying, looking back at me like a damned fool. *Voodoo priestess?* Those were old wives' tales, folklores. Out of all the life-empowering shit I had up in the library I just couldn't believe she'd actually read that particular one and tried to actually apply that shit to our life. What if I'd gotten addicted, or she'd gotten hold of some bad "pharmaceutical" shit and it'd killed me?

"I only did it—"

Holding up my hand I turned my face away, unable to look at her any longer. I didn't even want to hear it. I'd been drugged by my own wife. Never in a million years.

"Baby, I don't wanna lose you. I love you."

I ignored her. On one hand I had my ex trying to kill me, and on the other hand, my wife drugging me to keep me. *What the fuck kind of bullshit karma is this?* I just couldn't seem to catch a damn break.

CHAPTER 15

KARMA'S A BITCH . . . ONLY IF YOU ARE

They finally said I could be released after being stuck in that hospital for damn near two and a half weeks. Honestly, I thought Bird Bitch was just scared that me or Ris was gonna try to take her damn cookies when no one was looking. You know, since Ris rolled up in there and had her thinking we were lesbo, coke-sniffing, playing-in-ya-booty swingers. Wasn't nobody worried about Bird Bitch's old scary ass, I just wanted to go home. I'd asked Jim to arrange for a car to pick me up. I didn't want Ris driving me anywhere and definitely not in one of our cars until I could have them checked out. I guessed Rasheed thought he'd actually killed me or something, because the entire time I'd been in the hospital everything seemed to be pretty quiet.

"Michelle you *have* to use the wheelchair; it's policy."

I glared at Bird Bitch, happy that this was the last order and hopefully, the last time I'd ever have to hear her annoying-ass high-pitched voice. Reluctantly, I sat down and let the orderly wheel me to my car. Covering my eyes with my hand, I was momentarily blinded by the sudden exposure to the midday July sun. As the automatic door opened I welcomed the transition from hospital air to real air as it rushed over me. I waited for my eyes to adjust. I was literally thawing out. The transition from the cold, sterile hospital to the humidity and the sun on my skin made me feel alive again. Ris had brought my favorite turquoise sundress and flip-flops for me to wear home and I was thankful because any more clothing and I'd be sweating my ass off.

Walking into the house I couldn't help feeling a mixture of remorse and happiness. The place was just as I'd left it. Except for some ugly-ass oversized cream and tan couch where my old dark chocolate leather one used to be. *That shit better be stain guarded. Ris must've picked it out because there is no way I want the kids jumping they li'l asses all over a cream couch.* I frowned, the memory of why I needed a new couch suddenly making me feel sick to my stomach.

"Mommeeeeee." Trey ran up to me and I kneeled down and squeezed him so hard he squeaked. I loosened up, kissing his little cheeks. He smelled just like all little boys should smell—like cookies and dirt.

"You smell like a puppy," I teased him, rubbing my nose up against his neck, tickling him.

"I'm not a puppy. I'm a boy. Mommy an' me an' Taya have surprises for you."

The last person I really wanted to see was Ris, but I couldn't avoid her forever. "Okay, baby, where are they at?"

"Um I'm s'posed to keep you occ . . . occ . . ."

I smiled at his little scrunched-up forehead, deciding to help him out with the word before he developed a stutter. "Occupied, baby?"

"Yeah"—he was nodding his head like I'd solved a riddle—"dat's da word him used."

"*That's* the word *he* used. And, who is this 'he,' baby?"

"Ount know. Mommy said call him Daddy, but I didn't 'cause I wanted to ask you if he's Daddy, but Taya . . . Taya tried ta say it an' she said 'Da Da Da Da.'"

Lord, where the fuck is Ris at? What did Trey mean she told him to call somebody Daddy? I scooped Trey up, grabbed my cell, and marched toward the kitchen, confident that at any second I could have any one of my guys in there if I needed help. Hell, I done seen 101 movies where the psycho killer takes the whole family hostage and all kinds of crazy shit happens so I was ready for damn near anything. I guessed it was time to face the music and deal with this nigga face to fuckin' face. Man to woman.

"Trey, man, what happened to keepin' her occupied?"

"I'm only four." Trey shrugged in my arms. "Nex' time jus' lemme watch da cookies."

I couldn't believe who was standing in front of the oven with my favorite pink apron tied around his waist and pink oven mitt on one hand. He was trying to balance Lataya on one hip and pull the cookies out the oven with the other. Keyshawn looked awkward as hell, and right at home in my kitchen.

He was wearing a fitted black tank top and plaid tan and black shorts with some Perry Ellis boat shoes. *Damn.* Now this was a nice welcome home present. Looking around I didn't see Ris anywhere; agitation immediately set in. *She could've at least been here when my ass walked up in the house.* I put Trey down.

"Baby, go play in your room. I'll bring you some cookies as soon as they cool down."

Lataya was already asleep and once she was out, she was out. I peeled her out of Key's arm. My hand slightly brushed Key's skin and sparks shot through my body from the contact. The man looked like he was made out of solid muscle. I took Lataya and put her on the couch in the living room.

"So um, what are you doin' here and where's Ris?"

"Larissa told Lania 'bout the accident and shit. We both offered to help out. Lania jus' took her to get you a welcome home present so I volunteered to watch the kids. She thought you'd be home later than this."

I was scared to ask Key what exactly Ris had told him. Couldn't have been but so much or anywhere near the truth since the nigga was standing in the middle of my kitchen in a pink apron baking cookies. He pulled off the mitt, proudly examining his handy work. Smiling up at him I couldn't help teasing. "Well now, it's nice to see those hands are good for somethin' other than handlin' a damn basketball and jugglin' women, Betty Crocker." He gave me a mischievous grin back and I felt something I hadn't felt in years: butterflies.

"Oh no, they can handle plenty more than that and the women. They just keep me busy until the right one settles me down."

Somehow one of those cookies seemed to magically float its way up to my lips. Okay, the nigga fed me the cookie. But it was *the way* he did it. Once again I found myself as the focal point of his almond-shaped brown eyes. We were so close I could see that his lashes were short, thick, and extremely curly. I was just as mesmerized with him as he seemed to be with me. I could feel my heart starting to speed up; just being close to this man made my body follow its own agenda, no matter what my mind told it.

"So it seems as though we're both in completely unsatisfying situations. I think maybe we should join forces. Work on satisfying a few things."

That fool could've said "let's go sit and translate Latin in a library" for all I know and my ass still would've said "okay."

Warmth brushed up against my bottom lip and instinctively they parted. It could've been the fact that I'd been eating hospital food for the last couple of weeks but I couldn't help this shit, I had a straight-up big girl moment. Closing my eyes I moaned. This nigga made the *perfect* chocolate chip cookie. *Oh my God.* Ain't nothin' in this world like a cookin' or bakin' muthafucka. I lie to you not.

"My turn." I smiled, breaking one of the cookies in half, raising it up to Key's full pink lips.

He went in for his bite, and stepping in closer I moved ever so slightly, denying him his treat and leaving a trail of warm chocolate across his lower lip. He inhaled sharply, surprised when I leaned up on my toes and softly licked and sucked on his bottom lip until all the chocolate was completely gone.

"Mmmm." He raised an eyebrow, licking his lips. The action sent a wave of sexual awareness through my body. "I guess I get anotha turn since Michelle switchin' up the rules."

He was running his finger along the curve of my chin, toward my ear, down to my collarbone.

"Who the hell said we had rules?" I sounded like I'd just finished hiking up the side of Mount Everest.

He smiled at my comment before pulling me into a deep, long kiss that set my blood on fire and awakened the ocean in between my legs. It took my breath away and damn near made my knees give out at the same time. My eyes flew open and I gasped at the sudden warmth against my neck. *No, this nigga didn't.* But the light dusting of crumbs across my chest and all over the floor confirmed he'd just crushed that mu'fucka all over the side of my neck. He smiled against my lips before lowering his head, drifting his tongue lazily across my skin, treating the chocolate on my neck the same way I'd treated the chocolate on his lips. He stopped just long enough to lift me onto the counter beside the stove.

I untied my apron from around his waist and replaced it with my legs, my dress riding so far up my legs I could feel the cold counter against the back of my thighs. Sliding the straps to my dress down just past my shoulders, I took another cookie from the tray and stuck my finger into one of the gooey chocolate chips. I watched Key seductively as he watched me smear chocolate down the middle of my neck and even lower around my half-exposed nipple. He was rock solid; I could feel it through the barrier of his shorts pressed between my legs bulging up against me, the heat searing through my thin cotton panties. My thighs flexed involuntarily. He didn't need any more urging than that before lowering his head and pulling my chocolate-covered Hershey's Kiss nipple into the heat of his mouth, sucking hard.

Ripples of pleasure started at my hair follicles, and shot all the way down to my toes and back up again. Instinctively, I ran my hands underneath his tank top; he felt like warm marble covered in skin. His lips were working their magic on my nipples, left then right. Yes, he was definitely earning these milk and cookies. The top of my sundress had fallen almost down to my waist and I bit my lower lip hard when Key cupped my breast together with one hand and licked both nipples at the same damn time. We both moaned when my hand slid down into the waistband of his shorts, and all I can say is, feeling is definitely believing.

My hand closed around as much of him as it could. I twisted my wrist and gently stroked him upward; he took a sharp, quick breath. Like riding a bike, I started to remember how empowering it felt to be able to weaken a man with one hand. He was thick, thicker than I remembered him looking, and all of a sudden I needed something else wrapped all around that mu'fucka. As if he'd read my thoughts Key reached down and lowered his zipper, freeing himself through the hole in his boxers.

We didn't waste any more time. Our eyes connected for the briefest moment before he kissed me hard. The heat from his fingers grazed my inner thigh as he slid my soaked panties to the side, pulling me forward on the counter. He buried himself as deep as he could go in one fluid stroke.

My ass had completely forgotten what the fuck a real dick should feel like. I could feel every bit of me stretching around every single inch of him and it was a painfully pleasurable glimpse of heaven.

Breaking our kiss, I buried my face into his neck, biting into his skin to keep from moaning or screaming out loud. My nails had to be hurting him; I was digging them in like I was a rock climber and his back was the damn mountain. Every stroke sent a shockwave of pleasure through my body like one of those sonar pulses they use to ping the ocean.

"Damn, Michelle, you gonna have me all marked up. I got appearances to make, baby."

I kissed his skin, offering him a silent apology. "I wanna scream so bad, baby. I can't help it." My reply was no more than a breathless whisper against the side of his neck. I would've promised that I wouldn't do it again but I was used to being rough and being handled just as roughly in return. There was something about finding a bruise or a mark the next day that always made me smile secretively at the fun I had earning my "battle scars."

"Don't worry 'bout it, baby, daddy'll fix it."

My eyes drifted closed. I felt weightless. The nigga didn't miss a beat. He slid me off the counter and held me up against him. I tightened my legs around his hips and wrapped my arms around his neck. The excitement, the thrill of being caught, all of the above just acted as fuel to the powder keg about to explode inside my pussy, and this mu'fucka's dick was the damn fuse.

He palmed my ass in each hand, the heat from his long fingers searing my skin as he guided my pussy up and down the length of him. My head fell back, a soft moan leaving my lips. Fuck, he was about to get bit again and he must've sensed it coming because before I could even close my mouth or get anywhere near his neck, it was full of cookie. I glared at him, an angry frown creasing my forehead, and then I completely forgot why I was frowning in the first place. Mouth full of damn chocolate chip cookie, I chewed on that to keep from chewin' on him.

"Chelle, this shit so good," he moaned quietly in my ear, wrapping his arm around my body tightly he started to stroke deeper and harder.

I could feel every vein, every throb, my muscles contracted and the walls closed in around him. It hit me like a wall of electricity that started in my pussy, working its way outwards to my fingertips and toes—my powder keg *exploded*. I couldn't breathe, couldn't hold myself up. Eyes closed, I let myself float on each wave as it came in.

Key quickly pulled out and I felt liquid heat hit the back of my thigh as he stroked himself, his chest heaving like he'd just got off the court. He waited a few seconds before he sat me down.

I straightened my dress, wet a paper towel, and wiped myself down before sliding my panties back in place while he fixed his shorts, or at least tried to. There was no hiding the wet spot I'd left on them, and no, I wasn't sorry, but thankfully his shirt was long enough to cover it. I looked at the mess we'd made out of the cookies and laughed. *Lord, I might never let my babies eat another chocolate chip cookie again.*

"I'll take that as a yes?" Keyshawn walked over and smiled at me, expectantly waiting for a reply.

My response was to place a gentle kiss on his waiting lips because, honestly, I couldn't even remember the damn question.

It was another hour or so before Ris got back with nothing more than a flower arrangement, something that I was pretty sure Lania had a hand in picking out. It was way over the top, with birds of paradise and other exotic flowers. Ris knew for a fact that I loved lilies; they're the most fragrant and last the longest. I gave her a polite thank you and set the arrangement on the dining room table. I still wasn't ready to deal with her. It didn't matter how many times she apologized or tried to explain her side of the situation. The bottom line was, I'd have never drugged Larissa or given someone else permission to have access to her body without her consent. And, after the mind-blowing fuck session I'd just had with Keyshawn, there was the nagging question of whether I even wanted to be with her anymore. The constant uphill struggle of dealing with her on a day-to-day basis, constantly proving my faithfulness, and accounting for ever minor detail of my life was finally starting to wear me down. Aside from saying "thank you," I didn't bother speaking to her again until long after Key and Lania had left.

"Why you tell Trey to call that nigga Daddy?"

She was walking out of the bathroom, getting ready for bed. She tripped over the area rug at the sound of my voice. *I must have caught her off guard.*

"Huh? You talkin' 'bout Keyshawn?"

I sneered at her silently. Who the fuck else she think I was talking about?

"Oh, I was just playing—it was a joke. Trey pro'ly misunderstood it."

I didn't even feel like getting into it with her. As bad as I wanted to yell, "You don't joke with a two-year-old and a four-year-old about something like that," I just rolled over facing the opposite wall so my back would be to her for the rest of the night. It was definitely time for me to make a change.

The next morning I'd decided to skip work and just spend the day with the kids. We went out to breakfast and I watched my little boy put away a whole stack of pancakes like a grown-ass man. Lataya sat on my lap crushing bacon in her chubby little fists; she was getting more of it on me than in her mouth but she was quiet so I let her be. Trey chattered up a storm. I hadn't realized how much he'd grown up. It was like I'd missed the last two and a half years walking around in a daze. Ever since the move I'd made the mistake of puttin' another woman before my own flesh and blood and the thought pulled at my heart.

"Mommy, can we play wif Unca Key today?" He was so excited about the possibility of being around Keyshawn, his eyes lit up and he could barely sit still giving me his biggest "Mommy, please" smile. As bad as I wanted to tell him no, I had to admit it to myself: *shit, Mommy kinda wanted to play with Uncle Key too.*

"Let me text Uncle Key and see if he can come outside, okay?"

Good morning, Cookie Monster. Trey wants to know if you can come out and play?

I waited anxiously, worried that it was too early in the morning to be texting him or too soon to be trying to play house with this nigga. A few seconds later my iPhone whistled.

Sure, leavin' the gym. Gonna shower. Wanna meet me at my place?

"Well, sweetheart, it looks like we'll be hangin' with Uncle Key for a little while today."

The smile on Trey's face melted my heart. I never wanted to admit it but he needed a man's influence in his life—even if it was just for a few hours.

CHAPTER 16

CRIMES OF PASSION

A week had passed and Michelle still hadn't said more than a few words to me since being released from the hospital. It was eating me up inside. I'd apologized, begged, cried, and even cursed at her for making me do the things I'd do sometimes and still she wouldn't even so much as look at my ass. I couldn't think of anything else. She was s'posed to be on bed rest but decided to carry her ass to work against the doctor's orders. She even went so far as to take the kids with her, like I couldn't be trusted with them or some dumb shit. I called to check on her and my heart sank when every call went straight to voice mail. She was still heated. I guessed I just needed to face it. We were done and she was probably out seeing whoever she needed to see to talk about "Ris did this" or "Ris won't do that."

I'd tried to get my cousin Shanice to give me advice on the situation but she took Michelle's side, sayin' what I'd done was definitely fucked up and she'd be amazed if we weren't filing for divorce by the end of the damn month. Depressed and feeling completely fuckin' hopeless I hit up the connect I'd gotten from Keyshawn the day he'd dropped off my autographed basketball.

"This Tink, who this?"

That's how she always answered. The first time I'd called her to get the coke that I'd used on Michelle I thought I had the wrong number, but this time I knew better.

"Hey, boo, it's Ris."

"Hey. What's up, pud, you out lookin' at that silver BMW eight series again?" She was asking if I wanted an eight ball of the *good shit.*

"You know it. You know anyone who got a brand new one?" I answered the exact same way Keyshawn had told me to do the first time.

Tink's boyfriend, or King as they called him on the street, was the biggest dealer and the main supplier of the best shit on the entire East Coast. King's shit was pharmaceutical grade, so pure it was damn near translucent just like fish scales. It wasn't nothin' like that white powdery shit I used to get back home. Key hooked me up with Tink because she was what he called good quality and low risk. She only sold shit outta her personal stash that King gave her to use and she was under the radar. I just liked dealing with her because she was cute and cool as hell.

"Oooh, girl, I got you. Ya girl Lania jus' hit me up too. Why don't we have us a girls' day and hang out. We can go for a test drive, gas and drinks all on me."

Shit. If she was saying what I thought she was saying I ain't have no problem getting twisted for free. *Fuck!* I almost slapped my forehead in frustration. I'd forgotten all about Michelle's fucking hired idiots sitting outside. Even though they'd signed confidentiality agreements, basically meaning they couldn't say shit about what I did long as I ain't kill nobody, there was still no way I would expose Tink like that. I needed to think of a way to get rid of they asses so I could go out and have some playtime. I texted Lania to see if she could come by the house and pick me up, maybe bring Keisha or someone with her.

It wasn't long before I was standing in the doorway, my eyes the size of ostrich eggs, while Lania and her girls came in. The March of Dimes was what I'd call that shit. I was in lesbian heaven and I was sure the security guys outside were using all they expensive equipment to take close-ups so they could jerk off in the damn car later. Lania cat-walked over giving me her weird hug and air-kiss thing before introducing me to everyone.

"Larissa, you already know Keisha. This is Mercedes, Havannah, Sierra, Isys, Marisol, and Katia. They all work for me just like you, sweetie."

It was like looking at six of Baskin-Robbin's thirty-one flavors. These bitches was each as exotic as they names sounded and all of them were on some straight-up model shit. I mean makeup, pumps, hair, booty shorts, and baby-doll dresses all on point.

"It's nice meetin' all of y'all," I responded shyly.

All of a sudden I felt like the ugly duckling and even though she was being a complete bitch, being surrounded by all these beautiful swans made me miss Michelle even more. In all honesty Michelle never made me feel anything less than beautiful when we were around other women, and I could have used a little of that right now. I swallowed past the damn lump that formed in my throat and started to look each girl over. Lania stood beside me doing the same.

"You and Havannah look almost identical minus the eye color. She is sure to be perfect."

I was shocked. Havannah was the smallest of all the women and the second most beautiful in my opinion, the first being Lania. She was shaped like a mermaid, full and thick hips, small waist, and big old titties. She had what I'd heard white folk refer to as classical beauty. High cheekbones and pouty lips with sleek cat-like dark brown eyes similar to Lania's. I immediately fell in love with her eyebrows. I wish my shits would arch perfectly the way hers did. The only major difference was that her hair was dyed a funky platinum blond and my hair was reddish brown. But after looking her up and down I had to agree with Lania's observation; it could actually work.

I stared out the tinted window of Lania's all-white Range waving at myself standing in the doorway, wet from a shower, wearing nothing but a blue silk robe, hair tied up in a towel. I removed my hat and started unpinning my hair once she was out of view. I was actually waving at Havannah's sexy ass pretending to be me. I'd put on her clothes, pinned my hair up underneath a sun hat, and when the March of Dimes sashayed they asses out the house I went right along with them.

In a few hours Havannah would throw on a pair of jeans and a T-shirt I'd left out for her, call herself a cab, and by the time everyone figured out what had actually happened I'd be on my way back to the house high and happy. Of course Michelle's ass was gonna be madder than a muthafucka when she found out, but fuck it. In my opinion, since she hadn't been speakin' to my ass all this time what difference would it make?

We stopped just long enough to drop the rest of the girls off at some restaurant before going to meet Tink. *I swear, every house I visit in Florida just gets bigger and more bad-ass than the last one.* My jaw damn near hit the floor when I saw the house King had Tink set up in. We rolled through what seemed like a never-ending stretch of bare beach and palm trees before finally pulling up to this beach-side mansion, and that muthafucka looked like it was made completely the fuck out of glass. I mean almost *every* single wall was on some complete floor-to-ceiling window type shit. How this bitch did anything during the day or at night with the lights on my ass didn't know, but the shit was fuckin' beautiful.

Tink breezed her way outside as we pulled up. Imagine my surprise when I first learned li'l Ms. Tink was a white girl, and pro'ly one of the nicest ones I'd ever met, too. She led us through her glass house, the scent of gardenia and honey-suckle following us wherever we went, like she'd washed the windows in some smell-goods. I was relieved when she took us into a room toward the back that overlooked the beach. My ass wasn't tryin'a sit up in somebody's living room doin' some illegal shit. Especially not with all these damn windows.

The room was painted in a mint green or sage on some straight-up Japanese zen type shit, and I loved it. There was a lava lamp in one corner on a tiny pedestal, and tall green bamboo plants grew along the window facing the beach, giving us a li'l privacy. In the middle of the room lavender and cinnamon-colored Japanese-style zafu and smile cushions sat around a small marble table. Yeah, my ass knew a little somethin'. Stuck up in the house all damn day watchin' HGTV and decorating shows, wishing I could swap out Michelle's old-fashioned *Masterpiece Theatre* furniture taught me a thing or two. We each picked a cushion and sat down while Tink pulled a silver box about the side of a shoebox from underneath the table and the party began.

We were on our third or fourth line and my head was already buzzing. My nose had gone numb and I was trying to figure out if I wanted to buy me some of that shit to take home.

"Who the fuck you got up in here, Tink?"

We all jumped when we heard his voice boom through the house.

"Damn, King, what I tell you 'bout comin' up in here, yellin' all up in my damn house?"

I wanted to laugh because Tink actually *yelled* back, but my heart was already flying because of the coke and now this heffa was mouthing off to a kingpin. Lord, we was gonna die.

He hovered in the doorway, his bark way more intimidating than his look. He couldn't have been taller than five foot eight, with not a lick of hair on his face. Put some money on it, I bet someone could rub Taya's ass with one hand, King's cheek with the other, and not know the damn difference. He looked like a damn kid to me. I couldn't tell if he was Italian or what; his dark olive complexion could easily go either way. He had wolf-lookin' crystal-clear grey eyes, focused on Lania. I was thinkin' maybe we was s'posed to get up and kiss the muthafucka's pinky ring or some shit. I ain't know.

"Angelo, how are you sweetie?" Lania smiled at him and got up to give him a way-too-friendly hug.

"Ahh, Lany, baby doll." His tone softened and all his Jersey-boy accent came through. "I been lookin' for you's. Tell dat brother of *your's* my people are telling me that shit is gettin' very real and that deadline is close."

I looked at Lania. *What the fuck—Lany?* was written all over my face. He had a nickname for her ass and everything. *What kinda shit is she up to?* I tried my best not to make my "oh shit" face. Hell, I ain't know what the fuck kinda expression I was makin'—I couldn't feel my damn face anymore. I started touching my cheeks and my eyebrows, trying to keep my face straight while also wonderin' why this King person looked kind of familiar.

And then it clicked. I remembered the party at Curtis's place. King was this fool's street name. Standin' in front of us was Angelo Testa, the billionaire. The one Keyshawn couldn't stand for whatever reason and now I guessed I knew why. Because the muthafucka was a straight-up dope dealer. *Ooooooh.* I tried to keep quiet while he and Lania continued their conversation.

"I've spoken to him several times. He's just more resilient than either of us, but to you we owe many thanks. Your advice has always weighed heavily on my brother's decisions."

I was getting nervous. It felt like just being in this bitch and leaving alive meant I would owe this muthafucka a favor or some shit. Fuck that, I wasn't about to be drug mulin' shit across state lines for his ass. I breathed a little easier when he nodded and walked off, but my ass was ready to get the fuck up outta there.

"Lania, I kinda wanna be home close to when Michelle gets off work an' it's already four-thirty. You almost ready?" I really didn't want to go home. I just didn't want to be around a damn drug boss. After watching Rasheed and everyone around him crumble, I knew too well how bad shit could go for these types of people no matter how good it seemed to be going. Besides, I thought this bitch was s'posed to be low-key; this shit wasn't no kinds of low-key.

"Um, Larissa, Keyshawn told me Michelle would be showing him a house at five-thirty today, so you can relax."

I looked at her fuzzy, high, confused.

"She wouldn't do that. She took the kids into the office wit' her this morning. You sure he meant today?"

"Shit, Key wouldn't lie to me. If he wants to fuck he can fuck. We are open, he has no reason to lie or hide anyone from me. I'll call him and ask." She whipped out her little Prada something custom phone, speed dialing his number.

Only because my ass was high as fuck, I laughed dead in her face when that shit went straight to voice mail. Tink was looking back and forth between the two of us weak at whatever this little drama was we had going on.

"Larissa, call your woman and see where she is." Tink was grinning, her face all lit up with excitement.

I looked at Tink and smirked. "My *woman* ain't answering my calls—hasn't been all damn day and knowin' her, she pro'ly' been laid up with Lania nigga havin' family time and shit."

My words were like the negatives to a photo and the picture was developing crystal clear up in Lania's head. She was suddenly blazing mad and I for once was the calm one. *Somebody give my ass a trophy,* I thought, crossing my arms to the cheers of the fake studio audience in my head. The only reason I was so calm was because I was used to sharing Michelle with another man. This type of bullshit came with the territory as far as dealing with her ass was concerned and I'd been doing it for years, but Lania was shaking she was so pissed off. I couldn't resist; I had to ask.

"Um, Lania, if I'm not mistaken, weren't you tryin' to get with Michelle?"

"Fuck no, I had a bet with Keyshawn I could fuck her first. Usually if I get them before him, it makes him not want them so much after."

Smart bitch. I had to give her ass credit for that little plan.

"But, Larissa, I'm telling you right now. I will *kill* your bitch wife if I get my hands on her."

Her threat didn't sit well with me, high or not; something made me believe she'd do it. I pulled out my phone and dialed Chelle's number, praying she'd pick up and be at the house or at her job. Once a-muthafuckin'-gain that shit went to voice mail and *now* my ass was getting mad and the crowd booed.

"Fuck this, we're going. Now." Lania jumped up and stormed out of the house, leaving me no choice but follow her ass or get left behind. *Damn, she could have at least let me ask for a doggie bag.* In my dulled state our convo played back in my head, Lania's words finally catching up with my brain, and the audience in my head yelled, *Hold the fuck up!*

"Wait. Did you say Chelle was showin' Key a house today? I thought he closed on his house already. Michelle told me that's why we were celebrating that first night at LIV." I had to damn near run to keep up with Lania's long-ass legs. The sand didn't even slow her ass down. The coke we'd done gave everything a pink halo in my mind. Like none of this shit was real. She still hadn't answered me as she hopped her ass up into her Range. I finally caught up and climbed in as well.

"Key hasn't bought any damn house. He still in his same damn house. What lies your bitch wife tell you? I'll cut out her tongue and feed it to her, before I kill her."

This time I didn't get mad at Lania; oh no, this time my ass was furious and it was with Michelle. I couldn't believe she'd lied to me! We sped down the highway to Keyshawn's *real* house. I was thinkin' high thoughts the whole way. I imagined Keyshawn fuckin' Michelle and remembered Lania fuckin' her with her strap. The kids calling Keyshawn Daddy, me sitting in a cell by myself. Blood on wood floors, all kinds'a crazy shit.

A part of me wanted her to be there so I could actually catch her in the act. That way she wouldn't be able to lie to me or convince me of no dumb shit. Another part of me wanted her and the kids to be home, or on their way home, so we could try to get shit back to normal as soon as possible.

Lania started to slow down and we pulled into the driveway of a large cream-colored house with a red shingle roof. It wasn't as big as all the other homes I'd been to. Not the kind of house I expected Keyshawn "Keys to the City" Matthews to have, but I guessed that's why he was tryin' to buy a new one in the first place.

"I don't see Michelle's car nowhere." I looked around a few more times, scared to let myself feel any kind of relief.

"It could be in the garage or around the back, or they could have gone down to the courts by the lake. We will see." Lania grabbed her purse and dumped everything out into the floor of the Range, M•A•C makeup and NARS shit going everywhere.

Man, this shit was fucking up my free high. Two high bitches doin' some dumb-ass high-ass shit. She took her empty purse and cat-walked even now around to a side. My TV audience chanted the *Pink Panther* theme music in my head. I tried to shake them out as I followed her to a side door.

"Lania, you got a key?" I whispered.

"He took it back last time we had an argument but"—bending down, she picked up a smooth, large, round garden stone—"I do now." Dropping it into her purse, she tapped it against the glass in the door, which shattered instantly. She threw the rock back into the bushes and used her purse like a glove to reach in and unlock the door.

"Nigga never turns his alarm on. No matter how many times I fuss and tell him about it, he never listens." She tsked, and we crept in, careful to step over the broken glass. We were in the kitchen and straight ahead I could see the living room. Luther Vandross's "Here and Now" was playing loudly throughout the house over the intercom speaker system. There were two empty wineglasses sitting on the kitchen table. Looking at Lania my eyes involuntarily filled with tears, and as much as my heart was hurting it broke me down even further to see hers do the same.

"Where would they put the kids?"

Michelle wouldn't fuck no nigga in front of Trey and Lataya; she wasn't that damn trifling. Lania's eyes widened and her finger flew over my lips, silencing me. I stared at her—confused, waiting. I physically watched her heart break and fall into a million pieces. I saw my own sad reflection in a single tear that slid down her cheek in slow motion and I heard the splash when it hit the floor. Yeah, I was that high.

"Oh my God this shit feel so good . . ."

My own eyes filled with tears. High as I was I didn't care anymore; I just wanted to confront Michelle, make her be sorry, and then I could take her back and we'd be even. Lania turned and set down her purse before we started walking toward the stairs and I followed closely behind her. Not used to the house, I was making sure I stepped where she stepped so I wouldn't trip over anything or make a floorboard creak. The carpet kept our steps quiet as we went through the living room.

I saw a couple of Legos scattered around and my knees almost gave out but I kept walking—past the large black circular-shaped couch and wall-sized flat-screen TV. Past a room that looked like it wasn't nothing but a shrine Keyshawn devoted to himself, full of trophies, and life-sized posters, until we came to the stairs. The house surround sound was playing Aaliyah's "At Your Best" and I thought I was gonna be sick for a second. This was one of my and Michelle's songs back in the day.

We got up to the top of the stairs and every *I love you* replayed in my head, every kiss, every smile, every happy memory, and all I could think about was seein' her face so I could say, "Baby, I forgive you. Let's move on." I almost turned around and went back down the stairs, but we were right outside the bedroom door. You could hear Keyshawn more clearly now. Lania just stood there for a moment with her head down like she was 'bout'a just die. I couldn't see her face but I could tell by the way her shoulders were shaking, she was crying hard—trying not to make a sound. I felt so sorry for her. She turned the knob and I braced myself.

My eyes were ready for anything, Michelle naked and on top or Michelle on her knees getting it from the back, or, shit, Keyshawn on top and Michelle's legs around his neck. I already started picturing it so it wouldn't be as shocking when I finally got to see it. But I don't think anything we ever picture in our heads actually prepares our asses for reality. The door opened soundlessly and Aaliyah's voice sang the words directly into my ears over the speakers: "You may not be in the mood to learn what you think you know." It took me longer to find them because I didn't know how the damn room was set up or where the bed was. My high ass scanned everywhere like I was FBI, taking every little detail in at a glance. Pants, shirts, loafers all over, soft light brown shag carpeting, blue candles lit on a dresser. I could smell India Moon incense burning.

I stepped on the Trojan wrappers beside the foot of the bed and when I finally saw them, I probably lost a good five years off of my life based on the amount of time that my heart stopped. I'm pretty sure I sprouted 'bout fifteen grey hairs, too. Before I could say anything Lania was already across the room, and I tried, but I already knew I wouldn't be able to get to her fast enough. My TV audience screamed and I stood there, glued to the floor, watching everything in slow motion as she lunged at the bed, landing on top of the comforter. Landing right smack on top of Curtis's back.

"What the fuck, Yylannia? What the fuck you doin' in here?" Keyshawn jumped out the bed naked and, oooh, he was *maaaaad*.

I slowly backed my ass farther into the hall-way just to make sure he ain't see me. Ain't want the nigga not hookin' my ass up at clubs an' shit anymore. *Boy oh boy, if Michelle only knew 'bout this shit*. Remember now, I said I scanned the room like the damn FBI! I ain't see no women's clothes or panties up in there and and I ain't neva' *hear* a woman, but Lania, aka Mrs. Muthafuckin' Action Jackson, was already in the room before I could point that shit out. But the circumstances still gave her a damn good reason to be goin' the fuck off the way she was.

Soundlessly, Lania climbed off of the bed. I waited to see what Curtis had to say but he didn't dare move. Embarrassed, I guessed. All I could do was shake my head at Mr. Big-time NBA Owner fucking his damn . . . Gasping, my hand flew to cover my mouth as a red stain began spreading across the light blue comforter. So much for trying to remain unseen; my sudden movement caught Keyshawn's attention. His eyes locked on mine. Full of anger and fear he started to walk toward me, but my attention went back to Lania, who was now looking down at the knife in her hand like she didn't even know she'd picked it up. Hell I didn't even know she'd picked it up.

"Well Mr. 'Keys to the City,' think they'll give you the keys to your cell?"

"*Noooo*." Keyshawn's scream shocked me. My eyes widened 'cause I would've never pegged him as the screamin' type. Shit, I ain't see him as a bottom either but hey. He climbed onto the bed and grabbed Curtis's body, tryin' to stop the bleeding with his hands. Wiping the handle off with the comforter Lania laid the knife down. She smiled as she walked toward me, grabbed my hand, and we got the fuck from up outta there.

"Do you think he gonna call the police?" It was funny how we'd suddenly switched rolls and now I was frantic and on the brink of panic and Lania was calm as fuck.

"Who would believe him if he did? Someone broke in, took nothing, killed his gay lover who's also the owner of the team *and* left the murder weapon?"

We were now flying down South Dade Highway but in the opposite direction of home.

"Where are we going? I live the other way."

"To the beach for a little while. I know a shortcut so we can avoid traffic."

I checked my cell, disappointed that I only had one bar of battery power left and zero fuckin' missed calls. Well, for all the thinkin' I'd done about her ass earlier, if Michelle ain't miss me I sure as hell wasn't gonna miss her.

CHAPTER 17

STOP LOOKIN' AND LOVE
WILL SOON LOOK BACK

It was around six-thirty when I was sitting in the photo booth at Chuck E. Cheese and my phone went off. It was Jim's ringtone and my heart immediately went into a downward spiral. *Lord give me strength for whatever this man had to tell me.*

"Hey, Michelle, got some not so good news."

I waited, wondering what the hell could have happened now. Me and the kids were fine so the only thing I could think was that something had happened to Ris. 1001 worst-case scenarios flashed before me and even though I hadn't figured out whether I was more mad at her actions or hurt by them, I instinctively began to worry.

"All right, Jim, I'm listening."

"Welp, the other missus done up an' gone AWOL on us."

My hands clammed up in a nervous sweat. *Ris had gone what?* The photo booth flashed pictures of the kids' smiling faces, and me looking like I was gonna wring someone's neck the second I stepped out of there. I adjusted the kids on my lap, holding the phone with my shoulder.

"What do you mean by AWOL, Jim? Does that mean you lost her? Why wasn't someone following her? How'd they lose her? It's what the fuck I pay you guys for isn't it?"

Trey's eyes widened, giving me his "ooooooh, Mommy, that's a bad word" face, and I took a deep breath, trying to calm myself down. It wasn't working.

"Now, now. No need'n gettin' upset wit' my boys. They did what they was paid to do. She pulled a fifty-two switch up on 'em."

I started counting, but only made it to five before giving up. Rolling my eyes, I prepared myself for the bullshit. "CliffsNotes, Jim, quickly please, before I break somethin', an' what the hell is a fifty-two whatever?" You would think he'd be used to telling me shit by now. Used to me wanting quick details an' short answers in *plain English*.

After a long, drawn-out sigh he explained, "A damn gaggle of 'em, all lookers, showed up 'round 'bout three o'clock an' went inside. Apparently Larissa swapped outfits wit' one of 'em, matched her size an' build to a T. Walked out on her own free will, right dab in the middle of the flock."

I swore I needed my own Jimtionary. It took me a moment to figure out what a gaggle and a flock had to do with any damn thing. I was out of the picture booth, cell phone on my shoulder, Lataya on my hip, and Trey dragging his damn feet, pouting beside me before Jim could even finish his explanation.

"Mommeeee, you forgot our pictur—"

I shot him that mother's shut-up-and-bring-yo'-ass-or-meet-certain-death look, stopping him dead ass in the middle of his whining. I'd definitely perfected that shit over the years.

"Keith said he recognized one of the young ladies. The driver was the one y'all like to associate wit', Yylannia. She was a part of the high jinks. The decoy, as we called her, caught a cab 'bout ten minutes ago an' that's when he noticed it wasn't Larissa. He went inside to look fer her, put two an' two together."

I tried to feel a little more at ease knowing that she was with Lania, but I knew Ris all too well. With everything that'd happened lately, this shit was her way of acting out. She was trying to do something she shouldn't be doing in order to cope with our shit and all the drama. Lania just so happened to be her enabler.

I buckled the kids into their car seats, upset that once again my babies had to take back burner to some more bullshit.

"Thank you, Jim. I'll call her and Keyshawn to see if he's seen them. I'm on my way home now." I dialed Ris's number first, instantly becoming livid when my call went straight to voice mail. *Childish, absolutely fucking childish.* Yes, I'd blacklisted her number when I left the house with the kids but it was only because I already knew she would call me every five fucking minutes and I didn't want my phone going off all damn day. All it did was send her calls straight to voice mail and any texts she'd send would go to a waiting box. I checked my phone and was surprised when I saw zero voice mails and had zero waiting texts. This was just fucking great; now she wanted to be on some tit-for-tat petty shit by turning off her damn phone.

I dialed Key's number. It rang repeatedly before his voice mail came on. I hung up. It just didn't feel right to leave him a message about my wife missing, not after we'd spent such a nice day together. We'd taken the kids to the park and a duck feeding pond; afterward I sat with the kids and watched movies in his living room while Key was busy in the kitchen making us lunch. That's what a family was supposed to feel like. Not this constant push-pull, give and keep on giving situation I was in, that I had the nerve to be calling a damn marriage.

CHAPTER 18

IF YOU PEE IN RUNNIN' WATER,
IT DON'T MAKE NO SPLASH

My phone was completely dead by the time we got to the damn beach. It was a little ways away from the touristy area and quiet, which was good 'cause my ass needed some time to pull it together. I was glad the sun was starting to go down. The humidity was making me sweat up a storm. My borrowed clothes were sticking to my back and my hair was irritating my shoulders. I waited for Lania to pile all her shit back into her purse and we walked toward the ocean, looking for a good spot to sit down. My high was wearing off, the after-effects making me feel a little depressed.

"Want to try something new?"

I wanted to do anything that would make the sad hole in my heart go away. We sat down facing the water and Lania pulled a small white packet from her purse.

"Put a little of this under your tongue, it's better than sex—I promise."

"Shit. I doubt that, but we'll see." I cringed; it was bitter in my mouth like a crushed-up aspirin. "Ugh, you ain't got a Pepsi up in that bitch, do you?"

Lania laughed, dabbing a little of the shit underneath her own tongue. She waved at the ocean. "Water, water all around and not a drop to drink."

We both chuckled and stared out at the sea, waiting for our shit to kick in.

"Lania, you think Key been fuckin' dudes the whole time y'all been together?" I couldn't help it. Maybe the shit was working, making me ask questions I shouldn't be asking but I did. A few minutes passed before she answered me, her words floating to my ears like a song drifting in from the ocean.

"Keyshawn is not gay."

"Um I don't know if you just saw what I saw, but that looked pretty damn gay to me." This bitch was in de-fuckin'-nial.

"Some families have secrets buried so deep that it's the only thing holding the roots in the ground. You pull up those secrets, you loosen the soil, weakening the tree." *Shiiiiiit*. I glanced at Lania's ass out the corner of my eye. *If that wasn't the highest, most poetic shit I ever heard and ain't hardly understand.* I sat there, silently rolling her words through my brain.

"If I tell you something you have to swear you'll never repeat it."

Hell I forgot her ass was sitting beside me for a second. I mean, it's not like I didn't just watch her ass murder a muthafucka' or nothin'—but I guess maybe she wasn't counting that as a real secret, I don't know. "I promise. I'll even tell you one that you can't say shit about to no-fuckin'-body either."

She nodded, satisfied with our deal. "I owe a huge debt to Angelo Testa. It's the kind of debt that you repay for life, until either you die or Angelo dies. You see, I knew him long, long before he became the powerful man he is now."

I waited.

Lania took a shallow breath, her voice shaky as she continued, tears slowly welling up in her golden eyes. "Me and Angelo are bound by the blood of relation. We're brothers."

What the fucccccccccck! The TV audience in my head jumped back to life, screaming in unison as my eyes bulged out my damn head.

"You're . . . I mean . . . you were a man?"

"I'm completely post-op, did hormone injections, pills, all of it. My other brother, Keyshawn, met me long after it was all said and done and I myself never had the heart to tell him different."

The audience's heads tilted to the side in confusion. *Huh? Did he—she—just say . . . No. No.*

"Wait, Lania, you said Keyshawn is your . . . *other brother?*" Boy, these pills was definitely some goooood shit. 'Cause I could have sworn they was putting words in my ears that this bitch's mouth wasn't even saying.

"Right. Keyshawn is my stepbrother by marriage. We were dating and in love way before me and Angelo's mother met Keyshawn's father. We tried to stop seeing each other but it never lasted long, so instead we agreed to just keep a *very, very* open relationship, never revealing our relationship. Key was doing well and shit was going good until he was traded to Miami. Curtis had his eyes on Key the second he stepped out of that locker room. When Key turned him down not too long ago, Curtis started digging for dirt. He was a fool. He paid one of Angelo's goons to dig for him, so we've been feeding Curtis phony information and coming up with dead ends."

I sat there, staring at Lania, captivated. Their story was way more fucked up than the shit Chelle and I had done. No wonder we all got along so well.

"So, what happened back there with Curtis? Wasn't just you on some angry bitch, don't-touch-my-man type shit?"

"Fuck no. Last time I saw Angelo, he told me about a rumor in the owners' box. Something about Curtis wanting to trade Keyshawn to the highest bidder, like fucking livestock."

"That's nothin' new. Players get traded all the time, Lania, it's part of the game."

"True, but Angelo said the rumor also involved Curtis wanting Key injured after the trade so he'd never play again. I told Key about it and apparently he must've cut a deal with Curtis to stay in Miami *and* make more money. No person ever thinks they have a price until someone is willing to pay it. What Key didn't know was that Curtis was going to fuck him and trade him anyway. So, I deaded that shit . . . literally."

It was like hearing the ending of a long, dramatic bedtime story. The sun had almost completely set and every part of Lania's story made sense except for one little-ass piece. "Why would Keyshawn give up da ass just to keep playin' ball? That don't make sense, not when the nigga has the fuckin' Mafia on his side." I had a bitch thinking with that question.

"Only one way to find out."

Oooh, this is gettin' gooood. She whipped out that little phone of hers and dialed Key's number, hitting the speaker button so I could hear everything.

"You got some nerve callin' me right now." Keyshawn's voice came out of the speaker in a loud growl.

Even though it was just over the phone, instinctively, my ass leaned back.

Lania didn't look fazed. "Oh please, boy. I did you a favor and you know it." She started to sing into the phone while making some sorta kissy face. "There isn't even a mess for you to clean up now is there?"

"You already know ya Mafia brother done came over here wit' his fuckin' flunkies and mopped up. What I tell you 'bout callin' dat mu'fucka e'retime some shit go down? I'm tired of havin' blood on my hands, Yylannia."

"*I* kept your hands clean. Now shut up. I have a question," she snapped at him. In the blink of an eye her tone went from soft and playful to razor sharp. "Why did I catch you in the predicament you were in, given we could have resolved this in any number of ways with the snap of a finger and, eh-hmmm, saved your ass, sweetheart?"

We both waited for Key to answer, the phone hanging silently between us like a question mark.

"Because I fuckin' wanted to, Yylannia. You an' your damn brother got a problem with that shit? Huh? I *wanted* to!"

Triple whammy, were the words my mental studio audience shouted at the scene unfolding before me. I looked down and traced a heart in the sand with my finger; I knew exactly how Key must have felt, to have those kinds of feelings and be scared to act on 'em 'cause you afraid of what people might say or think. His family's approval obviously meant a lot to him. I scratched a squiggly break through the heart. That looked a lot better.

"But you told me you turned him down repeatedly and . . . and what about me, Keyshawn? I thought we had an agreement. You seemed happy."

"What about you, Yylannia? There ain't no we, jus' like there could never be anything wit' me an' Curtis. What would the star of the muthafuckin' team look like fuckin' the owner? If that shit got out it would discredit me, ruin my fuckin' career. Jus' like if anyone found out we actually kinfolk. *And, what the fuck was Ris doin' up in here with you?* Angelo know she was wit' you?"

"Of course not, and it doesn't matter, Key."

"So what you think he gon' say when he find out or . . . Oh, lemme guess, y'all cool now, you gon' save her ass too? You trust her like that?"

Lania glanced up at me nervously. I could see her doubting me all of a sudden as Keyshawn continued.

"That shit you pulled was sloppy and reckless, Lania. And, for future reference, I ain't askin' you or anyone else's *permission to use my own gotdamn dick.*" The phone went silent, his growl echoing across the beach out and into the waves.

Someone in the studio audience in my head held up their hand. *Sooooo, you mean to tell me, if Lania, who is a "she" now, woulda just kept her ass as Lance, a "he", then, um, he coulda been on some happily-ever-after shit with Keyshawn fo'reals, 'cause the nigga like dick any damn way?* The rest of the studio audience whistled and cheered and I shook my head. This shit was just too damn much for me. Here I was, all along gettin' jealous over Keyshawn spending time with Michelle and the kids. Thinking that nigga wanted to be *with* Michelle when, in all actuality, that nigga wanted to *be* Michelle.

"You know Keyshawn does have a point, don't you?" Lania was looking down at the sand.

I almost didn't hear her over the conversation I was havin' in my damn head. "Huh? What you say, *Lany?*" Laughin', I nudged her with my shoulder, and the movement made the entire ocean sway with me. "Ooooh, there goes that shit *finallllly* kickin' in. I was startin' to think it was a dud or sumthin'." I looked over at Lania, my mouth opening to ask her if she was okay, and I had to blink to clear the stars from my eyes, my ears suddenly ringing.

"Bitch, you hit me!" I already knew what was goin' on. One of us wasn't gonna leave that beach. Lania done sat there and spilled her fuckin' guts and now after listenin' to Key's ass she was second-guessing shit and trying to clean up after herself. Detroit raised my ass; I knew to throw punches that would break a bitch's nose before I could read or ride a bike.

Lania tried to hit me again and I grabbed her fist, twisting it until she screamed in pain. She grabbed my hair with her free hand and twisted it, tightening it around her fist and pulling my head back until it was in the sand. It felt as though each strand was being torn from my scalp; the pain made me lose my leverage on her hand and I let go. *Fuck, I really wanted to break that shit, too.* Lania climbed on top of me, straddling me, grinning. Her hands wrapped around my throat, and I clawed at the ground, reaching around for something, anything to hit her with and coming up with handfuls of sand.

The bitch laughed, taunting me. "Larissa, what's the matter? You're so pale. You look like you've seen a ghost."

Now I didn't know if black people could actually ever go pale and shit, but I could feel all the blood draining from my face. I stared over Lania's shoulder, tears welling up in the corners of my eyes and sliding down my face, splashing into the sand. I didn't know what the fuck was in that shit Lania gave me. I had to have been higher than the cost of living in California, giraffe pussy, *and* the cost of gas to drive me to the San Diego Zoo to look at the damn giraffe just so I could say, "Damn that pussy high." Because for all intents and purposes, for all my ass knew, I was staring directly at the Ghost of Christmas Past. And it was staring down at me, directly over Lania's shoulder, with a pistol pointed dead center at my muthafuckin' nose. For the first time, the studio audience was completely silent.

CHAPTER 19

DISAPPEARING ACTS

It was going on 2:00 A.M. and no one had bothered returning any of my phone calls. I was debating actually going over to Key's place just to see if maybe they were all over there drunk or high, or worse, having another one of their all-out fuck parties minus me, but I kept talking myself out of it. I refused to embarrass myself in front of him again. Aside from my time in the hospital I couldn't think of one night that Ris and I had spent apart since leaving Virginia. Call it paranoia or intuition, I didn't care; I just had a nagging feeling like something was seriously wrong and it wouldn't go away.

Jim had sent a few of his guys to check the club that we'd been to and a few bars in the area, but since she'd intentionally ditched his team he wasn't too enthused about putting too many man hours into a search at this point. I'd called

Keyshawn a few more times and Larissa's phone was still going directly to voice mail. I paced the house top to bottom and nearly jumped outta my skin when my phone rang.

"Keyshawn! Oh my God, Larissa—"

"So, I'm guessing I owe you some kinda explanation huh?" He cut me off before I could finish. He sounded tired, stressed.

"An explanation? About what?" *What the hell is this nigga talkin' about?*

"Wait, huh? I dozed off, I just woke up. What . . . what were you saying about Larissa?"

"Oh, God, Key, I think something's wrong. She left with Lania and a bunch of girls earlier today and I haven't seen or heard from her since."

"Woooow. I mean. You know how they are. So you haven't gotten a text, voice mail, no nothing?" He sounded strange, like he was amused or relieved, I couldn't tell. Maybe he was just happy that I was pissed with Ris because it would give him a chance to get in better with me.

"She's never done anything like this before. *Ever.* I don't know what to do right now. I'm losing my mind over here."

"You know it's fuckin' funny 'cause I haven't heard from Lania's ass all day either; her phone's been off too. You don't think the two of them . . . Nah." He cut himself off.

"Tell me, Keyshawn. The two of them what? What do you know?"

"Shit, don't quote me on this, but Lania had mentioned before that Keisha, the chick from the club—"

"Oh you mean the chick who was with ol' girl. Chanel, the one who was givin' you a hand job under the table?" I couldn't let that one slide. For him to be so interested in havin' me play the lead he sure did seem to have a lot of side tricks lined up waitin' to step in an' take the spotlight. The nigga definitely had ho tendencies and that was definitely a red flag in my book.

"Ah, that was when you was givin' me a hard time remember? I didn't even know I had a real chance wi'chu at that point. But nah, whenever Lania be on that phone off bullshit she's usually up to no good, and after the day I had wi'chu and the kids I gave her ass permanent walkin' papers. No more open relationship. I don't want that lifestyle anymore. I wanna build on somethin', I want a family—somethin' solid."

I was speechless. It honestly wasn't what I expected to hear, but everything I needed. "You know, comin' from a man, words ain't shit to me, Keyshawn. Far as I know you jus' another nigga promisin' me heaven, and for all I know you gonna take me through hell to get there. I got enough hell right now. I can't do this shit anymore."

"You won't have to. How 'bout I come keep you company—we can wait on Ris to call or not call, come home or whatever together. Either way you won't be doin' it by yourself. I make some mean hot cocoa, gurrrrl."

I laughed, I couldn't help it. Something about him just made me happy and the fact that he could do it even at a time like this, when I was actually worried sick outta my mind, made it that much more meaningful.

"Okay, you can keep me company, and I like marshmallows in my cocoa."

CHAPTER 20

UNFORGETTABLE
AIN'T IRREPLACEABLE

Almost a month had passed since Ris walked out of my life leaving the kids, her clothes, and everything we had together. There was always a shadow of doubt in the back of my mind that still carried the slightest fear that maybe something had really happened to her. It would nag me whenever my mind had a chance to wander, like when I was cooking, or taking a shower, or in those last few moments just before I'd fall asleep.

Lania had turned up within the next few days according to Keyshawn. She'd called him hung over and still high, claiming that Ris was of course laid up with that Keisha girl he'd mentioned. I was hurt, but Key turned out to be my knight in shining armor, gluing the pieces of my family back together little by little, even while dealing with the murder of Curtis, who I later found out was like his mentor, according to his teammates and all the news reports I'd read. They'd found parts of Curtis's body when some trappers caught a gator with a human arm in its mouth about a week after Ris disappeared. They never caught the killer or found the rest of his body; hell the only way they even knew it was Curtis was by his damn fingerprints. I could tell it still really bothered Keyshawn sometimes.

I'd decided to surprise him and make veal parmesan with bacon-wrapped asparagus for dinner. Closing my eyes I let myself enjoy something that I didn't get too often: a quiet house. The kids were at the park with Key, taking advantage of having him around since it was the off-season. I was in the middle of crushing garlic when that all-too-familiar alarm chimed on my iPhone. I hadn't heard from Jim in a while. Keyshawn insisted that I didn't need him since he had his own "special security" that he refused to tell me about. But until I knew Rah was back behind bars I kept Jim on standby.

"Hi, Jim, long time no hear."

"Ye know they say no news is good news. Well I've got some info that'll pro'ly have ya doin' a jig or whatnot."

"I'm ready." I took a deep breath, not sure if it would be about Larissa or Rasheed, but anxious either way.

"Not gonna sugarcoat this—they found Rasheed's body yesterday a few miles south of Emporia back in Virginia. Was burned up pretty bad; had to use dental records to identify it. He was inside one of those CMA CGM shipping containers. There was another corpse in there with 'im, one of 'em a female, but we're still waiting on more information. No ID on the Jane Doe as of yet. But I know you'll sleep better now knowing he ain't after ye."

I was dumbfounded. There were tears in my eyes from both sadness and joy.

"He wasn't alive . . . when they burned him, was he, Jim?" No one deserved that kind of death. Not even Rah.

"Not sure yet, sweetheart. We'll know more in a couple of days. I'll give you a ring back. 'Til then you be safe and enjoy yourself now."

I didn't know what to do with myself. I left the food and everything in the kitchen and walked out the front door; the humidity made sweat bead on my forehead almost instantly. I inhaled, smelling the rain that was coming and the rose bushes on the side of the house that'd just started to bloom. The sky was dark from the approach of one of our usual evening thunderstorms and for the first time in months I was able to just enjoy standing outside, not worrying about who, or if someone, was watching me or waiting.

***

"Woman, you got this house smellin' good."
Key walked in right on time with Lataya in his
arms and Trey following not too far behind him.

I'd already set the table and was just keeping
everything warm until they got back. Fresh basil,
garlic bread, bacon; yes, it did smell good and
my stomach growled in agreement.

"Everybody wash their hands, it's time to eat."

He came over and gave me a soft kiss, handing
me a small pink and white envelope.

"What's this baby?" I looked at it, amused; he
never failed to amaze me.

"Oh I don't know, let's open it later." Winking
playfully he marched off to the hall bathroom to
help the kids wash their hands.

The storm started to roll in just as we finished
up dinner. The thunder and lightning were scaring the kids and Keyshawn wasn't helping, jumping and yelling, "Boo," in between every damn
thunderclap. This was probably one of the worst
ones we'd had all summer; it was going on nine
and it still hadn't let up.

"Mommy, can we sleep wif you?" I looked
at Key and sighed. *Damn and double damn
because this is definitely some of that good
old-fashioned handling business weather.*

"Yes, baby. Let's go get our PJs on." Glancing
at Key, I led Trey to his bathroom.

He gave me a wink and my ass got excited. That shit meant, *oh we are gonna wait 'til they fall asleep and then the business is gonna get handled*. It didn't take long before all four of us were cuddled up in the bed and the three of them, with their bellies full, were of course unconscious before ten-thirty. Lataya was lying on Keyshawn's chest and Trey was all up in my back when I remembered the envelope he'd given me. I'd left it on the counter downstairs and now my curiosity was getting the better of me.

The storm was still on ten and I couldn't believe the thunder didn't wake the kids up. I'd stopped to look out the window and my mind couldn't help drifting to Larissa. We used to love to watch lightning storms together. "Nature's fireworks" was what she always called them. An exceptionally bright pinkish silver fork split down from the sky and I wondered if she was watching it now.

My phone dinged from its docking station on the kitchen counter. Slipping the small envelope into the top pocket of my pajama top, I checked my phone. It showed I had one missed call. Secretly, I hoped it was Ris. Every time I dialed her number it went to voice mail. Even though she was on my account, I never turned her line off, even though I pretty much assumed she'd probably gotten a new phone by now. I didn't know why I didn't just disconnect it. The missed call was Jim and I pressed the play button to listen to the voice mail he'd left me.

"Hey, Michelle. Funny thing. Was on the phone with the coroner's office in Virginia going over a few details. The body was set on fire after death. There was no burn or scar tissue on the inside of his lungs."

Well that was good; the last thing I wanted to think about was Rasheed suffering a painful, horrible death. He had a ton of enemies and I could only imagine who would do something like that once they got a hold of him.

Jim's voice mail went on: "Only problem is, tissue samples show massive decomposition. That man been dead for about three, maybe four months. Somebody got a hold of him and took him out *soon* as he got busted out of that prison, Michelle. So my question to you is—"

My iPhone slid from my hand, the glass shattering on the tile of the kitchen floor just as lightning split the sky open and thunder crashed so loud it sounded like a tree trunk being split in half like a twig. I didn't need to hear the rest of Jim's question because the answer was standing in my kitchen, soaking wet, staring me in the face. Rasheed was already dead but this could be the night I was going to die too.

CHAPTER 21

IF I SHOULD DIE BEFORE I WAKE . . .
(Two years earlier, December 25 . . .)

"Okay, sweetheart, you gotta trust me on this shit." Kita was a third-year medical school student who'd been workin' in the women's ward at the prison to finish up her residency or whatever the fuck they called it. She was one of the few people who actually took really good care of me during my pregnancy. She felt the worst 'bout what happened to initially even get my ass locked up, and e'reday when she could see me by myself all we'd talked 'bout was findin' a way to legally get my case appealed. When dat fell through an' every appeal I turned in got turned down, she started tryin' to find ways for me to get out illegally. Kita could lose her financial aid and all her school shit by doin' this, so even though my ass was scared as hell I wasn't gonna let her down.

"This is some experimental shit we been workin' on in lab back at Old Dominion. We've tried it a few times on animals, small pigs, and I'm gonna write my thesis on it and maybe earn myself an article in the *Medical Journal.* It's gonna slow down your heart jus' long enough for you to flat line. It disrupts the electrical transmitters that the EKG machine picks up on. But never mind; that shit's technical. Anyway, in three hours you'll go right back to normal. You still gon' be breathin'; it'll jus' be *extremely* shallow. So shallow nobody will even be able to notice."

We were sittin' in the post-delivery intensive care ward, if that's what you wanna call it. It was really just an area of the prison that they'd sectioned off with a few raggedy-ass hospital beds that had curtains in between 'em, but since there weren't a whole lot of pregnant women up in there it was pretty much all mine. A few days ago I'd been stabbed in my cell by my cellmate—the shit sent me into labor a couple weeks prematurely, but me and my baby were both some fighters and we made it out okay.

Kita was still goin' in, explainin' the plan to get me out. A plan she'd come up with one day outta the blue after my last appeal was finally turned down an' a few of the other inmates started gettin' hostile toward me.

Some shit went down where some of Rah's product was supposed to be killin' people out on the street. They was up in here takin' they anger out on me 'cause I was picked up wit' a loaded car full of his shit, even though my ass ain't even know it was there. But shit like that doesn't matter on the streets. When somebody lose a junkie cousin, brother, or auntie to some bad dope, first thing they wanna do is take out anyone they think coulda gave it to 'em. My question was always why couldn't they ass be as gung-ho 'bout takin' the damn needle or pipe *from* the person as they was 'bout takin' someone's life *over* that person?

"It'll be jus' like havin' one of those dreams where you can't move an' shit but you'll be able to hear an' feel everything."

Damn, she is still goin'. I needed to pay attention. I nodded, intent on keepin' my ass focused this time. The baby ripped me wide da fuck open wit' her water-head self when she came out. *She ain't get that big ol' thang from me. I'm blamin' all that dome piece on her damn daddy.* I was pretty sure my meds must've been wearin' off 'cause the stitches and the knife wound in my side was all startin' to throb again. Thinkin' about my baby made my eyes burn and I could feel the tears comin'. I started blinkin' quickly, tryin' not to cry, and counted the dirty yellow an' white checkerboard tiles along the ward floor. Some were cracked and peelin' up—others were broken in half, just like my family right now. We were separated and torn all apart. *I'd do anything to hold my li'l girl and my man again. Fuckin' worthless-ass prison bitches threw her in my arms and snatched her away before my blood was wiped off a her or her umbilical cord was even cut.*

"I'ma need you to be dat bitch, Honey. 'Cause they gonna tag you, bag you, and put yo' ass in the morgue, but you jus' keep thinkin' 'bout yo' li'l girl, okay?"

"I . . . I'm gonna be in there wit' dead bodies?" Jus' thinkin' 'bout not bein' able to move, freezin' inside a dead person storage locker, zipped up inside a body bag gave me chills. I was pro'ly gonna have nightmares 'bout this shit for the rest of my life.

"You'll be fine, Honey. My homeboy is wit' the coroner's office—he know what's up. Javis gonna get to you within the first half-hour of me declaring you dead 'cause you'll need to be put on oxygen ASAP. If we can help it you ain't neva' gonna make it to the freezer. You jus' gonna be in the morgue part—that's where they sit the bodies. Then it's a new ID, new name. New life."

"All right, you know I'ma do what it take to get back to Paris an' Rah. I ain' gonna do shit to get either of y'all caught for helpin' me. I'll even cut the skin off the tips of my fingers, like I seen some of the lifers up in here done did, if I have to so they can neva' link the 'new me' back to the me you talkin' to right now."

"Girl, you jus' find your baby, get to your man, an' live the life you was meant to live."

I closed my eyes, 'cause the pain from everything, from my wounds to my heart, was now too much to ignore, and the thought about the letter Kita had me write to Rasheed a few minutes earlier was just now startin' to sink in. In order for everything to work, everyone, including my love, had to believe I was dead. He could take care of Paris until I healed up and then we could all finally be together as a family. He was gonna be mad as hell at me for scaring him like this—I could already hear him cussin' me out now—but in the end it would all be worth it.

"All right, li'l momma, give me your arm."

Kita dipped a cotton ball in alcohol and I jumped when the cold cotton touched my bare skin. Visions flashed before me of the man I loved smilin' as he looked down for the first time at the li'l girl we'd made. I focused on what I wanted. This prison shit was the bad dream and when I woke up I'd be back waking up back in my normal life.

"You're gonna feel a little pinch. Now start counting backward from one hundred, and when you wake up . . ."

I closed my eyes, holding the image of the baby girl I'd just named and let go of, remembering the smile of the man I'd loved and held on to.

"One hundred, ninety-nine, ninety-eight . . ."

CHAPTER 22

THIS WOMAN'S WORK

I'd sat back an' watched these bitches livin' da life I shoulda been livin', raisin' da family I shoulda been raisin' for too damn long. Patience was not somethin' I was good at but I was learnin' it on a daily basis. Growin' up the old folk used to always say, "when you take things for granted, the things you are granted get taken"; well I was 'bout to do a whole damn lot of takin'. They owed me money, they owed me love, time, and sweat, tears, pain, and they owed me my damn daughter. They took Paris from me an' I'd do anything, an' I mean damn near anything, to get my baby back.

The good thing 'bout bein' dead—or I should say bein' thought of as dead—is you get to learn how people honestly feel. You get to see they actions an' compare all that shit to the words that they'd said to you to keep you faithful or loyal or, in my case, to keep you servin' a sentence for some shit you ain't even deserve to be servin' a sentence for. The whole time I was locked up all I could think 'bout was Rasheed. There was a few times when I called him an' he ain't take my call but I tried to be understanding 'cause he was goin' through so much back then. When I'd finally found a way to get out I almost lost my mind, 'cause the first thing I had to learn when I went lookin' for his ass was that my man's bitch-ass baby momma had done turned 'round an' gotten him locked up! It took e'rething in me to not go after her right then an' there.

Michelle an' Larissa. Michelle an' got-damn Larissa. Larissa, my damn cousin. We s'posed to be blood an' I gotta find out dat she the main reason why I know what the inside of prison walls is like, while she livin' in a fuckin' fairytale castle, pushin' Benzes an' shit. Hell da fuck no. First thing first was to get my money up an' that wasn't hard 'cause Rah had shit stashed in places jus' for shit like this. It was a weird feelin' bein' back in Norfolk without him.

January always reminded me of him. From the crunch and color of the leaves on the ground to the way the wind would blow an' it be so cold it damn near freeze ya skin even through your coat an' jeans. He called it get money weather, 'cause the air smelled crisp like brand new bills. And while lazy niggas was cuffed wit' they boos eatin' and gettin' fat, real niggas was hustlin'—out gettin' what them lazy niggas was passin' up. This weather was made for makin' stupid easy money. I smiled to myself and wished some of that stupid easy money would come to me now.

I went to the house where he stayed wit' his baby momma. It was still empty, thank God. I felt like a ghost; hell I was a ghost—creepin' through the dead grass in the middle of the night an' shit. My breath was comin' out in white clouds and my fingers burnin' in my gloves. His neighborhood always smelled like hickory 'cause all dem niggas out there got fireplaces an' they burn 'em hard in the winter. E'retime I smelled that smell it reminded me of him.

Police tape was still on all the doors an' windows, an' the Feds took e'rething up out the house down to the damn curtains. But I jus' carried my ass round the side like I remember Rah tellin' me.

"Any shit ever go down, a nigga grabbin' the burner from up unda the mattress, and if I can't get to a safe for some go paper, I gotta jus'-in-case stack up unda the li'l cement rain gutta on the side of the crib. Rainy day shit fo' sho'. Honey, a nigga stay ready so he ain't eva' and I mean so he ain't eva' gotta get ready."

Smiling, I crouched down as I got closer to the cement rain gutter on the ground. A few beetles ran from up underneath it when I slid it out the way an' it took me a minute to dig 'cause I forgot to bring somethin' to use an' the ground was half damn frozen. After a good thirty minutes I hit a li'l tin box an' uncovered it enough to get the lid off. He had at least seventy Gs in there and I stuffed it inside of the li'l blue duffel bag I had with me. It ain't have much in it, but it held everything I owned. This was more than enough for what I needed to start; the rest would find its way to me. I just needed to find my way out of Virginia until I could come up with a solid plan; it was too risky stayin' here.

They was both so damn stupid; like changin' names an' movin' all the way down the East Coast and whatnot would keep somebody from findin' 'em. I was gonna pay one of Rah's old homeboys to find 'em but I didn't wanna involve anyone else. So I used a pay phone outside the 7-Eleven not too far from Brambleton Street. Called the Norfolk district court one day pretendin' I was Michelle askin' if they could verify the forwardin' address for Paris's birth certificate. Some Latasha chick, or whoeva' she was, was all like, "Oh we mailed that already." So I said, "Well, ma'am, I ain't get it. Can you please verify where you sent it?" And just like that I knew exactly how to find they asses.

Soon as I knew how to find them, my next move was finding a way to get to Rasheed. I had to be able to pay the guards and COs and still have somewhere to lay my own head at night. I couldn't hang around Virginia to earn money for fear of someone recognizing me. I walked my ass to the Greyhound bus station and bought myself a ticket to Florida.

CHAPTER 23

KINGS AND QUEENS

That had to have been the longest fuckin' bus ride of my life. I was scared to sleep most of the way only 'cause I had so much cash on me an' I ain' want nobody to try to snatch my shit. I spent most the of trip tryin' to figure out how to get Rah out of prison an' the other half tryin' to figure out what to do with Michelle and Larissa in order to get my daughter back. I was stuck sittin' beside Baby Huey the first half of the ride. This fat-ass white corn fed–lookin' mu'fucka. He smelled like mustard and armpit sweat and kept fallin' asleep, snorin' loud as fuck wit' his head back; sounded like he was gonna jus' die. Stuck between his ass and the window was hell, but he got off in North Carolina and it was jus' me after that.

Miami compared to Virginia was a culture shock. It was already damn near sixty-five degrees outside and all over the place everyone looked tan, beautiful, happy. The first thing I did was find a cab to get my ass to the Ritz-Carlton hotel. When I was locked up, we'd see commercials for them hotels and I remembered thinkin' if I ever got up out of there and could do it I'd stay my ass in one of those—well that and I couldn't think of any other fancy places so that was that.

A short, little man with a hat and suit held the door with his white gloves as I walked into the lobby and I was in awe. There was floor-to-ceiling mahogany walls covered in mirrored balls that lit up. Cream-colored leather armchairs were all over the place and everything up in there looked like it cost a damn arm and a leg. There were live exotic flowers and this waterfall and stream with real fish swimmin' in it. The place was like a dream come true and I was only in the damn lobby. I wished Rasheed could've been there with me.

"Welcome to the Ritz-Carlton Hotel, South Beach Miami. Um, may I be of service?"

There was a snooty-lookin' older black woman behind the counter lookin' down her nose at me. "Umm. I'd like your biggest suite please."

"Ma'am, that would be the Ritz-Carlton Suite, it's approximately four thousand dollars per night."

I didn't see this bitch's fingers movin'. "Okay." I just stared at her blankly, and her dumb stuck-up ass just kept lookin' at me. Reachin' into my duffle bag I peeled off twenty Gs and laid the cash on the counter with the fake ID I had made before I left Virginia. I didn't think I'd seen strippers snatch up paper fast as that bitch scraped that shit up off the counter. I laughed—money always talks. But, shit, that was already twenty that I'd just dropped and it was only for a few days. I was gonna need to hustle that shit back, and fast.

"Here is your key. Brighton, will you show Ms. Lacroix to her room?"

It was weird as fuck hearing someone call me by that name. Kita, the girl who helped get me the ID, said it a few times out loud so I'd know how to pronounce it and I'd guess I'd forgotten since then. The desk clerk snapped her fingers and some redheaded white guy appeared beside me in the same uniform as the guy who held the door. He tried to take my bag but I refused, jerking it closer to my side. Fuck that—all my money was up in there and I had a death grip on it. Seein' that, he shrugged and led me to the elevator up to the fifteenth floor where he unlocked my door and showed me into my suite. I wasn't gonna tip his ass at first because I ain't have change for a hundred, but then I remembered when mu'fuckas used to say that shit to me when I was dancin' and I'd be thinkin', *you knew you was comin' up in here so why you ain' get change first?* Plus Rah used to always say to take good care of workin' men and women— waitresses, bus boys, bartenders and shit—'cause you never knew when you'd need 'em.

"Thank you so very much, Ms. Lacroix." His wrist went up in the air, and he had this cute little singy voice. *Aww, he's fam,* I thought, immediately feelin' homesick. I used to love goin' to the drag shows up in Nutty Buddy's an' watchin' the queens go in on some songs. They'd be on stage in heels, makeup, an' dresses, *killin'it.*

"Now look, this is for our exclusive VIP Ritz guests. I usually don't give it out because they worry me to death. Press this little button and talk into the light-up part and tell me what you need and Brighton will be your personal genie." He handed me the little silver radio and sashayed out of the room.

Lookin' around I'd neva' seen anything like this shit before. To go from the life I lived, basically sellin' myself on stage dancin' and sweatin' my ass off for a bunch of strangers, to bein' locked up an' sittin' in a cell and still having not a damn thing to show for it, to where I was now. Lookin' out a window at white sand an' clear blue ocean wit' more money in my hand than I'd ever seen or made in my entire life was a sign that I was on the right path. This shit was fuckin' bananas. I laughed like I was twelve again and jumped up on the infinity-somethin' cloud bed, sending all the pillows and the blue and gold Egyptian cotton 2,000-thread-count sheets flyin' everywhere. The entire room was decorated in blues and golds and I felt like Cleopatra sittin' in my empire beside the beach.

Tired, I fell out on my back and closed my eyes. Inhaling deep, I took in the smells of the ocean from the large balcony doors, citrus and coconut, and . . . *ugh,* my funky ass.

After my shower I decided to explore. I took $4,000 wit' me along wit' the *Star-Trek*-lookin'-ass communicator Brighton gave me an' locked the rest of the cash up in the safe. The hotel was like a damn mini resort. I stopped and bought myself a cute li'l black an' tan swimsuit outta the gift shop an' went lookin' for the hot tub so I could relax and think. First thing I needed to do was get my ass some clothes. It was a good thing where I was goin' was away from the main

lobby and all the guests. The Jacuzzi was in its
own area closed off from the main pool. I was
crushed when I got in there an' saw the OUT OF
ORDER sign on the door. Looked like I'd have to
settle for either sittin' in the steam room or the
sauna that was right behind it. I poked my head
into the sauna first and cringed. The heat was
so dry it damn near made my nose bleed so,
of course, I picked the steam room. I sat down
an' the machine scared the fuck outta me when
it cut on fillin' the room wit' steam. The smell
reminded me of Vicks VapoRub, but it was still
relaxing. It was makin' so much noise and there
was so much steam in the room I couldn't hear
or see outside the glass doors. When the steam
finally stopped I froze at the sound of the voices
outside.

"So we gonna meet wit' 'em at the bah an' then
what?"

"And then you's follow my lead. He shows us
the dope, we show 'em the cash but we ain' givin'
that Guido fuck nothin'. We gonna take his shit
an' dead his bitch ass."

"What if he don't let it go that easy or he put
up a fight?"

"What da ya mean, what if he don't let it go?
We make him let it the fuck go. We take this shit
tonight and *we*, you an' me, run this shit. This

tan, Botox, and tits city will be ours by morning. Bosses don't get made; bosses make themselves. You mark me on that shit."

I stayed my ass as still as possible in that damn steam room. I felt like I was gonna pass out an' hoped they ain' keep talkin' too much longer, but I'd rather die from the steam than from the hands of whoever those two mu'fuckas was. I waited until it got completely quiet before I felt like it was okay to leave. My head was spinnin' from the heat an' I ain' know if I was even gonna make it back to my room, but damn that shit was crazy. I shook my head. *Who the fuck was them two fools tryin' to set up?* That sounded like some straight up VA-dope-boy bullshit. I tell you what—ain't no sunshine in the damn dope game. The game stay on some shady shit no matta where you think you at or what side you on.

I made it to my room, thankful they had cookies an' shit in the lobby; it gave me just enough energy to stop at a boutique I'd noticed earlier to grab a few outfits so I'd have something to wear for dinner. I changed and went downstairs to one of the hotel restaurants to get a steak or something before my ass passed out and to look an' see what kind of strip clubs they had in the area. Damn, I ain't wanna go back to strippin' but I'd have to start somewhere. I was halfway done with my carne asada fries and jumbo mango margarita when I recognized the voices I'd heard earlier. They were sitting directly behind me, talkin' business at the bar. Turning slightly in my seat I glanced over my shoulder. I couldn't see their faces. I could only see the clean-cut dark-haired white boy they was talkin' to. My heart went out to him—poor dude, he ain't have no idea what he was in for.

"So you meet us an' you ain' bring shit, muda-fucka?"

"Maybe. Right now, you ain't showin' me enough to make a ten dolla' hooka' give you a second glance, *figli di puttana*. I got it, just not here."

I remembered hearin' those words a few times from the Italian chicks up in prison. This dude jus' sat there an' not only insulted 'em but he called these dudes "motherfuckers" to their faces. I listened for a few seconds; he was a cocky li'l somebody, reminded me of my baby. Damn, that could have been Rah—doin' some shit tryin' to make money wit' me at home waitin' on his ass an' these bitch-ass mu'fuckas was tryin' to take him for everything he was worth. Dead his ass and walk away with everything he'd worked for.

I had to do something. I pulled out the little radio and put the earpiece in so I could call Brighton. *Damn why didn't this shit come with fuckin' instructions?* It took me a second to figure it out but I finally got that shit.

"How may I help you, Ms. Lacroix?"

"Brighton, enough wit' that Ms. Lacroix shit. Jus' call me Honey—I need a favor." I held the earpiece in my ear, tryin' to keep my voice as low as possible.

"I'm in the Lapidus Lounge. Come get the guy at the bar. He's wearin' the green an' black striped shirt. The one talkin' to the two guys. Tell him he has a phone call in the main lobby."

"Okay, Ms. Honey. You talking about the cute li'l thang who came in with them grey eyes. I'm on it. I'll be right there."

I laid some money on the table an' went up to the front desk an' waited. When he walked out I grabbed his arm an' pulled him over into one of the side hallways.

"Them guys you talkin' to, they gon' take whatever it is you sellin' an' they gonna kill yo' ass. So if I was you—I'd leave now."

The mu'fucka actually laughed dead in my face. "I'm sorry. Excuse me for bein' so rude, beautiful, and who are you again?"

He was still chucklin', and all I could think was that this fool had to be dumb or straight-up crazy before answerin' him. "I'm nobody. Don't you worry 'bout all that. Did you hear what I jus' said?"

"Yes, gorgeous, I heard you." He looked around before leanin' down close to my ear like he had a secret. "That's actually the plan. They's been fuckin' wit' my operation since day one, ground zero. My boys is outside and when they make they move—we gonna' make ours. Bada boom bada bing,It's finished."

Well damn, I thought, *so much for tryin' to help; men always thinkin' they got they shit together.*

"So once again I'm askin' who's this li'l guardian angel who woulda saved my life, if it'd needed savin'?"

I looked up into the clearest grey eyes that I'd ever seen in my life an' all I could think was, *Damn, his eyes is sexy as fuck.* "Once upon a time, my name was Honey."

And that's how I met King Angelo Testa, the boss of Miami.

CHAPTER 24

BITTER HONEY

It didn't take me long to confide in Angelo. Eventually I broke down and told him every last detail 'bout my situation. In a way he felt as though he owed me a favor because if he was really in some shit an' hadn't known those guys were gonna set him up, I woulda gotten him out of it. When I finally told him everything that I wanted to do as far as gettin' my daughter back, he offered to let me stay wit' his cousin Tink out in Miami until I could get my money up an' get to Rasheed. He even came up wit' a way for me to get Rah outta prison. I worked wit' his sister Lania escortin', and did li'l odds an' ends bullshit here an' there until I was finally ready. It took me almost two years before I had enough money stacked up.

I flew to Virginia and put in a call to a couple of the COs out there just to test the waters and see who would play for money and who wouldn't. Most of 'em was scary as hell so it took a lot of fishing before I found any who were willin' to bite. When a couple of the K-9 trainin' officers were out in a bar one night drinkin', I decided to start buyin' rounds an' askin' questions. Recent freezes in pay raises and overtime cuts had 'em all a little salty and hard up for extra cash. It was nothing to throw 'em a couple thousand just to give me a few details on how the dogs are escorted in an' out, sick not sick, et cetera.

Findin' a CO to help Rah get out was actually easier than I thought it was gonna be, an' I shoulda known somethin' was up wit' that shit from the start. I had done the same thing as before. Hung out in a bar that the female COs went to and asked 'bout his ass. One CO, big ugly-ass heffa, was all like, "Oooh if I could get his fine ass," et cetera. So, end of the night I catch her outside an' offer her $50,000—half up front, the other half after he's out. She accepts and I tell her the plan and where to meet me. I pick a spot all the way out in Emporia, damn near in the country, away from the city, where I have a car hidden and everything. I let her know to leave him there, emphasis on the word *leave*.

I didn't trust no damn body after the shit Larissa an' Michelle pulled so I watched from one of the towers with another guard I'd paid. I saw when that big-ass Andre the Giant–lookin' bitch put Rasheed in that damn dog crate. I was parked nearby when she got outside the prison walls an' she let him out the crate. My heart hit the floor when he laughed, pulled her close, and they kissed. Yeah, I saw it all. Rah grabbed this ugly bitch ass an' was huggin' all up on her an' shit before he got in the passenger side of the car.

They were joy ridin' down the fuckin' road, stoppin' to get coffee an' junk food. I was followin' 'em the whole time. It took everything in me to just be still when they was stoppin' at hotels to fuck. Rah was probably tellin' her he loved her and whatever else she need to hear 'cause he thinkin' all this shit was on her, not knowin' someone else financed his freedom. They finally got to Emporia, to an address I gave her off a red clay-dirt road with a gravel driveway. It was actually an old abandoned house that I'd had decorated just so I could meet my man for the first time in two years. I'd handpicked out li'l shit like sheets and pillowcases. makin' sure there were steaks to cook for breakfast along wit' his steak sauce. I parked an' walked up, 'cause you can't drive on a gravel driveway without makin' noise. The way they was goin' at it the entire time I wasn't surprised when I walked in while they were fuckin'. Her big ass was sweatin' and ridin' him hard as hell. I closed the door behind me and stood there for a few minutes until Rasheed saw me. The look on his face was like he mentally shat a brick. Of course the CO's big ass didn't bother gettin' up.

I stood right there and I asked him, while his dick was still in her and e'rething, "So who you love, Rasheed? The bitch who done died an' paid to get you outta prison or the bitch who can put yo' ass right back?"

He looked at me and back at her. "What the fuck? I . . . They t . . . told me. Oh my God." He was lookin' exactly like he'd seen a damn ghost. Hell, everybody'd been lookin' at me like that; I was gettin' used to that damn look.

"No, nigga it ain't God. It's Honey." I watched the man I thought I loved so much debate between a life in prison—because he knew if he said he loved me that CO was gonna act like her ass had found him and take him right back to that prison so damn fast—and me . . . Well he already knew if he ain't say it was me . . .

"Honey, I thought you was dead. They had a funeral an' everything. It's been damn near two years. What the fuck you think a nigga was gonna do?"

"Okay, baby. Is that yo' answer then?"

He was starin' at me, wide-eyed, brain whir-rin', tryin' to spin me one of his famous "save a nigga" stories but too much time behind bars had slowed down that fast-ass mouth of his. Back in da day the nigga woulda told me some shit that woulda had me thinkin' I was wrong for havin' the nerve to even walk in the damn room while he was fuckin' somebody else. I shook my head at him.

His lack of an answer was all the answer I needed.

"I went to prison, Rasheed. I had our daugh-ter. I died, came back, sold my body, some of my soul, gave up things I can never get back. And you can't even look this bitch-ass correctional officer in the face an' say you love me over her ass outta fear that you gon' be locked back up!" I was done wit' both they asses.

"I could have her dead before she could even take you back, Rasheed, but fuck both y'all. You ain't even worth it to me anymore." I didn't know where the tears came from, but they were there. Tiny streams runnin' down my face, blurrin' my vision. It was one thing to dream and see us together but it was another thing to have all this shit shattered by the one mu'fucka who put the hope there to begin with. I'd opened the door to leave and almost screamed at the figure in front of me. I wasn't expectin' him to be standing there and it scared the fuck out of me. When I realized what his being there meant, I almost screamed for him to just leave.

"Angelo, what'chu doin' here?"

"Came to make sure you was good, princess." Head tilted to the side, muscles tensed, him and Rasheed was in a stare down.

"Really, Honey, you come up in here wit' the new nigga, worried 'bout what the fuck I'm doin'?"

"Rasheed, you don't know who you're talkin' to. Jus' shut up." I didn't even look in Rah's direction as I spoke. I was starin' in Angelo's grey eyes. They were cloudy like a storm was comin'. The muscle in Angelo's jaw was clenchin' and I put myself between him an' Rasheed, my hands up on Angelo's chest, trying to calm him down, but it was too late. Angelo's pistol was already drawn; they were both dead behind me before I could turn back around. I could smell gunpowder and the metallic coppery odor from all of the blood.

"I knew you would show that *figlio di una cagna*—son of a bitch—too much mercy, sweetheart." He lifted my chin, staring me in the eyes. "You won't make the mistake again will you?"

All I could do was shake my head no, stunned, dazed, speechless. I couldn't turn around. I didn't want to see Rasheed and that bitch laid out. Didn't want to be stuck with the visions of the brain splatter, blood, none of that shit. Revenge I wanted, yes, but the silent rage and cold mindset that someone needed to make that kind of shit happen was where I just didn't have the stomach.

"Good, baby doll." He wrinkled his nose. "I got the boys outside; let's get them to put the bodies in the container, and get the fuck outta this Podunk country-ass town. My woman's been hell bent on revenge an' neglecting her man." He leaned down and kissed me softly, my eyes closing by themselves at the touch of his lips.

CHAPTER 25

CAT AND MOUSE

Now that Rasheed was no longer an option or an idea or a dream, my next step was figuring out what to do with these damn thorns in my side, aka Larissa and Michelle. The flight back to Virginia was quick and painless. I was standing in the doorway of what would be Paris's bedroom. We'd gotten a crib and a bed and I'd picked out a sheep-skin fur rug that sat in the middle of the room. In the corner was her toy box, already full of brand new toys and baby dolls. I had no idea what size she was wearin' now so I was gonna wait and get all of her clothes after we picked her up.

"Tink say you spend more time standin' here starin' off into space than you do lookin' at the ocean."

I didn't even hear him come up behind me. I leaned myself back into his chest and tried to relax for once. "You think she gonna like the Gucci bedspread? It isn't pink but I'd heard you can do yellow for little girls, too." I couldn't make up my mind on the colors to pick out for her room. Since the house was so open to the ocean and the beach, pink and all that girly shit just didn't feel like it went well. I'd decided to go with soft yellows and oranges to complement the views of the ocean.

"*Il mio amore,* our little angel is goin' to adore any- and everything that you give her. I promise. Now stop. You worry too much."

He was right. I was worryin' 'bout all the wrong shit. I needed to start plannin' out exactly how I was gonna get to her and then get the ball rollin' on gettin' Paris back home.

"By the way, good news. Lania says her brother set up that meetin' with this Michelle woman. They'll be meeting him to look at a house and get things goin' next week. The mark is set; you ready this time?"

I thought about it for a split second. Was I ready to see the joy of my life again after two years? Yes. Was I ready to face the two bitches who'd taken her ass from me and deliver justice as Angelo had done with Rah? I wasn't too sure about that shit. I sucked it all up and straightened my shoulders. "I'm ready, baby."

The plan was simple. Lania was there to bait Larissa and Keyshawn's job was to bait Michelle. It was Angelo's idea to approach them on some divide and conquer–type shit instead of just goin in guns blazin' and wrecking shop.

"We gonna cat an' mouse these bitches, and when just when they think shit's at its worst, when they finally sayin', 'Oh my God, I can't do this anymore,' we gonna fall da fuck back. We'll wait until they sittin' there in they comfy li'l worlds, thinkin' they just dodged a bullet—then we gonna smack they asses like we the hand of God Himself."

Since neither one of they asses had any idea that I was still alive, it was gonna to be easy to bait and reel them in once they found out Rah was dead. Angelo kissed the side of my neck. I didn't think I'd ever get used to dealing with an Italian dude. It's not that his breath stank or anything like that. He just always smelled like garlic; the semi-sweet odor was always all over him. It even came out of his pores when he sweat.

Reaching down he cupped my ass in his hands. *I ain't feel like fuckin' this nigga, not right now.* It was like I'd traded the stripper pole for a long, skinny Italian one. Yeah, this one came with perks like money and power. When we went out people respected me simply 'cause they knew I was with King, but what I had for Rasheed was true, genuine love. This shit was just another job in my mind, and I couldn't wait until the day came when I could get promoted or better yet be my own damn boss.

Turning around I looked up into his eyes; they was the most attractive thing about him aside from his money. This fool had definitely fallen in love with me, it was written all over his face. Anything I wanted was mine; all I had to do was think about it and he'd make it happen. He'd do anything to make me happy.

"You wanna go upstairs, baby?" I already knew what his answer was gonna be. I could feel his long pencil dick already gettin' hard up against my stomach. *Why couldn't that shit be thicker? Then it would be perfect. Hell I'd take short an' fat as fuck over long and skinny any damn day.* Sex wit' Angelo was like bein' poked over and over with a long skinny finger. Then this fool wanna be doin' acrobatic shit, liftin' my legs and all kinds of foolishness; sometimes it would feel like he was stabbin' me in my fuckin' kidneys.

"I can't, *bella,* I've gotta go handle some business. But when I get back home best believe papa will be *handling business.*"

I breathed a sigh of relief and thankfully he mistook it for disappointment. At least while he was gone, I could go and get things rolling with Michelle and Larissa—maybe I'd get to see my baby.

I decided to take Angelo's silver Monte Carlo as planned. It was the one with the headlights that looked like blue beams of light when they was lit up. That shit was so sexy. It was decked out, too, with silver, grey, and black marble interior and all-black leather. It came with all this extra shit that I ain't have no idea how to use, OnStar navigation and whatever else. Long as that bitch went into drive and got me where I needed to go I was good.

I followed the address that the court had given me and drove the forty-five minutes from Miami to Fort Lauderdale where they lived. I couldn't help feeling awestruck as I parked across the street from a big-ass red brick two-story house with double glass doors on the front. The house was fuckin' huge; it was more long than it was tall, and had windows on one part that went from the ground all the way up. I wasn't completely sure about what I was gonna do until I saw her.

Tears were filling my eyes and it took everything in me not to jump outta the car right then
and there. I'd missed so much, her first teeth,
first smile, first words and steps. She was so
short. I laughed. Hell I wasn't that tall my damn
self but I was hoping maybe she'd have gotten a
little height from Rasheed. But she was standing
beside Trey, who looked like he'd shot up like a
damn bean sprout. Her fat little legs were pumping, trying to keep up with him. She tripped and
I thought she was gonna cry but she, my big girl,
surprised me; she just got back up and started
runnin' again.

Larissa came out the front door, saying something to the kids from the porch but I couldn't
make it out. I guessed she'd told the kids to come
inside, and they weren't moving fast enough. She
stormed off the porch, yankin' Paris up by her
arm, smackin' her butt, an' then smackin' Trey in
the back of the head as he walked past her. Nothing could have prepared me for seein' my child
being handled so harshly by another woman an'
not bein' able to do nothin' about it. It was time
for this shit to start. I pulled a piece of paper out
of the glove compartment and grabbed a pen. It
jus' so happened to be red, which was perfect,
because my ass was out for blood.

CHAPTER 26

RIGHT WHERE WE LEFT OFF...

Havin' Lania on the inside was a huge plus. I figured Michelle would go to some extremes once she got scared, but this whole security company shit was a bit hard to get around. They weren't hard to spot, though; you don't miss big-ass white dudes sittin' in cars twenty-four hours a day outside someone's house. One random day I'd decided to swim my ass back around the house just so I could get a look at what we were workin' with from the other side. Angelo took us out on one of his boats, and instead of sailing by the house and looking all suspicious, we dropped the anchor a few miles away and I swam. I'd tied my hair up and put on a wetsuit. It took me damn near an hour to get directly behind they house. Michelle was out there in the pool. I could see a third-level window back there, one that we couldn't see from the front. It looked like someone could climb up to it pretty easily. I was so excited about that window I sputtered and swallowed a mouthful of nasty-ass salt water, when I looked back down at the pool and saw Michelle looking right back at me. It had to be next to impossible for her to see me, but I dove and swam my ass away as many yards underwater as I could. I didn't come up until my lungs felt like they was about to explode.

When Keyshawn told me it was Michelle who'd crashed and almost died in the wreck and not Larissa I was in complete shock. There was no way that flashy piece of shit convertible was Michelle's car; she wasn't into shit like that. It had my cousin's name written all over it. Angelo found Candi, through one of his boys; she was loyal, young, and a straight-up little tomboy grease monkey. I told her a hundred times to make sure there weren't no car seats or no toys or shit like that in the car she fucked up. We ain't count on the babysitter seeing her when she was trying to leave. But Angelo was in good with everyone in Miami, it wouldn't take but so many phone calls and so much hand washin' or passin' money to get her cleared.

The whole car routine was really just to scare they asses. I was hoping Larissa would get banged up and then I could get her while she was in

the hospital on some real dramatic-type angel of death shit. Unplug her life support, put
somethin' in her IV, I didn't know. According
to Angelo, the bitch was doing side jobs with
Lania and her girls. I couldn't help smirking at
that shit. The thought of Larissa hoin' herself out
was a mess, enough to make me damn near piss
myself. Now that we knew she was gettin' close
to Lania it would be nothing to get her off by
herself and handle business.

I stood over her now with the barrel pointed
at her head.

"You look a li'l surprised, cuzzo, but it's nice
seein' you too. Get your ass up." I didn't know
what kinda shit Lania had them trippin' off of.
She and all them model bitches stayed high off
something. Larissa stood up, looking at me like
she couldn't tell if I was a hallucination or a some
kind of monster back from the dead.

"You dead, Honey. Either this some kinda
voodoo-zombie shit or I'm havin' the craziest
fuckin'. . . Lania, can . . . can you see this bitch
too?"

I almost laughed at her dumb ass. I don't
know why we wasn't filming that shit. Keepin'
the gun on my target I turned my head in Lania's
direction. "Lania? You good? Can you drive
yourself home or I need to get someone to take

you?" She was still sittin' in the sand lookin' like her world had ended or her heart was broken, I could never tell wit' her overly dramatic ass. Angelo told me all 'bout the little fucked-up love affair she was havin' with her stepbrother and shit. She was the main reason why he was so fuckin' timid and on the fence when it came to gettin' Michelle where we needed her. Some kind of brother-sister power struggle they all seemed to stay goin' through.

"I'm good. You're going to finish this now are you not?" She weaved where she stood, looking at me expectantly as if she didn't already know my answer.

"I am. This shit ends today."

Lania staggered to her feet and walked back in the direction I'd seen them approach from earlier.

"Honey, please, I'm sorry. We ain't mean to do shit to you. You just got caught up in—"

"Y'all ain't mean to get me locked up? What the fuck you think was gonna happen when you called and reported that car Rah gave me?" I stared at her, half expecting a real logical heartfelt answer, knowing her ass ain't have one.

"Honey, it was Rasheed we wanted to fuck up, ma. Not you. You don't wanna do this shit."

***

"The fuck you gonna tell me what I do an' don't wanna do? You don't even know *what* I'm gonna do."

"Anything you want you got it, just say the word. If I can't make it happen I'll find someone who can."

I couldn't hide the sneer that spread across my face. *Amazing how people will promise you shit they ain't got and don't even know if they can get when they got a gun pointed at their head.*

"There's nothing you can give me that my new man, Angelo, hasn't."

Even though her ass was high she knew what that name meant comin' out of my mouth. "How the fuck you get connected like that?" She whispered it, more like a thought out loud than a question directed at me.

"I want my daughter and I don't need *you* to get her back. All the times I sat and watched you put yo' hands on my child, like you was disciplining a damn dog. The way you talked to her."

Shock was written on her face. She didn't know I knew about the abuse, the welts, the bruises. The way she talked to the kids when Michelle wasn't around. From what I remembered Larissa couldn't stand kids, never really could. She just played the mommy role around Michelle's ass and that was it. Nothing could have prepared me for the anger that seared through me in a heated flash. The nozzle flared on the silencer, and I watched the shock in her eyes change to fear and then pain as she fell down onto the sand, holdin' her side.

"I ain' mean nothin' by it. How my momma and grandma raised me, even how Grandma did you. Remember? I ain't know no different."

She stared up at me until the pain faded from her eyes, until they were no longer the bright green I always remembered. Blood ran down the sand toward the ocean and I watched the trail for a second, wondering if I was gonna be just as bad with Paris because of how I was raised. I vaguely remembered being ordered to pull switches from rose bushes with the thorns still on 'em. Gettin' whoopin's across my bare legs because I'd fallen asleep in church or back talked. Extension cords, yardsticks, and flip-flops were regular weapons of ass destruction because we was always gettin' into something and doing shit we usually had no damn business doing.

"Good job; you are making me more and more proud each day. Pretty soon you'll be cold and calculated enough to be your own *capo*." Angelo had been watching me from the sidelines as usual, just in case I'd gotten cold feet again. He ain't have to worry about that shit happening, not when my daughter was involved.

"As much as I like it when you talk that talk, I have no idea what that means, baby." He always mixed that Italian shit in when he spoke and sometimes I could pick it up, but I'd never heard him use that word before.

"*Capo* means boss. You lookin' like a beautiful angel of death right now."

Boss. I liked the way that sounded comin' from his lips. I still had one more mu'fucka on my list to show exactly who's boss.

CHAPTER 27

SAVE THE BEST FOR LAST

After takin' care of Larissa's ass we had to chill for a minute so Angelo could cover up the sloppy work Lania did on Curtis. She was gonna get herself fucked up in the game if she ain't stop takin' all that shit an' then runnin' around makin' stupid decisions. Keyshawn was supposed to be keeping his eye on Michelle but something told me by the way he rarely checked in with Angelo, and how Lania seemed to stay upset with him, he was fallin' off. One of us needed to make a move before that nigga's puppy-lovin' ass slipped up and decided to either tell Michelle wassup or get her out the area.

It was one of those random days in August when Angelo hit me, letting me know they'd found the bodies in Emporia. That meant Michelle's little security team would probably be giving her the news that Rah was dead. Which meant it was time for me to make my move, end this shit for good, and get my child. All I could think about was holding and kissing her little chubby face. I walked up to the side of the house, pissed that it just so happened to be raining buckets from the damn sky. I was soaked, but I wasn't gonna let a little rain keep me from doing this shit. Lightning split the sky open as I thought this through one last time.

The back door was unlocked, just as planned. I was glad Keyshawn didn't back out on his word. Angelo was already on the verge of havin' that nigga killed just for GP. I let myself in as quietly as possible, the thunder coverin' up any little noises I might have accidentally made. I'd only been standing there for a few seconds when she came floatin' up into the kitchen, tall and regal. I'd always envied her. She was wearin' a man's red and blue checkered pajama shirt without the bottoms and her hair was tied up in a little scarf.

I looked at this other woman, who had captured the heart of my man and then thrown it away like it wasn't more than an empty soda can. Watching Michelle was like watching Snow White fuck around in the forest with all those damn animals. She floated over and looked at this, then floated over to look at her phone, before fluttering to pick up something else. It was like the bitch moved around in a dream bubble. I'd had enough of watching her flutter around the kitchen and stepped forward out of the shadows and into her line of vision.

"You look so shocked to see me. I was maybe hoping for—happiness."

She just stood there as her phone broke, glass scattering into a million pieces all over the floor. I could see her ass debating: run or fight; scream for Keyshawn or grab a kitchen knife. I shifted the gun from my right hand to my left, reminding her it was in my hand just in case she'd forgotten.

"You don't know how to speak to your house guests—offer 'em a glass of water or a dry towel, Michelle?"

"Legally she's my daughter. I've done everything for her—all the things you never could have done, even loving her like she was my own child. I've been doing it all, Honey."

What she was saying shocked me, and especially the way she said it, nothing like Larissa's dumb-ass begging and bartering. Michelle actually cared about Paris, that much was obvious.

"I'm tired of y'all bitches tryin'a tell me what the fuck I can and couldn't or will and won't do. You don't know *what* I can do now, Michelle."

"Honey, all I'm tryin' to say is that I took care of your daughter the best I knew how. I've raised Lataya right along wit' Trey like she was my own, at no point did I do for one and not do for the other."

"Who the fuck is Lataya? My daughter's name is Paris. Here yo' ass done renamed my child an' everything, what gave you the got-damn right, Michelle? And where were you when Larissa was out there talkin' to her like she wasn't nothin' but a damn dog? Where was you when she was puttin' her hands on my daughter, Michelle?"

She was starin' at me, tryin' to put the meaning to my words. "She'd never . . . Larissa wouldn't do anything like that."

"It's a shame you got cameras all up in here and still don't even know what's going on in your own damn house." I waved the gun, directing her to carry her ass through the door toward the car waiting outside.

"Wait, what about Trey? What's gonna happen to my child with me gone?"

Honestly I didn't feel like she deserved any kind of an answer; my ass didn't get one when they took my child away from me. "Rasheed's momma back in Virginia gonna keep him. Y'all took a lot from a whole lot of people on some straight-up selfish bullshit. His momma been depressed, not eatin', and everybody been worried about her. Having Trey and a little extra money might actually pull her out of the slump she in. Help balance shit back out."

"Can I tell him good-bye?" She had tears all up in her eyes and I almost felt sorry for her. Almost.

"You already know the answer to that. It's no. Now get ya ass outside. You ain' 'bout to get us off schedule."

CHAPTER 28

DON'T BE SO DAMN
SMART ALL THE TIME

I let Honey lead me out of the house, rain soaking through my nightshirt and plastering my hair down to my face and forehead. She forced me into the back of a silver Audi. Looking through the rain-streaked rear window I stared at the house. It would probably be the last time I ever saw it and I tried to remember every detail. Before pulling off she leaned over the seat and roughly handcuffed my hands together in front of me. In a sense I guessed I'd earned this shit. Larissa and I had played God, deciding who deserved to be met with what punishment; we altered peoples' lives and now everything was coming back on our asses full circle.

As the car started to pull forward I couldn't resist questioning Honey. I had no idea how she'd gotten out or how she'd found us. "So I'm

guessing it was you who murdered Rasheed?"
I knew her ass heard me. She was squinting
through the windshield, trying to navigate us
to wherever through the pouring rain, but the
car was dead silent aside from the sound of the
rain bouncing off of the roof. The wipers moved
back and forth, silently speeding up and slowing
down with the speed of the raindrops.

"No. I was actually gonna let his ass live.
Angelo made the decision before I could stop
him." There was sadness in her voice and regret
maybe. There were so many questions I wanted
to ask her, but I had to be careful. Honey was
hard to read and I didn't understand how Angelo
was tied into all of this. It wouldn't be long before
Keyshawn would wake up and notice I wasn't in
the house and call the police. She wouldn't be
able to get but so far if I could stall her.

I sighed, trying to sound empathetic. "Once
again we are at the mercy of our men; they make
all the decisions and our lives are either reactions or reflections of their choices." I waited.
If Angelo controlled whether Rah died, maybe I
could make Honey realize the situation she was
in now was no different than the one she was in
before, with a man controlling her, maybe even
her money, her home.

"I ain't at the mercy of shit. No-damn-body is makin' these choices. I decided to get Rah out of prison. You'd think the nigga woulda said thanks or showed me some kinda gratitude. But no, he ain't even bother showin' me the respect of takin' his dick outta the bitch he was fuckin' when I walked in to meet him—in the house I decorated for him to come home to." A flash of lightning lit up the sky, illuminating her face. I could see tears silently trickling down her round cheeks and I lowered my head. At least we were getting somewhere. I was getting to her. I just needed to keep her talking.

"Honey, I hate to say it but Rasheed lived and was always led by his dick, not his brain. For as smart as he was all that shit would go out the window once the blood left his head and that piece of meat between his legs stiffened up. It ain't neva' matter how good I was to him or how faithful or how beautiful he thought I was. It took years of dealing with him for me to learn that. He almost died, almost lost everything including me, and havin' his son wasn't even enough to make him change, Honey." Glancing out the window I tried to get my bearings, figure out where we were just in case an opportunity presented itself where I could bail out of the car.

"*You* wasted years because of him. Not me. I died and I came back just for my daughter. The time I spent, the pain I know, the shit I've seen was because of you and Larissa and no one else. Y'all wrapped everyone else up in y'alls plan to put him away. And what gave y'all the right to decide I deserved to be put away too? 'Cause we was fuckin'? 'Cause me and Rah was in love and you was the spiteful ass baby momma about to be cast aside?"

My mind was on overdrive trying to come up with something to diffuse the anger I could hear quickly seeping into her voice. The last thing I wanted to do was turn this into a power struggle between who deserved what punishment. We were wrong on many levels and I lived with our decision every day, but now wasn't the time to debate about that shit. Not with me handcuffed on a road to who knew where and Honey pissed the fuck off with a loaded gun.

"I didn't have anything to do with that, sweetheart. That was all Larissa. When I knew what she'd done the police already had you."

"Well you can talk that shit over with her when you see her. As far as y'all are concerned I'm done; this shit gonna end tonight and then I'm gonna get my daughter."

I was scared to even imagine Ris alive some-where being held all this time when I'd just assumed she'd left us. *I could have had people out lookin' for her if I hadn't just assumed the worst. Maybe we could have found her.* My stomach was in knots at the thought of seeing her, what I'd say, how much time we would have, how Honey was gonna end this. I could see the signs for the pier in the distance and I knew this was pretty much it for me. I didn't know what's worse: knowing you're going to die or knowing that death was coming and not knowing *how* you're going to die.

I lowered my head and I started to pray. It was the only thing I could think to do. That's when I'd noticed it. The color made it stand out in bright contrast against the dark red and blue of my pajama top. I'd forgotten about the little pink card Keyshawn had given me, and tears filled my eyes as I slid it out of my pocket as quietly as possible, opening the little flap on the back, and pulling out the card.

They told me my key to the city would unlock any lock, but you're the only one with the key to my heart—don't ever luse it. Keyshawn

I smiled at the typo; the poor thing was definitely an athlete and not a scholar. His words would have given me so much hope for a future and happiness and maybe even love. If only I'd have opened it when we were together, I could have said how I really felt. Instead I pressed the card to my lips, sending him a silent kiss. I was sliding the card back inside when I noticed something else. There was also a thin gold chain, attached to it a small gold skeleton key. I was scared to slide it over my neck; she might see it and take it from me. If I died I at least wanted to have it in my hand as close to me as possible.

"We almost there." She sounded cold and detached.

Glancing up I could see us pulling up to a loading dock of some sort. There were large storage containers all over the place, like the one Jim said they'd found Rasheed's body in. Panicking I tried to slide the gold chain over my wrist so I wouldn't drop it, but my handcuffs were in the way. On a desperate whim, a spur-of-the-moment thought, I glanced at the key and back at the lock on the cuffs. *Skeleton keys are supposed to be able to unlock any lock.* I looked up at Honey to see if she was paying me any attention. Nervously, hands shaking from the cold rain and adrenaline, I jammed the little key into the lock and twisted. I held my breath, squeezing my eyes closed tightly, thinking the cuffs would just clink, unhinge, and fall off at any second, and I could try to either roll out of the car or jump Honey when she wasn't expecting it. When nothing happened I damn near broke down.

"You ready to be reunited with your wife? Lania said y'all weren't gettin' along an' shit so I guess you can thank me for makin' the "til death do you part' part of your marriage happen so quickly."

I could feel myself giving up, or accepting my fate, to put it in better words. Lania, Angelo . . . So far this sounded like a bad joke and everyone in my life was in on it except me. Rasheed, and possibly Larissa, were both dead—it was starting to look like a bad dream come true, and I just didn't understand or know Keyshawn's place or his role in any of it.

The car came to a stop. Maybe it was the way the loading docks smelled or because I thought I was about to die; I was feeling like a complete idiot. The one time I decided to finally let someone else into my life they managed to shred it completely apart. My stomach was getting queasy, and I watched as Honey picked up the gun from the passenger seat and started to get out of the car. For some reason, even though it was pretty much over for me, a sense of desperation set in. I looked around, desperate for anything to help me out. I even tried the key again, twisting it frantically back and forth in both directions. I must've been turning the key in the wrong direction the first time. The lock on the cuffs clicked and they silently slid off. *Fuck. That's all the fuck I had to do?* I looked down, amazed that the key had worked. This was my chance, my last chance, probably the only opportunity I'd have at saving myself.

Honey was shielding herself from the rain as she got out to open the back door, ready to pull me out. I took that as my opportunity, and with the cuffs around my knuckles I pushed the door hard back at her, catching her off guard. Her feet slid in the mud and she fell backward.

The fact that I wasn't wearing any shoes worked to my advantage. I hopped out and dug my toes into the moist ground, giving myself better leverage as I lunged and climbed on top of her. Before she could raise her gun or get herself up, I hit her across the jaw. The inside of the cuffs cut into my skin and I ignored the pain shooting through my fist. I hit her three, four, five times, punching her repeatedly until the muscles in my arm started to shake and her body had gone limp, blood streaming from her nose and the corner of her mouth.

Searching her pockets I grabbed her cell, the pistol from her hand, and the keys to the car. I climbed into the driver's seat, intent on heading back to the house to get Trey and Taya and gettin' us the fuck out of town. *Damn.* Jim's cell number was programmed in my iPhone and of course I didn't have it memorized. If I could just get to the house, something in the contract had his number on it. He'd know a safe place for me to take the kids. It took me a few minutes to get used to the car's controls. I was flying in the direction of my house, hydroplaning on turns and curves, intent on getting myself there before Honey had another chance to finish me off.

Her phone started ringing from the seat beside me and my heart almost stopped beating in my chest when I saw Keyshawn's name. *Why is he calling Honey's phone? Should I answer it and let him know I'm okay? He gave me the key to my cuffs—obviously he wanted to help me. If I don't answer, what will he think had happened to me? What does he have planned for my children?* I couldn't risk it.

"Why are you calling this phone, Key?"

"Oh my God. No, Michelle! You didn't. What are you doing right now?" He sounded shocked and angry at hearing my voice, not the excitement I'd have expected hearing at me just barely escaping death.

"What am I doing? What the fuck are you doing, Keyshawn?"

"It's a lot to explain, baby. I've been helpin' keep you alive as much as possible without compromisin' myself. If you on Honey's phone I'm guessin' you in Honey's car?"

"Yeah. I used the key you gave me. In the envelope."

"*Fuck!*" Keyshawn rarely cursed and that one word scared the life out of me. *What did I "save" myself into?*

"Michelle, you gotta get out of that car, right now. Wipe your prints off the steering wheel and run from it. I'm packin' up some of your and the kids' things. I'm on my way to pick you up. I'll have the kids with me."

"Why? What's wrong, Key? You have to tell me." I pulled over to the side of the road and put the car into park. Using the bottom of my shirt I wiped the steering wheel. It was too late. I could see the red and blue lights comin' at me through the wind and rain. This bitch set me up.

"I didn't give you the key to use, Michelle; that's why when you set it down I ain't say nothin'. When I woke up and you were gone and it was gone . . ." His voice was drowned out by the sound of the sirens and the squad cars that surrounded me. That's when I realized he didn't spell "lose" wrong. He was trying to tell me not to use it. "Don't ever *luse* it." If I would've been thinking clearly maybe I would've picked up on that shit.

"Ma'am, get out of the car with your hands up." Slamming my hands up against the steering wheel I couldn't believe how stupid I'd been. If I'd have just run on foot I could have gotten away. That bitch anticipated my every fuckin' move just like I'd done with Rasheed, and like a mouse in a maze I'd blindly walked right into this brick wall, thinking it was a way out.

CHAPTER 29

IF YOU FAIL TO PLAN,
YOU PLAN TO FAIL

For half of a heartbeat I actually debated pushing the gas pedal to the floor and gunnin' it up out of there. I had no idea where I'd go or how far I'd get, but the image of every officer in the county opening fire and killing me before I could get more than a hundred yards away squelched the idea. I could only imagine the types of drugs Angelo and Honey would have stashed up in that damn car just to set my ass up—probably enough to put me away for life. Now I had an unregistered pistol with an illegal silencer on it in the passenger seat of a stolen car full of drugs, and no ID, with absolutely no logical explanation for any of it except that a woman who was supposed to have died in prison kidnapped me from my home at gunpoint and this was where I'd ended up. Yeah, I could see the cops believing that shit.

"Get on the ground now," someone yelled at me from somewhere in the rain. There were at least six different sets of high beams pointed in my direction, blinding me. I did as told. The cold, wet pavement scraped against my bare legs, rain ran into my eyes, for the second time in one night I was cuffed. A female officer grabbed my hands and forced them behind my back, almost pulling my arm out of the socket. I was pulled roughly to my feet and dragged over to stand beside one of the squad cars. Who knew what the hell Honey or whoever said when they called this bullshit in or how many drugs they told them I was carrying? I had a flashback of Rasheed being hauled out of his car and all I could think was that karma was definitely a complete and absolute fucking bitch.

One of the cops went through the glove compartment and came over to me with several pieces of paper in his hand. "Is there any reason why you're driving Mr. Curtis Daniels's vehicle, ma'am?"

I just stared at the officer blankly. No, I didn't have a damn reason. I was shocked—*why the fuck did Honey have Curtis's car?*

"Holy fuck, Miller. Come look at this shit!"

I was half pushed and half dragged toward the trunk of the car, where the other two officers were gathered. When my eyes finally landed on what they had back there that had them so in awe I almost fainted. They'd unzipped a large bag and the only thing I could make out was Curtis's body before gettin' sick. The smell of decaying flesh and the way he looked after being locked up in there decomposing in the heat for three or four weeks was unbearable. After that I was surrounded by pitch black. The haunting image of Larissa's face stuffed in the trunk underneath Curtis, the overwhelming smell of bodies, making everyone cover their mouths, fighting the urge to gag, her eyes dull and lifeless looking back at me, it was all more than I could handle at one time.

The smell of unwashed bodies and urine woke me up. I thought I was having a bad dream, that Honey and the car . . . everything was a bad dream. I opened my eyes. I was lying on a hard bunk, there was a toilet sticking out of the wall in front of me, and the realization set in that I was in a holding cell.

"Hello? Officer?" I looked out through the thin metal bars; there was a desk over in the corner but no one was there. Larissa's face . . . I couldn't get the image out of my head and I fought the urge to curl up in a ball and just cry. My clothes, well what little I'd had on, were taken from me and I was left in all-white cotton pants and a matching shirt.

"Look who's finally awake. Fuckin' Sleepin' Beauty over here." One of the officers walked in, eatin' pork rinds out of a bag, wiping the crumbs on his uniform. He was a pudgy pink-faced white man with a double chin that jiggled when he spoke.

"My name is Michelle Laurel, it used to be Michelle Roberts. I would like my one phone call please."

"Yeah, yeah, and motherfuckers in hell want ice water. You'll get your phone call when we ready to give you one."

"Stop fuckin' with her, Simmons, let her have her call." A female cop walked up, slappin' him playfully on his back. She was younger, probably about my age, brown skin, with friendly eyes.

"Can you look up a number for Jim Bartell please?"

Jim was the only person I could trust right now. She sat down at the desk for a moment, looking at her computer, before coming over to let me out, handing me the number on a Post-it note. She led me over to another room that looked like a cell, except it was surrounded with Plexiglas and had a phone in a center.

"I'm Officer James. Towanna James. Just let me know when you're done." She smiled at me and I liked her immediately.

I dialed Jim's number and almost cried when he answered. I was rambling and talking so fast, trying to tell him everything that'd happened literally overnight since he'd left that voice mail, it was a wonder he could keep up with me, but he did.

"This ain't as bad as you think, sweetheart. I'm sorry you're in there right now but be patient. Me and one of my boys will personally go by your place and pull all the security footage. I know you didn't commit them murders, sweet pea. I also record all of our conversations, so we have documented instances of you fearing for you and your late wife's lives. Our first suspect right now is gonna be that Honey woman, since she was the last person we saw Larissa alive with. It's a start and we'll go from there."

I hung up the phone, content that Jim would somehow work things out for me. I was confident that as long as the kids were with Keyshawn they were fine. Hopefully he'd grabbed enough Pull-Ups for Lataya to last a few days, and wherever he'd taken them, I just prayed it was someplace Honey and her people didn't know and couldn't find out about.

CHAPTER 30

AN UNMARKED MARKSWOMAN

"What the fuck, Honey?" Angelo was pacing back and forth lookin' like he was 'bout to burst a damn blood vessel. "Get the bitch, let her take the car. That was it. It was simple, so fuckin' simple."

"It was a mistake, she knocked me unconscious. I didn't know she'd take my gun."

Yes, we'd gone over the plan a million fuckin' times and had a million different scenarios. But not one included her whoopin' my ass with her handcuffs and takin' my damn pistol. We'd definitely underestimated little Miss "I'll Think You Into Some Shit Before I Beat You Into It," aka Michelle. I was still recovering from a broken nose, an' that bitch fractured the bone just beneath my fuckin' eye. I looked like I could be the poster child for spousal abuse.

"Yeah, but what the fuck have I always told you's? Neva', neva', leave your weapon or lay it down, right? I knew I shoulda went with you, sent someone with you."

I ain't answer. There was no point; he wasn't looking for no answer, he was just talkin' to hear himself talk right now and that was that.

"You my woman an' it's my job to protect you. I gotta figure out how to get us outta this city. We gonna have to lay low until this shit blow over."

"Ount need protectin', baby. I made a honest mistake an' I'ma fix this shit." We were sittin' up in one of Angelo's penthouses that was considered off the radar, one of his getaway spots for times like this when shit got too hot to be out on the streets. I was jus' sittin' my ass in one of the black ostrich recliners, starin' out through the huge floor-to-ceiling window in the sitting room at all the city lights that lit up Miami at night. From up here it looked like we owned this city, and somewhere down there, in spite of everything I'd planned, Michelle was still runnin' around a free woman.

"*Bella,* sweetie—you's got so much to learn. Up until that pistol *you* were the perfect weapon. A ghost, a ninja assassin, an unknown assailant who could strike anyone anywhere and vanish with no past and no file. You were untraceable.

But now, they know you're out there, and they know you're gonna come back."

He had a point. I wanted to get Paris back and Michelle knew I would die before I let her keep my child. If Lania coulda controlled her damn nigga we would not have had half of this problem. I went to Michelle's house afterward but Keyshawn's ass was gone. He'd taken Trey and Paris to who knew where and hadn't been seen since. I got up and walked into the bathroom.

"We not done talkin'; where you goin'?"

"I'll be right back, Angelo."

Walkin' into the penthouse bathroom was like goin' into a damn mini spa. Heated marble floors, crystal knobs on all the Koehler faucets, I was gettin' used to havin' the best of everything. I turned the water on, watchin' it swirl around the crystal bowl basin. I looked at myself in the mirror. *When did I become this woman, this rich man's canary to be kept in a cage—this bloodthirsty killer?* It was like I was living a double life.

The real me was hidin' away somewhere deep down inside, waitin' until the all clear was announced so she could come back out. *I should have done this shit a long time ago.* Reachin' into the medicine cabinet I grabbed a razor blade from Angelo's shaving kit and some alcohol to sterilize the blade. Trenisha's past was what got me caught up and I needed to erase that bitch once and for all.

"Angel face, you all right in there or what?" Angelo was knockin' on the door but at this point I couldn't open it. The shit hurt worse than I thought it would and shock and too much fuckin' pain was going through my arms for me to even move from where I was sittin' on the side of the tub to let him in.

"Honey? You good? What's goin' on in there?" He kicked the door open; wood splintered around the lock, and I looked up at him, teary eyed, tryin' not so fuckin' hard not to let him see me cry.

"I erased her, Angelo. There ain't no more Trenisha. There ain't no more Honey. That shit won't ever happen again."

"Fuck, woman, what the fuck did you do?"

Blood was all over me, it was all over the bathroom floor. He knelt in front of me and held up my bloody hands. I'd taken the razor blades and sliced the fingerprints clean off of my fingers one by one, cutting deep enough to where there were now only bloody pads where my skin used to be.

"No more mistakes, Angelo. I promise."

"Oh my God. Let me see. What made you do this shit?" He snatched his shirt off and grabbed my hands and started wrapping them up in it, trying to stop the blood.

I winced because it stung, but didn't pull my hands back.

"We gonna get my daughter. I don't care where I have to go or what else I have to do. All I want is my daughter."

"Yeah, Honey, we gonna get our princess I promise. On my life, I swear we'll get her back." He kissed my forehead, smoothing my hair back, and I drifted into sleep or passed out, I wasn't sure which. But my last thoughts were of a beautiful little baby girl with golden skin and chubby cheeks. Smiling at me though long, curly-ass lashes, it was a smile I'd seen a million times and I felt as though I hadn't seen that smile in a million years—it was my smile.

CHAPTER 31

WHEN IT ALL COMES DOWN

All the shit Honey and Angelo put me through to get me locked up and not one ounce of it could stick. Jim went to the DEA and all the charges against me were dropped within a week. The pistol that was used to murder Larissa was also the same gun used to kill Rasheed. There was no way I could have been in Virginia at the time he was murdered and when they ran the gun through forensics they found a second set of prints along with mine that belonged to Trenisha, also known as Honey. They did an autopsy on Curtis's body and his estimated time of death placed me at Chuck E. Cheese with the kids. They even pulled the photos from the hard drive in the booth from that day to help verify I couldn't have been the person to stab him and then cut off his arm.

It was such a relief to be treated like a normal member of society again. They'd reopened

Honey's case to determine how someone declared dead could be walking around committing murders. Honey was on all the bulletins and wanted ads; they had an older picture from her first prison arrest but it was a close enough resemblance for someone to identify her, and it did not surprise me at all that she'd suddenly vanished off the face of the earth along with Angelo and Lania.

With Honey and Angelo in hiding I was anxious to find Keyshawn and the kids. I'd asked Jim to pick me up a new phone since I'd dropped mine, and even though he was watching the house, I was still too scared to go back to that place. I dialed Keyshawn's number.

"Michelle?" he answered, and I could hear the kids screaming for me in the background.

I breathed a sigh of relief. "Yeah, it's me. They let me go. Honey fucked up and had her prints on the gun. I guess she wasn't expecting me to grab it, but combined with the footage from my home surveillance and Jim's security info to back me up they didn't have anything to tie me to the murders. I had an alibi and they had no material evidence. We even got records of Larissa's calls to Lania the day she disappeared."

I could hear the stress in his voice. I could only think what he was going through tryin' to keep up with two kids. "I'm so sorry. I tried to keep you and the kids safe for as long as I could, Michelle. Angelo's my half brother by marriage so goin' against him would have caused major shit with the family. I had to do whatever I could to keep me safe and pray you would still make it out of there okay. I had no idea why they wanted to get to you; all I knew is Lania and Angelo's new woman had it out for you since the day we met to look at that property, and, as part of the family, I either went with them or I was automatically against them."

I had to give Honey credit, she'd set this shit up damn near flawlessly. If I hadn't had the foresight to grab her gun after I'd knocked her unconscious there wouldn't be any reasonable doubt to stop them from pressing full double homicide charges against me.

"I wanna see my babies, Key. I miss you guys so much. Where are you?"

"Meet me at the spot where we first met. You already know Trey and Taya been missin' you something terrible. I have been too."

I was still paranoid as hell and I called Jim to make sure I wasn't being followed before I left the hotel I was staying in. I sent someone ahead to scope out the only place I could think of that Keyshawn could have meant. After getting the

all clear from Jim I rented a car and went to
see my babies, all of them. As I pulled into the
circular driveway I couldn't help but notice the
place was just as I remembered it; not a hedge,
leaf, or stone was out of place. So much of our
heartache started all because of this property,
and I couldn't help seeing the irony in the fact
that here I was once again, right back at square
one.

"Momeeeeeeee."

Tears streamed down my cheeks as I knelt
down to hug Trey. There was a point when I
thought I'd never see my son again; looking into
his bright eyes and kissing his smiling face filled
me with so much joy.

"I'm so glad you made it out of all this okay."
Keyshawn walked out of the back door holding
Lataya in his arms. They both had the biggest
grins on their faces.

Standing, I couldn't hide anything as I walked
over to kiss them both. I felt at peace and there
was so much love in my heart for Keyshawn.
No matter what doubts I'd ever had about him
or where our relationship would go, he'd saved
my children for me and I'd always owe him my
undying gratitude for that.

"So what do we do now?" I looked at him
still holding Lataya and tried to figure out how

we could still make it out of this and salvage something from our relationship.

"We leave Florida. Angelo and Honey gonna be lyin' low for a minute. Lania's pretty much wanted right now for her connection to Larissa goin' missing. I say we see what Cali is like, or Maryland."

I understood what he meant but I couldn't see me running from yet another situation. "I say, we like Florida, and we stay right here. You keep playin' ball for the Legends and I'll keep doing what I do. When they come for us, *if* they come for us, we'll be ready."

"So you wanna stay right here? Right in the middle of Angelo's stompin' ground?"

"Keyshawn, what good is leaving gonna do if they'll follow us wherever we go? If Angelo gonna send men out to wherever we are? We'll be runnin' our entire lives."

He handed me Lataya and was looking at me in disbelief, like he couldn't imagine me wanting to stay in Florida. "I can't do that shit, Michelle. I was supposed to take Honey her daughter that night and put Trey back on a plane to Virginia. They both probably want me dead. If not now then they will as soon as they've realized that I ain't do what I was s'posed to do."

"So what are you telling me, Key?" Looking him in his eye I dared him to tell me he was gonna leave me, standing right there with my son and my daughter like we weren't shit after all we'd been through together. I couldn't see it happening. But he didn't need to tell me anything. Kissing me on my forehead, he turned and walked toward his car.

I couldn't believe this nigga was walkin' out on us like this, but I expected it. These weren't his kids, I wasn't his wife, and he had his own problems to deal with. Grabbing Trey's hand I walked into this new, cold, empty house. It was time for us to start over. No drama, no bullshit, no ghosts, and no craziness. I didn't need anyone else to help me with my kids. I could and I would do this all on my own.

CHAPTER 32

MIGHT AS WELL GO OUT WITH A BANG

"Where's Uncle Key goin', Mommy?" Trey asked me quietly.

I fought the tears and the heartache; I needed to be stronger than what I thought possible. "He's going home, baby."

I'd barely closed the back door when I was knocked off my feet. All the air whooshed out of my body in one painful breath. Trey yelled and Lataya wailed.

"Trey, go upstairs! Take your sister upstairs!" I rolled onto my side, clutching my stomach as he scampered away, half dragging his crying sister behind him.

"How did I know this is where he'd meet you? Of all the places, he'd have you come here."

Lania was standing above me, her eyes wild with fury and hate. She glared down at me, shotgun in hand—muzzle to the ground. She was leaning on it like a crutch, slightly swaying back and forth.

"All he did was bring me my kids, Yylannia. There's nothing to us. You want him, you got him."

She sneered down at me. "You can't give me what's already mine, bitch. He's so damn caught up with your ass he's willing to die. I'm not worried about you. I just need the little girl so Angelo will let me and Key live in peace."

The meaning behind her words was all too clear. I slowly struggled to sit. No one was going to touch my daughter and the thought alone ignited a fire in my soul.

"You're going to have to kill me to get her. Is all of this really worth it? Do you think it's going to be that easy?" I glanced around, looking for something, anything to use in defense.

"Oh, Chelly. Poor Chelly. Misguided, thinks-she-owns-the-world little Chelly. I can do whatever the fuck I want, bitch! Angelo's my brother, sweetheart. We own Miami." She laughed, and it was the most deranged-sounding witch's cackle I'd ever heard in my life.

I watched helplessly as she raised the barrel of the shotgun. My mind was going berserk. I tried calculating how much time I'd have to stand and lunge or roll to the side. *Can I even make it to her before she pulls the trigger?* I didn't have a choice; my babies were not going to see me laid out in this floor.

"Stand the fuck up and take this shit like a woman. I'd hate to have to tell everyone I killed a cowering bitch."

Slowly I dragged myself upright. I didn't plan it and I sure as hell didn't fully think it through. I lunged at Lania's feet. The sound of the shotgun momentarily deafened me and she screamed as the bullet smashed through the door behind me. I didn't give her a chance to get any kind of leverage on that shotgun. I hit her in the jaw so hard I was sure my hand was broken.

Nothing prepares you for those split-second moments. They happen faster than lightning and you are all instinct and reaction. Before Lania could react I'd grabbed the gun, stood, and before I could think about consequences or anything else I fired. I hit her center mass—square in the chest. Shotgun still in hand I ran to get Trey and Lataya. They were hunkered together on the bottom of the stairs, crying hysterically.

"It's okay, babies. I promise everything is okay. Let's go get in the car."

I led them around Lania's body, turning their heads into my leg so they wouldn't look. There was a hole the size of tennis ball in the back door and the light from the sun cast a lonely ray through it. I turned the handle and nothing could stop the scream that escaped me. Nothing could have prepared me for what I saw and my heart split in two as tears streamed from my eyes. I dropped the shotgun and knelt down.

Keyshawn was lying outside the door. I already knew he was gone. His eyes stared unblinking toward the sky and blood covered his chest. He was still holding a bouquet of flowers in his left hand. *God, he must have reconsidered what I said and decided to come back.* There was so much bloodshed surrounding me and all of it was because of Rasheed and his hoing-ass ways. I was tempted to dig his body up from wherever it was buried and shoot him again, several times, just for all the pain we were going through.

I didn't know where I got the strength from but I stood. The kids were still beside me; their little scared faces would probably scar me for life. Kissing my fingers I touched Keyshawn's eyes and closed them.

"You two okay?" I asked quietly.

I looked at my babies, and I knew for a fact Honey wouldn't stop until I was dead and Lataya was back with her. I called the police and waited in my rental car for them to arrive. Officer Towanna, the one who helped me, was the first one to get there.

"Michelle, right? You all right?" She approached me with her weapon drawn.

"I'm good. You won't be needin' that gun though, they ain't gonna move."

She radioed for backup and smiled reassuringly. "Well, you sure do seem to keep a lot of drama surrounding your ass."

I smiled at her attempt to ease the tension. After I explained everything that had happened, Towanna offered to personally escort me and the kids to a new hotel while everything was being investigated. She didn't trust anyone else, since Lania and Angelo were known to pay off police officers and at the moment I didn't trust *anyone*.

"Y'all need me, you have my card and my cell phone number." She was standing at the doorway to the hotel room.

"Thank you for everything, Offi . . . Towanna. I just want a hot bath and sleep right now."

I watched as she closed the door and it felt as though a chapter was closing. My heart had been ripped out, replaced, and ripped out again, and I had no idea how to rebuild it this time. Every fiber in my body was screaming for me to just break down. I wanted to scream, cry, crawl into a hole, and never come out. There was now a gaping wound in my heart and nothing aside from my kids would ever be able to fill it again.

Everyone close to me was gone. It was just me and my two little ones, and if Honey wouldn't stop until I was dead . . . well, then it only made sense for me to try to kill her first. She'd made this game strictly life or death, and above all else I was choosing life.

"The end is a surprising, yet satisfying, conclusion to this series . . . another terrific story."
—*Fresh Fiction*

"The characters are intriguing and the romance is sexy and fun while at times heart-wrenching. The action is well-written and thrilling, especially at the end . . . *Dark Moon* is another powerful tale with a strong heroine who is sure to please readers and a hero who is worth fighting for. Handeland has proven with this trilogy that she has a bright future in the paranormal genre."
—*Romance Readers Connection*

"Elise is Handeland's most appealing heroine yet . . . this tense, banter-filled tale provides a few hours of solid entertainment."
—*Publishers Weekly*

"Smart and often amusing dialogue, brisk pacing, plenty of action, and a generous helping of 'spookiness' add just the right tone . . . an engaging and enjoyable paranormal romance."
—*BookLoons*

"A fantastic tale starring two strong likable protagonists . . . action-packed . . . a howling success."
—*Midwest Book Review*

"Handeland writes some of the most fascinating, creepy, and macabre stories I have ever read . . . exciting plot twists . . . new revelations, more emotional themes, and spiritual awakenings are prevalent here."
—*Romance Reader at Heart*

St. Martin's Paperbacks Titles
by Lori Handeland

THE PHOENIX CHRONICLES
Any Given Doomsday
Doomsday Can Wait
Apocalypse Happens
Chaos Bites

THE NIGHTCREATURE NOVELS
Blue Moon
Hunter's Moon
Dark Moon
Crescent Moon
Midnight Moon
Rising Moon
Hidden Moon
Thunder Moon
Marked by the Moon
(coming soon)

ANTHOLOGIES
Stroke of Midnight
No Rest for the Witches

THUNDER MOON

LORI HANDELAND

St. Martin's Paperbacks

This is a work of fiction. All of the characters, organizations, and events portrayed in this novel are either products of the author's imagination or are used fictitiously.

THUNDER MOON

Copyright © 2008 by Lori Handeland.
Excerpt from *Marked by the Moon* copyright @ 2010 by Lori Handeland.

All rights reserved. For information address St. Martin's Press, 175 Fifth Avenue, New York, NY 10010.

ISBN: 978-0-312-53263-5

Printed in the United States of America

St. Martin's Paperbacks edition / January 2008

St. Martin's Paperbacks are published by St. Martin's Press, 175 Fifth Avenue, New York, NY 10010.

10 9 8 7 6 5 4 3 2

ACKNOWLEDGMENTS

Grateful thanks to:

The guys who run a very funny Web site called "4q.cc".
They graciously gave me permission to use some of their Chuck Norris jokes in this book. Check it out at: http://4q.cc

Peggy Hendricks, who was so helpful in providing information about the technicalities of dying. Bet you never thought working in that funeral home would come in so handy—for me.

The usual suspects: My editor, Jen Enderlin, and all the people at St. Martin's who make it such a great place to work—Anne Marie Tallberg, Matthew Shear, Sara Goodman.

THUNDER

MOON

1

A STORM BENEATH the Thunder Moon is both rare and powerful. My grandmother believed that on that night magic happens. She neglected to mention that magic could kill.

Mid-July in northern Georgia was an air conditioner salesman's wet dream. In theory, the creek behind my home should have been balmy. In practice, it wasn't.

Nevertheless, I dropped my robe and waded in; then I lifted my face to the full Thunder Moon and chanted the words my *e-li-si,* my great-grandmother, had taught me.

"I stand beneath the moon and feel the power. I will possess the lightning and drink of the rain. The thunder is your song and mine."

I wasn't sure what the chant was for, but it was the only one I remembered completely, so I said those words every time I came here. The repetition calmed me. The memories of my great-grandmother were some of the few good memories I had.

According to her, a chant spoken in English was

worthless. Only one spoken in Cherokee would work. Unfortunately, she'd died before she could teach me more than a smattering of the language. I'd always meant to learn more, but I'd never found the time.

She'd left me all her books, her notes—what she called her medicine. But I couldn't read any of the papers she'd gathered into a grade school binder, so they accumulated dust in the false bottom of my father's desk.

I'd loved her deeply, and I mourned her every day. I missed her so badly sometimes a great black cloud of depression settled over me that was very hard to shake.

"Someday," I whispered to the night. "Someday I'll know all those secrets."

Lightning flashed, closer than it should be. The moon still shone, though clouds now skated across its surface. Thunder rumbled, a great gray beast, shaking the hills that surrounded me.

The Blue Ridge Mountains had always been home. I could never desert them. The mountains didn't lie, they didn't cheat or steal, and, most important, they never left. The mountains would always be there.

They were as much a part of me as my midnight hair, my light green eyes, and the skin that was so much darker than everyone else's in town. My ancestors had been both Indian and African, with a good portion of Scotch-Irish mixed in.

My toes tingled with cold, so I rose from the water and snatched my white terry-cloth robe from the ground. I slid my arms into it, and the silver glow of the moon went out as if snuffed by a huge heavenly hand. The wind whistled through the towering pines, sounding like an angry spirit set free of bondage.

I stood at the creek and watched the storm come. I

liked storms. They reflected all the turmoil I'd carried within me for so long.

However, this storm was different from those that usually tumbled over my mountains—stronger, quicker, stranger. I should have started running at the first trickle of wind.

Lightning flashed so brightly I closed my eyes, yet the imprint of the sky opening up and the electric sheen spilling out seemed scalded into my brain. The scent of ozone drifted by, and the thunder seemed to crash from below rather than from above.

I opened my eyes just as the lightning flared again far too soon. A horrible, screeching wail followed, and a trail of sparks tumbled from the sky in the distance.

"I got a bad feeling," I murmured, then watched the roiling sky for several minutes until the cell phone in my pocket began to buzz.

I don't know why I'd brought the thing. Half the time I couldn't get a signal out here. The trees were so high, the mountains so near. Often I got back to the house and realized I'd dropped the phone either at the creek or somewhere along the path. Nevertheless, I was too much my father's daughter to ever leave home without it. Dad had been the sheriff in Lake Bluff, Georgia, too.

"McDaniel," I answered, wincing as needles of rain began to fall, the wind picking up and driving them into my face.

"Grace?"

The connection crackled, the voice on the other end breaking up. Lightning flashed again, and I wondered if I should be out here with a cell phone pressed to my head.

Probably not.

I started for the house and—
Baboom!
Thunder shook the earth. The wind whipped my long, wet hair into my eyes. The world went electric silver as lightning took over the sky.

"Grace! You there? Grace!"

I recognized the voice of my deputy, Cal Striker. Cal had spent most of his life in the Marines; then he'd retired after twenty and tried to relax back in the old hometown.

Except Cal wasn't the relaxing type. I could understand why, after tours in the Gulf War, Afghanistan, and most recently Iraq, the pace in Lake Bluff had driven him bonkers. He'd begged me to hire him for the open deputy position. I'd been happy to.

"Right here, Cal." I wasn't sure if he could hear me. Above the wind and the rain and the thunder, *I* could barely hear me. "What's the matter?"

"We've got—" *Crackle. Buzz.* "Over on the—" *Snap.* "—problem."

Hell. *What* did we have on the *where* that was a problem? With Cal it could be anything. From a kitty cat up a tree to a domestic disturbance complete with shotguns, Cal handled every situation with the same calm surety.

Cal was a big fan of Chuck Norris, which had led to no small amount of teasing from the other officers, and someone had taken to leaving Chuck Norris jokes on Cal's desk. I thought most of them were hilarious. My deputy did not.

"You're breaking up, Cal. Say again."

Hurrying in the direction of home, I skidded a bit on the now-slick trail, hoping I wouldn't fall on my ass and wind up covered in mud. I didn't have the time.

I burst into my backyard and cursed. The house was dark. The storm had knocked out the electricity, probably all over Lake Bluff. The phones would be ringing off the hook at the station. I don't know why people thought the sheriff's department could do anything, but whenever when we lost power the switchboard lit up to tell us all about it.

"Grace." Cal's voice was much clearer now that I'd escaped the interference of the towering pines. "Look to the north."

I turned, squinted, frowned at the slightly orange glow blooming against the midnight sky, right about where that weird flash of sparks would have landed.

"I'm on my way," I said, and hurried into the house.

With no electricity and no moon spilling in through the windows, the place seemed foreign. Corners of furniture reached out and smacked my shins. I could stop and light a candle, try to find a flashlight, although it probably wouldn't have any working batteries, but I was possessed by a sense of urgency.

I kept seeing that orange glow in my head, and I didn't like it. Forest fires were extremely dangerous. They could sweep down the side of a mountain and right through a town. They've been known to jump highways and waterways, leaving behind acres of blackened stumps and devastated dreams.

I stumbled up the stairs to my room, found a towel, tossed the damp robe into the tub, then put on the same uniform I'd just taken off. As I shoved my .40-caliber Glock into the holster, I stepped onto the second-floor landing. The window rattled, and I turned in that direction, figuring the wind had shifted.

A great black shadow loomed, and my fingers tightened on the grip of the gun. Wings beat against the glass; a beak tapped. I couldn't catch my breath, and when I did I emitted a choking gasp that frightened me almost as badly as the bird had.

Then the thing was gone, and I was left staring at the rain running down the windowpane. How odd. Birds didn't usually fly during bad weather.

Heading downstairs, I dismissed the strange behavior of the wildlife in my concern for Lake Bluff and its citizens. I hoped the deluge had put out any fire caused by the lightning, but I had to be sure.

I ran through the rain and jumped into my squad car, then headed down the long lane that led to the highway. Once there, I hit the lights and the siren. I wanted everyone who might be stupid enough to be out right now to see and hear me coming.

My headlights reflected off the pavement, revealing sheets of water cascading over the road ahead of me. The trees bent at insane angles. My wipers brushed twigs, leaves, and pine needles off my windshield along with the rain. I glanced in my rearview mirror just as a huge tree limb slammed onto the road behind me.

"Great." I fumbled with the radio. "I have a ten-fifty-three on the highway just north of my place. Tree limb big enough to jackknife a semi."

"Ten-four, Sheriff."

My dispatcher, Jordan Striker, was mature beyond her twenty years and as sharp as the stilettos she insisted on wearing to work. She was Cal's daughter, and while the two of them didn't see eye-to-eye on much, they shared a sense of responsibility to the community that I admired.

Jordan's mom had hung around Lake Bluff after the divorce, but the instant Jordan turned eighteen, she was gone. I never did hear where.

Jordan dreamed of attending Duke University. She had the grades but not the money, which is how she'd ended up working for me.

"I'll send a car as soon as I can," she continued. "Everyone's out on calls. Storm's something else."

"Try the highway crew. We need to get that tree off the road. Some dumb ass who doesn't have the sense to stay in during a mess like this will run aground on the thing, and then we'll have a pileup."

"The world *is* full of dumb asses," Jordan agreed.

As I said, wise beyond her years.

I continued toward the place where I'd seen the orange glow. The sparks had appeared to fall near Brasstown Bald, the highest peak in the spine of mountains known as Wolfpen Ridge. Despite the name, there were no wolves in the Blue Ridge, hadn't been for centuries.

Static spilled from my radio, along with Cal's voice. "Grace, take the turn just past Galilean Drive. Careful, it's a swamp back here."

I followed his directions to the end of what would have been a dirt road but was now a mud puddle. Illuminated by the flare of headlights from his squad car, Cal wore a yellow rain slicker and the extremely ugly hat that came with our uniform. A hat I never wore unless I had to.

With a sigh I slipped into my own slicker and slapped the wide-brimmed, tree-bark brown Stetson wannabe on top of my still-damp hair.

"Where's the fire?" I asked as I joined Cal at the edge of the tree line.

"Not sure. I saw it. So did you. Hell, so did everyone in a mile radius. But by the time I got here, nothing."

Considering the wind and the rain, the fire had probably gone out. However, the proximity of the town required us to be certain. All we needed was for the thickness of the trees to protect one small ember, which would smolder and burst into flames the instant we turned our backs.

"You sure this is the place?"

Cal nodded. He wasn't a particularly tall man, maybe an inch more than my own five-ten, but he was imposing, still ripped, despite two years out of the Corps. I doubted I could even get my hands around his neck, if I was so inclined. Cal wore his light brown hair in the style of the USMC, and his face was lined from tours spent in countries that had a lot more sun and wind and sand than we ever could.

"Ward Beecher called it in," Cal continued. "Said all the trees were ablaze. He smelled the smoke."

I frowned. Ward Beecher wasn't a nut. He was the pastor of the Lake Bluff Baptist Church. I doubted he was much of a liar, either, and he lived not more than half a mile from this spot.

"There's nothing now." I walked around the clearing. The trees, the grass, the ground were all dripping wet; I couldn't find a single charred pine needle.

"'Cept this." Cal indicated an area in front of his car.

I joined him at the edge of a fairly large hole, which reminded me of photos I'd seen of meteor sites. Except there wasn't a rock of any noticeable size to be had.

"Could have been here forever," I said.

"Mebe."

He didn't sound convinced, but what other explanation was there? The hole was empty. Unless—

I went down on one knee, ignoring the mud that soaked through my uniform—I was already drenched— and studied the ground.

"You think someone was here before us?" Cal asked. "Took whatever it was that fell?"

I didn't answer, just continued to look. I was the best tracker in the county. My father had made certain of that. But sometimes, like now, being the best wasn't any damn good at all.

"The rain's washed away the top layer of dirt," I said. "An elephant could have come through here and I wouldn't find a trace of it."

I straightened, my gaze drawn to the tree line just as a low, bulky shadow took the shape of a wolf.

I didn't like that one bit. We'd had a little problem with wolves last summer.

Werewolves, to be exact.

I hadn't believed it, either—until some really strange things had started happening. Turned out there were werewolves all over the place. There was even a secret government society charged with killing them.

I'd thought they'd all been eliminated or cured—no one had died a horrific, bloody death in months.

But maybe I was wrong.

2

B Y THE TIME I drew my Glock, the animal had melted into the trees on the north side of the clearing and disappeared. I ran after it anyway, even though I didn't have any silver bullets.

In this gun.

"What's the matter?" Cal followed; he had his weapon out, too.

"You didn't see the—?" I stopped. Had I really seen a wolf?

Yes.

Did I want to tell Cal?

No.

"Never mind." I put away the Glock. "A shadow. Maybe a bear."

Not a wolf in these mountains, but bears we had.

Cal narrowed his blue-gray eyes on the trees. "They don't usually come this close to people."

"Which might be why it took off so fast."

"Mmm." Cal holstered his weapon, but he kept his hand on his belt just in case.

I was kind of surprised he hadn't seen the wolf. The animal had been right in front of him; he should have at least detected a movement, even if he had been focused on the mysterious gaping hole in the earth.

I checked the ground but found no tracks. Though the rain still fell in a steady stream, a bear would have left some kind of indentation. A wolf should have, too.

"We may as well head back," I said. "I'm sure Jordan has a list of problems the length of my arm for us to deal with."

"Probably," Cal agreed. "What do you think that orange glow was?"

"A reflection?"

"Off a UFO?"

"Okay." Hell, stranger things had happened—right here in Lake Bluff.

Cal laughed at my easy agreement. "Anyone else live out here we could talk to? Maybe they saw something."

"My great-grandmother had a friend who lived—" I waved in a vague northerly direction. "Although I'm not sure how much she can see or hear anymore."

I hadn't been to visit Quatie in a long time. My great-grandmother had asked me to check on her whenever I was in the area, but I'd had a helluva year, considering the werewolves, and I'd forgotten. I needed to remedy that ASAP.

"Probably not worth going over there," Cal said.

"No," I agreed, but made a mental note to stop by another day.

We got into our cars and reached the highway without getting stuck. Then Cal went one way and I went the other.

I decided to drive straight to the mayor's house. Claire Kennedy was not only in charge of this town, but werewolves had nearly killed her, and her husband, Malachi Cartwright, knew more about them than anyone.

Myself, I'd been skeptical about the supernatural. Even though my great-grandmother had been a medicine woman of incredible power and she'd believed in magic, I'd been tugged in two directions. I'd wanted to be like her; I'd wanted to believe. But I'd also wanted to please my father—hadn't learned until much later that such a thing was impossible—and he'd been a cop, filled with skepticism, requiring facts. I'd been confused, torn—until last summer when I'd had no choice but to accept the unacceptable.

I turned the squad car toward Claire's place, uncaring that it was nearly midnight and she had a new baby. Claire would want to hear about this.

Before my tires completed twenty revolutions, headlights wavered on the other side of a rise. I was just reaching for the siren when a car came over the hill, took the curve too fast, and skidded across the yellow line. Out of control, it headed straight for me.

I yanked the wheel to the right, hoping to avoid both a head-on collision and being hit in the driver's side door. The oncoming car glanced off my bumper, but the combination of speed and slick pavement sent me spinning. I was unable to gain control of the squad before I slammed into the nearest tree.

My air bag imploded, smacking me in the face so hard my head snapped back; then everything went black.

∞

I awoke to the sound of the rain and the distant beat of something that could have been a drum. Maybe thunder.

No, that wasn't right.

I frowned and then groaned as pain exploded across my face and chest. Slowly I opened my eyes.

The squad was crumpled against the trunk of a towering oak, my face squished into the air bag. I tasted blood.

The car wasn't running. The radio was smashed. I felt for my cell phone, peered blearily at the display, which read: No service.

I was dizzy, nauseous. A quick glance into the rearview mirror didn't reveal much, although from the dark splotches on my shadowy face, I just might have broken my nose.

I released the seat belt and fought my way from the car. Then I stood alone on a deserted, rain-drenched road. The prick who'd hit me had taken off. He was going to be toast when I got hold of him.

The rain had already drenched me to the skin. I'd removed my slicker when I'd gotten in the car. My head had been too fuzzy to remember to put it back on before I'd climbed out.

The trees spun. I wanted to sit. Instead, I leaned against the rear bumper and grasped for a coherent thought.

I was stuck in the mountains with no way to contact

anyone. I could walk back to Lake Bluff; I'd probably have to. Just not right now.

Branches rustled. I blinked the rain from my lashes. Everything was still blurry. I could see my nose swelling up. I was going to have two black eyes. Wouldn't be the first time. I did have four older brothers.

Not that they'd beat on me—much—but I'd always tried to keep up with them, and with the lack of supervision that came from a father obsessed with his job and a mother who'd taken off when I was three, I'd often ended up bruised and bloody.

I'd also ended up tough, able to take care of myself and compartmentalize pain, which were exactly the skills I needed right now.

"Thanks George, Gerry, Greg, and Gene," I muttered.

I'd often wondered if my mother had chosen names that began with *G* for sentimental reasons or because she hadn't cared enough to be original. Unless she showed up one day, and I wasn't holding my breath, I'd never know. My brothers had refused to speak of her, as had my father.

Had her desertion screwed me up? Sure. Whenever I cared about someone, I knew it was only a matter of time until they left. So far, no one had disappointed me.

I moved closer to the edge of the trees. Even though I was dizzy, my head ached, and I wasn't sure just how "with it" I was, those trees were bugging me. They weren't swaying with the wind, as I'd first thought, but shaking as if something was coming.

I drew my gun. Would I even be able to hit anything in my condition? Would a lead bullet do me any good tonight?

Why hadn't I given in to my own unease and started loading all my weapons with the specially made silver

"I've got brothers."

"Ah, then you know the drill."

I did, if I could only remember, which, come to think of it, was a symptom of a concussion.

He must have seen my confusion, because he kept talking. "If you start to throw up, get to a doctor. Have someone wake you once in the night."

I snorted, which made my head and nose scream. The only someone at my place was me. Not that I'd be getting any sleep tonight anyway.

"Ice for your face," he finished.

The wind picked up and slapped a hank of his hair across his eyes. He lifted a hand and shoved it back. A stray shaft of moonlight sparked off his ring. I couldn't tell if the circlet was silver or gold.

He turned his head as if he'd heard something and a single, thin braid swung free, tangled with a feather of some kind. In the slight gray light his profile revealed a sharp blade of a nose and a slash of cheekbones any model would kill for.

This guy was as Indian as I was.

Had he walked out of the past? Was he a ghost? An immortal? How hard had I hit my head?

"Let me help you stand," he said.

I wanted to lie there a while longer, but a flash of red and blue lit the sky, and beneath me the ground vibrated with the roll of tires approaching from the direction he'd been staring. How had he sensed the car before I had?

I managed to gain my feet. My rescuer let me go, and I was pleased when I didn't fall down.

The squad came over the hill. I lifted an arm, but Cal was already pulling over in front of my mangled vehicle.

He jumped out, ran over. "You okay, Grace?"

"So he says." I waved my hand toward the stranger.

Cal's face creased in confusion. "So *who* says?"

I turned to ask the man's name, but no one was there.

3

Y OU'RE STARTING TO WORRY ME," Cal said.

"I'm starting to worry myself."

I strode to the edge of the trees. Too much grass to distinguish any footprints. I found small areas of indentation, but with the rain they could have been from anything.

First the disappearing wolf and then the disappearing man. Were they connected?

"Yeah," I muttered.

"Grace?"

Talking to myself again. People who lived alone often did. I should probably stop, but I doubted I could.

"Never mind," I said. "How'd you find me?"

"Nine-one-one call from a cell. Probably the guy who hit you."

"Jerk," I muttered, although I was grateful someone had called. "I guess you'll have to take me home."

"I'm taking you to the hospital."

"No, you aren't."

"There's blood all over you!"

"Which is why I want to change my uniform before I go back out."

"You're not going back out. Not tonight."

"You seem to be under the impression that you're the boss of me," I said.

Cal's lips tightened, but when he spoke his voice was nothing but calm. Talk about the patience of a saint. "You can't drive around, especially in this mess, when you're dizzy. At least take the rest of the night off." He jerked a thumb toward my ruined vehicle. "You're going to have a hard time getting that thing to run anyway."

"I have a car of my own, Cal."

He mumbled something that I instinctively knew I didn't want to hear. Cal was just trying to look after me, but I wasn't very good at being looked after.

"Take me home," I ordered.

The short drive to my house was accomplished in total silence. When I tried to get out of the car, my head ached so badly my stomach rolled.

I glanced at Cal and sighed. "Okay, you win. I'll go to bed, but call me if anything serious happens."

From his somewhat sarcastic salute, there was nothing Cal would consider serious enough to wake me for tonight.

I hesitated. My father had rarely delegated authority. If he were here now he'd sneer and call me a girl. In my family, the ultimate insult.

"You need help getting inside?" Cal asked.

"Not since the mayor and I split a box of cheap wine when we were sixteen and I puked for three days."

"You two must have been a real treat."

"Oh yeah, we were swell."

I made it to the porch, then lifted my hand as Cal turned his car and went back to work.

I was mud splattered, blood spattered; my uniform had been soaked and partially dried so many times it was stiff and uncomfortable. My hair had come loose from its braid and slapped against my neck like wiry hanks of hay.

A long, hot shower eased the stiffness, the mud, and the blood from my body and face. I took a bag of ice to bed. It wasn't the first time.

I set my alarm for 3:00 A.M., happy that I woke easily when it rang. The ice bag was water. I tossed it to the floor and went back to sleep.

I dreamed of lightning and of birds trapped in a glass box so that the beat of their terrified wings sounded like distant thunder. My eyes snapped open as I realized what that odd sound had been in the woods last night.

"The wings of a really big bird." I shook my head and was rewarded with a dull ache behind my puffy eyes.

I was more concussed than I thought. I'd heard the wind, maybe thunder. There was no bird big enough to create the sound that had seemed to make the earth, the trees, the very air shudder.

Of course there weren't any wolves in Georgia, either, but last summer we'd had some. We might have some again, considering what I'd seen in the storm.

I climbed out of bed, got dressed, and went to see Claire.

Most nights it took me a while to fall asleep. As a result, I often overslept and had to race to work, hair still wet after I'd drunk a single cup of coffee in the shower.

This morning, dawn had just spilled over the horizon

as I drove my dad's faded red pickup down Center Street. A bread truck was parked outside the Good Eatin' Café. The *open* sign sprang to life in the Center Perk as I went by. The coffee shop specialized in the fancy lattes and teas popular in big cities—over the summer we earned a good portion of our income off the tourists—but the Perk also sold good old-fashioned java in a go-cup to appease the locals, like me.

A moving van idled in front of what used to be a doll shop, until eighteen months ago when the owner died. The store had been empty ever since. I made a mental note to see who'd bought the place and then welcome him or her to the neighborhood.

Claire owned the largest house in Lake Bluff. Not that she'd planned to, but when her dad—the former mayor—had died, he'd left her not only the family homestead but also his job.

Claire had never wanted to be the mayor. She'd wanted to be a news anchor, and she'd run off to Atlanta to do it. There she'd discovered that the talent and brains that had made her hot shit in Lake Bluff only made her average, or less, in the big city. She'd wound up a producer instead, and she hadn't liked it.

She did like being the mayor, and she was a good one. Much to her own, and pretty much everyone else's, surprise.

I was just glad to have her back. Claire and I had been pals since our mothers had left. Hers to Heaven, mine to Lord only knew where.

Our fathers had been friends, too—the mayor and the sheriff—and they'd thrown us together often, leaving one or another of my brothers in charge. Claire and I had survived. Then, as now, we'd depended on each other.

I parked in front of the white rambling two-story near the end of Center Street. Claire walked to work every day, as her father had before her. In a town of just under five thousand, nothing was very far away.

The door opened before I knocked.

"Who hit you?" Claire demanded. "And what did you say to make them?"

Her hands were clenched into fists, and she appeared ready to take on anyone who'd dared touch me. Not that she wouldn't get her ass kicked. Claire was a girl in the true sense of the word—soft, round, with the fire red hair, moon-pale skin, and clear blue eyes of her Scotch-Irish ancestors.

"Why do you think I said something?" I demanded.

"Because you always do?"

"Not this time. My face had an intimate encounter with an air bag."

Her fingers unfurled. "Are you okay?"

"Fine. But the squad car doesn't look half as good as I do."

She lifted a brow. "Lucky we can afford another."

Since Claire had taken over, the town treasury had done a complete about-face. Not only had our last Full Moon Festival been a huge success, despite the werewolves, but she'd also figured out a lot of other ways to bring tourists to town the whole year through, instead of only during that single week in August.

"There's something I have to talk to you about," I said.

Claire waved me inside and headed for the kitchen. "Coffee?"

"God, yes."

I glanced around for Oprah, the cat—named during Claire's talk-show-host phase—before I remembered that she'd developed an instant adoration for the baby and rarely left his side.

Whenever Noah slept in his crib, Oprah lay beneath it. If he fell asleep anywhere in the house, she stayed right next to him, and if anyone came in the room, she set up a squalling that would wake the dead yet never seemed to wake the baby. Oprah was the next best thing to a watchdog Claire could find.

"Where are the guys?" I asked.

"Still sleeping, thank God."

Claire had married Malachi Cartwright early last fall. Their son, Noah, had been born in May, which meant Claire was getting far too little sleep. Luckily, Mal took care of the baby during the day so she could take care of Lake Bluff.

Mal was an oddity here, and not just because he was a househusband. He had come to town with his band of traveling Gypsies to entertain at the festival. After a whole lot of spooky stuff had gone on, he'd stayed behind when the rest of his people left.

From the beginning a more unlikely pair could not be imagined—the mayor and the Gypsy horse trainer, the First Lady of Lake Bluff and the hired help. I could go on and on, making comparisons directly out of historical fiction. But the truth was, they'd been destined to meet, fated to fall in love, and they were the happiest couple I'd ever seen. I guess Claire had forgiven, if not forgotten, that Malachi had come here to kill her.

Claire set two mugs on the table, and we each took a chair. "What's going on?" she asked.

Quickly I told her about the previous night. The strange, flickering light. The fire that wasn't. The crater and the wolf.

"Not again," Claire muttered.

"I'm not certain I really saw it. When I checked for tracks, there weren't any."

"You expected to find tracks in a storm like the one we had last night?"

I shrugged. "You never know."

"Did you hear a howl?"

"Nothing but thunder and wind." And the rhythmic beat of the giant wings of an invisible bird. I decided to keep that to myself.

"There was also a man. He came from nowhere."

"As in now you see him, now you don't?"

"Not sure. He was in the woods. I couldn't make out his face clearly, but he was Indian. For a second I thought—" I broke off, remembering. "Grandmother used to tell a story about a band of Cherokee who'd hidden in the mountains to escape the Trail of Tears. They hid so well that eventually they become both immortal and invisible."

"I guess you *had* hit your head."

Though I'd thought the same thing, I couldn't resist needling her. I could rarely resist needling anyone.

"This from a woman who saw people turn into animals."

She toasted me with her mug. "Got me there."

I tapped my own mug against hers, then drank. "After my head cleared, it occurred to me that a wolf had gone into those trees and, not too long after, a man had popped out."

"Did the wolf have the eyes of the man?" Claire asked.

We'd discovered last summer that a werewolf resembled a real wolf in every way—except for the human eyes.

I tried to remember the eyes of the wolf, the eyes of

the man, but I couldn't. I would think I'd recall something as bizarre as human eyes in the face of a wolf, but with the residual effects of the concussion . . .

"I don't know," I admitted. "I have certain gaps in the gray matter since the air-bag incident."

Concern washed over her face. "You want an aspirin?"

"No, Mom, but thanks."

"Watch it, or I won't let you hold Noah when he gets up."

I had a serious weakness for Noah Cartwright. Who'd have thought that rough, tough, gun-toting, order-giving Grace McDaniel would go gooey over a baby? Certainly not me.

"Sadly, I'm not going to be able to wait for His Highness to get out of the crib." I stood, draining the rest of my coffee in one gulp.

"I'll mention what you told me to Mal." Claire and I went to the front door. "He's pretty good at spotting the unusual."

Considering Mal had been cursed to wander the earth for centuries, he'd had his share of experience with shape-shifters.

"That'd be great," I said.

I'd do it myself, but I had the distinct feeling I'd be a little busy with the human inhabitants of Lake Bluff for the next several days. Having never actually seen a werewolf, I was at a disadvantage. Not that I didn't believe they were real. Long before they'd shown up, I'd seen other equally amazing things, which had eventually made me a convert.

"I'll be in and out this week." I stepped onto the porch, marveling at the bright sunshine after such a terrible storm. "I'm going to have to check on all the people in outlying areas."

There were still quite a few old-timers who insisted on living in the mountains without a phone or even electricity. Hell, there were a few new-timers who thought it was all the rage. I thought they were nuts. Probably because every time a natural disaster occurred I had to check on them.

"Feel free to rack up the overtime," Claire said.

"Oh, I'd planned on it."

I headed down the hill where the sheriff's department shared a square of land with town hall. Instead of turning into the parking lot, I continued on to where the moving van had been parked earlier but was no longer. The front door of the store stood open, so I walked in.

I probably should have called out, but the place was empty. Had the moving van been taking things away rather than delivering them?

Smart thieves usually pretended they belonged somewhere, that what they were taking was theirs by right, and few people questioned them. What better way to clean out a place than to hire a moving van and dress like a mover?

I'd just turned, determined to find out if anyone had bought this place, when a floorboard creaked upstairs.

Slowly I lifted my head. I'd forgotten an apartment occupied the second floor.

Through the back door of the shop, in a small space that used to be a called a mudroom, lay a staircase. The stairs led up to a long, shadowed hallway full of closed doors, except for the last one at the opposite end, which gaped open. As I headed in that direction, I had the sudden sensation of being watched. A quick glance over my shoulder revealed nothing.

One door, two, three doors, four—I opened my mouth to announce myself and a whisper of air brushed the back of my neck.

Impatiently I turned, trying to stop my overactive imagination from harassing me by giving it a full view of an empty hallway.

The man was so close my breasts brushed his chest.

4

INSTINCT TOOK OVER, and I reached for my gun. He grabbed my wrist before I was halfway there. My left hand swung for his head, and he caught that one, too. Then we stared at each other, him grasping my wrists tight enough to bruise, our bodies so close every breath skimmed the front of me against the front of him.

He wore a black suit and tie with a shirt so white it glowed even in the dim light. But the suit wasn't what threw me—it was the long hair adorned with a single braid and an eagle feather.

At least I hadn't imagined him.

He didn't look Indian in this light, except for the feather. His skin was much fairer than mine, and his eyes were an oddly light shade—not brown, not green, not gray, but a swirling combination of all three.

"Hey!" I tugged on my hands.

He didn't budge; he didn't speak as his gaze wandered over my face. I struggled; I couldn't help it. Ever since my oldest brother, George, had held me down while Greg painted my face with maple syrup, I got a little wiggy when trapped.

I continued to thrash. He continued to ignore me. The friction created by all that rubbing started to feel better than it should. My nipples, despite the protection of a padded bra, responded, which only made my breathing and the subsequent friction increase.

I considered kicking him in the shin, but from the strength of his grip and the expression on his face, he'd continue to hold me anyway.

"You often sneak into private property and pull a gun on people?" he asked.

"Only when I see a previously abandoned storefront with an open door and then someone creeps up on me. You're asking for trouble."

"I hear that a lot."

"You're gonna hear more than that if you don't let me go. Catchy phrases like 'assaulting an officer' and 'held without bond.'"

His only response was a smile that flashed his slightly crooked but very white teeth. However, he did loosen his hold. I backed up, absently rubbing first one wrist and then the other.

My gaze caught on the eagle feather. In Cherokee tradition, only great warriors dared to wear the trappings of the sacred bird. Did he know that? Did he care?

"How's your head?" he asked.

"About to explode."

"It shouldn't hurt that badly still."

He moved so quickly I couldn't think, let alone escape, yanking me so close my nose scraped against his shirt as he began to probe my skull.

"Ow!" I shoved him away, even though he'd smelled

really good, as if he'd rubbed fresh mint leaves all over his skin.

He stared at me with a combination of bemusement and concern.

"My head's fine," I said. "Why'd you sneak up on me?"

"I didn't sneak."

"I didn't hear anything."

"I've always been quiet."

He was a lot more than quiet. *I* was quiet. My father had trained me to track both man and beast in complete silence, but this guy had tracked me. Something about him set my instincts humming—or maybe that was just my libido.

"Who are you?" I asked.

"I told you last night, or don't you remember?"

"You said you were a doctor, yet I find you creeping around abandoned storefronts manhandling women."

His lips curved. "You didn't mind."

If I could blush I'd have been beet red. As it was, my blood pressure went up so fast my pulse seemed to pound out a painful song behind my blackened eyes.

"I should take you in for squatting in an abandoned building."

"Do I look like a squatter?"

I took the opportunity to give him the once-over. In contrast to his expensive tailored suit, he wore sandals. His right ring finger sported the band I'd noticed last night, glaringly gold in the sunlight. I'd think it was a wedding ring, except he wore it on the wrong hand.

"Officer?" he pressed when I continued to stare.

He wasn't exactly handsome. The bones of his face were too sharp for that. But his hair was dark, his eyes light, and his skin just tan enough to make him memorable.

"Sheriff," I corrected.

His gaze lowered to my chest, and my pulse quickened again. " 'Sheriff McDaniel,' " he read from my name tag. "I'm Ian Walker, from Oklahoma."

Which explained the accent—not South, not North, but West, where most of the Cherokee had gone long ago.

"What brings you here?"

"To Lake Bluff or this building?"

"Both."

"I'll be opening an office as soon as I can get the place ready, and I chose Lake Bluff because . . ." His voice drifted off, as if he was trying to come up with a reason.

"Because?" I prompted.

"I traced my ancestors to this town. From the time before our people suffered on the Trail Where We Wept."

He used the Cherokee version of the historical term "Trail of Tears." They meant the same thing. Another example of the U.S. government's treatment of those whose only crimes had been to be here first and then arrogantly refuse to give up what was theirs just because they were told to.

"How do you know we're the same people?" I asked.

I could easily be descended from any tribe in the country. For all he knew I might not be Native American at all but African, Asian, Italian, Mexican, or any combination of the above.

"I ran across the McDaniels when I was researching my own family. You've been here since the beginning of time."

"Not quite that long." But close enough.

Legends say the Aniyvwiya, or the principal people, came from a land of sea snakes and water monsters near the place where the sun was born. In other words . . . east. But we'd been in these mountains so long that no one really knew when the first Cherokee had arrived.

"What clan are you?" Walker asked.

In ancient times, the question would have been unforgivably rude. Clan membership was a secret passed down from the mother to the children in a matrilineal society. To be without a clan was to be without rights, without protection, without family. Clan membership was everything.

Very few Cherokee knew their clan affiliation these days—partly because of the extreme secrecy that had been involved and partly because people no longer cared. However, I was one of the few who knew and who cared.

"Panther clan," I answered.

"A ni sa ho ni," he murmured. "Clan of blue."

Each of the seven clans had worn feathers of a different color to delineate them from the others. Panther, or the wildcat clan, was the clan of blue, referring to a certain medicine they'd made for their children.

When I was little and sick, my great-grandmother had often forced a disgusting blue concoction down my throat, and it always worked. I wished again that I could read her notes and discover what she'd put in that stuff.

"I'm A ni wo di," he said.

At my blank expression he frowned. "You don't speak the language of our mothers?"

I bristled at his tone. "I'm more Scotch than Cherokee."

I didn't bother to mention the African since no one really knew that for certain. Just because the Cherokee had once kept slaves didn't mean they broadcast the identities of the children they'd had with them. If secrecy was good enough for Thomas Jefferson, it was good enough for us.

"That's no excuse," he said.

"Who died and made you head of the Cherokee Nation?"

He contemplated me for several seconds, then dipped his head, the feather swinging past his ear along with the braid. "You're right. I just thought that someone descended from Rose Scott, one of the most powerful medicine women—"

"How do you know that?"

His lips quirked. "It's classified?"

"No." Although it wasn't exactly written about in the *Lake Bluff Gazette,* either. This guy knew an awful lot about me for someone who claimed to have been looking for *his* family tree.

"Your great-grandmother taught you nothing of the old ways?"

She'd tried, but my father had been adamant that there be no hocus-pocus or I'd lose my time with her. Since I'd known he was serious and that time meant the world to me, I'd balked at many of her teachings. Instead, she'd told me stories—legends of the origin of the clans, tales of the principal people being descended from animals.

As panther clan, we carried the spirit of the big cat within us. Some of us more than others.

Fascinated, I'd not only collected every stuffed and glass image of panthers that I could find, but I'd often pretended I was a panther, too. Slinking through the woods and the mountains, I'd often dreamed of actually becoming one.

However, I didn't want to talk about that, especially with him, so I flicked a finger at the feather in his hair. "You're bird clan?"

"That would be A ni tsi s kwa," he said. "Not A ni wo di."

"I don't speak the language," I said between my teeth.

He'd better not be wolf clan, or I just might rethink shooting him. At least I'd had the sense to load my gun with silver before I left home.

"I'm paint clan," he said.

"Medicine men. How convenient."

"I thought so."

My bad attitude didn't seem to faze him. He was a very calm guy.

"Too bad you had to give up the old ways when you became a doctor."

"Why would I do that?"

"I wouldn't think the AMA would be too happy about an M.D. who prescribes roots, berries, and bathing in a cool mountain stream."

"You'd be surprised."

"You do that?"

"If the illness warrants it."

My eyes narrowed. "Do you have a medical license?"

"Of course."

"From a real medical school?"

"Does Baylor College of Medicine suffice?"

Even I knew that was a good one.

"I also studied at the British Institute of Homeopathy in Canada."

I frowned. "Sounds like hoodoo to me."

"It's not."

I grunted, unconvinced. I enjoyed studying my heritage as much as the next guy. I was interested in the cures my great-grandmother had used. I might use them on myself, if I could figure them out, but I'd never presume to prescribe them to others. I considered a doctor who'd do so nothing less than a quack. People like Walker gave Native Americans a bad name.

I didn't trust him. I didn't much like him, although I did kind of like the way he smelled. I rubbed my forehead, wincing when I touched a bruise.

"Let me give you something for that." He inched past me and through the open door.

I caught a whiff of him again and had to bite back a sigh. I needed to get laid, then maybe this obsession would go away, but that wasn't as easy as it sounded.

In Lake Bluff everyone knew everyone and their mother, father, sister, and brother, too. I'd dated a few guys, slept with a few more. Every one had been a disaster of epic proportion.

If they hadn't expected special privileges from the sheriff's daughter, they'd definitely expected them from the sheriff. When they hadn't gotten them, each and every guy had turned into a whining child.

I'd sworn off locals, which meant the only sex I'd had in years had been during the festival when we were overrun with tourists. Sadly, I'd missed any kind of action last year due to our werewolf problem. No wonder I was so on edge.

Walker reappeared with a jar in his hand, unscrewing the top as he approached. The balm was pale yellow and carried a scent I didn't recognize.

He dipped a finger into the muck and spread some down my nose before I could protest.

"Hey!" I began, but he ignored me, smoothing the medicine over my bulbous nose and the bruised area beneath my eyes. The pain faded on contact.

"Close," he murmured, spreading one thumb over my brow bone.

What the hell? I thought. The stuff was already all over my skin. I let my eyes drift shut.

His fingers were gentle but firm. Everywhere he touched, the pain went away. He murmured words I couldn't understand, in the language of our ancestors.

Outside I heard again the low, rhythmic beat of wings. My eyes snapped open. His face was so close his breath puffed against the moisture on my face, and I shivered.

His eyes, eerily light, seemed to darken as his pupils expanded. I could see myself in them as he leaned closer.

My chest hurt; I wasn't breathing. He was going to kiss me, and I was going to let him.

My eyes fluttered closed again. I waited for him to take me in his arms, but the only place he touched me was in the light, feathery skate of his lips across mine.

I drew in a breath, captivated by the sensations. I was used to being handled differently. I was a tall woman who wore a gun. Guys never treated me as if I were spun glass. I didn't want them to.

My lips barely parted, his tongue flicked between, caressing both in one stroke. He lifted his mouth, I moaned in protest, but he pressed gentle kisses across my brow, beneath my eyes, down my nose. Wherever he touched, my skin warmed. I didn't want to open my eyes, to see his face, to remember who he was, who I was, how crazy kissing a stranger in an abandoned storefront on Center Street must be.

When he kissed me harder, deeper, his tongue delving in and stroking my own, my nipples went hard again; my whole body came alive.

He raised his head. I could feel him hovering, waiting and watching, his breath mingling with my own. Would we or wouldn't we?

Slowly I opened my eyes and stared at an empty hallway.

5

FOR AN INSTANT I doubted my sanity, until I caught and at last recognized the scent of the balm—fresh-cut grass beneath bright sunshine—then lifted a finger to my face. The tip came away shiny. Ian Walker was as real as the cream on my skin.

I strode to the open doorway. The room was cluttered with furniture, boxes, suitcases. I guess the moving van had delivered something. He stood near the window, shoulders slumped, head bent. What was wrong with him?

Then I saw the picture—a woman in a white dress, standing on a prairie as the wind ruffled her skirt. She was tiny, petite, young, with long hair like an inky waterfall against her smiling cheek.

The photo had been taken in black-and-white, then brushed with pastel colors, giving it the impression of age, although I'd seen the same technique used more recently, too.

Ian lifted his hand and shoved his own hair back

from his face. The wedding band flashed in the sunlight. No wonder he'd scooted off at the first opportunity. *Jerk.*

His shoulders slumped even more as he exhaled. He didn't turn around but continued to stare out the window as the streets below became busier and noisier.

If he could be this broken up about kissing another woman, maybe he wasn't such a prick after all. Then I remembered that kiss, what he'd made me feel, how my body still hummed with it, and my anger flared at the loss of something that could have been so good.

"Where's your wife?" My voice was as cold as my heart.

His shoulders twitched as if I'd slashed him with a whip. "Gone," he whispered.

The chill that had spread over me evaporated in the heat of embarrassment. Wedding ring on the right hand must mean widower, and I'd taunted him with the memory of his wife.

"I'm sorry—," I began.

"Not your fault. I forgot—" He stopped, shook his head, didn't finish.

I wondered how long she'd been gone. How she had died. If he'd ever get over her.

I was such an idiot. I didn't even like this guy. He'd kissed me once better than I'd ever been kissed before, and I was mooning over him like a lovesick teenager.

I'd been a lovesick teenager. Weren't we all once? I never wanted to be one again.

"Here." He snapped the cap back on the jar and held it out to me, though his gaze remained on the window. "Use it whenever the pain returns."

Right now my face felt great—as if I'd never been popped in the nose at all. I shrugged and took the jar.

"What's in this?" I asked.

"Rattlesnake oil."

I waited for him to laugh, but he didn't.

"You're serious?"

He turned. His skin pale, his pupils so large his eyes appeared black, fine lines bracketed his mouth. I re-arranged his age in my mind from late twenties to mid-thirties, which made more sense considering the medical degrees. If they were real.

"Rattlesnake oil is a common balm for rheumatism and arthritis," he said. "It works for bruises, too, if you say the right words."

I lifted my brows.

"Do you know anything about Cherokee medicine?" he asked.

"I thought we'd established I'm a cop, not a medi-cine woman."

"You're wrong."

I started to get annoyed again. Why did he have that effect on me? Maybe because he kept telling me what I was and who I should be.

"You think I wear this charming outfit because it flat-ters my ass?" I indicated the ugly brown uniform that bagged at the breasts and sagged in the butt. I didn't have a bad body, but you'd never know it by looking at me in this rag, which was probably the idea.

"You might be a cop," he said, "but you're a medicine woman, too. Even if you don't know the way. You were born to be who you are, and who you are is the great-granddaughter of Rose Scott."

I resisted the urge to roll my eyes again. "I'm sheriff of Lake Bluff. That's who I was born to be."

In truth, my dad had expected one of the boys to take over, but they'd hightailed it out of town the instant they'd turned eighteen. Good old Grace, who'd been begging for an ounce of Daddy's attention her entire life, had stayed and assumed the position when he died.

I didn't mind. I liked my job; I was good at it. Besides, there wasn't much call for medicine women these days.

"You'll discover your power one day." He tilted his head and the white of the eagle feather caught the sunlight and sparkled. "One day soon, I think."

I remembered how the small shaft of moonlight had glanced off the feather just last night. "What were you doing in the forest during a storm?"

"Is that a crime?"

"Not unless I can arrest people for stupidity, and as much as I'd like to, lawyers tend to frown on that."

"Lawyers frown on everything. Considering your accident, it was lucky for you that I was stupid."

"I'd have been all right. Why did you disappear?"

"I had things that needed to be done."

"Like what?"

"Things."

Before I could point out how uninformative that was, my cell phone buzzed. One glance at the display and I sighed. "Excuse me." I flipped the phone open. "What is it, Cal?"

"You okay?"

"Peachy. Cut to the chase."

"Sounds like you're back to normal. Nose broke?"

"I have no idea."

"Grace—," he began.

"My nose works, Cal. It's in the center of my face, and I can smell just fine with it." Against my will my eyes were drawn to Ian Walker, whom I'd been smelling far too much of. Walker lifted his eyebrows but said nothing.

"We've had a lot of calls since last night," Cal continued.

"I'm shocked."

Cal ignored me. He'd learned fast. "A lot of them dealt with birds."

"Whaddya mean?"

"Flocks of really big crows swooping low over cars. Birds flying into windows. Down chimneys."

"Is there a Hitchcock revival somewhere in the vicinity?"

"Very funny, Grace."

I hadn't been kidding. Every time a scary movie played in the area we had a rash of complaints that mirrored the plot. With every new *Friday the 13th* release— would they ever end?—people saw Jason all over the place.

"Could be the storm just threw them out of whack," I said. "Don't birds have radar?"

"I think that's bats."

"Whatever. We can't do anything about birds run amok. Anything serious I should know about?"

"Downed trees. Electricity out. Someone lost a carport to a falling branch."

"Injuries?"

"Nothing worse than that schnoz on you."

"Gee, thanks." I paused for an instant, thinking. A bird had smashed into my window last night. I'd thought it a fluke, but I guess not. I'd have to call the Department of Natural Resources and find out their take on it as well as— "Did anyone happen to see a wolf?"

"Why?" Cal asked. "Did you?"

"Maybe."

"But there aren't any."

"Could be someone has been keeping one as a pet and it got out during the storm."

"Could be," he agreed. "I'll ask around. You coming in soon?"

"Very," I said, and hung up.

"Pet wolves are more dangerous than real ones," Walker murmured. "They're often a wolf-dog mix, which makes them unpredictable. They aren't afraid of humans, but they're still wild in a lot of ways."

"How do you know so much about them?"

"I've known people who kept wolves. It never ended well."

I just bet it hadn't.

"If you've got a hybrid loose in these mountains you'd better catch it quick. Tame wolves tend to get themselves attacked by other animals, and then there's a danger of—"

"Rabies," I finished.

He nodded. "So you've got a wolf that isn't afraid of people, which is suddenly rabid."

I'd already been here and done this last summer. When a wolf that shouldn't exist in the Blue Ridge Mountains had attacked a tourist, we'd thought the wolf was rabid—never mind how it had gotten here. But when the tourist became extremely hairy and jumped out a second-story window before loping away, we figured that "rabid" was often a euphemism for "lycanthropic."

"I've got to go," I said, and did, ignoring the intent expression on Walker's face and the curiosity in his eyes.

A short while later I entered the Lake Bluff Sheriff's Department. The place was hopping.

We had nine full-time deputies and one part-time, along with three full-time dispatchers and one part-time on the payroll. Last night everyone had been called in, and from the crowd near the desks, most of them were still here. There had to be doughnuts.

I made my way through the outer area, nodding at the greetings. Sure enough, a box of bakery sat on a desk—more muffins and bagels than doughnuts, although I saw a few crullers with my name on them.

No one mentioned my swollen nose and dual black eyes. Cal must have warned them off. More and more I didn't know how I'd gotten along without him.

My office was a welcome respite from the chatter and the energy that come from having that many people in an enclosed space. I didn't like crowds. I did better one-on-one.

As soon as I'd taken the chair behind my desk, Cal appeared. "I've got every officer on the lookout for a vehicle with a dented front end. Also notified the repair shops in the county. We'll find whoever hit you and then took off."

"Thanks." I'd meant to do that myself, but I'd been a little distracted.

"I also checked the reports from last night," he continued. "No wolves. Just more of the really big crows and strange bird behavior."

"Wait a second," I said. "Really big crows—you mean ravens?"

"What's the difference?"

The knowledge wasn't common. The only reason I knew was because I'd done a report in eighth-grade science. Never thought that bit of trivia would come in handy.

"Ravens and crows aren't the same," I said. "You

could call a raven a crow, since they're in the crow family, but all crows aren't ravens."

"How can you tell them apart?"

"Ravens are about the size of a hawk and crows are more like pigeons."

"So people's complaints about really big crows are probably not about crows at all."

"Probably not, although I hardly think it matters in this case."

"True." He moved on. "I sent some of the guys out to check on the folks who don't have phones."

"Good." I began thumbing through my messages. Cal's silence made me glance up. The expression on his face made me set the messages down. "What?"

"One of them was dead."

"Who?"

"Orel Vandross."

"He was still alive?" The guy had to be a hundred.

"Until yesterday. According to the report, the officer found him in his bed."

"That's the way to go—in your own bed near the century mark."

"Definitely. The funeral home picked him up. There won't be a service. His family's gone and his friends, too."

"That's too bad."

"I don't think he'll care."

I cast Cal a sharp glance. Sometimes his gallows humor, no doubt learned on the front lines of several nasty wars, startled even me.

"I had another joke on my desk this morning," Cal said.

"Already?"

The Chuck Norris joke bandit had struck just yesterday with the ditty *When the boogeyman goes to sleep he checks his closet for Chuck Norris.*

Cal handed me a sheet of paper and I steeled myself before reading: *Chuck Norris ordered a Big Mac at Burger King, and got one.*

I bit my lip to keep from laughing. Cal didn't seem at all amused.

"I don't get it," he said. "Why would Burger King make a Big Mac?"

The man was so literal sometimes, he scared me.

"Anyone see who put that on your desk?" I asked.

"No, and I haven't had a chance to check the security camera. Not that it'll make a difference."

No matter how many times we ran over the security tapes, we never saw anyone put the jokes on Cal's desk. Which was impossible. Nevertheless, new jokes continued to appear.

"I'm going to call the DNR about the ravens," I said. "Can you do something for me?"

"Sure."

I wrote "*Ian Walker, Baylor School of Medicine* and *British Institute of Homeopathy—Canada*" on a piece of paper and handed it to him.

Cal frowned at the words. "What about them?"

"There's a new doctor in town. Or at least he says he's a doctor. Those are his credentials. Can you verify?"

"Shouldn't be a problem." Cal turned to go, then paused, peering at me closely. "I thought your face would be a lot worse today."

"You think this is good?"

"Considering how it looked last night, hell, yeah." He headed out.

I frowned, and for the first time since I'd been airbagged, the motion of my face didn't cause pain.

Reaching into my desk, I withdrew the mirror I kept there just in case I had to check my teeth for spinach or my nose for—well, what we check our noses for—and held it up.

My bruises were fading toward yellow, and my nose was half the size it had been an hour ago.

I lowered the mirror and stared at the jar of balm on my desk as if it were an actual rattlesnake instead of just the oil.

How could it have worked so fast?

6

M Y HEART WHISPERED, *Magic*. My mind scoffed. Too much in my life and my job contradicted any sort of fairy tale. But I'd also seen amazing, unexplainable things whenever I'd been around my great-grandmother, not to mention everything that had happened in Lake Bluff last summer.

So, on the one hand I figured the balm was just really good balm; on the other I wondered if the words Walker had murmured had been an equally powerful spell and, if so, where he had learned it.

Regardless, I rubbed more rattlesnake oil into my face before I picked up the phone and called the Department of Natural Resources.

After a few transfers I reached the office of Alan Sellers, bird geek. Quickly I told him what had happened in Lake Bluff.

"Odd bird behavior after a strong storm isn't unheard of," he said in a nasal whine that had me imagining his colorless hair, pasty skin, and watery eyes.

"So it's nothing to worry about?"

"Worry in what way?"

"Coordinated attacks. Bird rabies?"

His laugh disintegrated into a cough. I revised pale skin to the gray cast of a lifetime smoker. "You've heard the term 'birdbrain'?"

"Far more than I'd like," I muttered. It had been one of my brothers' favorite insults.

"Although recent studies have revealed that birds aren't as dumb as originally thought, coordinated attacks are beyond the capacity of most species. A flock may follow the leader, they can even communicate information about where to find food, but they don't have the brainpower to mount an attack."

"So Hitchcock was full of shit?"

"Most movies are."

Smart man.

"Also," he continued, "rabies is a disease passed from mammal to mammal, so birds can't get it. You say you have both crows and ravens?"

"Hard to know for sure. We've had reports of really big crows, which I took to be ravens. Crows have never been all that common in Lake Bluff."

"They usually congregate near larger towns; ravens like the mountains and forests. A sudden increase in crows in a rural area often follows a radical increase in the timber wolf population. I highly doubt that's the case in the Blue Ridge Mountains."

I opened my mouth, but nothing came out.

"Sheriff?" Sellers asked. "You there?"

"Yes. Sorry. Why would timber wolves increase the crow population?"

"No one knows for sure, but the two species have always worked in tandem. The crow leading the wolf to prey, and the wolf leaving carrion for his feathered friend to eat later—like payment, although we know they aren't so advanced in their thought patterns."

"Birdbrains," I muttered.

"Exactly. Wolves are quite a bit smarter, of course, but I don't think they have sufficient brainpower to account for a system of checks and balances. Of course there are quite a few Native American folktales that ascribe humanlike behavior to the beasts and the birds. I'm sure there has to be one somewhere that explains why the crow and the wolf are friends, although I haven't found it yet."

The slowing pace of his voice revealed he planned on remedying that lack of knowledge ASAP.

Too bad I couldn't ask him if werewolves followed the buddy system with crows, unless I wanted to be branded a nut job. Luckily, I did have a resident expert.

After thanking Sellers, I disconnected, considered calling Malachi Cartwright, and decided to walk over. That way I'd get to see Noah.

"I'm taking a stroll around town and then stopping at the Cartwrights'." Sharon Brendel, the dispatcher on duty, nodded. "You can raise me on the radio or my cell if you need to."

"How well do you know him?" Sharon asked dreamily.

Although she was probably only five years my junior, Sharon seemed very young to me. Probably because I'd never dreamed about anything the way Sharon did. Not my future, not boys, and certainly not men. I'd learned early and often that men were not very dream worthy.

"You mean Mal?" I asked.

"Mmmm." The girl actually licked her lips.

I had to resist the urge to laugh in her face. Malachi was way too old for her—by about two hundred years. Not to mention he was totally, hopelessly, in love with his wife. From the moment Mal had seen Claire, and vice versa, there'd never been anyone else for either one of them.

A prickle of jealousy burned just below my breast-bone. I was happy for Claire. She deserved some joy in her life, as did Malachi. But I'd never realized how lonely I was until Claire had come back and then gotten married. I wanted what she had so badly I ached with it.

Out on the street the sun shone with the wattage of a nuclear blast. I slid my wraparound sunglasses from the pocket of my uniform and onto my nose. No pain. God, that balm was good.

I hadn't gone half a block when an ambulance wailed down Center Street, pausing at a small white house only a few paces ahead of me. The paramedics jumped out and ran inside. There was no way I could walk past and not stop to see what was wrong.

Marion Garsdale appeared to have fallen asleep on her couch. It wasn't until I got closer that I saw she was dead. I should have figured it out from the sudden lack of hustle on the part of the paramedics.

"What happened?" I asked.

They glanced up—two young men who appeared just out of high school, although they had to have had some training for this job and could not therefore be "just" out.

"Sheriff." The dark-haired one, who must be at least a quarter Cherokee, straightened.

He was someone's kid; I just couldn't recall whose. My dad had always known everyone's name, their children's names, and their children's children's names, as well as their dogs'.

"She was gone when we got here."

He seemed a little nervous, as if afraid I'd blame him for something. But what?

I came closer, staring down at the face of Ms. Garsdale. Her eyes wide open, her mouth had frozen in an equally wide *o* of shock. I guess no one is really ready to go, despite any hopes to the contrary.

Ms. Garsdale had once taught English at the high school. Though she seemed like a caricature of an English teacher with her white hair, flowered print dress, and thick glasses on her thin nose, she had in fact been quite the hippie.

Her hair, when unbound, reached to her waist. The flower print dress had once been the height of fashion— a seventies maxi—and her glasses, while thick, were still the same granny frames that had once been popular in her days at Berkeley. I'd always liked her.

"I thought dead people were supposed to be peaceful," the dark-haired kid said.

I cut him a quick glance. He was paler than he'd been before. His blond sidekick appeared more green than white.

"First one?" I asked.

"We've been on calls before, Sheriff," the Indian boy said.

"I'm sure you have, but no one's been dead, have they?"

Both shook their heads so frantically their moppy haircuts flew over their eyes. Why did every kid want to look like a greasy, grimy rock star? I didn't see the appeal. But I wasn't a seventeen-year-old girl any longer. Thank God.

"What's the procedure for a death?" I asked.

"We need to have a doctor pronounce her."

"Here?"

"No. We take her to the hospital. Then she'll be DOA."

"Wouldn't it be easier to have someone pronounce her at the scene?"

"We'd have to call a doctor and wait for one to show. That's not a good idea, especially when a lot of times the families are watching and wailing."

"Speaking of—" I glanced around the empty house. "Who called you?"

The blond kid found his voice. "Neighbor. Said she heard shrieking last night but thought it was the wind from the storm. This morning Ms. Garsdale didn't show for coffee like she usually does, and when the neighbor knocked, no one answered, so she used her key and—" He spread his hands.

"The neighbor said she heard shrieking?" I asked.

Blondie nodded.

I stared at Ms. G. She'd never been the shrieking type, and if she'd died while reclining on her couch, what was there to shriek about?

"Which neighbor?" I asked. "North or south?"

"North," the two said as one.

"Don't move her," I ordered. "In fact, don't touch anything. Go back to your ambulance and play games on your cell phones until I tell you to do otherwise."

Their eyes widened, but they did as I told them.

I recognized the woman next door immediately. "Ms. Champion," I greeted. "Can I ask you a few questions?"

Without a word, she opened the door wider and stepped back.

Ms. Champion and Ms. Garsdale had been friends forever. They'd met at Berkeley and taken jobs in Lake Bluff the same year. Ms. C. had taught music.

Since they'd never married and they'd bought houses right next to each other, a lot of gossips whispered the *l* word. I suspected if neither Claire nor I had married, the same would have been whispered about us in a few years. Such was the way of things in small towns. I wouldn't have cared, and I never noticed Ms. C. or Ms. G. giving a shit, either.

Ms. Champion motioned me to a seat on her couch. She took a chair on the other side of the coffee table. She still wore her robe and slippers. Her hair was as short as Ms. G.'s was long and as black as Ms. G.'s was white.

"Can you tell me what happened?" I asked. Ms. C. seemed shaken, and I couldn't blame her. The average Josephine didn't often see dead people.

"She didn't come this morning. I figured she'd overslept, so I went over."

"Did she often oversleep?"

Ms. C. nodded. "She'd stay up late and watch shows, then fall asleep on her couch."

Which appeared to be what had happened, except—

"Did you turn off the TV?"

Ms. C.'s bright blue eyes jerked to mine and she frowned. "No. It wasn't on."

"You heard something last night?"

Her frown deepened. "Terrible shrieking. Like something was dying right outside my house. I had to put my hands over my ears, it was so awful."

Bing!

If I were a cartoon, there'd be a lightbulb blinking

over my head. The shower of sparks, the horrible sound, the fire that wasn't.

"What time was this?" I asked.

"I'm not sure. My electricity was out."

Which could explain Ms. G.'s turned-off TV.

"Probably three A.M. or thereabouts," Ms. C. continued.

Which was a lot later than I'd heard the sound, but who was to say Ms. C. could remember the day of the week, let alone what time it had been when she'd heard something in the middle of a storm without benefit of a clock?

"You didn't think the shrieking might be coming from Ms. G.'s place?"

She shook her head. "Marion never raised her voice."

I didn't want to point out that she might have if she was being attacked. Why upset the woman any more than she was already?

"The door was locked when you got there?"

"Of course." She straightened, appearing concerned. "Not that Lake Bluff isn't safe, Grace. I mean Sheriff."

I waved my hand. Ms. C. had been around since long before I wore diapers, let alone a sheriff's uniform.

"Okay, thanks." I stood, held out my hand, and she took it. But instead of shaking, she sandwiched mine between both of hers. Her skin was paper-thin, soft, and mapped with roads of blue.

"I'll be fine," she said. "I'd resigned myself to losing her soon."

"What?"

"When she had the diagnosis, I was upset, but I had time to make my peace."

"I don't understand."

"Marion had congestive heart failure. The doctors

didn't give her long, although she'd been doing so
well . . ." She spread her hands. "I'm glad she went in
her own home in relative peace."

There went whatever theory I'd had about the
shrieking being connected to some unidentifiable monster that was killing little old ladies.

I returned to Ms. G.'s house. Just to cover all my
bases, I walked around the yard, and didn't find a single track. Big shock with all the rain.

Then I checked every window—locked, with no
sign of forced entry—and I did the same for the doors.
Beyond Ms. G. being dead, nothing was out of place—
neither outside nor in.

I should have been happy that she'd gone to her reward without any help, but I had a funny feeling, and
I'd learned long ago that my funny feelings were often
premonitions.

7

B ACK AT MS. G.'s I discovered Ian Walker bending over the corpse as the two baby paramedics looked on.

"What are you doing here?" I demanded, even though his stethoscope made it fairly obvious.

"Pronouncing her," he said. "Now she can go directly to the funeral home instead of making a detour to the hospital."

I scowled at the boys. "What did I tell you?"

"But he's a doctor," Blondie said.

"I'm the sheriff. What I say wins." I cast Walker a quick glance, but he was still messing with Ms. G. "The jury's still out on if he's really a doctor."

That made him glance up, but instead of being angry or even annoyed, he appeared amused. "Oh, I'm a doctor all right."

"I'm just supposed to take your word for it?"

"Sheriff, I'm sure you've checked my credentials, or

had one of your underlings do it. If you don't have my
info yet, you will soon. If I'm lying, you'll arrest me.
Since I've got better things to do than sit in a cell, believe me when I say I have a medical license and I
know how to use it."

"Just because you were certified as a doctor in Oklahoma doesn't make you one here."

"I'm a doctor everywhere, regardless of if I'm licensed in that particular state or not."

I narrowed my eyes. "You're not licensed?"

"I didn't say that."

I'd had enough. Not only was the scent of him reminding me of the kiss we'd shared, but it also was
making me want to kiss him all over again.

"You two go play cell phone." I jerked my thumb toward the door, and the kids left.

I had a shoulder mike, which would raise Cal quickly,
but what I had to ask him I didn't want everyone else to
hear, so I yanked my own cell phone off my belt, and
seconds later my deputy answered.

"I don't suppose you checked those credentials yet?"
I asked.

"Of course."

"And?"

"Top of his class at both places."

"His license to practice in Georgia?"

"Funny you should ask." I scowled at Walker, but he
didn't appear concerned. "He's got one."

"Why would that be funny?"

"His application was scooted through damn quick.
He must have friends in high places."

"Terrific," I muttered.

"What's the rush?"

"He's running around town pronouncing people. Wanted to make sure he was legal before I let him sign any death certificates."

"Who's dead?"

"Ms. G."

"Ah, hell," Cal muttered. "I liked her."

"Me, too." I disconnected, then contemplated Walker. "You're good."

I heard the words an instant too late and wanted to snatch them back before he made some sexual innuendo. But Walker wasn't the type. He merely contemplated me with an expression that said, *Told you so.*

"How did Ms. G. die?" I asked.

"I can't say for certain without an autopsy, but if I had to make a guess, I'd say it was her heart. Did she have a history of problems with it?"

He *was* good.

"Congestive heart failure, or so her friend next door told me."

He sighed as if I'd said something he expected but didn't much like. "Well, that would explain it."

"What about her face? She looks . . . scared."

Which was what I couldn't get past. Ms. G. had died at home in a way she'd been warned she might, yet her expression said otherwise, and that made all my nerve endings hum.

"She was alone," he said. "Probably in pain; she could have gone into shock. No matter how prepared we might think we are, when the time comes, we aren't."

Walker moved back to the couch, brushing his hand over Ms. G.'s eyes and chanting a short, quick chant in Cherokee. When he turned, his face appeared drawn. But why would he be upset over the death of an elderly woman who'd lived a full life, one he hadn't even known when she was alive?

"You okay?" I asked.

"Yeah." He rubbed his forehead. "Why wouldn't I be?"

"You seem upset."

"Death pisses me off."

"You can't win them all, especially when you weren't even her doctor."

"I know. It's just—" He shrugged.

Walker was a mystery. He seemed to mourn Ms. G.'s passing with a sorrow that mirrored my own. Although I was no longer completely suspicious of him, I *was* totally curious.

"What did you say?" I waved at Ms. G. "The chant?"

"The Cherokee equivalent of last rites."

"She's not Cherokee." Or Catholic.

"Doesn't matter. I told her spirit to go to Usûñhǐ' yi."

"Translation?"

His lips curved, reminding me of how they'd tasted on mine. "The Darkening Land in the West."

"Where the spirits go after death."

"You do know something."

My eyes narrowed. "There's no need to get snotty."

"You can, but I can't?"

"Now you're catching on. Why would you send a little old white lady's spirit to the Darkening Land?"

"You don't want her hanging around here, do you?" I snorted, and his head tilted, making the eagle feather swing free. "You don't believe spirits can come back from Tsûsginâ'ǐ?"

"Hard to say when I don't know what Tsûsginâ'ǐ is."

"The ghost country."

Something in my expression must have revealed my skepticism.

"You don't believe in Heaven? No Hell below us, above us only sky?"

"A John Lennon fan," I murmured. "Imagine. You have a lot of strange beliefs for a man of science."

"And you have a strange lack of belief for a descendant of Rose Scott."

"I didn't say I didn't believe in Heaven, even though I've seen no evidence of it."

"Belief in something for which there's no evidence is called faith, Sheriff."

"So I hear."

I *did* believe in things I had no proof of.

Werewolves, for instance.

8

I FINALLY MADE it to the Cartwrights' around noon.
The day, as usual, got away from me.

I tapped on the front door, unwilling to ring the bell
for fear I'd wake Noah from his nap. Then I heard
voices in the backyard, so I skirted the wide veranda
and found Malachi pushing Noah in his red plastic
baby swing. For a minute I just stood at the corner of
the house and watched.

Mal had the dark hair, dark eyes, and bronzed skin
of his Gypsy heritage. Combined with the brogue of
Ireland, a place he'd once called home, he'd been a
lethal combination of looks, charm, and danger. Claire
hadn't stood a chance.

He'd come to town searching for a way to break a
curse of immortality and found it in her. He'd also
found love and a family.

Since last summer, Mal had cut his hair and removed the earring from his ear, but he still stood out

as a stranger in Lake Bluff, though folks had accepted him for Claire's sake.

My gaze turned to Noah. The kid was only two months old; I don't know why I had such an incredible crush on him. Could be because he was too young to run out on me.

Today a tiny Braves baseball cap covered his bright red hair. His blue eyes were scrunched up as he did his best to keep his gaze focused on his father's face.

"Will ye be fallin' asleep soon, son? You've worn me out, and the day's not half yet gone."

The light shone so brightly it hurt my eyes, typical of the day after a horrific storm. It was almost as if the sun had to prove itself stronger than the wind and the rain and the moon.

"I can take over," I said.

Noah kicked his bare feet at the sound of my voice and gurgled. Mal didn't even turn around. He'd been aware I was there from the moment I'd set foot on their front walk. In truth, he'd probably known I was coming for a visit before I did.

In the Gypsy tradition only the women had the gift of sight; however, Mal had a few gifts of his own. According to him, those who possessed the pure blood of the Rom—the name the Gypsies called themselves—were magic.

I'd witnessed a few parlor tricks—appearing and disappearing coins—as well as a near-supernatural ability with animals and, according to Claire, a very convincing knowledge of things yet to come.

I moved forward, taking Mal's place behind the swing. Noah's eyes followed me, and he kicked harder as I got closer. His father sat in the grass and stretched out with his hands behind his head.

Mal and I hadn't gotten on at first; I'd known he was up to something. But in the end, he'd sacrificed everything for Claire, earning not only my thanks but also my friendship.

"I heard you saw a wolf last night," he said.

"I'm not sure what I saw. Any tingles on your end?"

"I haven't had a vision, if that's what you're askin'."

"I don't know what I'm asking. Claire tells me you know things. I've seen how you are with animals." I shrugged, then gave Noah another soft push. His head was beginning to sag against the headrest. Nap time would soon be at hand. I could use a nap myself.

"I've had dreams that come true, but I've had just as many dreams that didn't. Since I stopped living as a Gypsy, the ability's fading." He held out his hands as if he wasn't sure what to do with them. "I dinna mind. The magic for me now is in Noah and Claire."

I smiled, leaned over, and kissed Noah's sweet cheek. He murmured sleepily. "Well, if anything comes to you—"

"I'll call."

"Thanks."

"I don't suppose you've contacted the *Jäger-Suchers*?"

I paused. That hadn't occurred to me.

Last summer the *Jäger-Suchers,* translation "Hunter-Searchers," a Special Forces monster-hunting unit, had come to town. We wouldn't have even known they were there, as they'd planned to slip in, shoot the werewolves, then slip out again unnoticed—their modus operandi—but things had gotten more complicated, and they'd been forced to reveal themselves.

I knew that the *Jäger-Suchers* had resources beyond anything a small-town sheriff might. I still didn't want to call them when I wasn't exactly sure if anything supernatural was going on.

"I think I'll wait," I said.

"Wait too long and they'll just show up and take over."

"Like they won't do that anyway," I muttered. The *Jäger-Suchers* had a lot in common with the FBI when it came to sharing cases. They didn't.

A shadow passed over the yard, and I glanced up just as a great bird seemed to sail through the rays of the sun. Something tumbled out of the sky, sifting slowly downward on the current. Mal snatched the feather from the air before it got anywhere near the ground. "I didn't think you had any eagles here."

I stared at the feather, white with a dark tip. I couldn't recall the last time I'd seen one, and now I'd seen two in as many days.

"We don't," I answered. "Not really. They live in the south, though sometimes, in the winter, they'll travel to the mountains."

"Mmm," Malachi said, twirling the feather around in his nimble fingers.

"What do you think it means?" I asked.

His eyes met mine. "There's an eagle where one isn't supposed to be. What do you think it means, Grace?"

In the lives of most women, that would mean a bird whose sense of direction was on the fritz. In mine it meant the very real possibility of a shape-shifter.

"Hell," I muttered. I was going to have to call the *Jäger-Suchers*.

I headed to my office, trying to figure out a way to avoid the inevitable. The only thing I knew about shape-shifters was that touching some of them in human form with silver caused a nasty burn, and if you shot them with a silver bullet, whether they were on two legs or four, great balls of fire were the result.

Some of them, but not all. An unpleasant fact we'd learned the hard way last summer. Those cursed to shape-shift, rather than having been turned by another shifter, followed different rules depending upon the nature of the curse. However, it wouldn't hurt to try the silver test; it was all that I had.

Since the only new person in town was conveniently the same person I'd seen step out of the woods after the wolf had gone in, *and* he was the same person who'd shown up in town wearing an eagle feather in his hair, *and* he was a self-admitted member of a clan of medicine men, I had a pretty good idea where to start.

"Is he an eagle or a wolf?" I murmured. Did it really matter?

What good was a were-eagle anyway? I could see the advantage of a werewolf—faster, smarter, stronger, they had the abilities of wolves, with the addition of human intelligence and a lack of human compassion. Werewolves were the perfect killing machines.

So if a man became an eagle, he'd theoretically have human intelligence with the abilities of a bird. Big deal. Sure the eagle was considered a great and terrible war beast by most Native American tribes, mine included. But that basically meant eagles could kick the crap out of every other bird on the planet. Humans? Not so much. What then was the advantage?

I guess I'd just have to pin one down and ask him.

Unfortunately, it appeared that everyone else in town had the same idea—not that Walker was a werewolf or even a were-eagle, but that they wanted to meet him, talk to him, welcome him to the neighborhood. His storefront was packed.

I approached the nearest loiterer, a member of the town council and former bank president, Hoyt Abernathy. "What's up?"

Hoyt shuffled his feet, clad as always in a pair of slippers. When Hoyt had retired from the bank, he'd made a dress-shoe bonfire and worn nothing but soft soles ever since. In my opinion, a fantastic idea.

"Folks heard about poor Ms. G.," he said, in a voice reminiscent of Eeyore on a very rainy day. To Hoyt everything was an indication of upcoming disaster. In a lot of cases, he was right.

"And?" I asked.

"They wanted to pay their respects, thank the new doctor."

"What did *he* do?"

"Helped out one of our own in her last hour of need."

"She was already dead when he got there," I pointed out.

Hoyt shrugged. I scowled at the sea of people in line ahead of me.

Though I wanted to march right in and toss a silver bullet at Walker's head, I was going to have to wait.

Probably a better idea to do this in a more private place anyway. What if he exploded on Center Street? How in hell would I explain that?

I'd do better to ask Walker over to my place tonight for a get-acquainted drink. After the kiss we'd shared, he'd probably think it an invitation, and if his reaction this morning was any indication, he'd turn me down—unless I went about asking him just right.

Sadly, since I'd been elected sheriff, I had no patience for bullshit, and I'd lost any social graces I'd once had. Although most people who knew me would argue that I'd never really had any. Maybe a note would be a better idea than letting my mouth run free.

I caught a glimpse of Walker beyond the crowd, his long dark hair a delicious contrast to his stuffy suit and tie, and the idea of my mouth running free took on a whole different meaning.

Why did I keep having these flashes of lust? The guy could be part wolf, part eagle, 100 percent monster.

Maybe that was the attraction. For years I hadn't felt a thing beyond a passing interest in any man from Lake Bluff, the same went for any of the tourists, but Walker, with all his secrets and contradictions and baggage, fascinated me.

I scribbled a note, then waded through the crowd making official noises. Unfortunately, by the time I got to the front of the line, everyone had gone silent, wondering why I was here. Walker was no help; he merely contemplated me with a slight curve to his lips and a lift of his brow.

"I . . . uh—" Hell. I couldn't exactly hand him the note like a ten-year-old with a crush on the new kid, and I couldn't ask him over to my place tonight without the same problem.

"Thank you for your help today." I held out my hand. He took it, and I pressed the note into his palm.

Not even a flicker passed over his face when the paper transferred between us. No doubt he'd had this happen to him before, which only embarrassed me more.

"You're welcome." Ian released my hand and casually put his into the pocket of his pants.

I turned away, nodding at the townsfolk, noticing people from every walk of life—old, young, rich, poor, white, black, and Indian—although the majority had to be twentysomething single women. A new man in town, they couldn't help themselves. They probably thought I couldn't, either.

I was not a desperate old maid hitting on the new young stud. I *wasn't*. I'd invited him to my house to figure out what he was.

Man or beast? Human or monster? What if he came to my place in animal form?

I gave a mental shrug. That would only make it easier to shoot him. Because, despite my tough exterior, my determination to keep Lake Bluff safe from anything that might threaten it, I still wasn't certain I could put a silver bullet in a man just to be sure.

The rest of the day was full of both the mundane tasks of a small-town sheriff and the atypical happenings that came with tourists and the aftermath of a hellish storm.

I mediated a dispute between two neighbors over dog poop—they both had dogs; how in hell did they know that each other's pet was pooping in the opposite yard, and what possible difference could it make?

I had a case of shoplifting (local kid), a case of bullying (a tourist), and four calls from former residents whose loved ones weren't answering their phones after the storm.

I arrived home with an hour to spare before the appointed time with Walker—if he showed up. No messages on my machine telling me anything one way or another.

I was hot and sticky, compliments of a scalding day in Georgia and a lack of air-conditioning in my dad's old pickup. I smelled bad courtesy of both, as well as the little girl from Michigan who'd gotten lost, eaten too much ice cream, cried bloody murder, then upchucked on the front of my uniform.

The shower was heaven. I washed twice with scented soap and worked conditioner into my hair all the way to the ends; then I stood under the lukewarm spray and let my blood settle.

I opted for a loose white cotton skirt that fell to my ankles and an equally lightweight fuchsia top. I didn't bother with shoes—not after a day in cop boots. I had just enough time to walk to the water and stick in my feet.

I saw no reason to drag along my gun; the sun was still up, although I did tuck a bit of silver into my pocket for later. I planned an impromptu shape-shifter test.

As soon as I left the yard and the trees closed in behind me, I took a deep breath full of the scent of grass, leaves, and sun. I loved Lake Bluff, but here in the shadow of the mountains was where I truly lived.

Tiny animals scuttled in the bushes. Birds rustled in the trees. A snake slithered through the fallen leaves, hurrying away from me as fast as it could.

I reached the creek, lifted my skirt, and stepped in. The chill of the water on my tired feet was bliss. I wished I could throw off all my clothes and sink in as I had last night.

At the creek I felt the closest to E-li-si. When I went to the water, I could almost hear her speak. Under the moon and the stars, I missed her the least.

The sun tipped toward the horizon. Soon shadows would spread from the mountains through the trees, dappling everything with the approaching coolness of night. Dusk was my favorite time of the day. If I didn't spend it here at the water, I usually spent it on my porch just watching the evening come.

I glanced at my watch. Best be on the porch tonight. Best to get out of the woods before the sun died and the really dangerous things began to roam.

I turned and froze.

Like that wolf.

9

"S HIT," I MUTTERED.

The animal tilted its head, growling as if it understood the word and did not approve.

I took a step backward; my foot slipped on a flat slick rock, and I nearly fell. The wolf gave a sharp yip, but it didn't attack, just continued to stare at me, half in and half out of the underbrush.

I couldn't run, couldn't hide. The only weapon I had was the silver bullet. Fat lot of good it would do me without a gun. I could toss the bit of metal at a person, and if they caught it and smoke began to pour from their hand, they were a shifter. However, the wolf was a little short on fingers for that test.

I hadn't thought I needed a gun before sundown. Frowning, I glanced at the sky, then back at the wolf. What the hell?

The sun was still up, and while I knew there were monsters that walked in the daytime, werewolves weren't one of them.

I peered at the wolf more closely. Black with silver threads in its fur. Long, spindly legs. Dark, dark eyes, with not a hint of white.

Just a wolf.

I sighed with relief, although there was still the issue of a wild animal choosing to come near me—not something a healthy wild animal would do—and the strangeness of this thing being here in the first place.

"Nice doggy," I murmured.

The wolf snorted. I could swear the animal understood me.

"I don't suppose you want to turn tail and run away from the big bad sheriff."

The wolf blinked once but didn't move.

"That's what I figured."

I cast my gaze around for some kind of weapon. Plenty of big rocks, but I'd never been much of a softball player. To hit the thing, I'd have to get much closer than I wanted to.

I spied a long branch—thick enough to do some damage—and slowly lowered myself until I could pick it up. The beast's upper lip curled.

"I won't hurt you if you don't hurt me," I said.

The animal charged.

Despite my lack of talent with a ball and bat, I hauled back and swung away. Not only did the branch pass right through the wolf, but the wolf passed right through me also.

For an instant I stood there gaping, shivering at the sudden chill; then I spun around. The animal sat placidly behind me, tongue lolling.

I couldn't see the grass through its body, nor the creek on the other side. The wolf seemed solid.

I poked at it with the stick. The end swept right

through its body. The animal lifted a paw and swatted at the branch, leg swooshing from one side of the stick to the other with no resistance.

"What are you?" I whispered.

The wolf cocked its head, staring at something behind me.

"I know that trick," I said. "I turn, and you jump me." Or maybe I should say *jump through me*.

"Can we have a drink first?"

I spun around despite my resolve not to. Ian Walker stood at the edge of the trees.

"I was talking to—" I glanced at the wolf, which was, of course, gone.

I didn't bother to check for tracks. Been there, done that, saw the movie.

"I . . . uh—" That seemed to be the extent of my conversation around this man.

"Did the wolf come back?"

I glanced his way; he nodded at the club. I dropped it to the ground. "Did you see anything?"

"No. But you obviously did."

"Maybe." I looked around the empty clearing. "Then again, maybe not."

"You want to explain that?"

"Not really."

He moved forward, lifting one arm, which held a six-pack, and another, which held a bottle of wine. "I didn't know what you liked."

"Thanks. But I invited you—"

He shrugged. "My mother taught me never to arrive at anyone's home empty-handed."

"We can go back—"

"No. I mean, if it's all the same to you, I'd like to sit here. I don't get much chance to go to the water."

I started at the term, but why shouldn't he know it? Despite his light eyes and skin, he was Cherokee, too. Or so he said.

Walker leaned over and set the beer and the wine in the creek, then sat on the grass and took off his shoes. He'd changed from the suit he'd worn in town to a pair of jeans and a blue button-down shirt. The color only served to make his eyes glow eerily golden in the fading light.

The sharp crunch of a beer can being opened made me jump. Walker held one out to me. "I didn't bring a corkscrew," he said. "Or a glass."

"This is fine." I took the beer but hesitated at sitting next to him. I'd asked him here to see if he was a shape-shifter. I needed to do what I'd planned before I got too close.

"I—uh—found this," I said, and before I could change my mind, tossed the bullet at his head.

He snatched the lump of silver out of the air before it hit him between the eyes. After shooting me a puzzled glance, he opened his palm and stared at the metal. No smoke rose from his burning flesh. *Yippee.*

"Strange bullet," he mused. "You find this out here?"

"Yeah," I lied.

"Huh." He put it into his pocket and took a swig of beer. "Thanks."

I blinked. I hadn't meant for him to keep the bullet, but I guess it didn't really matter. I had a hundred more just the same.

"You going to have a seat?" He tilted his head. "Or make me get a crick in my neck talking to you."

"Sure. I mean no." What was it about this guy that turned me into a gibbering idiot? I began to sit next to him, and he jumped to his feet.

"Wait." He yanked off his shirt and spread it on the ground. "You can't sit here in a white skirt."

I tried not to stare at his chest, but it was a really great chest. Ridges and dips, smooth, flawless, the dark circles of his nipples like melted caramel against the paler skin. I fought back a groan—two years of celibacy—then took a quick sip of beer to stop the drool from running down my chin.

"Grace?" He patted his shirt, which was far too close to him for my comfort.

I smiled, set my beer down, then pulled the shirt farther away under the guise of smoothing it. However, when I sat, he merely scooted closer, tilting his can toward me. "Cheers," he said.

I grabbed mine, clinking it against his a little too hard, so that beer sloshed onto my wrist. I licked it off, caught him watching my mouth, and stopped. Silence that wasn't really silence descended. In it I heard all sorts of things.

Want me. Kiss me. Do me.

"I was surprised you came," I blurted, then bit my lip at the dual meaning to the sentence. Why did everything have to remind me of sex around him?

Luckily, he didn't have the same problem, because he answered with an easy curve to his lips. "If you didn't think I'd show, why did you ask?"

I'd asked Walker here to test him for shape-shifting, but I couldn't exactly say that. "I—I'm not sure."

"Are you uncomfortable?"

"What?" *Yes.* "Why?"

"The wolf. We'd discussed it being rabid."

Oh, the wolf. Right.

"I don't think it is," I said. I wasn't sure what the beast was, but "rabid" wasn't on the list anymore.

"They say the wolf is a messenger from the spirit world," he murmured.

I started again, sloshing beer, *again*. This time I left the spill where it was.

"Why would you bring that up?"

"A wolf that appears and disappears in a place no wolf should be. Don't tell me you hadn't thought of it yourself."

I hadn't. Until now.

The wolf wasn't a shifter—or at least not any kind of shifter I knew about—so maybe it *was* a messenger. Since I was the only one who'd seen the thing, I had to think the message was for me.

"What do you know about messenger wolves?" I asked.

"Only what the legends say."

"Which is?"

"Your great-grandmother never told you?" I shook my head and he frowned. "What *did* she tell you?"

"Family stuff mostly."

Since my mother had taken off and my grandmother died before I was born, Rose had been concerned that the family history would die with her. Unfortunately, all that time spent on who was related to whom had left precious little for lessons in language and mysticism, even if I'd been open to them.

"This is what the old men told me when I was a boy," Walker began. "When someone from the Darkening Land must commune with those still of this world, a messenger wolf is sent from the west."

I glanced at the trees where the animal had appeared. Yep, west all right.

"To the Cherokee the wolf is sacred," Walker continued. "He is not to be killed for fear we might extinguish."

"I never heard that."

"Have you ever killed a wolf?"

"Not yet." I paused, thinking. "How would you kill a spirit wolf anyway?"

"I always figured the messengers were actual wolves," he said, "hence the taboo on killing them. Unless you're a wolf killer."

"Is that like an eagle killer?" My gaze rested on his feather.

"Exactly."

In Cherokee tradition, only certain people could kill an eagle—those who'd been trained in the method and the prayers that would allow such a great warrior bird to be taken without having a curse fall on the hunter and all his descendants. I'd heard the same rules applied to wolves—kill one and be cursed forever, along with your children.

"Are you an eagle killer?" I asked.

Though the title was one of honor, the words sounded more like a taunt. I hadn't meant for them to.

"I'm not," he said.

"You know only great warriors are supposed to wear the feather of an eagle?"

He turned away, resting his gaze on the slowly falling sun. "I know," he whispered.

I meant to ask what he'd done to be considered a warrior, but when he faced away he presented me with his back, and I saw the tattoo.

High up on his left shoulder blade flew the image of an eagle, talons outstretched as it swooped down on unsuspecting prey. I'd never known a Cherokee to have a tattoo. Slowly I reached out and touched it.

He moved so fast I didn't have time to draw back, let alone get away. The beer I'd been holding fell to the ground, tipped over, and melted into the grass. My hand was left hanging in the air where his shoulder had been; his fingers closed around my wrist.

"What—?" was all I managed before he kissed me.

I didn't fight; I didn't want to. His mouth was already familiar, his taste one I already craved. The air hummed with awareness, or maybe just cicadas.

His tongue tasted of beer, not unpleasant considering the heat and my thirst. I licked the inside of his mouth. His lips were cool; I wanted them to touch me everywhere.

Wait. There was a reason I shouldn't be doing this.

I tugged on my wrist; he let me go, his mouth stilling on mine as our breath mingled. Instead of pulling myself away, pushing him away, I let my hand trail over his beautiful skin, down his belly around to his back, then up to his shoulder. My finger worried the area of the tattoo—it felt almost feverish—so much so that I remembered everything I should never forget.

Sometimes people weren't people all of the time.

A shadow passed over the dying sun. An eagle lazily circled the creek. And if the eagle was up there and Walker was right here—

Well, there could be two, but since there weren't even supposed to be any . . .

My mind filled with all sorts of interesting codas to that sentence, even as my libido screamed for the only one that mattered—*forget about shape-shifters and kiss him again*—still, I hesitated.

Earlier a simple embrace had sent him to a darkened room where he had mourned next to a picture of his lost wife. I didn't want to upset him further, but I also believed that he needed to move on. Probably because I wanted him to move on to me.

I stood, and Walker eyed me warily, as if he thought I would stomp my feet and order him to leave in my best Scarlett O'Hara voice. I might be Cherokee, but I was also Scottish and Southern. I could Scarlett with the best of them.

Instead, I pulled off my shirt, my skirt, my underwear; then I held out a hand for his. "You say you never get to go to the water?"

He shook his head mutely, his gaze wandering from my thick dark hair tumbling over my breasts to my waist, past where other thick dark hair swirled, all the way to my toes, which wiggled in the steadily cooling grass.

Mist tumbled from the mountains, skating across the tops of the trees, reflecting every shade of sunset. Soon it would settle over the water, going silver along with the moon. I wanted to bathe in that mist, sink into the creek, as Walker sank into me.

I flexed my fingers, and spellbound, he put his hand into mine.

10

H<small>E WOULD HAVE</small> walked into the water still wearing his pants if I hadn't stopped him with a hand on his chest. The heat of his skin distracted me, the smoothness of it beneath my own, and I lifted both arms, running my palms across his pecs, over his shoulders, down his biceps.

The scent of him mingled with the scent of the trees, the mist, the water. I had to taste him or die, so I put my mouth where my hands had been, running my tongue from his collarbone to his nipple, then tracing the line of his ribs.

His fingers clenched in my hair, not pulling me away but holding me close. Slowly I straightened, cupping him through the thick material of his jeans, sliding my thumbnail down the zipper until he moaned.

"The water," he said almost desperately.

"We'll get there." I flicked open his jeans and reached inside.

Hard and hot, thick and full, he pulsed against me. "Grace, I haven't—"

I squeezed him once and he came, spurting against my belly. "You have," I murmured, continuing to work him in my fist.

His face was beautiful in the fading light, his profile harsh yet familiar, eyes closed, mouth slightly open and relaxed. Leaning up, I brushed my lips against his, and his eyes opened, staring straight into mine. "I'm sorry," he whispered.

"I'm not." I'd followed my instincts, and they'd been right. He hadn't done this in so long, he had no control. Now he would.

I waded in until the water reached my waist, then turned and waited for him. He stood on the bank, staring at me as if I were a water nymph emerging from the depths.

As I did every time I came to the water, I lifted my hands to the moon and said the words of my great-grandmother. When I lowered my arms, he still watched me.

"There is another world beneath our own," he said. "It's like this one in every way, except the seasons are opposite. Which is why the moving waters are warmer in winter and colder in summer than the air."

I smiled, enjoying the way he told the tales he'd heard from the old ones whenever something reminded him of them.

"To reach the other place we walk the trails of the springs that come down the mountains. The doorway lies at their head where we can slide in and the beings there can slide out. You're so beautiful, Grace, you seem from that other world."

I shook my head, and my hair skated across the surface of the water, tossing droplets every which way.

As a child I'd been stared at and pointed at so much that by the time I'd grown into my legs, my mouth, my nose and teeth, I no longer believed I was anything but strange.

"I'm cold," I said, as my nipples tightened, and my body seemed to come alive in a rush of blood just beneath my skin. "Warm me."

Ian stepped into the creek and immediately went below the surface, bobbing up, then dunking himself again. Once, twice, he kept at it until he'd doused himself seven times. Most every Cherokee ritual involved the sacred number seven.

At last he burst from beneath and stayed there. "Before you come to the water you should fast." He cast his eyes to the rising moon. "The ritual is performed at daybreak."

I reached out and pulled him closer. "Forget about the old ways for a minute."

I slipped my arms around his waist and licked a cool drop from his hot skin. At first I thought steam rose from his body, until I realized the mist skimmed across the surface of the creek like a snake, swirling around and over us.

"Grace," he began. "I haven't been with anyone . . ."

His voice faded, and his face darkened. He stiffened as if he might pull away, and I kissed him. Open-mouthed, lots of tongue, as I gripped his biceps and poured all that I wanted, all that I needed, into this single embrace.

He hadn't been with anyone but his wife—maybe ever, but considering his reaction to just the sight of my body, the touch of my hand, definitely since he'd lost her.

Walker was a naked man in the water with a naked woman. Eventually he kissed me back. He didn't stand much of a chance.

I believed he needed to connect with someone; I certainly needed to, and not in a nudge-nudge, whisper, snicker, connect-with-me-baby kind of way. I needed a *connection*, the sharing of bodies, some kindness and awareness in a world where there's so very little.

If, in some tiny corner of my mind, I thought, *Maybe he's the one, the one who won't leave,* I didn't know it then. Then all I knew was the taste of his mouth, the sleek, wet expanse of his skin, the scent of the water and the wind and the night. We both belonged right here, right now, with each other. I'd worry about later . . . later.

His hands raced over my body, slipping, sliding both above and below the water; the sensation of his hot flesh and the cool creek, his slightly roughened fingers on skin that hadn't been roughened at all, made me moan. He traced a palm over my hip and swooped up, cupping one breast, then the other, before scraping his thumbnail over each peak.

My head fell back, my eyes half-open so I could watch his head descend and his lips close over me. His tongue pressed my nipple against the roof of his mouth, suckling me as one finger dipped below the surface of the water and stroked.

The moon was satin on my cheeks, his mouth like silk. The lap of the creek, the pressure of his hand, I came apart in his arms just as he'd come apart in mine. He held me as I gasped, and pressed soft kisses across my chin, even as his fingers drew out the magic.

I lifted my head and met his eyes. "Sorry," I said, and he smiled, hearing the echo of himself.

"That was . . ." He paused, uncertain.

"Amazing? Astounding? Fantastic?"

"Yes."

"How about one more?" I headed downstream, tugging him along after me.

"Life-altering? Mind-boggling? Mood-shifting?"

I glanced over my shoulder, smiling at the happiness on his face. Until now, he'd only looked sad.

"When I said, 'How about one more?' I didn't mean an adjective."

The water deepened until it was over our heads. I dropped his hand and began to swim.

"What did you mean?"

He swam, too, following me around the bend and into the secluded cove where the water remained warm nearly the whole year through. I don't know if an underground spring fed the pond or if the smaller, somewhat enclosed area held the heat of the sun longer than the moving length of the creek. Either way, this was my secret place. I'd never brought anyone here, not even Claire.

At the center, I let my feet drift to the soft bottom, then rose into the moon-shrouded air like a mermaid. The water lapped at my rib cage. Droplets shone like pearls on my skin.

"I meant, how about one more?"

"Oh!" He dragged his gaze from my chest to my face. "Yes."

I floated across the few feet separating us, stopping when I was so close my breasts brushed his chest. Then I bobbed up once and sank beneath the surface.

11

"GRACE!" HE GRABBED at me, but I was too quick. As soon as my mouth closed around him, he understood I'd meant to submerge.

I could hold my breath for a very long time, even without the added incentive. The water was warm, welcoming. Beneath the surface everything was dark.

He was already hard; I wasn't surprised. Even though I'd taken the edge off earlier, he was still a desperate man. I'd never known I had a thing for desperation until I'd tasted it in him.

Lazily I ran my tongue along his length, then drew him deep within. The swirl of water past my face revealed movement even before his hand cupped my head, showing me the rhythm. In and out he pumped against my lips. Long before I was ready, he urged me upward. I shook my head, suckling him hard, grazing him with my teeth before I gave in and burst from the water.

His hands found my arms; he dragged me against

him, the poke of his erection insistent. He tasted of need. I wrapped myself around him and held on.

He fell back, taking me with him, and side by side we floated, kissing, touching, arousing. My shoulders bumped against the mossy bank, and I twirled with the current until he was braced against it, then slid up his body until we were face-to-face. His hands spanned my waist; my legs opened, then closed around him.

He seemed to know my body better than, or at least as well as, I did, slowing, shifting, taking the pressure away from one place and applying it to another.

His lips traveled everywhere, first soft, then hard, a nip of the teeth, a stroke of the tongue, just enough, not too much. There, yes there. Again.

I wanted the release; I begged for it, too. He made me wait, nearly gave it to me, then made me wait some more. The moon shone, round and impossibly white on my upturned face as I rode him, desperately seeking something.

His body convulsed, triggering an answering convulsion in mine. The sharp, hot puff of his breath against the damp skin of my breasts made my nipples tighten, the reaction echoing in the deepest part of me.

In the aftermath, I lay draped over him. He was strong; he kept us both above water. The warmth, the gentle lap of the waves that slid into the cove from the moving creek, lulled me. I almost fell asleep.

"Is this where you bring all the guys?" he murmured.

I stiffened, lifted my head, and met his curious eyes. I could see how he'd think that. We'd only just met and now we were naked. Maybe I *was* a slut, but most men had the sense not to say so.

"You're the first."

He frowned. "I don't think so."

"Ass." I shoved myself off him, scooting backward in the water. "I didn't mean first, first. I meant first person I've ever brought here. This place is special, but you, Doctor, are not." I began to swim home.

He caught me before I reached the colder, faster rushing water of the creek, grabbing me around the waist and hoisting me against him. I struggled, but he was bigger, stronger, more determined than me.

"Hey," he murmured, putting his forehead against mine. "I'm sorry. That was . . . stupid."

"You think?" I kicked him in the shin. Since I had no leverage and the water dulled the blow, it was a childish gesture, but I felt better.

"I'm sorry," he said again. "I'm no good at this."

"What? Speech? Social niceties? Tact?"

"All of them. Since my wife—" He sighed, his chest rising and falling against my own. "I haven't been with anyone and I've never been very good at keeping what's in my head from shooting out of my mouth. I like you and I didn't want—" He broke off. "I'm making a bigger mess of this now than before, aren't I?"

"I don't think that's possible." I pushed against his chest, and this time he let me go. "Listen, I don't sleep around. This is a really small town, and it's bad for business." I shoved my hand through my dripping hair. "Sleep with a guy, he expects privileges."

"What kind of privileges?"

His face had hardened, his biceps, too, as his hands curled into fists. I found myself charmed by his defense of me, as well as the flex and flow of his muscles. God, I was pathetic.

"Fixed parking tickets. Free rein to speed wherever and whenever. Leniency for all his kith and kin."

"Seriously?"

"Seriously."

"I can see why you'd be leery. So why me?"

I didn't want to explain about two years of celibacy, exacerbated by the way he smelled, the way he looked, how he'd made me feel when he'd touched me. I was pitiful, but I didn't want him to know that.

I let my gaze wander from the top of his sodden feather to where his spectacular chest disappeared into the water. "Why not you?"

"You don't think I'll ask for favors?"

I tilted my head. "Will you?"

"No."

"We're adults," I said. "We both needed the release. We can just leave it at that and go back to being . . ." I spread my hands. "Whatever."

"You think I can go back to being *whatever* with you, after this?"

I held my breath. I so didn't want to go back to being "whatever" with him, but I'd had too many years of being the one left behind, even figuratively, to put myself on the line like that ever again.

I thought about the guys who had come before. Not a one of them had ever had a problem with a few days of sex and then never seeing me again. Of course none of them, for several years anyway, had lived in Lake Bluff. Not that any of the townies had had a problem calling it quits with me, either.

For that matter, neither had my mother. . . .

When I didn't answer, he made an aggravated sound. "I'm not a robot, Grace. If I share myself with someone, I do it for a reason."

"Sex."

"I'm not made that way."

"You're a guy. Don't tell me you haven't had meaningless sex and walked out the next morning."

"I didn't say that. But this wasn't meaningless and you know it."

I did, although I wasn't exactly sure what it was. Not love. But something a step above a quickie in the night.

Something swirled through the water near my hip. I jumped, thinking snake, until his hand slid into my own. "Why don't we see where this goes? We kind of went at things out of order, but what would you say to a date?"

My face must have revealed my confusion, because he continued with a laugh in his voice, if not his eyes. "You know, dinner, a movie, maybe a walk beneath the moon?"

"Sounds vaguely familiar."

"I thought it might. Tomorrow night?"

I nodded. I couldn't believe we were standing in my pond, discussing dinner and a movie while naked. Talk about back assward.

Walker stared up at the towering hills, navy blue against the indigo night. "I'd like to see Blood Mountain sometime. Have you been there?"

"Sure. My great-grandmother used to take me."

His gaze lowered. "Why?"

"It's beautiful. We had a picnic."

Waterfalls and hiking trails surrounded the peak. We'd eaten on the banks of Lake Winfield Scott. It was one of my fondest memories.

But we hadn't gone there just to eat in the sun. According to Grandma, Blood Mountain was sacred. Our ancestors had once worshipped it. On Blood Mountain the greatest of magic was born. She'd done some awesome things there, things I'd never told anyone about.

"The history books claim the mountain was named because of a battle between the Cherokee and the Creek."

"People still find arrowheads," I said. Though no one had been able to decide for certain what year the battle had occurred.

"The Cherokee won."

"Of course."

He smiled. "And the Creek gave them Blood Mountain. It's a holy place."

A spooky place, that's for sure. I'd often wondered if the blood that had been spilled there had turned the very earth and the air of that mountain into something otherworldly.

"Usually the Cherokee revere the highest point," Ian mused, "like Brasstown Bald, so it's odd they took such a shine to Blood Mountain."

"Not really," I muttered, thinking of the way the light hit the lichen and rhododendron, turning the mountain the shade of freshly spilled blood.

"What was that?"

"Nothing. It's a great place. Lots of hiking trails. Neat-o."

Ian lifted a brow. "I'll take your word for it."

A sudden and disturbing thought muscled into my head. "I left my phone at the house." The whole town could have gone up in flames while I'd been banging the new doctor. That would play great during the next election. "I have to go."

Ian tugged on my hand, and I paused, glancing at him. "You have every right to a life, Grace. That's one thing I learned—though a little too late for Susan."

"That was her name?"

He appeared startled he'd said it out loud. "Yes. I shouldn't talk about her so much."

"Yeah, you've been a real chatterbox on the subject."

"Feels like it."

"I don't mind, Ian. You obviously loved her; you lost her; you miss her."

"Obviously," he murmured, then dived into the creek and swam away.

⟨◯◯◯⟩

I offered Ian the use of my shower, but he seemed in a sudden hurry to leave.

His taillights disappeared down the drive; then the sound of his tires rolling faster and faster across the pavement of the highway that led to town drifted on the wind. Despite our supposed "date" tomorrow night, I wondered if I'd ever set eyes on him again.

I shrugged it off. I was used to seeing men's taillights. So why did it seem so much worse this time?

Because I'd felt something, just as he'd said. A kinship. Perhaps just the shared heritage and the interest in our past, maybe more. Did it matter? I had a full life—a busy job, a friend or two, a community. I didn't need Ian Walker any more than he needed me.

Inside, I checked all my phones and messages.

Relieved to find nothing that couldn't be handled tomorrow, I headed for the shower, but before I got there a slight scratch at the back door drew my attention.

I glanced out the window, didn't see anyone, shrugged, and turned away.

Yip.

My eyes narrowed as the scratching began again.

Not wanting to meet whatever was out there while I

was stark naked, I grabbed some jeans and a tank top from the clean pile atop the dryer, found my gun where I'd left it in the junk drawer, loaded it, and slowly opened the door.

The wolf sat right on my porch.

I tightened my finger on the trigger. The animal tilted its head, unconcerned. Since a stick had passed right through it, I had no doubt a bullet would do the same. I eased my finger away.

"What do you want?" I asked.

The beast tilted its head in the other direction. There was something about the eyes that disturbed me. They weren't human; they didn't seem crazed or evil, but they did seem familiar.

"Do I know you?"

Yip!

Swell, was it one yip for yes and two for no or the other way around?

The wolf got to its feet and my finger went back to the trigger. Spirit wolf or not, I didn't plan to let the thing jump me without trying to stop it.

However, the animal whirled and trotted down the steps, pausing at the bottom to peer over its shoulder at me as if waiting.

All I could do was stare. The wolf had passed right through me earlier, yet it was capable of scratching at the door. How could that be?

The beast ran a few feet toward the woods, then waited. I contemplated the Lassie-like behavior. "You want me to follow you?"

Yip.

I was starting to think one was for yes.

According to Ian, a wolf was a messenger from the spirit world. If so, I really wanted that message.

The animal whined, scratched at the ground, trotted to the tree line, then halfway back again.

"What the hell?" I slipped my feet into the sandals on the porch, shut the back door, and followed my messenger into the mountains.

12

THE WOLF LED me through thick towering spruce, so close together the silver light of the moon barely penetrated their branches. I glanced back, but the trees had already swallowed the white gabled roof of my house. I did see a few of the bats that I couldn't seem to oust from the attic flitting in front of the moon.

The night had cooled, but the air was muggy, hard to breathe, especially when we continued on for the better part of an hour.

I'd been this way before. My great-grandmother had lived at the foot of the mountain, preferring a remote cabin to putting up with my father, whom she'd never had much use for.

According to Rose, men were good for two things: providing children and hunting. Other than that, they could go to the Devil. I guess it was lucky for them both that my great-grandfather had died young. I didn't think Rose had ever been easy to live with.

At first I wondered if we were going to her cabin—maybe someone was squatting. Why such a minor offense would warrant a messenger from the Darkening Land I had no idea, but when I took a step in that direction the wolf growled and kept on what appeared to be a straight arrow to someplace else.

My mind began to wander. Where were we and why? What possible message could there be for me up here where the mist began?

The sudden silence made me pause. I looked ahead, to the side, even behind me, but the wolf was gone.

"Nice one, Grace." I rubbed my sweating palm against my thigh and took a better grip on the gun. This suddenly smelled very much like a trap.

The wind lifted my hair, which had dried once again into stiff-straight hanks, and slapped them against my face. The trees rattled like dry bones, and dead needles tumbled from the sky like spruce-scented rain.

The underbrush moved, first here, then there. Ah hell, everywhere. I turned a slow circle, searching the darkness, twitching at every slinking shadow.

Something flew across the moon—a bat, a bird, a beast? I glanced up, but it was already gone, and when I lowered my head a human-shaped silhouette emerged from the night.

An old woman, bent but still strong, her hair long and black, with strands of silver lit by the moon. Clothed in what appeared to be traditional Cherokee dress, a sleeveless shift made of deer hide, belted at the waist and ending at midthigh, complemented by a knitted underskirt with beaded fringe that fell to the ankles. Her feet were covered in soft moccasins to the knees.

I was again reminded of those who had disappeared into these mountains during the removal, hiding so well from the white soldiers that to this day no one had ever found them.

The woman lifted her head, and the outline of her face was familiar. "E-li-si?" I whispered. "Grandmother?"

"Gracie?"

The voice wasn't hers. How could it be?

"Quatie." I stowed the gun and hurried forward to help the woman who'd been my great-grandmother's best friend. "What are you doing out here in the dark?"

Quatie was a full-blooded Cherokee, very rare in this day and age. She'd lived in Lake Bluff her entire life, as had her mother and grandmother and great-grandmother before her. She knew every tree, every trail, every stream and hill. But she was old, arthritic, and half-blind.

I took her arm. She was thinner than I remembered and less steady on her feet than I liked.

"I could ask the same of you," she said.

My gaze flicked to the trees. "Did you see a wolf?"

Her laughter was more of a cackle before it turned into a long hacking cough. I supported her until she was able to straighten, then speak. "Messenger?"

I wasn't surprised that Quatie knew what a wolf meant. The surprise would be if she hadn't.

"What did she come to tell you?" Quatie asked.

"She?"

"Who would bother to come all the way back from the Darkening Land with a message for you?"

"E-li-si," I whispered.

Quatie patted me on the arm. "What did she say?"

"The wolf's supposed to talk?"

She shrugged. "I've never seen one."

"What do you know about them?"

"Only what my own grandmother told me. A messenger from the Darkening Land is not of this world. Once their message is delivered, they will return to the west. Until you understand the message, expect visits from your *e-li-si*."

Now that I had a hint of who the messenger was, I had a pretty good idea of the message.

The wolf had first appeared on the night of the Thunder Moon, when magic happened, and she had shown up not far from here. Grandma and Quatie had been friends. Quatie was obviously ill, fading. She needed help, and Grandma had come to make sure I gave it to her. She'd led me to Quatie and then disappeared. I doubted I'd see the wolf again.

Which was fine with me. Messenger wolves were spooky, even if they were Grandma in disguise. Too Little Red Riding Hood for my comfort.

"I'll walk you home," I said.

"No need, child. I come out here every night for a little exercise before bed."

I frowned. What if she fell and broke a hip? She could be on the ground for days, weeks, before anyone found her. We might not have wolves, but we had bears. They'd love to come across a crippled little old lady buffet in the forest.

"Don't you have any relatives who could stay with you?" Despite her protest, I walked with her in the direction of her cabin.

"Why would anyone want to stay with me out here?" She patted my arm again. "And I'm not leaving. The place belonged to my own great-grandmother. My children are in their seventies, their children in their fifties." She waved an arthritic hand as if to say, *And so on.* "No one wants to spend time with an old woman who has no indoor plumbing."

"I do," I said.

"No, you don't."

She appeared almost scared, or maybe just embarrassed. I was the one who should be embarrassed. My great-grandmother had asked me to check on Quatie, and I'd done a shit-poor job. No wonder my *e-li-si* had come from the Darkening Land in the guise of a wolf. I was lucky she hadn't ripped me limb from limb. If a spirit wolf even could.

We reached Quatie's cabin. Though the building lacked certain amenities, like plumbing and a furnace, it possessed a good foundation, a solid roof, and weathered log walls, which had been chinked recently. The place appeared cozy, friendly, warm.

I caught a whiff of tobacco. Had Quatie walked into the woods to smoke? Why, when she lived alone?

Perhaps she'd been performing a ritual. Many of the Cherokee spells involved blowing smoke to the four directions.

I didn't ask what she'd been doing. Some spells were secret, known only to the one who'd invented or inherited them. These were sacred and could be ruined just by talking about them.

The place was the same as I remembered—one room that served as a bedroom, sitting room, and kitchen. What more did Quatie really need? Scattered across every surface were papers scrawled dark with the Cherokee alphabet.

Quatie and my great-grandmother had always conversed in Cherokee and written everything that needed to be written the same. They'd both been terrified that the language would be lost.

"Quatie, could you teach me Cherokee?" I blurted.

That would kill two birds with one stone; I'd learn the language and I'd be able to keep an eye on her.

"No, Gracie."

I blinked, stunned. I hadn't expected her to refuse.

"My eyes are going. I can barely read the books. My hand shakes too much to write anymore, and I'm just too tired and impatient to teach."

"Oh," I said, my voice faint with disappointment.

"You know more than you think. From the day you were born, Rose spoke to you in our language. If you let yourself, you will remember."

I had my doubts, but I nodded anyway.

"I'd better get back," I said. "Let you sleep."

"I don't sleep much anymore, but I think I will lie down. That walk nearly did me in."

"Maybe you should take it a little easier. What if you fell out there?"

"Then I fall."

"And if you fall and die?"

"Better to die against the earth, beneath my brother the moon and a hundred thousand *năkwĭsĭs,* than to fade away hidden from the sun."

"Năkwĭsĭs," I said softly. "Stars."

"See? You do remember."

I wasn't sure if I remembered or if I'd just figured it out from the context. Regardless, I liked how knowing the word made me feel. As if I'd connected to my past and in doing so made possible a brighter future.

"You're taking good care of her papers, aren't you?" Quatie asked.

"Of course." They were irreplaceable—in both emotional value and ancient lore.

"They're in a safe place?"

"Very."

I thought of the false bottom in the right-hand drawer of my father's desk—the one I'd only learned about from his lawyer after he'd died. In it I'd found all the pictures of my mother that had disappeared soon after she'd died. Now the photos were in my bedroom and my great-grandmother's papers were in the drawer.

"I'll come back in a few days," I said. "Is there anything you'd like me to bring for you?"

"I hear there's a new doctor in town."

My eyebrows lifted. The gossip grapevine never ceased to amaze me. The proof of its far-reaching voice also soothed my guilt just a little. If Quatie was getting the news that quickly, then she was in contact with townsfolk other than me, and if there'd been anything seriously wrong up here, I'd have heard about it just as fast.

"There is a new doctor," I agreed.

"He knows the old ways?"

"So he says."

"I'd like to meet him."

"Are you ill?"

Quatie glanced up and her lips quirked. "Child, I'm *old*."

"You've never gone to a doctor before." Or at least I didn't think she had.

"Rose took care of me. Her cures were all I needed. But since she's been gone, I've just made do. I'd like to hear what this young man has to say."

"I'm sure that could be arranged. I'll bring him with me the next time I come."

Quatie's eyes brightened. "He'll come here?"

"Of course." There was no way Ian would make an

arthritic old woman come to see him. I didn't know him well, but I knew that much.

"That would be lovely. Thank you."

"No problem." Quatie shifted in her chair and her mouth tightened with pain. "You're sure you're going to be all right?"

"I'll be fine, Gracie, and my great-great-granddaughter is coming soon."

"Really? When?"

She glanced out the window. "Hard to say."

I had the feeling there was no great-great-granddaughter, or at least not one who was coming to visit. Quatie just didn't want to burden me.

I'd come back in a few days with Ian. Who knows? Maybe that would be all it would take to keep Grandmother in the Darkening Land and off of my back porch.

13

I RETURNED TO my house without incident. No wolf in the woods. No bats in the belfry. No messages on my voice mail. A good night.

Nevertheless, I slept badly—my dreams full of Ian Walker's body entwined with mine, wolves howling somewhere in the darkness, and the whisper of words in Cherokee that I could almost, but not quite, understand.

The shriek of a diving bird woke me to a misty dawn. I sat straight up in bed clutching my chest, my breathing too hard and fast, so that at first I didn't realize the shriek was nothing more sinister than my phone.

I snatched it up. "McDaniel."

"Having trouble with the wildlife again, Sheriff?"

I recognized the voice at once because it made the hairs on the back of my neck lift like the ruff of a dog. "Dr. Hanover, what an unpleasant surprise."

Malachi had been right. If I waited too long to contact the *Jäger-Suchers,* they'd just contact me. Or worse, show up.

"Are you in town?" I asked.

"If I were in town, I'd knock on your door, or perhaps break it in."

She could, too. Dr. Elise Hanover was both a virologist and a werewolf.

According to everyone who knew her, she was "different," a werewolf that wasn't evil, as long as she took her medicine—a serum she'd devised to keep the bloodlust at bay. Though she was able to cure some of those afflicted with lycanthropy, she'd never been able to cure herself. I would have felt sorry for her if she didn't irritate the hell out of me at every opportunity.

"What do you want?" I asked.

"I'm following up on a report we had from the local DNR. Birds run amok? Imagine my surprise to see your name on the complaint."

"How do you always know every damn thing?"

"Just a service of your federal government, ma'am."

Sometimes the services of my federal government were downright creepy.

"If I'd wanted *J-S* help," I said, "I'd have asked for it."

"You don't have to ask; we freely give."

I snorted. "Force yourself in and do whatever you like, you mean."

"Goes without saying."

My lips twitched. She was kind of amusing when I didn't have to look at her. Elise was a perfect example of Aryan beauty. Hitler would have loved her.

"Listen," I said. "This wolf's a messenger wolf—a spirit, maybe a ghost. No worries."

Silence came over the line. *Shit.* I hadn't complained about a wolf but birds. I should never be allowed to speak without first drinking at least two cups of coffee.

"There's a wolf in Lake Bluff and you're asking questions about ravens and crows?"

"The wolf's nothing. My great-grandma came back from the Darkening Land. Wants me to keep an eye on her friend. Forget it."

"I've often wondered what people would say if they listened in on some of my conversations. This one's a beaut."

"Lucky no one can listen in, then."

The *Jäger-Suchers* had all the best toys in security and electronics.

"I've dealt with ghost wolves before," Elise said. "They aren't anything to screw with."

"Ghost wolves?"

"Ojibwe legend. Witchie wolves guard the resting places of warriors, and they aren't nice about it."

"How much damage can be done by a non-corporeal animal?"

"You'd be surprised," Elise murmured. "You do realize that crows are an indication of werewolves?"

"And ravens?"

"Them, too."

"I'd heard that crows increase in rural areas when the timber wolf population increases. I wasn't sure about werewolves."

"Works the same way."

"I've only seen one wolf and, as I said, not really a wolf. You don't need to get your knickers in a twist, Doctor. I know what I'm doing."

"That remains to be seen. So what, exactly, have your crows and your ravens been up to?"

I told her, finishing with, "I think the birds are out of whack because of the storm. I even saw an eagle a few times."

"And that's out of whack why?"

"They usually stay south, especially at this time of year."

"I don't like the sound of that. Let me do a little checking on eagle shifters."

I opened my mouth, shut it again. What could it hurt?

"Next time you see any bizarre animal behavior, call me first," Elise said. "Don't make me hear it through the grapevine. That always pisses me off."

"And I do live to please you," I muttered, but she'd already hung up.

I was wide-awake now. No chance of going back to sleep. Usually I hit the snooze three times before rolling out of bed, but today I was so far ahead of schedule, I not only made coffee and toast, but also read the paper while I enjoyed them.

Since our last newspaper editor was still listed as a missing person—though Claire and I knew better—we had a new one who was doing a very nice job. Balthazar Monihan had treated the *Gazette* like a small-town *Tattler,* printing all the gossip and running embarrassing photos of the citizens, which is probably why no one made much of an effort to find him. Not that they would have.

I turned the page, planning to glance over the smattering of obituaries published weekly, and paused.

An entire section was taken up with names, dates, and survived bys. Mostly elderly, a few terminally ill, nothing odd in the least—except for the large number.

I knew that during storms maternity wards were packed, with deliveries taking place in the hall, the elevator, the lobby. I blamed the barometer.

So if there were more births during a storm, maybe there were also more deaths. I'd just never noticed it before. All of these people *had* died of natural causes. If there'd been a hint of anything hinky, I should have been called to the scene. Nevertheless, I made a mental note to speak with the funeral director.

Since I was up so early, I stopped at the clinic. The doctor was in. Where else would he be?

"Grace." Ian's smile was full of the memories of the last time we'd met. Though I'd like nothing better than to step inside and have a repeat, I couldn't let myself be distracted. I had far too much to do.

Especially if I wanted to be ready for our date tonight—if he'd actually been serious. From the expression in his eyes, he had been. Very.

"Would you make a house call?"

His smile widened as he reached for me. "Anytime."

I stepped back, laughing. "Not that kind of house call. A real one, to a friend of my great-grandmother's."

"Oh." The hand that had been extended toward my waist lifted to push his hair out of his face. "Sure. I thought—" He stopped. "Well, you know what I thought."

"Yeah." I couldn't say that I wasn't tempted, but if I was going to take Ian to Quatie's, then get to work on time, I couldn't allow the temptation to become reality.

"Be right back."

He disappeared into the clinic, returning a minute later with a doctor's bag that looked like something straight out of a seventies TV show–*Marcus Welby, M.D.,* or maybe *Medical Center.* My brother Gene had always watched the reruns. He'd wanted to be a doctor, but he hadn't had the grades or the money. Last I heard, he was a paramedic in Cleveland.

Ian and I piled into my truck—if I had time, I'd check

on my new squad later—and I pulled a U-turn, then headed for Quatie's.

"You want to fill me in on this friend of your great-grandmother's?" he asked.

I did, giving him what facts I knew, which weren't many—an approximate age, no real knowledge of her medical history, my armchair diagnosis of age and arthritis.

"I've got more balm in my bag."

Only a few days ago I'd have rolled my eyes, snorted, or laughed out loud at the idea of herbal balm healing anything. But my nose didn't hurt and the skin around my eyes was fading from green to yellow already. I had to admit, I'd become a believer.

At Quatie's, we found her sitting on the porch as if waiting for us. When we climbed out of the vehicle, she frowned in my direction. "You didn't have to come, too, Gracie. You're busy."

I stifled a wince. Was that a dig?

No. Not Quatie. She just didn't want to burden me.

Right now, I wanted to be burdened. Maybe coming here often enough would ease my lingering guilt; I hoped it would send the spirit wolf back where she had come from.

"I brought Dr. Walker," I said.

"You didn't have to rush." Quatie moved to the steps and began to descend, slowly, painfully.

Ian sprinted forward. "Don't bother, ma'am. I'll come up."

Her round face became even rounder as she smiled. "Sweet boy. I'm so glad to see you."

Ian took her arm, and she leaned on him, patting it as he led her toward the door. But she sat in the chair she'd just vacated with a heavy sigh, her smile fading, her face strained.

I stood in the yard uncertain if I should return to the truck. Was this a case of doctor/patient privilege?

Ian glanced my way. "Could you grab my bag?"

He'd dropped it when he leaped to help her, so I scooped it up and climbed the stairs as he knelt at Quatie's feet.

"If you could stay and give me a hand." He looked at Quatie. "All right with you?"

She seemed to hesitate, and I couldn't blame her. Illness was private. But then she met my eyes and nodded. "Of course. I have no secrets from Gracie."

Ian got to work with his stethoscope. Asking soft questions. "Where does it hurt?" "How do you feel?"

Making quiet demands. "Take a deep breath." "Say 'ah.'"

Now and then he'd ask me to fetch him something from his bag—a small rubber hammer to check her reflexes, an instrument to look in her ears, eyes, nose, and mouth. As he continued to poke and pry, she began to question him.

"Where are you from?"

"Who are your people?"

"What clan is your mother?"

"Who taught you the old ways?"

"Why did you come here?"

"Do you plan to stay?"

And last but certainly not the least embarrassing: "Are you married?"

Ian answered every query with jovial patience. However, by the end of the inquisition, my patience was frayed. Quatie was obviously checking him out to see if he was good enough for me.

At last the exam, and the interrogation, was finished. Ian straightened and stepped back, leaning over his bag and pulling out a jar of balm that matched the one he'd given me.

"Use this for your aches, ma'am. I think it will help."

She screwed off the cap, took a whiff, then nodded in approval. "Rattlesnake oil. I'd run short."

I couldn't help but smile at that before asking, "How is she?"

"I'm wearing out," Quatie said, and shot me a glare when I began to protest. "Truth is truth. The body wears down. The only way to completely cure what ails me would be to get another."

"Barring that," Ian said, "use the balm. Take aspirin. Alternate ice and heat. Rest. Eat well. Exercise as much, but as carefully, as you can."

"Thank you, Doctor." She reached for his hand, then sandwiched it between hers, peering at him as if he were a long-lost grandson. "I'd love to talk to you more about the old ways."

He patted her shoulder with his free hand. "I'd be happy to."

"Now?" she asked.

Ian glanced at me.

"I . . . uh—" I had to get to work, but I didn't want to take him away when she was so clearly enjoying him.

"I'm afraid I have appointments." Ian tried to remove his hand, but Quatie held on, and he let her. "Contractors. Painters. But I'll come another day."

Quatie nodded and released him.

We left her on the porch enjoying the sun and returned to Lake Bluff.

"Sorry about that," I said.

"What?"

"The third degree. She was my great-grandmother's best friend and—" I broke off.

"She wants to make sure my intentions are honorable. I understand."

I kept my eyes on the road; I couldn't look at him.

"She doesn't want you hurt," he continued softly. "Neither do I."

I glanced over. There was something in his voice I couldn't read. But his face was open and honest. I wasn't sure what to say, so I said nothing.

A short while later I pulled up in front of the clinic. "I'll see you tonight," he said, then leaned over and kissed me. Before I could respond, he was gone.

I thought back over the last hour's happenings. I hadn't seen Quatie in nearly a year—my own fault—but despite my neglect, she'd stepped right into my great-grandmother's role. That she had made me a little choked up.

Though I didn't need anyone to protect me, it was nice when someone tried.

14

I WENT TO work, meaning to check in, then head to the funeral home as planned, except the day got away from me—extensive cleanup after the storm, electricity still out in several places, dogs gone missing. We'd had a bit of looting, too.

And the Chuck Norris bandit was back.

Today's chuckle went like this: *MacGyver can build an airplane out of gum and paper clips, but Chuck Norris can kill him and take it.*

"I never liked *MacGyver*," Cal said. "That wasn't realistic."

"And *Walker, Texas Ranger* is?" Jordan asked.

Cal scowled at her as if she were nuts. "Of course!"

There was really no talking to him.

I handed the joke to Jordan. She was keeping a file, not so much for investigative purposes as for the employees. Whenever anyone needed a laugh, they pulled out the Chuck Norris file. Cal didn't know. He'd have a cow.

Jordan went back to the switchboard. A tiny thing, despite her father's bulk, Jordan reminded me of a pixie with attitude. Maybe it was the way she kept her dark hair cropped close to her head. Could be the sharp edge to her chin or the spark in her blue eyes. Maybe it was just the collection of killer spike heels. But I liked her, and while she was the best dispatcher I'd ever had, I still hoped she earned her college money soon so she could live out her dream.

I glanced at my watch. Only an hour until change of shift. I needed to walk across the parking lot to the funeral home.

"Cal, can you take over here?"

He nodded, staring morosely at his desk. Were the jokes making him sad or was his inability to nab the culprit making him crazy? Perhaps a little of both.

Five minutes later I let myself into Farrel and Sons Funeral Home. Strangely, none of the viewing rooms were open for business. With the number of deaths, you'd think they'd be stacked like cordwood. I winced at the image.

A shuffle of a shoe against carpet announced Grant Farrel even before his Lurch-like bass murmured, "May I help you, Sheriff?"

Grant might have sounded like the butler of *Addams Family* fame, but he didn't look like him, being short, round, and sweet in both face and nature. I'd never understood how anyone could be a mortician, but I guess someone had to. I'd heard many people say that Grant's gentle and discreet manner had eased their grief. The man had a gift.

I gestured at the empty rooms. "What gives?"

His nearly invisible white eyebrows lifted toward his receding baby-fine silver hair. "Excuse me?"

"I saw in the paper that we'd had a rash of visits from the Grim Reaper. So where are the bodies?"

Grant's round gray eyes widened. Why I felt the need to be flippant whenever I entered this place I had no idea. Must be my way of coping with the uncopeable.

I cleared my throat and tried to be a good girl. "Mr. Farrel, considering the number of obituaries published in the *Gazette* today, and taking into account you're the only game in town—" He frowned and I rephrased. "You're the only funeral establishment in Lake Bluff, I'd think you'd have several services tonight."

"Oh no, Sheriff, not a one, considering. Was there someone in particular you were interested in? I could arrange for a private visit."

It took me a minute to realize he was offering to show me a corpse. "Uh, thanks. Maybe some other time. Let's get back to the lack of funerals. Why isn't there even one?" I lifted my hands and made quotation marks in the air. "Considering."

"Ah, I see what you mean. A layperson such as yourself wouldn't know."

"Know *what*?" Grant's discreet nature was starting to get on my nerves.

"In many of these cases the deceased was quite elderly. Most of their friends have already passed and some of their family members as well."

"Cut to the part where there's no funeral."

Grant's well-manicured hand fluttered up to his chest, and he cleared his throat. "The families, or sometimes the deceased, will make arrangements for a graveside service only."

"Straight from hospital to cemetery in one easy payment?"

He winced. "It is cheaper, no doubt."

"So everyone who's died lately has been on the 'do not pass go, do not stop for a funeral' plan?"

"Not everyone. There is one service tomorrow for the family of an Alzheimer's victim."

He lowered his voice on the last two words, as if afraid that just by speaking them aloud he'd give the disease the power to rise up and grab him.

"There was nothing unusual about any of these deaths?" I asked.

"Unusual? In what way?"

I shrugged. "Seems strange to have so many."

"It happens that way sometimes, Sheriff."

"I guess you'd know."

Grant beamed. "Been in the business for forty years. Be sure and come to see us when you're ready to plan ahead."

I don't care what anyone said, Grant Farrel was ghouly.

I thanked him for his time, and as I headed for the door, Grant's phone rang.

"Hello?" He paused, listening. "Another one?" I turned. Farrel's eyes met mine and he nodded. "All right. Send him over."

⚭

The most recently deceased citizen of Lake Bluff was an octogenarian by the name of Abraham Nesersheim. There hadn't been a thing wrong with him until he'd come down with a summer cold that had turned to bronchitis.

His doctor, not Ian Walker, had ordered amoxicillin and rest. The next day Abraham's niece had found him in his bed after a long night of eternal rest. She'd called

911 and his doctor. In a replay of Ms. G.'s death, the doctor had pronounced the body and the EMTs had contacted the funeral home for direct delivery. I gave in to temptation and called the medical examiner, Dr. William Cavet.

Grant was beside himself. "Can you just order an autopsy, Sheriff, without even consulting the family?"

"When there's suspicion of foul play, yes."

"What foul play? You didn't even see the body."

"I'm afraid I can't tell you that," I said in my best cop voice.

"Of course." Grant practically bowed as he back-pedaled. "Police business. I'll just get the embalming room ready. Doc Bill has used it several times before."

I don't know that it had been several. We didn't have a lot of suspicious deaths in Lake Bluff—until last summer anyway—which is why we shared a medical examiner with the nearest town, Bradleyville.

Still, I supposed Doc Bill had used the room enough to feel comfortable there. I doubted I ever would. Not that I fainted at the sight of blood. Far from it. But I'd never been thrilled at observing an autopsy.

Looked like I didn't have much choice in this case. I wanted it done, I'd have to suck it up and watch. Twenty minutes later, the door opened and Doc Bill walked in.

He'd been a doctor for over fifty years, beginning as a GP, then becoming the ME. The man knew more about the human body than anyone I'd ever met. He also knew more about werewolves than anyone in town, even Malachi.

According to Doc Bill, Adolf Hitler had ordered his favorite Doctor Death, aka Mengele, to create a were-wolf army. Doc had been there when that army had been unleashed, just after the Allied landing. The fruits of that experiment were still running around causing havoc at every opportunity.

"Sheriff." His eyes met mine, and he lifted his bushy white eyebrows.

I knew what he was asking without the words, and I shook my head. "Not this time."

"Then what's the rush?"

"That's what I want you to tell me. Am I nuts or is something weird going on?"

"Better be more specific."

Quickly I told him about the strange increase in mortality since the Thunder Moon.

"No wolves?"

I hesitated, then decided to keep Granny to myself. She wasn't relevant.

"Not this time," I said. "No wounds on the body. No visible signs of death."

"You're pushing it, Grace."

"Humor me."

"You're the sheriff," he said, and headed for the embalming room.

The place smelled of chemicals that I really didn't want to put a name to. Everything was sparkling clean, though I didn't see the point of sanitization for the dead.

Grant had decamped after leaving the shrouded body next to a stainless-steel table covered with instruments and bowls, a scale, and a saw.

"You going to watch?" Doc Bill washed his hands and put on a gown, cap, gloves, and paper boots. I nodded. "You'll need to gown up. Don't want any of your hair or skin cells finding their way into a specimen."

I did as he asked, then stood as far away as I could get and still see.

Doc Bill turned back the shroud, revealing a marble-pale Abraham Nesersheim. I started at the expression on his face, which was very similar to the one I'd observed on Ms. G. after her death.

"Is that common?" I asked.

Doc, who'd been scribbling on a clipboard, paused. "Is what common?"

"He seems frightened to death."

Doc Bill stepped back, tilted his head, contemplated Abraham. "Not common, no. But not necessarily unusual."

He returned to work. Since there was no convenient X-ray machine at the morgue, he skipped that step and moved on to describing the outer appearance of the victim, then weighing the body.

Next, Doc sliced Abraham's chest open with what I knew to be a solid-silver scalpel. If Abraham were a werewolf, we'd already know about it.

But nothing happened. No smoke, no flames, no explosion. No shouts, no screams, no getting up and running off. Abraham was definitely dead.

Doc Bill worked with painstaking efficiency. As he did, he spoke of his findings into a tiny mike he'd pinned to his collar.

The smell of chemicals was beginning to make me light-headed when suddenly Doc froze, making a strangled, garbled sound of surprise.

I took a step forward, hand already on my gun, expecting Abraham to sit up, despite the hole in his chest, grab Doc Bill, and snap his neck like a twig. However, the corpse lay there, as a good corpse should.

"What is it?" I drew my gun. No point in being un-prepared.

"Impossible," Doc managed, his voice hoarse and thin.

"What's impossible?"

His hand shook as he directed my attention to the chest cavity.

I'd never been a whiz at anatomy, but I knew what a heart looked like.

Abraham didn't have one.

15

A HUMAN BEING can't survive without a heart," I said.

"Precisely."

"So what is he?"

Doc lifted his hand to rub at his face, saw his bloodied glove, and lowered it again. "I don't know."

My mind ran in several directions at once, searching for an explanation.

"The heart wasn't removed after death?" I asked. Anything could have happened between the time Abraham had died and Grant had been called.

Doc shook his head. "No scar."

"So what kind of monster looks human but doesn't have a heart?"

"A woman?"

I gave Doc a quick glance. "Sorry," he said. "I make jokes when I'm nervous."

"You and me both." Unfortunately, I couldn't think of a single one, not even about Chuck Norris.

"He's not a werewolf," Doc mused.

"You're sure."

He lifted the silver scalpel. "As I can be."

Problem was, according to the *Jäger-Suchers,* there were more supernatural beings out there than either they or anyone else knew about.

I glanced at Abraham. *Obviously.*

"What else was Mengele making?" I wondered.

Just because Hitler had ordered a werewolf army didn't mean he hadn't ordered a whole lot more. He'd been a greedy bastard. Start with the Jews, why not toss in the Gypsies? Create a werewolf? Well, hell, let's see what else we can come up with.

"I don't know," Doc repeated. "I was just a kid, dropped behind enemy lines, fighting my way back home. We dealt with the werewolves, but I didn't see anything else."

"Did you hear of anything else?"

"No. For years when people brought up the war, I didn't listen. I didn't want to know."

"What walks like a man, talks like a man, but isn't made like a man?"

Doc spread his hands. "Zombie? Ghoul? Vampire?"

I rubbed my forehead. "Hell."

"On earth," he agreed.

Mengele's monstrosities weren't the only beings we had to consider. Many of the legends that had come down through the ages, terror-inducing tales told around campfires in every culture, were real. Which just meant I had no idea what we were facing or any hint where to begin looking for clues.

"Finish the autopsy," I ordered. "Let me know if any other crucial body parts are missing. Then get going on the others."

"Others?"

"Abraham isn't the only one who's died around here since the storm."

"You want an autopsy on every one of them?"

"Yep."

"Some of them were buried already."

"Dig them up."

"Grace—"

"Do it, Doc."

I only hoped they were still there.

I headed straight for Claire's office. She needed to know what we were up against. Too bad I didn't.

On a typical day there would be several constituents waiting in the outer office for a moment of her time. Today there weren't any, which should have struck me as strange, but I was on a mission.

"Grace!" Claire's assistant, Joyce Flaherty, jumped between me and the office door. "She's in a meeting."

"Not anymore." I moved to the right. So did Joyce.

I narrowed my eyes, trying to decide if I could take her. Probably not.

Joyce was at least six feet tall and built like the lumberjack her father had been. Though her hair was as dark as the day she'd been born, most estimates put her between prehistoric and antique.

She'd been a high school phys ed teacher before she'd become assistant to the mayor, Claire's father. Joyce had mothered both Claire and me for most of our lives, and she wasn't about to start taking shit off of either one of us now.

"It's an emergency." I moved to the left.

So did Joyce. "Can't it wait?"

"What is it about 'emergency' that you don't understand?"

"Do you really want to be sarcastic with me, Grace?" she said with deceptive gentleness.

I gulped. "No, ma'am."

"I didn't think so. Now sit down and wait until Claire's done."

I turned away. Joyce went to her desk; I turned right back and opened the office door. Then I shut it again. I should have caught a clue when I noticed that all the shades on the outer windows were drawn.

"Told you so," Joyce murmured with gleeful satisfaction.

"My eyes." I shaded them with my palm. "I've been struck blind."

"Karma." Joyce began to hit the keys on her computer in a *rat-a-tat-tat* rhythm that only made my brand-new headache worse.

The door to Claire's office opened. She scowled as she buttoned her blouse and motioned me inside.

"You missed one." I pointed to a gaping hole in the center of her chest, which revealed she'd forgotten to put on her bra. Or maybe she'd just lost it.

I used one finger to lift the lacy white garment from under the visitor's chair. Claire snatched it out of my hand and shoved it into a drawer.

Malachi lounged against the wall completely dressed except for his feet—bare. He lifted a brow and shrugged. I couldn't help but smile.

Claire was on the floor picking up papers and pencils, which appeared to have been swept from the desk by a whirlwind, or maybe just an arm.

I stifled a sigh. I wished I had a husband who'd

come to my office for a nooner—even when it was long past noon.

The thought made me straighten. I had more important things to worry about than my love life, even if it had taken a turn from loserville toward exceptional.

"Next time lock the door," I said.

"Next time keep your ass out unless you're invited in," Claire snapped, her fair Scottish skin beet red.

"Where's the baby?"

Mal pointed toward the car seat, which had been hidden by the desk.

I gasped. "Won't that cause irreparable psychological damage?"

"He's asleep, Grace."

"Oh." I knew nothing about babies. Only that I wanted some.

"What's so important that you had to interrupt the only alone time we've had in weeks?"

"Sorry," I said, then went silent.

"You want me to go?" Mal asked.

"No. You'd better stay. We've got . . ." I paused. What did we have?

Claire glanced up from putting her desk in order. "Werewolves?"

"No."

She frowned. "Something worse?"

"I don't know."

"Is this twenty questions? Because I'm really bad at games, Grace, and my patience right now is shot."

I told her everything, from last night, when I'd seen the messenger wolf on my porch, until ten minutes ago, when I'd seen a gaping hole where Abraham's heart should have been. I purposely started the tale after I'd had sex with Ian. Just because I'd walked in on

Claire and Mal didn't mean they got to walk in on me, even in their imaginations.

Besides, I knew what Claire would say. The same thing I'd said to her when I found out she'd kissed an itinerant Gypsy horse trainer.

He's out of your league.

I hadn't said it to hurt her but rather to keep her from getting hurt. Mal had looked like a player—a love 'em and leave 'em kind of guy. How could he not be when he'd once performed in a different town every week? What I hadn't known then was that he'd been searching for Claire for centuries.

In the same way, Ian was out of my league. He might not leave town at the end of every week, but he was just as emotionally unavailable. The man was still in love with his dead wife.

Boy, could I pick 'em.

At any rate, I didn't want Claire worrying about my love life any more than I needed to worry about it right now. We needed to focus on what was ripping apart our town.

"You talked to Doc Bill?" Claire asked.

"He only knows about werewolves."

"And the *Jäger-Suchers*?" Mal put in.

"Elise called this morning."

"Figures," he muttered.

"That must have been a pleasant conversation," Claire said.

"It wasn't bad, considering."

"What did she have to say after the two of you got done with your pissing contest?"

Claire knew me so well.

"She was going to check into eagle shifters."

"Huh?" Claire's face went blank. I guess I hadn't told her everything.

"Grace has seen an eagle a few times," Mal explained. "According to her, they're rare around here in the summer."

"They are." Claire bit her lip and studied me. "I hear the new doctor wears an eagle feather in his hair."

"He does. Though if he were the shifter, do you think he'd be that dumb?"

"Maybe not so much dumb as arrogant, which a lot of supernatural creatures are. With good reason."

"I doubt an eagle's our problem."

"Because?"

"The heart wasn't ripped out of the victim's chest by a bird beak; it was just gone. Or maybe never there in the first place."

"So you're thinking the *victim* is a supernatural being?" I nodded. "But if that's the case, then what killed him?"

"And why?" Mal added.

I sighed. "So many questions, so little time."

"Let's get cracking." Claire pushed her intercom. "Joyce, cancel all my appointments."

"Already done."

My eyes met Claire's and we shared a smile. Joyce could be downright supernatural herself sometimes.

"We need to call Elise."

"Your turn," I said quickly.

"Fine. Mal, any ideas about what we could be dealing with?"

His forehead creased. "I only know Gypsy legends. The *chovhani*, the witch."

We'd already dealt with the effects of one of those.

"Any bird legends?"

"Crows are good luck." I opened my mouth, but he beat me to the answer before I got out the question. "Ravens, too. The hoot of an owl is a harbinger of death, as is the howl of a dog."

"No shape-shifting birds?"

"No. The leading supernaturals for Gypsies are the werewolf and the vampire."

"I don't suppose the Gypsy vampire has no heart?" I asked.

"I haven't heard that, although one of my uncles told of a *mulo*—a vampire—literally one who is dead, that returned without a finger, and another who was marked by the tail of a dog."

I made a face; so did Claire.

"But for the most part, the *mulo* look like every other person on earth."

"Except they were dead and buried, which could be a little noticeable to the ones who buried them."

"Giving rise to that popular invention, the torch-carrying mob," Claire said.

Malachi gave her an exasperated glance. "I've met a few torch-carrying mobs in my time, and they aren't anything to joke about."

"Sorry."

Sometimes it was easy to forget that Mal had been born in a world completely different from our own.

"My people believe that the dead are angry at being dead and come back as vampires. Most often the *mulo* is someone who died by accident or design, and returned for vengeance."

"Doesn't really fit," Claire said. "The victims are dead, right? None have come back?"

"Not that I know of, though I'm having Doc do autopsies on the ones who've died since the storm."

"How do you kill a *mulo*?" Claire asked.

"The Rom use a *dhampir*—part human, part vampire—the only being capable of hunting down the undead and ending their existence."

"A Gypsy vampire killer?" I asked, and Mal nodded. "Know any?"

"As a matter of fact, I do. However, there's no need to call one."

"Because?"

"None of the victims are Gypsies."

"We did gloss over that one very important point," Claire murmured. "Any other ideas?"

"If we're going with the notion that the victims are the ones with the powers, maybe we need to research Scotch-Irish legends."

Claire nodded. "And what about the one who's killing them?"

"Once we know what they are, it should be easier to figure out what or who's after them," I said. "But first, let's make sure it isn't a *Jäger-Sucher*."

Claire frowned. "Wouldn't Elise have mentioned that?"

"You'd think, wouldn't you?" I motioned to the phone.

Claire sighed and made the call.

16

F IVE MINUTES LATER, Claire hung up.

"Elise insists there are no *Jäger-Suchers* in town."

"I don't trust her."

"She'd have no reason to lie, especially since we already figured out there's something rotten in Lake Bluff."

"I suppose she's sending an agent to take over for us idjuts and save the day."

"Not so much," Claire said. "According to her, all their agents are otherwise engaged. The last full moon was a doozy."

I didn't like the sound of that. From both Claire's and Malachi's expressions, they didn't, either. If supernaturals were acting up all over the place, that more than likely meant they were acting up here, and we were on our own.

Nothing we hadn't been before.

"Any advice from the great werewolf in the impenetrable fortress to the north?"

"Sounds like a fantasy novel," Claire murmured.

"Never sell," I said. "Too unrealistic."

"Got that right. Elise thought we were doing all that we should—exhuming the bodies, ordering the autopsies, checking the legends."

"Damn, we're good."

Claire shot me a glare, and I shut up.

"She hadn't uncovered any eagle shifter information, but suggested we check local Native American traditions, as they've been having a few problems in that direction."

"She mentioned witchie wolves." At Claire's lifted brow, I elaborated. "Ojibwe. Not from here."

"Doesn't mean they couldn't catch a plane, train, or automobile."

"Most Native American legends are tied to the land of their people, the way those people are part of the land they love."

"Like you and these mountains."

"Exactly."

"So we should be checking Cherokee legends," Claire mused. "You do that. I'll take the Scottish ones and Mal can take the Irish."

"Unless he already knows them."

Malachi shook his head. "We lived in Ireland, but we weren't truly Irish. We were Gypsies, remaining outside of every society we lived among, only trusting of ourselves."

His gaze went to Claire and softened. He'd been trusting of no one but other Gypsies until her.

I cleared my throat; they stopped mooning at each other and returned their attention to me. "We're going to have to tell the populace something once they get wind of the autopsies and the exhumations."

"Something that won't cause a panic," Mal murmured. "Mobs come in all shapes, sizes, and centuries."

People did get up in arms very easily, and around here that would mean a lot of guns in the streets—a cop's nightmare.

"What about a virus?" Claire proposed.

"Maybe." Better to have people staying at home, wearing masks to the store, rather than running around in the forest with their weaponry. "I'll talk to Doc. I'm sure he'll have an idea."

"Good." Claire tapped her keyboard, and her computer came to life. "Let's meet tomorrow."

"Same bat time?" I asked.

"Same bat channel," Claire answered.

We'd watched a lot of classic TV as kids—my brothers' favorite way to shut us up so they could do whatever it was older brothers did when forced to babysit.

As I closed the door behind me, Mal asked, "What's a bat channel?"

I glanced at my watch. My shift had ended over an hour ago. A quick call to Jordan revealed there were no pressing emergencies that required my attention.

"I'm headed home," I said. I could do my research in the office, but I'd learned it was better to do anything funky on my personal computer.

All I needed was to be under investigation for blowing up a citizen with a silver bullet and have the investigators discover I'd been researching werewolves during my on-duty hours.

I checked in with Doc Bill on my cell as I drove out of town. He was on top of things—having already done the paperwork for the additional autopsies and the exhumations. The lack of a heart in Abraham had freaked Doc Bill out as much as it had me.

"What are you going to tell the relatives?" I asked.

"As little as possible."

"Seriously, Doc, we should get our stories straight."

His sigh sounded tired, and I felt kind of bad. The man was at least eighty and should have retired years ago. But his wife had died, and he'd kept working. He'd always seemed happy about it, until now. Can't say that I blamed him, but I needed Doc on the job. I certainly couldn't explain this mess to someone who wasn't already with the program.

However, when he spoke again, he seemed stronger. Doc knew what was at stake; he wouldn't fail me.

"I'll tell anyone who insists on an explanation that we're doing a study for the Centers for Disease Control."

"Okay."

"I can make it sound official. Government ordered. Hush-hush. Blah-blah-blah."

"And when they panic about the Ebola virus?"

"I'll swear whatever this is, it isn't contagious."

"In other words, you'll lie your ass off."

"Without a qualm, Sheriff. We don't know what we're dealing with, and a panic won't help anyone."

"I like how you think, Doc."

"That's because I think like you."

"And smart, too. You're my kind of co-conspirator."

He chuckled. "I'll get back to you," he said, then hung up.

Another thing I liked about the man—he didn't bother with niceties. He got the job done. I only hoped he'd get *this* job done before we had more bodies on our hands.

I turned into my long dirt drive, holding tightly to the steering wheel as my dad's truck jerked over the muddy ruts left by the storm. I hadn't had a chance to ask Claire about my new squad car, but since the truck worked so well on the still-saturated side roads, that was probably for the best.

The wheels bounced over a particularly large hump and rolled down the other side, sliding into my front yard and nearly slamming into the car already parked there.

"Crap." I'd forgotten about my date.

Ian Walker wasn't in his car. He wasn't on the front porch. I glanced toward the trees, wondering if he'd gone to the creek, hoping to find me there as he had last night. How mortifying that he might think I'd actually wait for him at the water for more of the same . . . although it wasn't a half-bad idea.

I had to remind myself that this was an affair, nothing more. Even though I'd broken my self-imposed rule on sleeping with a resident of Lake Bluff, that didn't mean this was going to be anything more than a short interlude that would end badly.

If that's all this was, then where lay the harm in going directly to bed? After the day I'd had, I could use a little comfort, a chance to forget for a few moments everything that was whirling in my head.

I climbed the porch steps and opened the door. Ian sat at my kitchen table.

I looked at the door, then at him. How had he gotten in?

"The door was open," he said.

Which wasn't like me. Of course I had been distracted lately—hot doctor, messenger wolf, ravens, crows, eagles, dead people.

"I forgot," I said. "There was—" I stopped. I couldn't tell him even if I knew.

"It's all right." He got to his feet, hovering by the table as if uncertain.

"It isn't. I didn't think. I'm not good at—" I waved a hand.

"Talking?"

"No, that I'm good at. I suck at dating."

"Then we're two of a kind. I haven't dated since . . ."

His voice trailed off, and he glanced down, his braid and the feather swinging across his face. I'd reminded him again of his dead wife. Maybe I wasn't as good at talking as I'd thought.

"I wrecked everything. I'm—"

His head came up. "Don't say you're sorry. I'm glad you forgot."

My eyebrows lifted. "Glad?"

"Grace, I'm a doctor. I'm going to forget a lot of things. Dates. Birthdays. There'll be times I'm so wrapped up in something, I might forget your name." My eyebrows lowered, and he laughed. "Kidding."

"You aren't mad?"

"Of course not." He brushed his hair out of his face. "There was something we didn't discuss the other night."

Discussion hadn't been on my list of options, but I had a pretty good idea of where this was headed.

"Protection," I said. We hadn't used any.

"Yes. I . . . well—I didn't think."

That made two of us.

"I'm on the pill," I said. Had been for years. I wanted children, but a surprise pregnancy was not the way I planned to get them. "And I've never had unprotected sex."

"Never?"

"Until you."

That admission made me look away from his intent gaze. It felt like more than it was. It felt like some kind of promise.

"I haven't either," he murmured.

I looked up. Was he serious? From his expression, very. I wasn't sure if I should believe him, but what reason would he have to lie? Besides, that milk had already been spilled, so to speak. No sense crying over it now.

I smiled and his shoulders relaxed. He was as glad to have that conversation out of the way as I was.

"What was so engaging that you didn't get home until nearly nightfall?" he asked.

"The usual."

"Which is?"

He seemed awfully interested, but maybe it was just the natural curiosity of a non-cop for a cop's life. I'd fielded such questions a hundred times before, but I really didn't want to now.

"Cats up trees, dogs in the garbage. Such is the life of a small-town cop." Most of the time—just not lately.

"Hear anything from Quatie?"

"No." I tensed. "Did you? Is there something wrong?"

"Not that I know of." He spread his hands. "I was just making conversation."

"Oh. Right." I shuffled my feet. "Thanks again for seeing her."

"My job and my pleasure. She's a neat old lady." I warmed at the description. She was. "Did you still want to go out to dinner?"

He seemed so out of place wearing a suit and tie in my eighties-style peach and teal kitchen. I'd run out of remodeling money a long time ago.

His ring reflected the overhead light, flashing silver

even though it was gold. His feet were bare; he'd kicked his sandals off at the door.

I think it was the feet that got me—long, slim, tan. They made me want to take off my shoes, too, along with everything else. I crossed the room and kissed him.

I needed to get to work, but right now I needed this more. From the way he kissed me back, he did, too.

My fingers tangled in his hair, the sweep of the strands, the braid, the feather over my wrists made me shudder in anticipation. What would that feather feel like drifting over my breasts, my stomach, my thighs? I intended to find out.

I backed away; he reached out, then stopped, clenched his fingers, and let his arms fall slowly to his sides. "I'll go. You're tired."

"Do I look tired?"

"No." He moved closer, his gaze wandering over my face, staring at me as if I were fascinating. "You look . . . amazing." I smiled. "That balm really worked."

My smile faded, but he didn't notice.

"I wasn't sure it would." He began to pat his jacket, his pants pockets. "I have to make a note. Check Quatie in the next few days and see if the results are the same."

I saw now why he'd warned me about forgetting things. Give him a medical miracle and he was in another world. I couldn't blame him, but now was not the time.

Taking his hand, I led him toward the stairs.

17

H E HAD THE good sense to keep quiet as we climbed to the second floor and entered my room. Once there I pulled off my gun belt, unloaded my Glock, and shoved everything into a drawer.

I turned, expecting him to be stripped to the skin. Instead he stood in the doorway staring. Well, I had used most of my remodeling money here.

We'd walked into a forest—or at least that was the impression I'd wanted to convey. The walls, the bedspread, the heavy curtains were green, with detailing that made them seem like long, swaying blades of grass. The carpet held the blue of a mountain lake reflecting a sunlit sky. I'd bought sheets and pillowcases in a muted violet, the same shade as a lily pad. A miniature fountain in the corner spread the peaceful sound of running water.

"You must sleep right through the night in a place like this."

The way Ian said it, the way he stared, made me think he didn't sleep through the night often. Some people didn't. My dad had been one.

He'd wandered the house at all hours, making it extremely difficult for me or any of my brothers to sneak out. When we were kids we'd thought he did it on purpose, but now I realized he'd been troubled—by my mother's desertion, the stress of raising five kids on his own, the job, probably all three.

Then, just when he and I were starting to get along, bonding over the job in a way we'd never bonded over anything else, he'd died on me. Massive coronary, just like Claire's father. My dad had been older than hers by at least twelve years, me being the youngest and Claire being the only. However, Dad had shared with Jeremiah Kennedy not only a close friendship but also a deep love for booze, cigarettes, and red meat.

However, I didn't want to think about my father, or anything else, right now.

"Shut the door," I said.

When the door closed, this room became an island, filled with the sight and sound and scent of serenity. I pulled candles out of the nightstand, fumbled a bit for a match. A soft glow swirled through the room—the forest beneath a murky moon.

Ian took a deep breath. "Grass, water." He frowned and breathed in again. "The air right after a thunderstorm. Where did you get those candles?"

"My great-grandmother made them."

Another thing I couldn't do if I couldn't read her papers. She'd always made the most amazing candles that gave off scents no one in the world could duplicate. She'd lived on the proceeds from the ones she sold to a gift shop in town. Every time I went past the place, the owner begged me to tell her how Grandmother had done it, but I didn't know.

"These are the last of them." I peered into the flames, mesmerized.

I felt him come up behind me. "Thank you."

That he understood what the candles meant, and what it meant to use them, made my stomach flutter. When he kissed the back of my neck, my stomach dropped toward my toes.

His hands slid around my waist, his palms resting on my belly as if he knew the turmoil going on beneath my skin. I leaned back, absorbing his heat, enjoying the pressure of him against my spine. Arching, I rubbed myself along his hardness, and the hands that had been gentle were gentle no longer.

He gripped my hips, pulling me more tightly against him, then running his palms up my ribs, cupping my breasts through the heavy material of the ugly sheriff's uniform. I had to get it off; I had to feel all of him against all of me.

Buttons opened under my busy fingers. His were occupied releasing my pants.

"Wait," he whispered as I began to shrug out of the shirt, his breath tickling the moistness left on my neck by his mouth and making me shiver. "Let me touch you like this."

Before I could ask or even wonder what he meant, he spun us around so that we were facing the mirror above my dresser. The candles gave off just enough light so I could see everything.

My uniform blouse gaped open, my lacy white bra peeking from beneath. My pants unbuttoned, unzipped, the silken V of my panties revealed, as well as the swirling, curling darkness that lay beneath.

His hand stark against my belly, his skin lighter than mine, our hair the same shade of ebony. Him wearing a suit, all buttoned up and stiff. Me in my uniform, unbuttoned and loose. We looked like an ad in *Hustler.*

His fingers slid beneath the tan waistband; then lower still, they crept beneath the white silk, one finger unerringly finding the center and stroking.

I arched, my shirt parting as my breasts thrust upward, seeming to strain at the soft white cups of my bra.

He nuzzled my ear; his teeth worried the lobe, as his finger continued to stroke. I was so interested in that finger, I didn't notice his hand releasing the catch on my bra until the pressure eased and his palm swept over the tingling peaks.

My eyes remained open, watching him, watching me, watching us. I couldn't see what he was doing beneath the cover of the bra still hanging over my shoulders, shrouding my breasts; I couldn't see what his finger was doing beneath the white silk of my panties, which only made what I felt more exquisite.

His thumb rolled my nipple, then joined with the forefinger to pluck me in a rhythm equaled by the strokes between my legs. His tongue swirled into my ear with a similar beat as my blood pulsed in time with the throbbing of his penis pressed to the curve of my spine.

One more hard thrust of his finger and I cried out, riding the wave, riding his hand as he drew out the orgasm. Lights flashed in front of my open eyes so brightly I was forced to close them, even though I wanted nothing more than to watch the two halves of myself—the woman and the warrior—cry out as one.

When it was over, he turned me around and kissed me. He was still hard against my stomach. I wanted to touch him as he'd touched me.

My fingers worked at his belt, his buttons, the zipper. He began to protest and I bit his lip, just a nip, one I could soothe with my tongue.

As he'd done, I slid my palm down his stomach, enjoying the flutter of the muscles beneath his skin; then my fingers slipped beneath the waistband of his briefs, immediately encountering the smooth, hard length of him.

I took him in my hand, rubbed my thumb over his tip, then worked him until his tongue was darting in and out of my mouth and his hips were pumping in time to the flick of my wrist. When he was so close I didn't dare go any further, I shrugged out of my shirt, my bra, then stepped out of my boots, my slacks, my socks. Holding his gaze, I dipped my thumbs into my underpants and lost them, too.

His eyes flowed over me like water over rocks; smooth and cool they caressed. When he reached for his tie, his fingers shook, and I took pity on him.

"Let me." I undid the knot, tossed the length of silk aside. Made short work of his buttons, revealing his beautiful smooth chest inch by glorious inch.

Shoving the jacket and the shirt from his shoulders, I couldn't help but pause to taste him; then I became distracted by the slope of his collarbone, the flat, dark disc of his nipple, and the spike of his ribs and hips.

"Grace," he muttered. "You're killing me."

Lifting my head, I smiled. "Not yet."

I stripped him of the rest, admiring the way his penis sprang out of his underwear ready for anything.

Then I inched him backward until his legs met the bed, and gave him a little shove.

He fell, bouncing once and laughing. The sound was so light, so uncommon coming from him, that I paused just to listen. But when I didn't join in, he began to sit up, so I straddled him.

I didn't think I could be ready again so soon, but I couldn't wait; I didn't want to, and from the way he cursed when I pressed my damp curls against him, he didn't want to, either.

Lifting myself, I took him in, my breath coming faster as he filled me, stretched me, took me. His palms cupped my hips, pulling me down as he pressed up, and I began to move.

"Wait," he managed, voice hoarse, the desperation at its edge a contrast to the word. He tightened his fingers, stilling me.

"Are you crazy?" I asked, fighting against his hold, needing to move as much as I needed to breathe.

"Shh," he murmured, then yanked the band off the end of my braid. "Shake it out."

I did, my hair flying, sliding across his chest, flicking his face, cascading over my shoulders, my breasts, rippling all the way past my hips.

"Now," he said, and I clenched my thighs, ready to ride.

But he flipped me onto my back, the movement so sudden, so unexpected, all I could do was fall.

I landed with an *oomph,* and I had no time to recover as he slid into my body once more. We were both on the edge, so close we shook with it. I lifted my legs, crossing my ankles at his spine, the movement pressing us together just so.

The lights went off in front of my eyes again, even

though this time they were closed. He pulsed inside of me, his sigh in tandem with mine. He buried his face in my hair, kissed my neck, then my cheek, then my mouth.

He grew heavy, lax with satisfaction and languor. I had the same problem. All I wanted to do was sleep, but I wanted to breathe, too. I shoved at his shoulder, and he tumbled onto his back. As he did, his eagle feather brushed my skin and heat trailed in its wake.

I rolled onto my side, fingered the feather. "I was wondering how this would feel against my—"

He turned his head, lifted a brow. "Your what?"

"Use your imagination."

He lay back and closed his eyes. "All right."

I hadn't meant "use your imagination" literally; then again, round three was beyond me right now. I'd just hold that thought, or maybe dream a little dream.

From the smile on Ian's face, he was already doing just that.

18

I AWOKE TO complete darkness, disoriented. I'd forgotten the candles.

Panicked, I turned in that direction and bumped into
someone. The sense of dread increased momentarily
before everything came flooding back.

Ian. The date that wasn't. The sex that was.

I relaxed, allowing my thigh to press against his.
This was nice, though I didn't dare get used to it. Once
I did, he'd be gone. I knew that as surely as I knew he
was going to break my heart if not sooner, then definitely later.

Now I couldn't sleep.

I glanced at the clock. Four A.M. I might as well get
up and do the work I was supposed to have done last
night. When I met with Claire and Mal I certainly
didn't want to do so empty-handed. They'd wheedle
out of me why, and I really didn't want to say.

I slid from the bed, snagged my robe from the closet,

and slipped out the door without Ian ever moving. He seemed to be sleeping well, and I was glad.

I'd left my laptop downstairs, so I padded in that direction rather than to my office. I'd installed wireless Internet the week after I'd buried my dad.

In the same way that Claire's father had sneered at air-conditioning, calling it a sinful waste of money, mine had refused to allow the Internet in his house. Anything that needed to be done in that direction could be done at work or at school.

Personally I'd thought he was scared of computers. I never had seen him use one when he could get someone else to use one for him. He'd called it delegating; I'd made chicken noises when his back was turned.

At any rate, I now had wireless Internet and Claire had central air. The times they were a-changing.

In the living room, I curled up in the recliner, tucking my bare feet beneath the hem of my robe. It might be summer, but the nights often turned cool, especially this close to the mountains. Right now the windows had fogged over with the mist that would shroud everything until the sun burned it off.

The computer connected, the cursor blinking, waiting for me to proceed. I bit my lip. It was kind of hard to look up creepy crawly things when I didn't know which creepy crawly things I wanted to look up.

I typed in *supernatural creature without a heart.* I got back nothing useful.

I tried *heartless,* which was worthless, as were any other combinations of "creature," "paranormal," "supernatural," and "heart."

Next I tried *Cherokee myths.* I didn't discover anything I didn't already know—legends of creation, stories that explained the sun, the moon, the thunder. Tales of the little people and the immortals, beings who were often invisible until they wished to be seen. The rabbit as trickster, the hummingbird that brought us tobacco before tobacco was common.

No mention of eagle shifters, although there was the belief that a great warrior could change his shape at will, and I found it quite interesting that the symbol of a great warrior was the eagle. Still, none of these stories gave any clue as to why Abraham had no heart.

I searched my mind for some other possibility. In desperation I typed *ghoul.*

A monster from Arabia or Persia, I read. *Appears in graveyards. A desert-dwelling, shape-shifting demon that can take the guise of a hyena.*

That wasn't very helpful, either.

Lures unwary travelers into the desert and devours them. Robs graves. Eats the dead.

Well, there wasn't a desert anywhere near here. Still, a ghoul might have eaten Abraham's heart, although how that could have been accomplished without tearing open the chest, and in the small window of time between his dying and his being found, I wasn't sure.

No matter which way I sliced this, it came back to the heart being missing without a single scar. Which to me meant the heart had been missing all along, and that in turn meant the dead person wasn't a person at all.

I sighed and rubbed my face just as a board creaked upstairs. I didn't want to explain any of this to Ian, so I shut down and went back to my room.

He wasn't there.

I checked the bathroom, the next bedroom, and the next. Another creak, from the third floor, had me scowling and climbing the last flight of stairs to the office that had once been my father's and was now my own.

I'd re-done that room, too, at first using it to attempt some of the spells and cures my great-grandmother had shown me. But the time between when she'd died and my father had was a period of several years, during which Dad had forbidden any hoodoo, and I'd been too busy learning to be a cop to care. The problem was, when I went back to it, I couldn't remember enough to do anything right.

I reached the open door; Ian stood at the window. The bulb had burned out in here long ago, and I hadn't replaced it, preferring instead to use candles as *E-li-si* always had. With the moon falling down and the sun not yet up, the room was cast in navy blue shadows.

Books and beakers, a few test tubes, and the toad. The amphibian had been dead a long time. Grandmother had kept it in an aquarium, so I did, too. She'd told me she was waiting for it to turn to dust, then the powder could be used for a very powerful spell. Unfortunately, I didn't know what spell that was.

I'd brought everything she'd left me here. Crystals lay scattered about; dream catchers hung from the ceiling. E-li-si had enjoyed all things magical, trappings from every culture. The room had a fantastical air, especially in candlelight. I loved spending time here.

Alone.

My gaze went to Ian. The slump of his shoulders took away any annoyance at his intrusion. Yes, this was my private place, but since he'd pretty much been in all my other private places, what difference did it make?

He hadn't bothered to put on any clothes, and for an instant I wondered if he was sleepwalking; then he spoke. "I didn't realize this was where you kept your great-grandmother's things. I intruded."

I opened my mouth to deny it, then said instead, "Why did you?"

"Where I lived in Oklahoma, everything was flat."

I blinked at the randomness of his statement, then gave a mental shrug. "I thought all of Oklahoma was flat."

"A lot of people do. But we have mountains, though nothing like these; canyons, rivers, plains. Oklahoma is the most geographically diverse state in the union. We're proud of that. Though I was born there, I never felt like I belonged. I never felt like I belonged anywhere until . . ." He pointed toward the Blue Ridge. "I saw those. I wanted to be closer to them."

As a kid I'd often snuck up here for the same reason, even though my father had warned me to keep out. I would stare out this highest window, and I would know that there was somewhere that I belonged.

"Sah-ka-na-ga," he murmured.

I crossed the room and looked past him at the horizon. "The Great Blue Hills of God."

"I heard about them all my life, but I didn't believe anything could be so beautiful." He reached out and touched his fingertips to the window. "I was wrong."

His eagle tattoo caught my gaze. Reaching out myself, I touched it. The muscle jerked beneath his skin, and I froze, hand hovering in the air.

Slowly he turned, his eyes dark when I knew they were light, his face shadowed.

"I've never seen a tattoo like that," I said.

He didn't answer, just kept his gaze on mine, waiting.

"What does it mean?"

He turned away, stared out the window again as if he couldn't bear not to see the mountains for a moment longer. "Only warriors can wear the eagle."

"The feather?"

"Yes. But feathers can be lost, stolen, ruined. I got the tattoo so I would have a reminder to be a warrior always. Warriors do what must be done no matter the cost to themselves or anyone else."

Something in his voice, a starkness, a desperation, made me move so I could see his face. What I'd heard I saw reflected there, and it made me shiver. Despite his calm demeanor, his vow to harm none, I recognized a ruthlessness in this man; I sensed secrets and danger, and I was enthralled.

"Come back to bed," I murmured.

He followed me downstairs, where he trailed that eagle feather all over me. I shuddered and writhed; I begged and then I came, clutching his shoulders, holding him close. Sated, we slept, only to be awoken by the doorbell.

Shoving my tangled hair from my face, I stared at the clock. "Nine? Hell."

I was late. So why hadn't Jordan or Cal called?

Ian turned over; I became distracted by the way the sheet twined across his waist, the outline of his legs, how his skin shone in the small ray of sunlight that strayed past a slight gap at the side of the heavy green drapes.

"I'll have to go right to the office," he said.

"Sorry."

He looked up, and in his eyes I saw a reflection of our memories. "Don't be."

I threw on my robe. "Use the shower, whatever you want."

As I ran down the steps, the doorbell chimed again. I threw open the door and discovered why my deputy and dispatcher hadn't called.

They were here.

Cal stood on the porch; Jordan leaned against a brand-new squad car. A second was parked behind it. The mist that so often swirled in from the mountains shrouded my yard. Beyond the cars lay the trees; I just couldn't see them.

"You sick?" Cal strode past me without being invited.

"Not yet. What's the matter? The Chuck Norris joke of the day too good to wait?"

"Huh?" Cal appeared preoccupied. "Oh, well, there was a joke, but it wasn't good." He reached into his pocket and handed me a crumpled sheet of paper, which I smoothed, then read.

There is no theory of evolution. Just a list of animals Chuck Norris allows to live. I thought it was pretty good. But— "You came to show me this?"

"Of course not. Claire dropped off the keys for your new squad car. We figured we'd bring it out so you could drive it in."

"Thanks."

Cal moved to the door. I followed, thinking he meant to leave. Instead, he shut the door and turned with a serious expression, even for him. "There's something I wanted to tell you, but not at the office."

He was acting strangely. Showing up at my house. Not noticing there was an extra car in my yard and asking about it. Bringing me the squad without calling first. Not commenting that I'd left the shower running upstairs.

Cal seemed . . . well, my great-grandmother would have called him "out of sorts." Something had gotten him worked up, and today it wasn't Chuck Norris.

"What is it?" I asked.

Ducking his head, he began to pace, and I caught a clue. Cal must have observed something supernatural, and being Cal, tip-top, tough Marine, he didn't know what to do about it. Anything that didn't make sense could not be true. Poor guy. I was surprised his head hadn't exploded in confusion.

"Cal, I—"

"I found out more about the doctor."

My mouth snapped shut so fast I narrowly missed biting my tongue.

"The doctor?"

"Ian Walker. You wanted me to check on him."

"His credentials, which you did."

"I kept digging." He shrugged. "Figured it wouldn't hurt."

From the expression on his face, he was wrong. This *was* going to hurt.

"He has a wife."

"Had. He *had* a wife. She died."

The fine lines that had been etched around Cal's mouth and eyes by the sun and the wind in countries I never wanted to visit, deepened. "She didn't die, Grace. She disappeared. There one day, gone the next. Not a trace of her anywhere, ever."

"How long?"

"Five years."

"He was a suspect?"

Cal tilted his head, his eyes sympathetic.

Of course Ian had been a suspect. In cases of spousal

death or disappearance, the husband or wife is *always* a suspect.

"They could never pin anything on him," Cal continued. "No evidence of foul play."

"Alibi?"

"Squat."

"Where's he been in the five years since?"

"Not in the town where she disappeared. He left as soon as the cops said he could."

"Odd," I murmured.

"Especially since I've had a hard time tracing exactly where he went, but I will."

"What made you suspicious? Why'd you keep checking?"

Cal glanced away, then quickly back. "I saw you go into his store that first day, and I waited until you came out."

I thought back. I'd gone into what I'd thought was an abandoned building, ended up kissing a stranger. Cal had called my cell phone. He'd been checking up on me.

I could imagine what I'd looked like when I emerged onto the street. I hadn't been kissed in a very long time, and I hadn't been kissed like that in . . . forever.

"You need to stay away from this guy, Grace."

Into the silence dropped the sound of a door closing. The shower had stopped running. I had no idea when.

Cal frowned and glanced up, then back at me. Understanding dawned in his eyes even before Ian Walker came down the staircase.

His hair was wet; his shirt wasn't buttoned; his tie was looped around his neck and his jacket over his arm. His feet were bare. From where I stood, I could see his sandals near the back door.

"Jeez, Grace," Cal muttered.

"I didn't know."

"Know what?" Ian asked, pausing five steps from the bottom.

Cal opened his mouth, and I elbowed him in the stomach. He didn't react—his gut was a brick—but he did shut up.

"Thanks for bringing me the new squad," I said, my eyes on Ian. "I'll see you at the office."

Cal hesitated; then after giving Ian an evil glare, he opened the front door and slammed it behind him, which was probably the most emotion I'd ever seen from Cal—unless you counted his reaction to the joke bandit.

Ian came the rest of the way down the steps. "What's wrong?"

I peered into his face, searching for something, I'm not sure what. A scarlet *M* didn't magically appear on the foreheads of murderers. More's the pity. It would make law enforcement so much easier.

"Did you think we wouldn't find out?" I asked.

He frowned. "Find out what?"

"That your wife isn't dead, Ian!"

He jerked as if I'd slapped him. "You ran a check on me?"

"You told me to."

"My credentials."

I shrugged. "Two for the price of one."

"It isn't what you think."

"You mean I haven't slept with another woman's husband?" I hadn't realized when I'd quipped that I wasn't sick *yet* just how prophetic my words would be.

Nausea rolled through me. I'd seen enough domestic

disputes, enough ruined families, to swear I'd never be a part of that. But here I was.

"I haven't been a husband for five years. I know she's dead."

I glanced up, suspicious. "How can you know?"

"She was gone without a trace. She didn't come back; she didn't write; she didn't call. People don't drop off the face of the earth like that anymore, Grace."

"You'd be surprised," I murmured.

The *Jäger-Suchers* were experts at making people disappear. I wondered if Ian's wife had been the victim of some kind of monster. Another question for the great and powerful Dr. Hanover.

"I thought you were mourning her. That—" My voice broke; I was horrified. I'd thought he was coming back to life because of me. I'd known this man was going to hurt me, but I hadn't expected it so soon.

"I was," he said. "I am. I loved her and she—" He stopped, cursed, shoved his hand through his still-damp hair. "She left me. She didn't love me enough. Do you know how that feels?"

I did. My mother had left. She hadn't loved me enough. I still looked for her in every dark-haired, green-eyed woman who passed through Lake Bluff.

I clenched my hands into fists against the twinge of sympathy that swirled through my chest. Just because I understood his anguish didn't mean I could, or should, forgive him. He'd lied, or at least misled me over what "gone" meant. I guess I could have asked more questions, but wasn't that considered rude when dealing with a dead wife, even when she wasn't dead? The lines on rude had always been a little unclear to me.

"Get out," I said. I knew *that* was rude, but I didn't care.

"Grace—"

I narrowed my eyes, and he clamped his lips shut, then walked to the back door, slid his feet into his sandals, and left.

I felt a twinge when his car started, when I heard his tires crunch on gravel. There'd been something between us, something that could have become a whole lot more.

If he hadn't had a wife.

I kicked the door. I was late for work. What else was new?

I ran upstairs, tore the covers off the bed, and tossed them into the clothes chute. I couldn't sleep on sheets that smelled of him. Even now the minty fragrance lingered. I'd have to burn candles in here for an hour before I could bear to lie down and rest.

I showered, soaping up twice for the same reason, then dressed in a fresh, crisp uniform, strapped on my weapon, braided my hair. I stared at myself in the mirror.

My nose was back to normal; the only remnant of my two black eyes was a slight yellow shading across one brow bone. I could use Ian's balm, but I didn't want to. For all I knew, the stuff was an aphrodisiac or some kind of lust potion, which would explain my hopping into bed with him so easily.

"It couldn't just be that you were horny and he's hot?" I asked the woman in the mirror.

She gave me the finger.

My boots made a satisfying thunder against the wood as I ran downstairs. I concentrated on the rhythmic thud and not the pain in my chest.

The best way to forget all of this was to throw myself

into my work; it wasn't as if I didn't have plenty to do. I had a dead citizen minus one heart, and a lot of relatives to interview.

I opened the front door and stepped onto the porch.

"Déjà vu," I muttered.

The wolf was back.

19

THE ANIMAL STOOD on the hood of my brand-new squad car. If I hadn't known she was a messenger, I might have been worried about the paint job. Those claws appeared awfully sharp for a spirit wolf.

"Now what?" I asked.

The beast tilted her head.

"I got the message. Watch over Quatie. I'll go there later today. You don't have to keep coming back, Grandmother."

The wolf growled and jumped off the hood. The car bucked up and then down as if something heavy had just been removed.

"What the—?" I took one step forward. The wolf turned and ran. I followed, but by the time I reached the trees, she was gone.

The mist was lifting; the sun shone through, sparking brightly off the droplets of moisture on the grass, the branches, my shiny new car. Come to think of it, the spirit wolf had looked a little wet, too.

"Damn." Too much was going on this morning. Far too much had been going on all night. I sat on the hood and put my head in my hands.

"What's done is done," I murmured. "If the wife ever turns up, I'll apologize. Let her pop me in the nose."

I probed my recently healed appendage. It was only fair.

"Until then," I continued, "leave him alone and you're good." Or at least as good as I was going to get.

Standing, I peered at the smooth finish of the car. Not a mark on it. I hadn't expected there to be.

I peered in the direction the wolf had gone. North, just like last time. I hadn't figured to see the wolf again since I'd gotten the message, but either I'd gotten the wrong message or there was a new message.

I wished I could ask Ian about this, but I was going to have to make do with my own investigative skills from here on out.

Inside I found a book I'd bought on Cherokee traditions—sad that I had to get a book off of Amazon for something I should already know, but I didn't have much choice.

I turned to a section on directions. As Ian had said, to the west lay the Darkening Land, a place of thunder, its color black. In the east was the land of the sun, triumph, power, the color red. The south held Wahala, the white mountain where peace and good health were found. To the north waited the Frigid Land, a site of sadness and trouble, its color blue.

The wolf had materialized each time either before Ian had shown up or after he'd left, then run north. Was she trying to tell me that Ian was trouble?

As if in answer, a sharp, insistent howl rose from the

distant hills. I'd never heard a wolf howl in the daytime. Hell, I'd never heard a wolf howl at all until last
summer. As previously stated, we didn't have them.

If the messenger wanted me to help Quatie, I would.
If the wolf wanted me to be careful of Ian, I'd already
figured that out for myself. And if she came back?

I almost wished the thing *were* a werewolf, because
then I could shoot it.

◯◯◯

I didn't bother to go to the office. I didn't want to see
Cal or Jordan. I called in, said I was going on patrol.
I could do whatever I wanted. I was the boss.

Pulling out the obituary section, I headed for the
first house on the list. Before I got there, my cell
phone buzzed. I nearly let it go to voice mail, figuring
the caller was Cal or, worse, Ian. But I was too responsible to ignore what could be an emergency, so I
glanced at the display, then I jerked my car to the side
of the road, nearly dropping the phone under my seat
in my haste to answer.

"Doc?"

"Freaking caller ID," he muttered. "I hate progress."

"Tell me you've made some."

His exasperated sigh came over the line. "Have you
ever known me to dawdle? I've performed autopsies on
two of the bodies still at the funeral home. No hearts."

I sat there, uncertain what to say. I'd suspected as
much, but now what?

"Don't you want to know what killed them?" Doc
asked.

"Not the lack of a vital organ?"

"No."

Which led me to believe that my initial diagnosis was correct: The victims weren't people, but creatures we hadn't identified yet, and there was someone in town who knew not only how to recognize them, but also how to kill them.

"Okay," I asked when Doc didn't elaborate, "how did they die?"

"From the exact cause you'd expect in the particular circumstance of each victim."

"Which makes no sense."

"And human beings without hearts do?"

"I'm not so sure they were human."

"I didn't find any indication of that," he took a deep breath, then let it out, "except for the pesky tin-man syndrome."

"I don't understand how this wasn't discovered before now," I said.

"In the case of these victims, I'm not surprised."

"Why not? I'd think that a dead . . ." I paused, not wanting to use the word "person" but being unable to think of a better one, since we had no idea what they were. I gave up and moved on. "They come into the funeral home with a gaping hole in their chest cavity and no one notices?"

"The chests were unmarred, so the lack of a heart would only be found during an autopsy, and there wouldn't be an autopsy ordered in any of these cases. Nothing suspicious."

"What about during the embalming process?"

"None of them were embalmed."

"But isn't that required?"

"Embalming's only used to preserve the body for the

funeral. If there's a quick, planned, small ceremony, no ceremony, or a cremation without a viewing, no embalming."

Since I'd already had a variation of this conversation with Grant, I nodded.

If the dead were some kind of supernatural creature, then how could they be dying from a human ailment?

Maybe they hadn't been, but the "hunter" was able to kill them so it looked as if they were, or perhaps infect them, somehow, someway, so that they died in a manner that wouldn't begin a rash of autopsies.

Which was pretty far-fetched, but I wouldn't put it past the *Jäger-Suchers*.

Except Elise insisted none of them were here. I wasn't sure I believed her; however, plenty of people in the world had seen strange things and might have decided to kill them. Neither me, Mal, Claire, nor Doc was a *J-S* agent, but we all kept silver weapons close at hand.

"None of the deceased showed any signs of waking up and walking around?" I asked.

"Not when I was through with them." I grimaced at the image of what had been done. "You're thinking zombie? Vampire?"

"I have no idea."

"Huh," Doc said, as if we were discussing the new special at the Good Eatin' Café. "I saw no evidence of movement or reanimation. If they were capable of it, I'd think they'd do so before I—" He stopped before elaborating, and I was glad. "But who knows? I've scheduled an exhumation for this afternoon. Three o'clock."

"That was fast."

In most places, exhumation of bodies is a long, drawn-out, expensive process. Here we did things with a bit less fanfare.

"You need to come," Doc continued. "If we open up the grave and there's no one home, you could be on to something."

∞

I agreed to meet Doc at a quarter to three; then I continued on my way to the house of Barbara O'Reily, daughter of Peggy, who'd passed away the morning after the Thunder Moon from complications of Alzheimer's and whom Doc Bill had just sliced up like a Thanksgiving turkey. How was I going to explain that?

Barbara opened the door wearing a black dress and heels. Today must be the day of the small ceremony. Could I have picked a worse time?

"Grace."

Those of my father's generation or older continued to call me Grace instead of Sheriff, and I didn't mind.

"I'm sorry about your mother," I said.

"Thank you." She stepped back, inviting me in. "It's nice of you to come by."

I followed Barbara into the living room, accepting her offer of a seat before I disabused her of the notion that this was a condolence call.

"Ms. O'Reily—"

"Call me Barbara. I've known you since you were four."

Which would be a good reason for me to continue to call her Ms., but I smiled and said, "Thank you, Barbara. I need to ask you a few questions."

Her distracted, artificial smile faded. "Questions?"

"About your mother."

I decided to leave the autopsy news until last. Some people tended to get pissy when you ordered knives and saws applied to their relatives. In case Barbara was one of them, I wanted my questions out of the way first.

"All right." She glanced at the clock on the mantel. "I've got a little time before I have to meet my sister at Farrel's."

The O'Reily sisters were twins. Betty had married and moved to Atlanta. Barbara had stayed home with her mother. Since Betty's husband had already died and she'd never had any children, that would make for the small ceremony that seemed to be a requirement of this strange rash of deaths.

"I can't imagine what you'd want to ask," Barbara continued.

I wasn't quite sure myself. "Can you tell me how she died?"

Barbara frowned. "Alzheimer's."

"I know. I mean *how*? Was she conscious? Did she say anything? Did she seem—" I remembered Ms. G. "Afraid?"

Barbara's eyes widened. "How did you know?"

Bingo.

"What happened?"

She hesitated, as if she didn't want to speak of it, and I couldn't blame her.

"Where are my manners? Would you like some coffee? Tea? A soft drink?"

"No thank you," I said politely, though I wanted to snap, *Get on with it.* I patted her hand awkwardly. "Just tell me."

I *had* learned to be a little less short and sharp with people since being elected.

Barbara bit her lip, nodded, and began. "Mom was in a home. I couldn't keep her here anymore. She'd take off in the night. She was always looking for Dad. Didn't remember he'd been dead for a decade." Her lips trembled.

I made noises of commiseration. At least my dad had gone quickly. There was something to be said for a massive coronary.

"I'd gone to see her after work. I always did."

"Was she any better, or worse, than usual?"

"That was the strange thing—she was better. The doctor thought she'd last a few more weeks. I wasn't sure how I felt about that. Her going was really a blessing."

I nodded. She was right.

"So I sat with her longer than usual, but she got agitated. Said there was someone in the room."

I stiffened as an icy finger seemed to trace my neck. "Who?"

"She was paranoid, a symptom of her disease. I didn't think anything of it until she screamed and began to thrash, clawing at her throat like she was fighting for breath."

"How strange."

"The doctor had warned me. Some of them forget how to eat, how to swallow, and literally starve to death. Some forget to breathe and—" She lifted one shoulder. "Struggling for breath sent her heart into overdrive, and it just couldn't handle the stress. She died of a heart attack."

We seemed to be having a rash of those, too.

Barbara took several deep, slow breaths. "Her face when she died . . . She was so afraid."

"Not being able to breathe would scare the crap out of me," I agreed.

Barbara gave a wan smile. "I don't like to believe that in her last moments she thought someone meant to hurt her. I'd hoped that when she went, she'd do so peacefully. I guess that was too much to ask."

I didn't think so. Unfortunately, no one had asked me.

"Was there anything else about the night that struck you as odd?"

She cast me another quick, suspicious glance. If I weren't careful, people would be whispering that I had the sight. Too bad I didn't, because it would make interrogations a whole lot easier.

"There was a scream," she said. "It didn't sound—" She broke off, then dropped her gaze to her lap, where she began to pick imaginary bits of lint from the black material.

"It didn't sound what, Barbara?"

"Human."

I blinked. *Uh-oh.*

"Screams probably sound a whole lot different than a person's voice," I managed, "and if your mom was scared—"

"Maybe. I was in the hall, and then there was this horrible, blood-curdling shriek. I thought someone was in there with her, even though I knew no one could be."

"You didn't see her scream?"

"I was talking to the nurse, and—" She made a vague motion with one hand. "We both froze for a second, then ran in. Mom was gasping, choking, struggling."

"But she was alone?"

Barbara nodded. "I was right outside the door. No one went in or out."

"The windows?"

Barbara's gaze met mine. "She's an Alzheimer's patient, Grace. There were no windows."

20

WHY ARE YOU questioning me about my mother's death?" Barbara asked. "It was pretty cut-and-dried."

Except for the scream, the choking, the mask of fear upon dying, and the lack of a heart, but I decided to keep that to myself.

One thing I couldn't keep to myself, no matter how much I might want to, was the autopsy I'd ordered.

"There've been more than the usual number of deaths in town over the past few days. Doc Bill has been asked by the CDC—" At her blank stare I elaborated. "The Centers for Disease Control want him to do some tests."

"Why?"

"Hard to say. But I authorized an autopsy on your mom as well as the others."

Her eyes widened. "You didn't ask me."

"It had to be done right away."

"Is there some kind of epidemic?" Her hand fluttered up to rest, trembling, at the base of her throat.

How had I known that would be the first question? Maybe I *was* psychic.

"Doc assures me nothing's contagious. Just a precaution. Tests." I spread my arms, trying for the good-old-boy grin my father had used so well. "You know how those folks from Atlanta are."

Barbara nodded. To the citizens of Lake Bluff, Atlanta was a strange and foreign land, a place of crime and dirt, one that dazzled the youth of our town into absconding down the mountain, then spit them back out when they were ruined.

Claire had come home from Atlanta a ghost of her former self. If it weren't for Mal, I wasn't sure she'd have been able to get over what had happened to her there.

At any rate, playing the Atlanta card usually worked to bring people into an "us against them" partnership. I just wasn't sure how many times I'd be able to get away with using it today.

"Did Doc find anything?" she asked.

"I'm going to have to get back to you on that."

"What? But—"

"It's an ongoing investigation." I stood. "Until we've come to some kind of conclusion, I won't be able to give you any answers."

"Well, as soon as you know anything—"

"Of course." I headed for the door. "One more question—was there anything different about your mother lately?"

"Besides her thinking I meant to kill her every time I walked in the room? Or the charming way she started to keep her shoes in the refrigerator and the milk under her bed?"

"Sorry," I said. "We're just looking for a pattern."

"To what?" Barbara threw up her hands.

"I—"

"Can't tell me. Right. Never mind." She patted her hair. "I need to go."

"Thanks for your time."

When I left, Barbara shut the door a little harder than necessary. I headed for the residence of the next name on the obituary list.

The interviews were all eerily similar. Walking down Center Street after the last one, I was cataloging those similarities in my trusty notebook when I bumped into someone.

A sharp, horrified gasp, followed by, "Oh no!" made me glance up as a glass jar of something sped toward the ground. I snatched it out of the air before it smashed into the pavement.

"Grace." Katrine Dixon set her perfectly manicured hand against her great big breasts. "You always were the quickest gal in these mountains."

I handed her the jar, which appeared to be a jelly container full of swirling liquid the shade of skim milk. I glanced at the nearest storefront. "Did you come out of there?" I nodded at Ian's clinic.

"Have you met him? I think he might be able to help me."

Lake Bluff being what it was, I already knew that Katrine didn't need any help. There wasn't a thing wrong with her that a good, swift kick in the ass wouldn't cure. Katrine liked attention, hence the balloon breasts and itty-bitty skirt.

"What did he give you?" I demanded.

She blinked at my tone. "A natural cure. Suzanne Somers used natural cures on her breast cancer, and it went all away."

"You don't have breast cancer, Katrine." What Katrine had was a raging case of hypochondria.

She sniffed and stuck her suddenly pert nose in the air. Hell, had she had that fixed, too?

"Ian takes me seriously. He gave me a *complete* physical." She drew one bloodred nail over her left breast. I half-expected the pointy tip to pop the silicone like a balloon. I took a step back just in case. An explosion like that could put out an eye.

"He gives great physical," she purred.

I narrowed my eyes. I could imagine.

Katrine had once been a knobby-kneed, flat-chested, stringy-haired whiner. But she'd left Lake Bluff after high school—no one knew for where—and come home a completely different person, except for the whining.

I eyed the short white skirt and the tight red top, which showed off the body she'd returned with to perfection. I wondered how many plastic surgeons she'd had to blow to get those breasts. I wondered how she planned on paying Dr. Walker for his exam. Despite the shiny new exterior, Katrine was *poor* white *trash*—emphasis on "poor," double emphasis on "trash"—and she always would be.

She worked at the Watering Hole—a local tavern, located as far away from Center Street as it could get and still actually be *in* town—as a bartender. The place was rough. I'd been there half a dozen times in the last month on disturbance calls, and I usually worked the day shift.

The door to Ian's clinic opened and another woman stepped out, in her hand a similar jar, although the liquid inside held a greenish tint. I recognized Merry Gray, and I left Katrine behind without so much as a good-bye.

"Well, ain't that just like you, Grace McDaniel,"

Katrine shouted after me. "You always did have the manners of a savage."

Since I didn't particularly care if I did or I didn't, and I certainly didn't care if Katrine thought so, I kept right on going.

The clinic had improved a lot since I'd been there last. The lower floor had been cleaned and painted a calming pale blue. Someone had thrown up drywall, creating a separation between the waiting room and the receptionist's desk, although there wasn't any receptionist. Past that, three exam rooms had been roughed in. A fourth appeared to be done, since Ian walked out of it wearing the traditional white coat over a pair of khaki slacks, a mint green shirt, and a tan tie.

He stopped dead at the sight of me. "Grace, I—"

"How did you get all this done?" I blurted. He'd only been in town a few days, and a lot of that time had been spent with me.

"You'd be amazed at what you can accomplish if you're willing to pay for it."

"What did you give Mrs. Gray?"

He stiffened as if I'd jabbed him in the butt with a stick, which wasn't a half-bad idea. "That's none of your business, Sheriff."

"It is if you're selling her lime-flavored water and calling it a miracle. She's dying."

"Then I doubt lime-flavored water would hurt her." His voice and posture gentled.

The entire town knew Merry Gray had endured every cure available to modern science in an attempt to kill the tumors raging inside of her. Instead of growing smaller, the cancer seemed to feed on the chemo and the radiation, multiplying out of control and making her sicker and sicker.

"I don't want her hopes up," I said.

"Why not?"

"You give her green water and tell her it'll heal her, then it doesn't? That's criminal, Doctor."

"I'd say what's happening to her is criminal. I've given her nothing that will hurt, and I have every reason to believe it could help. She's exhausted all other avenues of treatment."

"I don't want her disappointed."

"It's been proven that a person's attitude can mean as much or more to their health than the actual medicine."

"Did you give her a placebo?"

"I'm not telling you what I gave her."

"What about Katrine? There's nothing wrong with her."

"I know." His lips quirked. I had a strong feeling that Katrine was the one with the placebo.

"The way you do business doesn't sit right with me." The way he did a lot of things no longer sat quite right.

"Let's make an agreement, Sheriff. You don't tell me how to deal with my patients, and I won't tell you how to beat a confession out of a subject."

"I don't do that."

"And I wouldn't give people anything I didn't think could help them. When I take an oath, I live by it."

" 'Do no harm,' " I murmured.

"Among others." I opened my mouth to ask, *What others?* and he stepped in, quick and close, startling me so much any questions I'd been about to ask got caught in my throat.

"The balm I gave you worked." His long, slightly rough fingers brushed my cheek, and my eyelids fluttered closed.

The scent of him brought back the feel of his body

in mine. His breath stirred my temple. I wanted so badly to touch him, to have him touch me.

"You should trust me," he whispered.

My eyes shot open; my chin came up. His face was so close our lips nearly brushed before I backed away. "You haven't exactly been trustworthy so far."

"You took me to see Quatie; you had to have trusted me then."

Which only made the loss of trust in him now hurt worse. "If you lie about one thing, you'll lie about everything."

His mouth tightened, as if he were trying to hold his temper. But when he spoke his voice was so calm I wanted to shriek. "You're not mad about my business; you're mad about my wife."

"I'm pretty sure I'm mad about both. I don't trust you. For all I know you could be doling out poison."

A surprised bark of laughter escaped him, more convincing than any denial would have been. "Why would I do that?"

"Why would you tell me your wife was dead when she'd disappeared?"

"I never said she was dead."

"You never said she was alive, either."

He sighed. "This is getting us nowhere."

"Where did you want to go?"

The look he sent me left no room for misunderstanding. He wanted to go back to bed—immediately.

My body reacted as if he'd run his beautiful hands all over me. I longed for him, and I hated myself for it.

"Put that right out of your head," I snapped. "We won't be going there. Not ever again."

"You're overreacting."

"Marriage means something, Ian." I thought of my mother. "Or at least it should. And lying—" I stopped.

Why did it bother me so much? Probably because so many men had told me what I wanted to hear, then walked out on me.

You're beautiful, Grace.

I love you, Grace.

I'll never leave you, Grace.

My wife is gone, Grace.

So I'd started saying good-bye to them before they could say good-bye to me. It was the only way I could keep from getting hurt. I'd waited too long this time.

"This was crazy from the beginning," I said. "We met three nights ago. Two nights ago we went to the water and—"

"Had sex," he finished.

"It was too much, too fast. I thought—"

I broke off, unable to finish. He took a step forward, and I narrowed my eyes, daring him to come any closer. His fingers curled against the legs of his slacks, the scritch of his fingernails loud in the sudden silence.

"Thought what?" he asked softly.

I'd thought it had meant something. I should have known better. Just because he was Cherokee didn't make him any less of a man.

21

I WALKED OUT, and Ian let me. I hadn't really expected anything else. It wasn't as if he loved me. It
wasn't as if I loved him.

No time to weep and wail—as if I would. I had an
appointment at the cemetery.

Luckily, all of the churches still buried their dead
outside of town. We'd have fewer gawkers that way. Not
that word of what we were doing wouldn't get around,
but the longer it took, the better.

I turned my car in the opposite direction of Lunar
Lake. In the old days it was common practice to con-
struct burial plots as far away from the populace as possible, mostly to keep the roving bands of wild animals
from dragging a stray leg or arm under your porch.

As time went on and Lake Bluff grew, there wasn't
room for a cemetery in the town proper, but there was
plenty of space to expand out where the dead had already been established.

I turned into the gate of Mountain View, saw Doc

Bill's car parked near what must be the grave we were interested in, and pulled up behind him.

Doc was already giving instructions to the man standing next to the machinery. Since he'd only been buried yesterday, no grass covered the grave of Alec Renard, just dirt. According to his obituary, Alec had expired from a stroke.

However, according to Alec's granddaughter, whom I'd spoken with fourth on my happy hit parade of interrogation, Granddad had been as healthy as a horse.

Until he died.

Doc finished speaking with the worker and headed toward me across the lush green carpet that covered the majority of Mountain View.

There truly was a mountain view here, not that any of the residents would benefit by it. Or maybe they would. What did I know?

This would have been a nice place for my father, except he'd been cremated per his instructions. I'd wanted to keep his ashes with me in the town and the home he'd loved, but he'd specified that all five of his children would take turns. You'd be amazed at some of the stuff people put in their last will and testament. Sheriff McDaniel, senior, had been no exception.

Grandmother had been buried like a true Cherokee on the slope of a forest-clad mountain. Illegal as hell, but by the time I'd told Dad about it, the deed was done.

He hadn't been happy. My father was the law here, and even if he hadn't disliked Grandmother with an intensity rivaled only by her dislike for him, he would have put a stop to her being buried as she'd wanted to be. To him, the law was the law and human remains were not to be put into the earth without observation of the required legalities.

I glanced at the white stone markers. It would have been nice to have her closer, in a place like this where I could visit. Although, according to Quatie, Grandmother wasn't available for visits since she was running around on great, big wolf paws trying to tell me something.

I choked back inappropriate laughter just as Doc Bill joined me.

"You okay?" He thumped me between the shoulder blades, just in case.

"Yes. Thanks." I stepped out of his reach. He might be old, but he still packed quite a punch. "Everything set?"

I indicated the grave, where the man fiddled with a machine as if he were dealing with a recalcitrant child. I even heard the distant murmur of his voice, cajoling, praising. As I watched, he started the engine, then patted the metal monstrosity gratefully.

"He's going to dig up the vault, remove the top, then leave it to us to open the casket." Doc cast me a sidelong glance. "In case the thing's empty."

Which would be a little hard to explain.

"I doubt that'll happen," I said.

"No?"

"I've been interviewing the relatives."

"Do tell."

I motioned for Doc to follow me farther away from the grave site, since talking for any length of time where we stood would have necessitated shouting over the sound of the machinery.

I told him everything. When I was through, Doc asked, "Conclusions?"

I pulled out the notebook I'd been scribbling in when I ran into Katrine. "The deceased were either old or ill. They were expected to die, though, in most cases, not quite yet. They all passed on in the night, seeming to gasp for breath in their last moments."

"But none of them died from asphyxiation," Doc murmured. "Or with any signs that they'd been deprived of oxygen or any bruises that would match strangulation."

He'd answered my next question before I'd even voiced it. I liked that in a doctor.

"Those who could speak," I continued, "and had a nurse or family member present to hear them, believed there was someone or something in the room, though no one else saw or heard anything."

"Could easily have been the presence of a loved one who'd gone before."

I lifted my eyebrows. "Seriously?"

"You think only evil entities come back from beyond?"

"I hadn't thought of anything coming back from beyond." I scowled. "But now I will. Thanks."

He quirked a bushy white brow and shrugged in lieu of apology. "I've been in attendance at enough deaths to know that there's something waiting on the other side. Sometimes, the other side comes over and gets us."

His face took on an appearance of rapture at odds with the slightly cranky Doc Bill I knew and loved. I wasn't sure how to deal with him, except to move on.

"Since all of our victims died with an expression of surprise, perhaps shock, or even fear on their faces, maybe every one of them was visited by a loved one they'd hoped never to see again."

Doc shook his head. "Everyone I've ever observed in that situation dies at peace. It's made me believe in the afterlife along with the ghosts and goblins, witches, warlocks, and werewolves."

Since I knew he wasn't kidding about the werewolves,

I had to figure he wasn't kidding about the other entities, either, but right now I really didn't want to know.

"So you think our victims aren't getting a glimpse of the great beyond," I continued, "they're getting a glimpse of their killer—invisible as he or she might be?"

"Perhaps," Doc said slowly. "Don't forget, the lack of a heart has made us conclude that the victims themselves could be supernatural."

"That doesn't preclude them being frightened of whatever's killing them." Doc frowned. "What?"

"I was just imagining what might frighten a being that has no heart. I don't think I want to meet it."

I didn't, either, but I had a hunch I was going to.

The sudden cessation of sound had us both glancing toward the grave site. A coffin-shaped vault now rested aboveground rather than below. The worker indicated with a wave of one gloved hand that Doc and I could return.

"One more thing," I said as we headed across the grass in that direction. "In several of my interviews, relatives or friends who were either with or near the deceased reported hearing an unearthly shrieking right before the victim began to gasp for breath."

"Shrieking from the victim?"

"Some didn't know, but the ones who did said it definitely didn't come from the victim. The scream was so loud it seemed to come from the air itself. A few saw bright sparkling lights as well."

"So the killer, whatever it is, announces itself with a shriek and some sparks?" Doc contemplated my face. "What else?"

"I heard a shriek and saw a trail of sparks fall from the sky on the night of the Thunder Moon."

"The what?"

"The full moon in July is known as the Thunder Moon. After that, people started to die."

"That was the night of the big storm."

"According to Cherokee legend, when thunder arrives on that night, magic happens."

We reached the grave site. Doc nodded to the worker, and he strolled off to have a cigarette under a tree at the edge of the last line of stones. The top of the vault rested against the side, leaving the rectangular container open.

"You think we've got an alien?" Doc asked.

I gaped. "What?"

"Falls from the sky in a shower of sparks, then invisibly starts to kill people—or perhaps unpeople—definitely heartless people, literally, which cannot by any stretch of the anatomy *be* people. What do you think?"

"I think you've been watching a little too much *Predator,* pal."

Although now that I thought about it, there had been that weird crater Cal and I had found after those sparks tumbled from the sky.

"*Predator*?" Doc asked. "Is that some new reality show?"

"Arnold, Doc. He commandos in to some bizarre jungle and fights a monster from another planet." At his continued blank stare, I gave him one more clue. "Schwarzenegger?"

"The governator? I never much cared for him. Too puffy." He made a fierce face and brought his scrawny arms into a muscleman pose in front of his body. "*Errrr!*" he growled.

I had to laugh, though I sobered quickly enough as I stared at the vault in front of us. "You really think we've got aliens in Lake Bluff?"

"We had werewolves."

The man made an excellent point.

"What if we have aliens in town, then an alien hunter arrives on a sparkling trail of stars?" Doc murmured. "And when he—she—it kills the aliens he—she—it screeches, like a battle cry."

"If that's the case," I said, "then where did the original aliens come from?"

"Pods?" Doc slid a glance my way. "*Invasion of the Body Snatchers.* That one I know." He jerked a thumb toward the vault. "Shall we?"

We stepped forward until we could see the casket ensconced within. A lot of people don't know that you need to purchase not only a casket for the deceased but also a vault for both to go into before the burial. Even if the loved one is cremated, a casket is still required. The item is just burned with them. Death is both a huge and a strange business.

Doc leaned over and went to work removing the top of the casket. Of its own accord, my hand went to the butt of my gun. Unfortunately, a bullet, silver or lead, could do nothing to eliminate the smell.

"Why?" I asked, putting my other palm to my nose.

"No embalming, Sheriff, and it's July in Georgia. What did you expect?"

I wasn't sure. More action from the corpse, less smell than we had. Wrong on both counts.

"Although . . ." Doc paused. "For an alien, this corpse is behaving pretty human."

"Whatever he is," I said, "he's here." Which took care of any vampire, zombie, ghoul theories, not that I'd been all that wild about them. "Now what?"

"Now I open him up and see what made him tick,

unless he didn't tick, which seems to be the case with everyone I've opened up lately."

Doc's gaze went past me. He lifted a hand, and I turned. A hearse bounced toward us over the rutted dirt path.

"What's that for?"

"You didn't think I was going to crack his chest right here in front of God and the cemetery guy, did you?"

I hadn't really thought of it at all.

I was trying not to.

22

After making Doc promise to call me as soon as he had news, as if he wouldn't, I left him to deal with the hearse and the body. I went to meet Claire and Mal.

As I drove back to Lake Bluff, I considered Doc's "alien" theory. I didn't buy it; however, if it were true, then these people had to have become "other" sometime in their lifetime. They couldn't have been born that way.

Lack of a heart would have been revealed, if not when they were a baby, then somewhere along the line. People didn't go through an entire lifetime without having a chest X-ray.

Well, one person might, but not several. At some point, they must have had bronchitis, pneumonia, or—

Wait, Ms. G. must have had a chest X-ray. Since she'd been diagnosed with congestive heart failure, she'd definitely had a heart to congest somewhere along the line. So when had the thing gone poof?

I pulled up in front of town hall and hailed Joyce, who was just leaving, as I got out of the squad.

"You've lived here since the dawn of time, right?" I asked.

She lifted her black brows. "Do you *want* me to smack you?"

My lips twitched. Joyce always cracked me up. "Anyone in town strike you as different?"

"Different how?"

Yeah, how? "I don't know, just weird. Not like everyone else."

"No one's like anyone else, Grace."

"Okay, let's try it this way. Did anyone leave Lake Bluff and come back later acting strangely? Or maybe disappear without a word for a few days and come back without ever saying where they'd gone?"

"Do you have a fever?" She reached over before I could stop her and placed a palm against my forehead.

"Stop that!" I stepped out of her reach.

Joyce narrowed her eyes. "The only one acting weird is you. What's going on around here this time?"

We'd kept what had happened last summer under wraps. The only people who knew the truth were me, Mal, Claire, and Doc, but Joyce wasn't dumb. She knew something bizarre had gone down, but so far we'd been able to put her off the scent by ignoring her questions.

As long as we stuck together, she'd never find out, because the *Jäger-Suchers* had, as usual, done a bang-up job of lying their asses off to explain away any out-of-the-ordinary weirdness.

"We got another rabid wolf in the woods?" she asked.

J-S doublespeak for werewolf.

"Not this time."

"Then what?"

"Nothing, Joyce." Or at least nothing I could put a name to.

Yet.

She opened her mouth, and I jumped in first. "Gotta go. You know how Claire is when I'm late."

Her teeth came together with an annoyed click. "Oh yeah, she's a regular slave driver."

"Mmm," I said, and fled.

If Joyce set her mind to discovering what was going on, I'd cave. The woman had been like a mother to me—hell, she'd *been* a mother to me and to Claire. The only reason we'd kept the truth from her so far was because she'd let us. And she'd probably let us because she understood, on the level that all great mothers have, that she really didn't want to know.

Six o'clock and town hall was deserted. My steps echoed in the cavernous marble foyer. They didn't build places like this anymore. Between the labor, the materials, and the slashing of municipal budgets, they couldn't afford to.

Claire, Mal, and Noah reclined on the floor of Claire's office, Claire making fart noises by placing her mouth against her son's stomach and blowing. He thought it was hysterical. Typical man.

I stopped in the doorway and watched them for a second. Noah kicked his legs, wiggling with joy. Claire's expression was full of a happiness I'd feared I would never see on her face again. And Mal—

His eyes were full of love and wonder. I had to glance away. I wanted someone to look at me like that so badly I ached with it.

"I see you're bringing him up right." I flopped into

the nearest chair. "Can't start too early teaching them how funny farts are."

"Boys will be boys." Claire lowered her head and blew one last, loud raspberry on Noah's baby belly.

God, I wanted one just like him.

Claire got to her feet. Noah made a squeak of protest and Mal scooped him up.

"Who wants to go first?" Claire asked as she rummaged in the bag on her desk, then tossed a bottle to her husband.

Mal caught it with one hand, flipped the top with a thumb, and popped the nipple into Noah's mouth. "That'll be me," he said. "The only vampirelike creature in Irish legend was the Dearg-dul, or red blood sucker—an unhappy maiden forced to marry not for love, but by arrangement, and so commits suicide. Then she walks the night luring first her husband, then her father, to their doom. Ever after, she leaves her grave several times a year to prey on any young man she sees."

"I don't think we're dealing with a vampire," I said.

"She's also a shape-shifter," he added, "turning into a lovely bat-winged creature as soon as her victim is in her clutches. The other Irish shape-shifters are the Children of Lir, who became swans, and a host of others who turn into various creatures, including insects, as a result of a curse or magic."

"I don't think we're dealing with any of those, either."

"Don't you now?" Mal murmured softly as Noah's eyes fluttered closed. "What, then?"

"Hey," Claire interrupted, "don't you want to hear what I scrounged up on Scottish shape-shifters?"

"If we must," I said.

"Well, I did spend a lot of time searching. Apparently the Scots aren't big on shape-shifting. I found only one."

"Which is?"

"Selkies—seal shifters. Since we're not anywhere near the sea, I'm not feeling the magic on that one. So there goes our theory that the victim is the supernatural."

"Not necessarily," I said.

The two of them exchanged a glance, then sat back in their chairs. "Get to it," Claire ordered.

I told them all I'd discovered, and they didn't laugh, though Claire did roll her eyes at the "alien" theory.

"You got any better ideas?" I asked.

She glanced at Mal and together they shrugged.

"We're at a dead end. I'm not sure what to do next." I hated to admit that. I always knew what to do. That's why I was the sheriff in these parts.

"We'll keep searching for a connection," Claire said. "Sooner or later something's going to pop, and then we'll be on whatever demon or monster or alien like white on rice."

I never had understood the "white on rice" adage, but now didn't seem the time to bring that up.

"Maybe one of us should check in with Elise," Claire said.

"I will."

"*You* will? No way."

Since I wanted to ask about Ian's disappearing wife, I didn't have a problem calling the wise and furry doctor, but I wasn't going to tell Claire that. I didn't want her sympathy about another doomed affair, especially one she hadn't even known I was having.

"I'm a professional." I lifted my chin. "If she knows anything worth knowing, I'll get back to you later."

"Okay," Claire said, though she stared at me suspiciously. I got out of there before she pulled out the thumbscrews.

Since I hadn't been to the office all day, I stopped before I went home. Both Jordan's and Cal's shift had ended hours ago. Cal had left a note on my desk—or at least I thought he had. When I picked it up, I saw it was merely another Chuck Norris chuckle.

When Chuck Norris crosses the street, the cars better look both ways.

With a smile, I set the sheet aside to give to Jordan to-morrow.

Several other messages lay beneath Cal's, people who had called during the day but not been urgent enough to contact me about.

I shuffled through them. All were from citizens, wanting to know why I was ordering autopsies and dig-ging up corpses. Well, I wasn't going to tell them. I'd already met with the next of kin and shared what I could.

I tossed the messages into the trash. I was certain citizens would accost me on the street if given a chance, so I'd do my best not to give them one.

I snuck out the back door and slid into my brand-new squad car. At home I changed out of my uniform into jeans, a red tank top, and sandals. Then I headed upstairs to the third-floor office to call Elise.

Like Ian, I was drawn to that room. The view of the mountains from the window soothed me. I sat at the desk facing them as I dialed the super-secret phone number of the *Jäger-Suchers*.

"What now?" Elise asked without benefit of "hello." The longer I knew her, the more like her grandfather she became.

Edward Mandenauer had founded the *Jäger-Suchers*

over sixty years ago. From what I'd seen of him in the short time he'd been in town, he wasn't much on "hello" and "good-bye," either. Edward liked to shoot first, ask if you were human later. It saved time.

"Caller ID is wrecking polite conversation as we know it," I said.

"If I know who's calling, why waste time making nicey-nice?"

See what I mean? Edward junior.

Well, two could play at this, and I didn't want to chitchat with wolf girl any more than she wanted to chitchat with me.

"We've got a new kid in town, and I was wondering if you had any info on him in your handy-dandy 'Big Brother is watching you pee' database."

"You'll be glad we've got that database if he's in there."

I didn't argue.

"Name?"

"Ian Walker."

"What do you think he is?"

"If I knew that, I wouldn't be calling you."

"Nothing here," she said, and started to hang up.

"Wait!" I shouted. "I was actually more interested in his wife."

"Oh, really? Why's that?"

"Because she disappeared without a trace, which sounds suspiciously like your work."

"Doesn't it though? Except it wasn't."

"You know that off the top of your head?"

"If we'd disappeared her, we'd have a record of that right next to any record on her husband, which there isn't. We like to keep our lies straight, and the only way to do that is to keep track of them."

"Well, when it comes to lying, I guess you'd know."

"Got that right." She sounded proud, and maybe she was. Her lies, and those of her colleagues and underlings, were what allowed the world to continue turning on its merry axis, secure in the false knowledge that monsters were not crawling all over the place.

I opened my mouth to thank her, but Elise was already gone.

23

As I ended the call on my side, something howled out there in the night. Spirit wolf or real wolf, didn't matter. The sound reminded me that I needed to check on Quatie. I got to my feet and headed for the door.

The rush of air from my movement caused something to swoosh out from under a bookcase against the front wall. Whatever it was, it was as light as a—

"Feather," I murmured, and snatched it up.

I'd never had a feather in here that I could recall, except for Ian's, and this wasn't his. Not only had I seen the eagle feather in place in his hair earlier today, but the one I held in my hand wasn't from an eagle.

Big and black without a hint of white, I had no idea what kind it was or how it had gotten here. Feathers this big didn't appear out of nowhere. Or maybe they did in this new world evolving every day in Lake Bluff. I put the feather into the top desk drawer for later perusal.

Aaaewww!

I jumped. The howl seemed to come from right outside my window.

"Coming," I muttered as I ran down two flights of stairs.

However, when I went outside, the wolf wasn't there, and she had gone as silent as the ghost she no doubt was. I jumped into my dad's pickup and headed north.

Quatie sat on her porch. As I got out, she stood, moving a lot easier than the last time I'd visited. That balm of Ian's really needed to be bottled and sold.

Seeing her get around so much better, I was relieved. I'd brought Ian to Quatie—at her request, true, but I never would have forgiven myself if his cure had harmed rather than helped.

Several sticks lay on the ground in front of the house. Kindling, most likely. I scooped them into my arms, frowning when I saw the ends had been honed to points.

"I whittle," Quatie said without my asking. "Not very good at it."

If she'd been trying to make a mammal or a bird, she wasn't. If she'd been aiming at poking out someone's eye, I'd have to change my mind. Physicians recommended handiwork to soothe arthritis, the movement working out the kinks. Quatie must have taken up whittling for just that reason.

I wondered if Ian had been back to visit without me and had suggested it, but I wasn't going to ask. The subject of Ian Walker was still a little raw.

She'd shoved one into the ground at the corner of the house; the pointy end stuck straight up.

"A little dangerous." I indicated the stick.

"For squirrels," she said.

I wasn't sure if they were meant to keep the squirrels

away, entertain them, or skewer them, and I had no chance to ask since she turned and went into the house.

As I followed, I marveled again at how much her gait had improved. Even with the miracle balm, the progress was amazing. Then I saw a probable reason why on the table and forgot all about pointy sticks and squirrels.

"Moonshine's illegal," I said.

"You going to turn me in, Gracie?" She squinted through cataract-murky eyes. "This settles the pain in my old bones."

It would probably eat her old bones if she drank too much. I was concerned it might eat right through her stomach lining, too, but she slammed back a shot, licked her lips, and smiled with more teeth than I recalled her having. She must have gotten dentures. I only hoped the moonshine didn't ruin them.

I shook my head when she offered me a shot. I spent a lot of time chasing stills in these mountains. Theoretically, moonshine was dangerous. Too much alcohol and a person could go blind. In truth, the old folks who made it had been brewing the stuff for decades and they knew what they were doing.

I could tell by the jar and the shade of the brew that Quatie had gotten hers from Granny McGinty, the biggest moonshiner in the county because she made good hooch for a reasonable price.

Since Quatie appeared a lot better now than she had the last time I'd seen her, I wasn't going to complain. In the old days, people doctored quite a few things with moonshine—rheumatism, arthritis, toothache. They managed with what they had. I couldn't fault Quatie for doing the same.

"I wanted to see how you were doing." I took a seat.

"Better." She took another gulp. "You don't need to

keep checking on me, child. I've been alone a long time."

"Is your great-great-granddaughter still coming to visit?"

"Soon." She laughed with such pure joy I had to smile.

"Where's she coming from?"

"Not far. Enough about me. How's your young man?"

He wasn't my young man. But the eagerness on her face, her genuine fondness for Ian—I couldn't tell her he was a lying, married weasel. At least not today.

"He's fine, Quatie."

"Very fine." She winked and took another sip of moonshine.

I frowned. "You aren't going to take a walk later, are you?"

"No. No walking tonight." She didn't seem affected by the alcohol at all. I suppose familiarity bred resistance. "Have you read your great-grandmother's papers yet, Gracie?"

"No, ma'am."

"Mmm." She seemed to think about that. "That's probably for the best."

"Why?"

She got up from the table and walked without a wobble to her couch, where she lay down. "They'll just make you sad." She closed her eyes.

The silence that settled over the room was so thick I began to get nervous. She hadn't died, had she?

"Quatie?" I called softly.

My only answer was a snore.

⚭

I went home. I didn't have much else to do.

Heading down the highway, I let my mind wander.

I'd driven these roads a thousand times; I knew how they twisted and turned. I considered ignoring my house and returning to work or maybe going to Claire's or even—

The wolf appeared as if from nowhere, right in front of my truck. I slammed on the brakes, but it was too late. I braced for the impact, but the truck passed right through the animal and came out the other side.

I looked in the rearview mirror. The wolf stood behind me, not a mark on it. I got out of the vehicle.

A flurry of movement, the scrabble of claws against pavement, and the animal ran through me again. Cold wind, a heavy rain, I felt thick and full, then thin and empty. I had a mental image of my body and the wolf's melding, stretching, coming together, then suddenly flying apart.

I swayed, and when I could see clearly once more, the beast had stopped several yards ahead. She glanced back, then ran a few feet.

"If you wanted me to go in that direction, all you had to do was wait," I said. "I was already doing it."

The wolf snorted and I remembered. I'd been thinking of going anywhere but home.

"You can read my mind?"

I wasn't sure how I felt about that. It wasn't as if the wolf could tell anyone my thoughts, but they were *my* thoughts, and I preferred to keep them that way.

I scowled at the furry beast. "What difference could it possibly make if I go home or not?"

As if in answer, the air seemed to shriek. I put my hands over my ears and glanced up just in time to see a shower of sparks falling from the sky.

The wolf whined. I would think a noise like that

would hurt her ears worse than mine, even if they were spirit ears.

The animal ran south again, then turned, waited. South, the direction of peace and good health—the direction of home.

I peered at the area of the sky where the sparks had disappeared. Just like last time, orange glowed against the night.

Cursing, I jumped into my truck, fumbling for my cell phone even as I thrust the vehicle into gear and drove over the messenger wolf. The animal didn't seem to mind, catching up in seconds and loping alongside, oblivious to the trunks of trees that lined the road. The wolf just ran right through them.

I reached the fire department and gave them the approximate location of the blaze; then I called Cal.

"Remember when the sparks came down and started the fire that wasn't?"

"Where is it this time?"

"I think it's my house."

"I'll be right there."

I continued to drive as fast as I could on the narrow, winding roads, praying that this fire was as much a myth as the last one. The wolf ran beside me until I turned down my long, rutted driveway; then she disappeared.

The orange glow had only brightened as I approached. I knew even before I shot out of the trees and into my yard that my house was toast.

The fire department had arrived ahead of me, as had Cal. A scuffle was going on near my front porch. Cal and the fire chief held on to someone who seemed to be fighting to get inside.

"What's going on?" I called.

The three men stopped struggling and turned. One of them was Ian.

"You're okay," he said.

"Not really. My damn house is on fire."

"I told him you weren't in there, but he didn't want to listen," Cal said.

Ian had been trying to run into a burning building to save me? I couldn't help but be touched. Because I was, I turned away to look at my house. I almost wished I hadn't.

The roof was completely engulfed. There wasn't much I could do except watch the fire department do their thing and wonder what in hell had fallen from the sky onto my house. Whatever it had been, it wasn't there any longer.

Ian and Cal joined me, staring at the flames, too.

"What are you doing here?" I asked Ian. Cal took one look at my face and walked off.

"I wanted to talk to you."

"Was the house on fire when you arrived?"

"Yes."

"So you didn't see what started it?"

He frowned. "You're thinking arson?"

I hadn't said that, but I found it interesting that he'd heard it.

"I'm a cop," I said. "I think a lot of things. What did you see?"

"I drove up, and the roof was on fire. I thought you were inside. The place was locked. I pounded on the door, shouted for you; then those guys grabbed me."

"I appreciate your concern, but I'm fine. You may as well go."

"I'm not leaving you."

His voice was too loud, and I winced, then glanced

over my shoulder toward Cal, who, from his scowl, had heard. He took a step in our direction, and I shook my head. I didn't need my deputy to step in when I had man trouble.

I faced Ian. "I'm a big girl, Doctor. I can take care of myself."

"Where are you going to sleep?"

"Certainly not with you," I snapped.

"That wasn't what I meant."

Too bad, I thought. Despite all my protestations to the contrary, I wanted to sleep with him, to hold him and have him hold me. If I'd lived in another town, one that wasn't so small, so conservative, so judgmental . . . No, that wouldn't matter.

If I'd been a different person, one who didn't care about what was real or true or right, I'd have agreed with him that a missing wife was as good as a dead wife. But I wasn't and I didn't. However, that didn't keep me from wanting what I couldn't have.

"Thanks," I said softly. "But I can't."

"Grace, you have to listen to me—"

I held up my hand. "Not now. Please."

He pressed his lips together, then gave a sharp nod. "It's just that I came over here with my speech all prepared and then—"

"My house was on fire."

"Yeah."

"Grace?"

I turned as the fire chief, Sam Makelway, strode up. He'd taken over recently from Joe Cantrell, who'd been the fire chief as long as my dad had been the sheriff. Sam was more than qualified since he'd joined the department right out of high school.

A few years older than me, Sam was broad and tall,

with short red hair and a round, pale face that got ruddier and ruddier the closer he got to a fire and the longer he had to stay there. Right now his facial barometer hovered between salmon and rose, and I let out a relieved breath. Couldn't be too bad.

Sam had been in the same class as my brother Gene. They hadn't been pals—my brothers had been pals only with one another—but they'd been friendly enough. I liked Sam. He knew his job, which made mine so much easier.

"We've got it under control." He waved at the roof, which was only smoking now, no longer shooting spiky tendrils of flame toward the slightly lopsided silver moon. "Looks like just the top room is ruined."

"Well, I guess that's better than—" I stopped as I realized what that meant.

"Grace?" Ian took my arm, shook it a little. "You need to breathe."

I not only couldn't breathe, I couldn't stand, so I sat with a thud on the ground at Ian's feet.

Both men went to their knees next to me, Sam bellowing for Cal to call the paramedics.

"No," I managed, then drew in a huge, loud, gulping breath. "I'm okay."

I wasn't, but I didn't need a paramedic. No one, nothing, could fix this.

Grandmother's papers had been in that third-floor room, and now they were gone.

It was as if I'd lost her all over again.

24

IAN'S LONG FINGERS wrapped around my wrist as he took my pulse. From the expression on his face, he didn't like what he'd found.

"You need to calm down," he murmured.

Cal hovered; so did Sam. They weren't used to seeing me sitting down on the job. The way I'd hit the ground, they probably thought I'd fainted. How would that appear to the general public? *Lake Bluff sheriff faints at the sight of her house on fire.*

Not that I wouldn't have every reason to, but people liked their sheriffs tough. Can't say that I blamed them. I forced myself to my feet.

"I'm good." I yanked my wrist out of Ian's grasp, even though his fingers felt pleasantly warm and dry against my cold, clammy skin. "I just thought of all I kept in that room. Things that can't be replaced."

"You can't be replaced," Ian said, and I cut my gaze to his. What I saw there made me look away.

"What do you think started the fire, Sam?"

Sam stared at me for several beats, decided I wasn't going to swoon, and got on with it. "Hard to say. I'll have the investigator over here first thing tomorrow. You better not stay tonight. Even though the lower floors weren't burned, there's going to be water damage and the smell—" He spread his huge, hard hands. "You'll have to hire a professional cleaning company."

"Ka-ching."

Sam grinned at the evidence I was back to my old self. "Yeah. But you've got insurance, right?"

"Of course."

My dad had been big on insurance. We'd had a couple of crosses burned on our lawn back in the old days—which weren't all that old.

When Dad had taken over as the first Cherokee sheriff in Lake Bluff history, there'd been some who hadn't been as happy about it as we were. We'd never been quite sure if it had been the Cherokee sheriff part they objected to or the African-American part. Maybe both.

If it hadn't been for the sparks I'd seen tumbling from the sky, accompanied by the supernatural shrieking, I'd have figured someone who wasn't happy about a female Cherokee, African-American, Scotch-Irish sheriff had lit up my roof to express their point of view. From the expression on Sam's face, he'd had the same thought.

"I'll take care of it from here," I said.

Sam nodded and returned to his men.

I considered going inside, maybe grabbing some clothes, but I knew from past experience with other fires that everything I owned would smell like wet charcoal. I was going to have to live with what I had until I could buy new underwear and enough casual clothes to last me a few days. Luckily I kept some spare uniforms at the office.

I hated to knock on Claire's door this late and scare the crap out of her, so I decided to rent a hotel room. We had plenty in town, and since the Full Moon Festival was still several weeks away, there should be a lot of vacancies.

"Stay with me," Ian murmured.

I didn't even dignify that with a glance, let alone an answer.

Instead I strode to where Cal was talking into his car radio. I meant to tell him where I'd be and get gone, but as I approached, his words made me pause and listen.

"She's dead?" he asked. "They're sure?"

"Dad," Jordan said with a scorn that made me want to reach through the radio and strangle her, "I think people know what dead looks like."

"Not as often as you'd think," Cal muttered. "I'm on my way."

He glanced at me. "You heard?"

I nodded. The sound of a car starting made me glance over my shoulder. Ian had at last taken the hint and left.

"Who's dead this time?" I asked.

"Merry Gray."

"But—" I stopped before I blurted something I'd have to explain later. I guess Merry *did* fit the profile. She was dying.

"But what?" Cal asked.

As far as Cal knew, we'd only had a rash of deaths. I wasn't going to tell him about the supernatural questions. He was a straight shooter, an eternal Marine. He'd never believe in aliens, or anything else out of the ordinary for that matter, and I didn't have time to convince him.

"I'll take the call," I said.

"I'll go with you."

"No." I was going to have Doc go with me. "I need you to hang around here. I—" I forced my voice to break. It wasn't that hard. "I can't do it."

Sympathy washed over Cal's face. "Of course. I'll stay."

He tried to pat my shoulder, fumbling the gesture and smacking me in both the chin and the neck. I stepped out of his reach. "Where'd they find Merry?"

"Died in her bed, I hope in her sleep. Poor woman."

"Yeah," I agreed. It would be nice if we had a plain old death for a change, but I doubted it. "I'll see you tomorrow. I'm going to stay in town. You can raise me on my cell."

Cal lifted a hand in good-bye and took off with long, sure strides toward the huddle of firefighters on my lawn.

In the past few days, Doc had moved up on my speed dial to the number-one position. He answered on the second ring, and I gave him directions.

"I'm getting real sick of seeing your number on my caller ID," he said.

"Be honest, Doc: Did you ever really like it?"

⚭

I reached Merry's house, which stood on one of the many side streets in Lake Bluff. Despite the hour, the place was lit up like the Fourth of July. Merry's husband, Ted, opened the door before I even knocked.

His face was pale and tear-streaked. He tried to speak and choked, then turned and walked into the living room, leaving the door open.

I'd dealt with hysterical relatives before, but they were usually women. Ted was six-four and weighed about three hundred pounds. He was a mason, and his hands were as big as bricks. I guess size didn't matter when it came to heartbreak. Still, Merry had been sick a long time and, according to all the gossips, there'd been no hope. I don't know why I'd thought he'd be ready for the inevitable by now, but I had.

"Ted." I crept into the room, not wanting to disturb him but needing to ask questions. I was going to try to finagle an autopsy out of this man—it wouldn't hurt to actually have permission from the family member on record—but I couldn't do it if he was incoherent.

"Grace." He paused, trying to breathe, but his chest kept hitching like a child who's sobbed too long and too hard.

"Take your time." I perched on the edge of the couch. He stood by the window.

"She—she—she—"

"I know," I said gently.

"She wasn't supposed to die."

I stilled. "What?"

"She went to the doctor yesterday. She was in remission. It was a miracle."

"Miracle," I murmured, wondering what in hell Walker had put in that jar. I meant to find out.

"What, exactly, did her doctor say?"

"Just that. Remission. She had more time."

"How much?"

"He wouldn't say, but then—" He lifted his huge hands and let them fall back to his sides, helpless.

"Tell me what happened."

"She went to bed early; she always did. I watched the news, then Leno. I heard this horrible noise." He winced and put his palms over his ears. "So I went up and she was—" He choked, dropped his arms, and began to sob again.

I wanted to check on her, but I didn't want to leave him. Thankfully, Doc arrived.

"Stay with him," I said, and before Doc could protest, I hustled up the steps.

Merry lay on her bed. If it weren't for the expression on her face, I'd have thought her sleeping. Her body was in repose, thin hands folded over a concave stomach. But her eyes were wide open, her mouth twisted in pain or fear.

I pulled the sheet over her face and went back downstairs, jerking my head at Doc, who joined me in the hall. Ted still stared out the window, shoulders shaking.

"Same as all the others," I said. "Her face, the shrieking before she died. Except, according to Ted, she'd just gone into remission."

"She wasn't dying?"

"Not today."

"I told him I needed to do an autopsy," Doc murmured, and I stifled an inappropriate hoot of happiness that I wouldn't be the one who had to ask. "He was agreeable. I'll do it right away. Maybe this isn't even related."

"Maybe," I agreed, but I didn't think so.

⚭

I called Ted's sister to come and sit with him, then left Doc to deal with Merry. I headed for Ian Walker's place; I didn't even take my vehicle, just stalked downhill toward Center Street.

His building was dark except for a tiny glow on the second floor. I pounded on the back door loud enough to wake everyone on the street. Luckily, all of the establishments nearby were retail. Walker was the only person I knew who lived above his business.

He opened the door and smiled. "I'm so glad you—"

I put my palm in the center of his chest and shoved. He stumbled back a few steps and I followed, kicking the door shut behind me. "What did you give her?"

He lifted one hand and rubbed at his sternum. "Who?"

"Merry Gray."

"We already had this conversation, Sheriff. I'm not going to tell you."

I began to walk forward, my steps echoing on the wood floor. He stood his ground, chin lifting, the smooth silver light of the moon through the windows glancing off his cheekbones and nose, sparkling in his dark hair, and playing hide-and-seek with his eagle feather.

Why was it that in the darkness he looked like a warrior and in the daylight he just looked like a man? Without the feather, no one would ever mistake him for Cherokee between nine and five. After midnight, he could be mistaken for nothing else.

"You think you can take me?" he murmured.

I stopped with the toes of my sandals just brushing his bare feet. He'd removed his jacket and tie, loosened the buttons at his throat, rolled up his cuffs. His skin gleamed in the half-light. Taking him took on a whole new meaning, one I was tempted to explore—until the moon's glow glanced off of his wedding ring.

"I don't have to take you," I said. "I can get a warrant."

"Good luck with that."

I wanted to scream. He made me so mad.

I took several breaths and tried a different tactic. "What's the big secret? She went into remission. I'd think you'd want everyone to know what a great doctor you are."

"Remission?" His brow creased. "Really?"

"You seem surprised."

"I am. What I gave her—" I perked up, but he paused, shrugged. "I'm glad she's better, but I had nothing to do with it."

"She not so much better as dead."

"But you just said—"

"Yeah, things change fast around here." I headed for the door. He wasn't going to be of any help, and if I stayed I'd only want to jump him, which just made me madder at both him and myself.

I slammed the door, then stood in the silvery light trying to think of what to do. I wasn't trained for paranormal investigation; I was getting nowhere and people were dying.

If they were people. The committee was still out on that.

Regardless, beings that inhabited my town were turning up dead, sans hearts, and I had no idea why. Pretty soon someone besides me was going to notice the epidemic, and then there'd be real trouble.

Inside I heard the faint mumble of Ian's voice. Either he was talking to himself or he'd called someone. I inched closer to the door, noticing that I'd shut it so hard, the latch hadn't caught, and now it stood open a few inches.

"A woman in remission died tonight."

I frowned. Who could he possibly be calling about that?

"I gave her one of my healing potions. Herbs, vitamins. Nothing major. Believe me, if I could cure cancer, I'd be doing it."

My lips curved. Wouldn't that be something?

"I know it doesn't make sense. The Kâlanû Ahyeli'-skĭ steals the lives of the dying."

I froze.

The *what*?

25

While I wanted to bust right in and demand answers to a whole lot of questions, I forced myself to remain where I was and listen.

"No one's reacted to the feather."

His feather? I'd reacted to it, though I certainly hoped he wasn't sharing how.

"Buzzard," he continued, "just like the legends said."

Buzzard feather? I flashed on the huge black feather I'd found in my office at home—the office that was now toast. What in hell was Ian Walker up to? Who in hell was he? And who was he working for?

"I'll keep looking." His voice faded, and the stairs creaked as he went up them. I leaned back as his shadow passed in front of the second-story window. Before I confronted him, I needed some answers. Namely, what did a buzzard feather repel and what in hell was a Kâlanû Ahyeli'-skĭ?

Leaving the door ajar—I'd definitely be back—I headed for the sheriff's department.

The place was quiet at this time of night. My third-shift dispatcher, a semi-retired lawyer by the name of Catfish Waller, manned the phones. Catfish was the only lawyer left in Lake Bluff. Since we didn't have much need for a lawyer, that worked out well.

Catfish had come to work for me when his insomnia had gotten so bad he never slept a wink between midnight and 9:00 A.M. He not only was responsible, but he also knew the law. If I could only get him to stop writing his memoirs during his shift. Not that there was all that much else to do, but he had a bad habit of reading them to anyone who would listen. There'd been complaints.

"Grace!" he greeted. "Chapter seventeen, where I lose my virginity."

Oh, God.

"Sorry, Catfish, gotta hit the Internet. Maybe later." I made a dash for my office.

"Real sorry about your house," he called.

"Thanks!" I waved as I escaped inside, then locked the door behind me and pulled down the shades. I didn't want Catfish deciding he really needed my opinion any more than I wanted him seeing what I was researching on the Internet.

I also wanted to change my clothes, which reeked of the fire, so I stripped and donned one of the extra uniforms in the closet, exchanging my sandals for sneakers, then made my way to the computer and typed in *buzzard feathers*.

I got back a whole lot of ways to use them for decorating or arts and crafts. Did people have lives? Who spent their time thinking up this stuff? Psychotic Martha Stewart clones?

Native American legends, buzzard feathers, I pecked out next.

That got me a hit right away.

> *The Cherokees believed that by placing a buzzard feather at the entrance of any dwelling, a witch would be unable to cross the threshold.*

"Oookay."

I'd overheard Ian say that no one had reacted to the feather, which led me to believe he was looking for a witch, and I wasn't the only one he was looking at.

My heart pounded in my throat, not with fear so much as excitement. I'd been at a dead end. I'd had nowhere else to turn for answers, and suddenly answers were falling into my lap. I just didn't know the question.

The Internet had been of no use to me before, but I hadn't had enough information. Now I had a name.

"Kâlanû Ahyeli'-skĭ," I murmured as I typed, then hit *enter* with a flourish.

> *Of all the Cherokee witches*

"Well, that explains the buzzard feather," I murmured.

> *the most feared is the Kâlanû Ahyeli'-skĭ or the Raven Mocker.*

"Could also explain the sudden increase in ravens." I frowned. "Maybe."

The Raven Mocker robs the dying of life. Flying through the night with arms outstretched trailing sparks, the witch announces its approach with a horrible shriek.

The Raven Mocker eats the victim's heart, stealing whatever days the person has left on the earth. Because the Raven Mocker is a witch, it is able to remove the hearts without leaving a scar.

Well, at least that took care of our theory of alien invasion. I can't say I was sorry to see it go.

Now I knew what we were dealing with, kind of. I had no idea what this thing looked like, how it worked, a way to kill it, but I had a pretty good idea who did.

∞

Since the door was still partway open, I walked right into the clinic. Out of curiosity I glanced up. A buzzard feather had been tacked to the wall directly over the entrance at both the back door and the front. Obviously not taking any chances, Ian had placed one over each window as well.

I'd already broken in, so I took off my shoes, snuck up the stairs, and headed for the only room where a light remained burning. No one was there.

I allowed my gaze to wander over the area. Desk, books, papers—his office, not his bedroom. He'd probably gone to bed and forgotten to shut off the light. Before I woke him up and questioned him mercilessly, I'd take a look around.

I wasn't worried any longer about a warrant. No court in the land was going to believe any of this anyway.

Medical texts. Medical journals. Tiny bottles of oil.

Colored liquids. Bowls of herbs. A bag of what appeared to be grass. I opened it and took a whiff, determining it was the kind that cows ate, before setting it down.

I made my way to the desk where several loose sheets of paper lay on the blotter. The words were in Cherokee. I couldn't read them, but there was something familiar about them.

I threw a quick glance over my shoulder; I'm not sure why. The place was as quiet now as it had been when I'd walked in.

Ian stood right behind me.

I let out a pathetic squeak and stepped back, stumbling over a stack of books next to the desk.

He reached out, quick as a snake, and snatched me by the forearms, hauling me against him. His eyes caught the golden glow of the lamp, flickering topaz, even as the pupils dilated so large they nearly obscured the lighter shade of his irises.

"What are you doing here?"

I opened my mouth to answer, or maybe to question, and he kissed me. That seemed to be his prelude to everything.

I tasted desperation on his tongue, lust, desire, need, on his lips. My body responded; I couldn't make it stop. I felt all those things, too, even though my mind knew better.

But right now my mind seemed to have gone on vacation. Something nagged at the corner, but I couldn't quite grasp it with him kissing me like this. Then he was touching me, too, and I couldn't do anything but respond.

My thighs hit the edge of the desk, and I sat abruptly. He stepped between my legs, nudging them farther apart. Looming over me, his shadow blotted out the light. His hair sifted over my face, creating a curtain between us and the world.

"Grace," he whispered, as his lips trailed across my jaw, down my neck. My head fell back; to keep my balance I wrapped my legs around his, hooking my ankles.

His fingers popped the buttons on my uniform seconds ahead of his mouth. He traced his tongue across my collarbone, then dipped it into the valley between my breasts and up and over the swell. One tug and he bared me to the night air, then his mouth closed over a peak, and he suckled.

Somehow my shirt came off, my bra, too. I was naked from the waist up, clothed from the waist down, but wrapped around him, center to center; his erection rode me right where I needed it to. My gun belt thwapped against the desk in an enticing rhythm, which only added fuel to the arousal.

He lifted his head, reached behind me, and flung the papers and pencils and books off the desk in a single sweep of his arm. For an instant I was stunned and excited; then I saw again those papers, the writing, and I remembered where I'd seen it before. I shoved him away and drew my weapon.

His gaze shifted slowly from my bare breasts to the Glock. "You have an odd idea of foreplay."

"Then you're really not going to like the climax." I lowered the barrel until it was pointed at his crotch. He took a step backward. "Don't move."

I got off the desk, ignoring the sudden chill as the air drifted over my skin. I wasn't going to give him the satisfaction of covering myself. It wasn't anything he hadn't seen before.

Keeping my eyes and my gun on him, I bent and retrieved one of the papers he'd swept so grandly to the floor. I would have known sooner if I hadn't believed they'd been burnt to cinders in the fire at my house earlier that night.

Straightening, I held up a paper covered in my great-grandmother's handwriting.

"Who in hell are you?" I asked.

26

"YOU KNOW WHO I am."

"I may know your name but not *who* you are. Not why you're really here." I set the paper on the desk, then leaned my hip against it. "Tell me more about the Raven Mocker."

His eyes widened. "I should have known you'd figure it out."

I didn't bother to tell him I'd only figured it out because I'd been eavesdropping.

"You left a buzzard feather at my house?" He lifted one shoulder, lowered it. "You thought I was a witch?"

"Someone is."

"Why me?"

"You were out in the forest the night of the Thunder Moon."

"So were you."

"I was looking for the Raven Mocker, and there you were."

"You knew it was here?"

"I knew it was coming."

"How?"

He tilted his head. "You wanna stow the gun, maybe put on a shirt so I can think straight?"

"No."

"Grace, I won't hurt you. If I planned to, I could have a hundred times already."

"Well, that makes me all warm and fuzzy," I muttered, my stomach rolling.

I'd believed he wanted me for me, just as I'd wanted him. But like so many others, he'd wanted something *from* me—to get close so he could see if I was evil and then steal my great-grandmother's medicine.

I stared at him, uncertain what to do. Scream, shout, shoot? None was a good idea, so I put up my gun and reached for my shirt, keeping my eye on him the whole time.

"Talk," I ordered as I buttoned the last button.

"I'm a member of an ancient society."

I sighed. "I am going to kick Elise Hanover's ass."

"You know about the *Jäger-Suchers*?"

"They were here last summer."

He frowned. "Werewolf troubles?"

"Like you wouldn't believe."

"I hadn't heard. I run into a *Jäger-Sucher* here and there on various assignments. It's hard not to since we're both hunting supernatural creatures, but I'm a member of the Nighthawk Keetoowahs. You've heard of them?"

I nodded. I'd learned about the Keetoowahs in school. They'd been formed in the eighteenth century for the express purpose of keeping Cherokee history and language alive.

"So you're a member of a Cherokee society devoted to preserving the traditional ways," I said. "Big deal."

"That's what the Nighthawks are on the outside, but on the inside we're sworn to track down and eliminate evil supernatural entities, like the Raven Mocker."

"If you know about the *Jäger-Suchers,* then it would follow that they know about you." Especially since they seemed to know about everything.

"Sometimes we make use of the others' resources."

I wondered momentarily if Edward had used his influence to get Walker's medical license approved so fast or if perhaps the Nighthawks had their own Edward on staff.

"I asked Hanover about you, and she said she'd never heard of you."

He smiled. "She lies."

"No shit."

"You don't like her?"

"No," I said shortly. "We rub each other the wrong way."

"Wolf and panther." He was suddenly right next to me. "I can understand why you would."

"Back up." I shoved at his chest. I couldn't think when he was so close. He smelled too good and his body lined up with mine just right. Damn him. "I'm not a panther."

"You are." He reached out and drew one finger between my breasts. "Here. Just like I'm an eagle." He pointed at himself. "In my heart."

"Speaking of hearts, I have a sudden rash of missing ones, which I hear is the fault of the Raven Mocker."

"Yes."

"But no one's seen this thing."

"It's invisible."

I *had* suspected that.

"Though not all the time. It's a person and a raven. Witch and shape-shifter. The Raven Mocker enters the rooms of the dying by becoming invisible."

"The shrieking?"

"Frightens the victim to death."

I remembered the terror-stricken faces of the dead, and I wanted the witch to die as frightened as all of its victims had been.

A little vindictive? Sue me.

"How do we find it?" I asked.

"That's the problem. I don't know."

"I thought finding these . . . things was what you did."

"If it was that simple, everyone would do it."

I narrowed my eyes. I was in no mood for jokes. "Why isn't it simple?"

"Do you know what a witch looks like?"

"Bad teeth, warts, long, gray scraggly hair?"

"Could be. Could also be you, me," he spread his arms wide, "everybody."

"How do we figure out who it is before someone else dies?"

He jerked his chin, indicating the desk. "That's why I'm translating your great-grandmother's papers."

"I thought those were cures."

"Cures can have more than one meaning—medicinal cures for human ailments and supernatural cures for monstrous entities. Most of the papers of great medicine men and women also contain legends that were passed down through the generations. Stories of beings from ancient times—both good and bad."

"Why do you think my great-grandmother's papers

contain information about the Raven Mocker?" I paused as another thought occurred to me. "Wait. You were already here when the storm arrived on the night of the Thunder Moon. You said you knew the witch was coming, but how?"

"I'm A ni wo di."

"A paint clan medicine man. I know."

"Paint clan are more than medicine men; some of us are sorcerers."

I waited to see if he'd laugh, but he didn't. "You've been reading way too much Harry Potter."

His lips curved. "While I do enjoy Harry and clan, I was a sorcerer long before he showed up. Besides, I think he's a wizard."

"Wizard, witch." I threw up my hands. "What's the difference?"

"I've never met a wizard, so I'm inclined to believe they don't exist, but I could be wrong. A witch can be either good or bad, depending on the witch. And a sorcerer, in the world of the Nighthawks, is a medicine man with a little something extra."

"What?"

"Magic."

"Right," I said. "You bet."

"You don't believe me?"

I hesitated. I'd seen magic, both as a child and as an adult. I'd shoved aside the memories of my great-grandmother's gifts, refusing to believe what my eyes had seen. Then last summer I'd had no choice but to believe when I'd witnessed men and women turn into beasts and back again.

"What kind of magic are you talking about?" I asked.

Ian didn't answer, at least with words. He closed his eyes and began to chant in Cherokee. The air thickened, shimmered, changed, and when he opened his eyes, they weren't human anymore.

"Eagle eyes," I murmured. "You're a shape-shifter?"

"Not completely. After years of practice, I can draw the essence of my spirit animal, take on some of its powers."

I thought of the eagle that had been seen soaring over the mountains. "Can you fly?"

He smiled. "Not yet."

"There's been an eagle spotted near town."

"I'm sure it's just drawn to the . . . ," he shrugged, "vibes. When I call on my eagle spirit, something must go out into the air."

"Okay." That could explain the sudden influx of ravens, too. If this witch was a raven shape-shifter, that would put "something" into the air as well and perhaps draw them in. "If you can't fly, what can you do?"

"I see."

"Me, too, pal, and I'm not even magic."

"You're a descendant of Rose Scott, one of the most powerful medicine women in recent history. With some training, you could easily do what I can and more."

"No thanks. I'm not much of a bird lover."

He gave me a knowing look. I *had* been a bird lover, several times.

"You're A ni sa ho ni," he said, letting me off the hook without comment. "Clan of blue. The panther. You have powers beyond your wildest dreams. If you study, if you practice, there's nothing you can't do."

I'm not saying it wasn't tempting. The long-ago childhood dream of actually *becoming* a panther, of course it called to me. But I was no longer a child, and I'd had to put away childish things. Like my panther collection.

"You're starting to make me think more of a snake in the garden than an eagle in the medical clinic."

He tilted his head with a birdlike flick that kind of gave me the willies. "What do you mean?"

"You're tempting me, Ian. I've seen what werewolves can do, and I want no part of that, regardless of how powerful I might become."

"What do werewolves have to do with anything?"

"Shape-shifters are shape-shifters. Just because I'd be a panther wouldn't make me any less . . ." I waved my hand. "Evil."

"Why would you be evil? I'm not evil."

"That remains to be seen."

"You've got this all wrong, Grace. I was born to be a sorcerer, a Nighthawk, and a warrior. Accessing the eagle spirit is part of who I am, just as your panther is part of who you are. Elise sensed it in you, just like you sensed the wolf in her. You think if she believed you were evil she wouldn't have shot you in the head the first chance that she got?"

He had a point. I had no doubt Elise Hanover would have blown my brains out gladly if she sensed any threat to humanity. I might not like much about her, but I did like that.

"Tell me more about what you can do."

"I have the eyes of the eagle, so I can see farther, better. At times I can see the future. Which is how I knew to come here before the Raven Mocker appeared."

"If you can see so damn well, why can't you see who it is?"

"The Raven Mocker has powers, too. We just need to find a way to be more powerful."

"Yeah, that oughta work."

He ignored my sarcasm and continued. "He or she is

invisible when stealing lives and probably too visible when not stealing them."

"Too visible?"

"The witch blends right in."

"How does the Raven Mocker thing work?" At his puzzled frown, I elaborated. "Is it, *shazam,* there's a new person in town, and he or she is a witch?"

He was already shaking his head. "The Raven Mocker is born during a storm on the night of the Thunder Moon. You saw the sparks trail down to the Di'tatlaski'yi?"

"English," I ordered.

"The place where it rains fire."

"Yes," I said slowly. "Twice. Once on the night of the Thunder Moon, and once when my house almost burnt down."

"You saw the sparks that night?"

"Didn't you?"

"No, but that doesn't mean they didn't happen before I got there."

"I also had reports of sparks before the shrieking, though no other fires," I said.

"The legends say the Raven Mocker arrives in a shower of sparks. I'd thought that just meant original arrival, but I guess not."

"On the night of the Thunder Moon I saw the sparks, heard the shriek, saw what seemed to be a fire, but when we got there all we found was a crater."

"Where the Raven Mocker was born."

"The crater was empty."

"You think it would wait around to be captured or killed?"

"What *was* it?"

"An evil spirit."

"Which is so easy to capture and kill. Where did it go?"

"If we knew that, we'd know who it was."

"You said the Raven Mocker wasn't a new person."

"No. Someone called on the Ani'-Hyûñ'tĭkwălâ' skĭ."

I just stared at him until he translated.

"The thunder beings. They released the Raven Mocker from the sky vault. The spirit rode in on the lightning, then possessed the one who called it."

"You're saying someone in my town is possessed by a shape-shifting witch who eats the hearts of the dying and steals their lives?"

"That about sums it up."

27

"WHERE DO WE go from here?" I asked.

Ian stared at me intently with his all-topaz eyes.

"Can you put those back the way you found them?" I waved vaguely at his head.

He murmured an indecipherable Cherokee word, gave one slow blink, and voilà, his eyes were light brown again, surrounded by normal, human white.

He flicked a finger at the papers all over the floor. "I need to translate those and hope I find something that will help us."

"For instance?"

"How we identify a Raven Mocker, how we kill one once we do."

"And why would you think my great-grandmother knew this?"

"I saw her before I came here. She showed me her papers, told me where I could find them."

"You know she's been dead for seven years?"

"So?"

"Was she a wolf when you saw her?"

His brows lifted. "Should she have been?"

"Hell if I know."

"The wolf you saw at the pond . . . You think that was your great-grandmother?"

"She's not a real wolf. Thing ran right through me." I shuddered at the memory of the sensation. "Ran through a couple of trees, too. They didn't even slow her down."

"Messenger wolf."

"That was my vote."

"What did she want to tell you?"

"She wasn't inclined to chat." If it had even been my great-grandmother. Who knew? "I thought she wanted me to keep an eye on Quatie, which I have been. But then she kept appearing and running north."

"Sadness and trouble," he murmured.

"She showed up quite a few times either before or after you did."

"Me? What'd I do?"

"Seduced me? Stole my papers?" I scowled. "Seduced me *to* steal my papers?"

He didn't deny it.

"If I hadn't stolen them, they'd be incinerated."

"That doesn't excuse it."

"No?"

"No!"

"I've learned in my business that the end justifies the means."

"You *should* be working for the *Jäger-Suchers*," I muttered. They were mavens of the "end justifies the means" philosophy. "And while I'm on the subject, why *aren't* you working for them? They've got government funding up the wazoo. You're both looking for super-natural entities; why split your force? Isn't that how Custer got his ass kicked?"

"So I hear," Ian drawled. "We don't join forces for several reasons. First of all, the Nighthawks began hunting in the eighteenth century. The *Jäger-Suchers* are a little kill-them-come-lately. They can join *us* if they like, but why should we join them?"

I opened my mouth, though I wasn't sure what I meant to say, but Ian continued without pausing. "Second, pardon us if we don't trust the government. They don't have the best record when it comes to Indian affairs."

"Don't you think it's time we got over that?"

"No," he said succinctly. "Third, we specialize in Cherokee spirits, though we have branched out into the spirits of other tribes, and we aren't averse to putting any old evil entity to rest if we happen to run across it. You can ask Dr. Hanover, but I don't think they have the best luck with Native American spirits."

"She said something about witchie wolves. Ojibwe. Considering how she likes to howl at the full moon, I was surprised at how little she cared for them."

"Just because they're wolves doesn't make them pals. Same goes for the Nighthawks and the *Jäger-Suchers*. We might both be monster hunters, but that doesn't mean we'd work together very well. I've talked with Edward. He was perfectly agreeable to our continuing in our way and the *Jäger-Suchers* in theirs. Many of the Cherokee spirits require someone with knowledge of the language to understand what they are and how to get rid of them."

"Hence your assignment to my fair town." He dipped

his chin. "So the Raven Mocker has possessed a Cherokee?"

"Not necessarily. Anyone in possession of the spell
can call the Raven Mocker, and since it's an ancient
legend, there are no doubt a lot of old ones who know
it. Although the Raven Mocker is a Cherokee spirit and
therefore the incantation must be spoken in Cherokee,
if someone read the words—"

"My great-grandmother always said a spell would
only work if the caster spoke the Cherokee with true
understanding."

"Understanding would only require a translation,
which is easy enough to get if you really want to. Even
if the Raven Mocker does need to be of Cherokee de-
scent, around here that could be anyone."

He was right. There were very few full-blood Cherokee left, but just about everyone could claim at least one
ancestor who had a drop or two of Aniyvwiya blood.
Basically, we were screwed.

However, I didn't plan to just lie down and let everyone in town get their hearts ripped out by an invisible
raven witch.

Try saying that five times fast.

"I guess you'd better get cracking on that translation," I said.

"I guess I'd better."

"I'm going to find a hotel."

Ian had already knelt and started gathering the tumbled sheets, but at my words he glanced up. "You don't
have to."

"Yes, I do."

He stood, hands full of paper. "I'm going to work all
night. You can sleep in my bed." My lips tightened, but

he didn't notice. He'd already turned away and begun shuffling the mess into some semblance of order. "As soon as I find something, I'll come and get you. It'd be easier if you were already here."

Since he had a point and I was tired, I gave in. He'd slept with me to get Grandmother's papers. Now he had them, so I doubted he'd be crawling between the sheets with me any time soon.

I don't know why that bothered me. I should be glad I wouldn't have to keep fending him off. I should be happy it had ended before someone—me—got really hurt. I should remember that he had a wife. Somewhere. But all I wanted was to take him by the hand and lead him to his own bed.

And because I wanted that, I turned and left.

◍

Grace!" Someone shook me.

I'd fallen asleep easily, deeply, the scent of Ian's sheets, of him, more soothing than it should have been.

My eyes snapped open. Papers rustled; a switch clicked. As shards of light pierced my brain, I moaned, then flipped the covers over my head.

Ian tugged them right back down. "I found something."

That woke me quicker than a cold shower and a hot cup of coffee. "What?"

He scooted next to me on the bed as he laid the papers on my lap and pointed. In the jumble of words I recognized one.

" 'Kâlanû Ahyeli'-skǐ,' " I said. "Raven Mocker."

"Yes. The word actually means 'killer witch.'" He shrugged, and his shoulder rubbed against mine. "Same difference."

I'd removed my uniform and stolen a T-shirt from his drawer to sleep in. Beneath the sheet my bare legs tingled with goose bumps. I gritted my teeth and willed them to go away.

"So my great-grandmother's papers did contain the legend."

"Better than that," he said. "She included a way to banish it."

The goose bumps, which had at last been fading, came back. "How?"

He leaned closer, and his feather brushed my cheek. Was he trying to drive me crazy? "Here." His long finger tapped the papers that lay at the juncture of my thighs. The vibration started goose bumps somewhere else. "If a sorcerer of great power sees the Raven Mocker in its raven form, the witch will die."

I shifted on the bed. My hip bumped his. We both froze. I picked up the papers and handed them back without meeting his eyes. "How are you going to accomplish that when the thing's invisible?"

"Your great-grandmother included a revealing spell."

"Nice of her."

"I thought so." He stood, and I was able to breathe again. "Get dressed."

My gaze flew to his. Was he kicking me out?

He smiled gently. "I know you're tired, but I'd like you to go with me. I'll put together what I need for this spell, and then we'll destroy a Raven Mocker."

"How will we find it?"

"The witch feeds on the lives of the dying, and I've

got a patient who's doing just that. If we sit with him we should be able to end this. If not tonight, then tomorrow night, or the night after."

"Why would it choose your patient over anyone else?"

"In a town of this size, there aren't a lot of people who fit the profile, especially when the Raven Mocker's already sucked the life out of so many."

"Eventually it'll run out of the ill and the elderly," I murmured.

"Then it'll move on."

I imagined a trail of towns with dozens of fresh graves. And what happened when the Raven Mocker reached a big town like Atlanta? The carnage would be mind-boggling.

"We need to kill it before that happens." I threw the covers off, forgetting I wore only a T-shirt that ended at mid-thigh and a pair of white nylon panties.

When Ian didn't answer, I glanced over my shoulder and found his gaze on my legs. The goose bumps sprang up again, making me shiver. I shoved my feet into my uniform trousers and covered myself, turning so that I couldn't see the heat in his eyes that called to the chill in my soul.

When I faced him again, he was gone. My phone beeped with a message, so I checked it while Ian rustled around first in his office upstairs and then in the clinic downstairs.

"You have one new voice message."

"I locked up the house," Cal said. "The fire investigator should be there at eight A.M. Sam will get you a report as soon as he has one. Don't bother to come in tomorrow if you aren't up to it. I can take care of things. Oh, and we found the man who hit you."

I blinked. The accident now seemed so long ago, I'd nearly forgotten all about it.

"Guy in Bradleyville. Was probably drunk and that's why he ran, but we'll never prove it now. Sheriff over there said the guy's always been a model citizen, so he gave him a ticket and a stern talking-to. You can call him if you want."

I turned off my phone and tucked it into my pocket. I had bigger problems right now than some guy from Bradleyville.

"Ready?" I jumped as Ian spoke from the hall. I hadn't even heard him come back upstairs.

"Are you sure it's okay if I come along? I can't see how a dying man would want an audience."

"Better an audience than the Raven Mocker."

Though I still felt uncomfortable, I followed him through the clinic and out the front door.

"Who's your patient?" I asked.

"Jack Malone. You know him?"

"Of course." I'd arrested Jack a dozen times since I'd become sheriff. He had a little drinking problem.

"Advanced cirrhosis," Ian murmured.

I wasn't surprised. "How did you get his case so quickly?"

His gaze slid to mine, then away.

"No one else wanted him," I guessed. Jack was a mean drunk. "He doesn't really like me."

"I don't think he likes anyone, but that won't matter. He's close to the end. I doubt he'll even know we're there."

Jack's sister—the only one who could stand him, and I'd never figured out why unless he'd been a much better boy than he was a man; it wouldn't have been hard—let us in, nodded when Ian asked if we could sit with him, and disappeared.

I followed Ian into the room, and he sprinkled whatever he'd brought along in a brown paper sack in a circle around the bed, chanting in Cherokee; then he set a buzzard feather on Jack's pillow and we sat in two folding chairs near the door.

"If the Raven Mocker goes near the bed, the spell should make it visible, and then—" He spread his hands.

We both stared at Jack. He appeared more peaceful now than I'd ever seen him before.

"Don't the buzzard feathers have to be at the entrance of a home to work?"

"Just being near one should do it."

I glanced at my watch. Four A.M. We didn't have long until dawn. I had my doubts the Raven Mocker would show up here tonight, but one could always hope.

Since we couldn't really talk or risk waking Jack—that was something neither one of us wanted—time passed slowly. The room was warm. I was tired. My head would dip toward my chest; then I'd jerk awake and stare bleary-eyed at Malone, who hadn't moved but still breathed.

Ian took my hand. "You can sleep."

I shook my head. I didn't want to be awakened by that unearthly shrieking. I'd have a heart attack myself.

Ian's fingers clenched on mine so tightly my bones crunched. I glanced at him and froze. He stared upward as if he'd heard something; then his gaze lowered. I couldn't look away as he jibber-jabbered words in Cherokee I didn't understand.

"Repeat that," he ordered.

I did, mangling it so badly he said it again, his voice, his face, urgent. This time I got it right.

"What was that?" I asked.

"A charm of protection." His head tilted. "Something's coming."

The air felt close, as if a storm approached. In the distance, I could have sworn I heard the call of a great black bird. My gaze switched to Jack, but he slept on undisturbed and I was glad. As much as I disliked him, I didn't want him to die afraid.

Thunder rumbled from a clear sky. Both Ian and I came to our feet. He whispered in Cherokee, blinked once, and his eyes went eagle. His gaze swept the room.

"Nothing," he muttered, and the shrieking began.

I slapped my hands over my ears. Ian flinched, the movement alien and birdlike. Through a slice in the curtain, lightning flashed. He crossed the room and threw back the drapes. Sparks flickered. Slowly I lowered my hands and watched the sparks fall.

28

THE SHRIEKING STOPPED; the sparks faded away, but we could see the house over which they'd tumbled. The roof still glittered as if the sky had rained diamonds, but not a flicker of flame rose toward the star-studded sky.

"Fitzhughs," I said. "Ben and Nora. Young couple in their twenties. No children. Run the ice-cream shop on Center." As far as I knew, neither one of them was sick, let alone dying.

Ian dropped my hand and ran. I was right behind him.

Two blocks down and on the other side of the street, Ian went to the front door and turned the knob.

"Hey!" I put my hand on his shoulder. "You can't—"

He shook me off and went in anyway. Years of training and a cop for a dad made me hesitate. But when I heard the crying and the shouting, I followed. With those kinds of noises, I could easily claim probable cause.

I found Ian tossing his herbs around the room again. Nora was crying and pointing at both him and what appeared to be her dead husband. I already knew, even before I saw his fear-frozen face, what had happened.

"What-what-what's wrong with his eyes?" she sobbed.

I looked at Ben, whose eyes were a little bugged out. But Nora shouted, "Him!" and jabbed a shaking finger at Ian.

He still had eagle eyes. Hell. How was I going to explain that?

I put myself between them and murmured, "Ian. Your eyes."

"I don't see anything," he said. "I think it's gone."

"Put them back before she strokes out."

"Huh?" He glanced at me, and I gave an exaggerated blink. "Oh." He did as I asked.

When I turned to Nora, she sat on the bed. "Ben?" She patted his face, his hand, his chest. "It's okay. Wake up."

I doubted she'd remember any of this in a few hours. I knew shock when I saw it.

I yanked a handmade afghan off the recliner in the corner and draped it around her shoulders. "Nora?"

She didn't answer. I opened my mouth to say her name louder, and Ian murmured, "Shhh."

The tiny shushing sound fell into a silence broken only by Nora's murmurs and pats. Ian stared upward, tense, alert.

Slowly I stood, feeling it, too, something hovering above us, peering back and forth, picking, choosing, who would die and who would not.

"Say the charm, Grace."

Ian didn't even glance my way, but his voice was so

sharp and intense, I began to recite the words as if my great-grandmother herself had ordered me.

Whatever was here with us drew a breath. Shock? Fear? I paused, listening, and something bitch-slapped me across the room.

I flew off my feet; my shoulders hit the wall. My head snapped back. I heard the sick crack, a thud as I fell, then nothing.

⬤⬤⬤

"G race?"

I opened my eyes. I couldn't remember where I was. From the pain in my head, I was half-afraid I'd landed in the hospital, but then my senses came back one by one.

The soft sound of Nora weeping.

The hardwood floor beneath me.

The scent of Ian, the heat and strength of his hand in mine. His expression so worried, I got worried, too.

"Am I bleeding?"

His smile was strained. "No. Though not for lack of trying. What happened?"

"Your charm *sucked*!"

"Did you say it right?"

"Exactly the way you did."

"It's always worked for me."

"Saying the words without understanding them is worthless." I put my hand to the back of my head, wincing at the bump. "I guess Grandmother was right again." If we'd had more time, I might have remembered that.

Suddenly Ian leaned over and kissed me. I was so startled, I let him.

"This was my fault," he said.

"You didn't throw me across the room."

"I brought you into this situation; you weren't prepared. You could have died. Or worse."

"Worse?"

He looked away, his face haunted. There was more to this, which I'd get to the bottom of later.

I sat up, gritting my teeth against the pain. I had things to do and no time for a headache. Ian reached for me, hands gentle, and I shoved them away. "I'm fine."

I was able to get to my feet under my own power. Nora still sat on the bed with Ben, whispering to him as if he'd wake up sooner or later.

"I should probably call Doc," I muttered.

"I'm a doctor."

"He's the medical examiner. He can deal with Ben; you can deal with Nora. She's going to need sedation, but not before I talk to her."

"You might not get anything useful."

Maybe not, but I had to try. I inched closer and put my hand on her shoulder. "Nora?"

I half-expected her to keep whispering, lost in another world where Ben still answered, but instead she said, "Hey, Grace."

We'd gone to high school together, though she'd been a few years younger than me. However, in a town like this, everyone knew everyone else and most of their business, which made me wonder why I hadn't known her husband was sick.

"What was wrong with Ben?" I asked.

"Wrong?" Nora's forehead wrinkled. "I think he's dead."

"I meant when did he get sick? What did he have?"

"Ben's never been sick a day in his life. Hardly even a cold. He made me so mad."

I glanced at Ian, who shrugged. "You're sure he didn't see a doctor lately?"

"He hated doctors. No offense," she threw in Ian's direction.

"I'm not wild about most of them myself," he said, and Nora's lips curved just a little.

"Can you tell us what happened tonight?" I pressed.

Nora's smile faded, but she nodded. "I got up to get some water, and there was this awful noise. I ran back to bed, and he was gasping, clutching his throat." Her voice broke; she buried her face in her hands.

"Okay." I patted her, as clumsy with it as Cal had been, then moved to where Ian stood by the door.

"I've got a bad feeling," he said.

"I've had one for days. What's going on?"

"I can't be sure until we've got an autopsy report, but I think the Raven Mocker's figured out how to steal the lives of the living."

I got a sudden chill, even though the room was July-in-Georgia warm. "But that's not what the legend says."

Ian's eyes met mine. "Legends are made to be broken."

∞

M erry was as heartless as the rest of them," Doc said in lieu of "hello." He complained about caller ID, but he had it, too.

"I've got another one."

Doc sighed, sounding as exhausted as I felt. "Who is it this time?"

I'd moved out of the bedroom and into the hall, not wanting Nora to hear me call the medical examiner and order an autopsy. Ian had run back to the clinic to get his bag so he could sedate her if she didn't stop whispering to the dead. Before I'd called Doc, I'd called Nora's mother, who was on the way.

"Ben Fitzhugh," I answered.

"What the hell? He's maybe twenty-five."

"He doesn't fit the profile," I said, "but then, neither did Merry. At least when she died." An idea flickered. "I wonder if the Raven Mocker didn't know that until it was too late?"

"The what?"

Whoops. Doc was still under the impression we were dealing with aliens. I hated to burst his bubble, but quickly I filled him in.

"You think that makes more sense than alien invasion and pods in the basement?" he asked.

"You're kidding, right?"

"Not really," he muttered.

"All the evidence points to the killer being a Raven Mocker. The loud shrieking, the lack of a heart in the victims, lack of a scar from the removal, and the storm on the night of the Thunder Moon."

"Except the Raven Mocker steals the lives of the dying. So what about Merry and Ben? If Ben's actually a victim and not just a fluke. We won't know for sure until I crack his chest."

Sometimes Doc was too blunt even for me.

"Legends are made to be broken," I murmured.

"True. When dealing with the *super*natural, it's good to remember that anything can happen. You have a theory?"

"Yeah," I said slowly. "What if the Raven Mocker

didn't know Merry was in remission, killed her anyway and discovered it could, so it moved on to a completely healthy victim with Ben? In killing a person who has years left, the witch would gain so much more time than it's ever gained before."

"If that's the case, no one's safe."

I didn't bother to curse, even though I wanted to.

"I'll be there in ten," Doc said.

"Thanks." I hung up. Ian stood just inside the front door. "You heard?"

He nodded. "We'd better figure out how to identify this witch before the thing eats every heart in town."

"Works for me," I said. "Got any ideas?"

"Actually, I do."

29

IAN'S IDEA FOR identifying our culprit involved visiting every elderly man and woman in Lake Bluff and surrounding areas and gifting them with a buzzard feather.

According to him, the Raven Mocker should appear as a withered senior citizen—cronelike with the weight of the days it had stolen. Such an appearance for a witch seemed too cliché, but then, clichés became clichés for a reason.

Before we'd left on our odyssey, we'd stopped in town, where I'd bought enough underwear, jeans, and shirts to last me a week. Ian had bought postcards to run through his computer.

While I'd taken a shower and changed, he'd made up fairly professional-looking flyers for his new clinic, then attached a buzzard feather to each of them.

People didn't seem to think that was any odder than the sheriff, wearing jeans and a plain white T-shirt, escorting the new doctor, also in jeans and a black T-shirt, but wearing cowboy boots instead of sneakers, from door to door. No one had burst into flames or cried, "I'm melting!" Not one person had hesitated to take the buzzard feather at all.

"How many buzzards are now bald?" I asked.

Ian shrugged. "Buzzards are kind of bald anyway."

"Are you sure these things repel a witch? What's supposed to happen?"

"Extreme aversion to the feather."

"Cringe, cry, run away?"

"Maybe all three."

I narrowed my eyes. "How many witches have you dealt with?"

"Enough."

"Any Raven Mockers?"

"Not personally, no."

"Swell." Was it too much to ask that he'd be an expert in this field? Apparently.

We continued to visit the elderly. We continued to have no luck. We never ran out of feathers, though. I swear the basket was like the proverbial fish and bread for the masses; the more elderly there were, the more feathers we had.

I'd checked in and told Cal I was taking a personal day, which he assumed was because of the fire, and I let him. Once Claire got to work and heard about the incident, she called and made me promise to come to dinner.

Since I needed to update her on the latest in paranormal occurrences, I accepted. When she found out I was spending the day with Ian, she invited him, too. I felt weird about that, like it was a date, but the least I could do was provide him with dinner.

Later, Sam called. The investigator had ruled the fire

accidental. Even though the night had been clear, enough people had heard thunder and seen what they swore was lightning to blame just that for my torched roof. I knew better, but what could I say? A shape-shifting witch had thrown sparks out her ass onto my shingles? I'd get the insurance money regardless, so I kept my mouth shut.

We finished my list of old folks without having one person behave oddly. However, there were at least half a dozen on the list who hadn't been home, including Quatie, which disturbed me more than I liked. Where could she be? It wasn't as though she belonged to the local book club or women's society. She didn't even drive.

Ian must have sensed my unease. "We'll make Quatie's place our first stop tomorrow," he said.

Just as we had at every house where we hadn't been able to hand one to the resident directly, I tacked the buzzard feather to the front porch. If it didn't reveal the Raven Mocker, the feather could then protect the holder *from* the Raven Mocker. Ian's test became a charm.

We rang the doorbell at the Cartwrights' at 6:00 P.M. Ian had insisted on stopping at Goldman's Save U and buying a bottle of wine and some flowers for Claire. I brought the bright orange pacifier in the shape of a basketball that I'd been unable to resist buying for Noah. Malachi would just have to be content with the pleasure of our company.

The door flew open. Claire didn't even say hello before she hugged me so hard I coughed.

"Hey. What's wrong with you?" She had me worried. "Where's Noah? Mal!"

Malachi appeared in the hall with the baby, saw Claire mauling me, and shook his head. "Ye scared her

half t' death, Grace." His Irish accent was more pronounced than I'd heard it in a long, long time.

"What'd I do?"

"She finds out your house was on fire and you didn't
call, you didn't come to us?"

I leaned back, met Claire's eyes. "Sorry. I—"

Her gaze went to Ian and she smiled. "Dr. Walker,
come in. Are these for me? Thank you."

Suddenly all mayoral, she turned and headed for the
kitchen. Now that she'd hugged me and made sure I
was in one piece, she was going to make me pay. I suppose I deserved it.

I should have called. I'd have been pissed if the situation were reversed. Hell, I'd given her a seriously
hard time for taking off to Atlanta and leaving me behind, even though the only way she could have gotten
me out of Lake Bluff would have been to shanghai me.
We were best friends, and we were supposed to share
everything, depend on each other. Just because she was
married and I—

I glanced at Ian. Well, I wasn't. That didn't mean I
shouldn't follow the best-friend rules. They were women
law. Break them at your own risk.

I took Noah and offered him the new pacifier, which
he promptly started drooling on as he laid his cheek
against my chest.

Something bumped against my ankles, and I glanced
down to see Oprah rubbing her head on me just like she
used to. I went down on one knee and scratched behind
her ears. She began to purr.

One of Noah's wildly waving hands smacked Oprah's
tail. Before I could stop him, his fingers latched on and
yanked. Instead of hissing, Oprah went still and let him
tug. Definitely true love.

I pried Noah's fingers loose. They came away covered in cat hairs, which I began to pick off one by one.

"Come along and have a drink on the deck." Mal led the way through the kitchen.

Claire had opened the wine and put the flowers in water. She was messing with something on the stove that didn't appear to need messing with, but what did I know about cooking?

"Need help?" I asked. She snorted. "Guess not."

"Ah chroi," Mal murmured, and her shoulders raised and lowered on a sigh.

"I actually could use a hand bringing the drinks out. Does anyone want anything other than wine?"

We declined, so she began to pull out wineglasses. I turned to hand Noah to Mal, but he'd already stepped outside.

"Here." Ian held out his hands. I hesitated, and he tilted his head. "I'm a doctor, Grace. I've held quite a few babies. Haven't dropped one yet."

"Of course not." I handed Noah over, and he curled up on Ian's chest with as much trust as he'd cuddled against mine.

The men disappeared outside. Claire poured four glasses of wine, then handed me one and took a sip of her own.

"I screwed up," I said.

"Big-time. Don't let it happen again."

"Yes, Madame Mayor."

Her blue eyes narrowed. "I thought we were making up."

"We are. But sometimes I just can't shut my mouth."

"Most times," she muttered. "Now tell me what's going on around here, but first take the boys their drinks."

She handed me a bottle for Noah, which I tucked in

a pocket, then picked up the other two glasses of wine. Mal and Ian faced the trees that lined the property, watching the sun fall and chatting about—

"NASCAR?" I said incredulously.

Mal shrugged. "I like fast cars."

"And you?" I asked Ian.

"What's not to like?"

Noah spit his basketball pacifier directly into Ian's face. Ian caught the thing before it fell to the ground and laid it on the table. He really did seem to have a knack for kids.

I set the bottle between the two men, figuring Ian would turn Noah over to his dad for the feeding. But they continued to talk about drivers I'd never heard of. I couldn't stand car racing, probably because all of my brothers had watched it incessantly. Around and around and around. Crash, bang, explosion. Snore.

I reached the sliding glass doors that separated the deck from the kitchen and glanced back just in time to see Ian shift Noah into the crook of his arm and pop the bottle into his mouth as if he'd done the same thing a hundred times before.

My chest tightened; my eyes went hot, and I had to turn away before I embarrassed myself. The sight made me want him in ways that didn't involve being naked in the night. Ways that were far more dangerous.

I practically dived inside and nearly smacked into Claire, who was watching him, too. Her gaze met mine. "He could be a keeper."

"Too bad someone else is already keeping him."

"He's married?"

"That's the word on the street."

Claire looked at him again. "He doesn't seem married."

"How does someone seem married?"

"They just do." She handed me my wine, which she'd topped off to the brim in contrast to every Southern Belle Rule of Etiquette.

Claire and I had always done our best to break all those rules as often as we could. I took a swig instead of a dainty sip; she did the same and we clinked glasses, then leaned against the counter, as I filled her in on everything that had happened.

"Raven Mocker," she murmured. "That's a new one."

"So was werewolf, but we handled it."

She lifted her glass in a salute. "And now the thing's moved on to the young, the strong, the healthy."

"Yeah." I took another swig of wine.

Doc had tagged me by noon with the news I had dreaded. No heart in the chest of Ben Fitzhugh, either.

"Maybe we should call Elise again." Claire glanced toward the deck where the men continued to lounge. "At least see what she knows about this other secret society."

Since I did want to give the woman a piece of my mind, I dialed the number.

"What can you tell me about the Nighthawk Kee-toowahs?" I asked as soon as she picked up. I could ignore "hello" as easily as she did.

"He told you," Elise murmured. "Interesting."

"You said you knew nothing about him."

"I said he wasn't in my database of paranormal baddies."

I wondered if she knew about his tendency to go eagle eyed, literally, then decided I wasn't going to be the one to tell her. Two could play at the secret game.

"I called you for help and you didn't give me any."

"Listen, Sheriff, there are quite a few ancient groups that were fighting evil long before the *Jäger-Suchers* showed up. We work with them sometimes, but against them never, which means I don't give away their identity to anyone who calls and asks."

"I'm not just anyone."

"The secret was his to share, which he did, so what are you whining about?"

God, she was annoying.

"We've discovered we have a Raven Mocker in Lake Bluff."

"I haven't heard that one before."

"Ian seemed familiar with it."

"Then you're lucky he's there."

"We could use a little help of the *J-S* variety."

"Can't do it. We've got . . ." She paused. "Issues."

"What kind of issues?"

"Creepy things are crawling all over the place. Like I told you before, I can't spare anyone, especially when you seem to have things under control."

"People are dying here!"

"People are dying everywhere, Sheriff, and at a lot higher rate than usual. I have confidence you and your people will prevail just as you did the last time you were visited by supernatural creatures."

In the background I heard phones ringing, people shouting, buzzers buzzing. Sounded as if all hell were breaking loose.

Elise hung up, or maybe the line went dead. I couldn't tell. I glanced at Claire, lifted a brow.

"I got the gist," she said. "They aren't coming."

I shrugged. "She annoys me anyway."

"What is it with you two?"

"Ian thinks her wolf smells my panther and the other way around."

Claire's eyes sharpened. "You been turning furry and not telling me about it?"

"No. But according to legend, my clan descended from panthers."

"Which kind of explains your collection obsession," she said. "You believe that?"

"I'm not sure. Stranger things have happened."

Claire tilted her head with an expression that said, *Got me there,* then finished her wine without further comment.

We ate dinner outside—grilled fish, garlic potatoes, steamed broccoli, and a lot more wine.

Noah sat in his swing and watched us, wide eyes on Ian all the time. I think he had a crush. Which just made two of us.

As darkness fell, we said good night. Though Claire had insisted I stay with them, I'd refused. I was going to get that hotel room tonight.

Really.

Ian and I could have walked from Claire's to his place and then I could have gone on to a hotel. Except I had my truck, and it was full of packages, and I'd need it in the morning, so I drove down the hill, slowing as we neared the clinic.

Someone stood outside. "Hell." Ian lay down, putting his head in my lap. "Keep driving."

Katrine leaned against the brick wall. The streetlight spilled down, revealing her usual tight, low-cut blouse and short skirt. Her hair had been curled and teased into the trademark trailer trash big hair, and she wore a shade of lipstick that must be labeled Ruby Red Botox.

"Go to the hotel," Ian whispered, as if she could hear

him. "I'll help you check in and then walk back. Hopefully she'll be gone by then."

His breath puffed against my knee, warm and moist. I shifted in the seat as other places grew warm and moist. I wished I could forget the times he'd touched me, but I wasn't sure I ever would.

"She's been hitting on you?"

"A little."

Knowing Katrine, a little was more like a lot.

"You tell her you were married?"

"Yep."

"She didn't care?"

"Nope."

"I think you can sit up now."

I'd turned at the end of Center and wheeled onto the next block toward a decent bed-and-breakfast run by the Fosters, a retired couple from Ohio. They'd come to Lake Bluff for the Full Moon Festival five years ago and loved it so much, they'd snapped up the eighteenth-century hotel as soon as it had gone on the market. They were now as much a part of Lake Bluff as I was.

"That woman scares me." Ian lifted his head, tentatively checking the dark streets around us. "She's got more replacement parts than a Fiat."

"A Fiat?"

His smile was quick and sheepish. "I had one in college. You know what it stands for?" I shook my head. "Fix It Again Tomorrow."

I laughed.

"Wasn't funny then," he muttered, and got out of the car.

He grabbed my shopping bags and started up the walk, pausing at the porch and reaching into his pocket.

As I joined him, he handed me a bag and used his free hand to tack a feather on the underside of the handrail.

Jordan sat behind the desk. "What are you doing here?" we both said at the same time.

I glanced at Ian, and my cheeks heated, which was silly. Not only was Jordan twenty years old, but I was certain most of the town had figured out there was something going on between Ian and me.

"He's helping me with my things," I blurted.

Jordan just grinned.

"My house is trashed. I need a room. What are you doing here?" I repeated.

"Mrs. Foster hurt her back. Mr. Foster needs to sleep since he worked all day. I'm filling in."

Jordan filled in a lot around town. Everyone knew she needed every penny for Duke.

"Didn't you work the switchboard today?" I asked.

"Yeah. But I'm a night owl. I don't sleep much."

I recalled Cal saying she'd been a difficult child, only sleeping a few hours each night and then being up the rest of the twenty-four. She'd driven her mom nuts, and more often than not, Cal had been off in a war zone unable to help. Which kind of explained how Jordan had wound up an only child.

I handed her my credit card; she handed me a key, then offered her hand to Ian. "Jordan Striker."

"Sorry," I said. "I should have done that."

The two ignored me, shaking hands and making nice. When Ian snatched the key from me and turned toward the stairs, Jordan wiggled her eyebrows and made kissy noises in my direction.

What had I said about her being mature beyond her years? I took it back.

"He's just going to take up my bags," I said. Ian was already tramping up the steps.

"I don't care, Grace. This isn't an all-girl dorm in the 1950s."

She returned her attention to the notebook she'd been scribbling in when we arrived. I glanced at it and stilled.

Because my brothers had always tried to hide things from me, I'd become very good at ferreting out secrets. I'd learned how to read upside down at almost the same time I'd learned to read.

What I read this time was: *Hand sanitizers claim they can kill 99.9 percent of germs. Chuck Norris can kill 100 percent of whatever the fuck he wants.*

"You're the Chuck Norris bandit?"

Her eyes widened and she slapped the cover shut, but it was too late. I'd already read another: *Chuck Norris's calendar goes from March 31 directly to April 2. No one fools Chuck Norris.*

I bit my lip to keep from snickering. "Why do you want to make your dad crazy?"

"I don't. I write these jokes for a Web site. They pay me. Not a lot, but—" She shrugged. "The best jokes are always the ones that make him turn purple."

"You're a bad girl," I said, but I smiled.

"You aren't going to tell him, are you?"

"No, but he'll catch you sooner or later, and then you're on your own. How did you bypass the security cameras?"

"It wasn't hard. Your security is lame. Have you even updated it since your dad was king?"

"No."

"Of course, who'd want to break *in* to a cop shop?"

"Besides you?"

"I didn't break in."

"What *did* you do?"

I knew Jordan was smart. She'd have to be to have any prayer of going to Duke. But bypassing a security system—even a lame one? I wasn't going to tell her so, but I was impressed.

"A little computer mumbo-jumbo," she said. "A screwdriver here, a wrench there, and—" Jordan flipped her hands in a voilà gesture. "Just call me the Invisible Woman."

30

I HALF-EXPECTED TO meet Ian coming downstairs as I went up. How hard was it to drop shopping bags on the bed?

Apparently pretty hard. The door to my room was open and Ian stood at the window, staring at the night, the bags still in his hands.

"You okay?" I asked.

"There's something I have to tell you."

From the tone of his voice, this might take a while, so I stepped inside and shut the door.

The room was clean and quaint, with a carved wooden headboard and a homemade quilt for the queen-sized bed. An overstuffed flower-print love seat hugged one wall, and a thoroughly modern bathroom lay behind a recently refinished door. There was even a desk with a lamp, chair, and Internet connection.

I took the bags and set them on the floor, but Ian continued to stare out the window so intently he started to worry me. I laid my hand on his shoulder, tracing the material that covered his tattoo with one finger.

"When did you get this?" Maybe if he started talking about that, he'd segue into whatever it was he was having such a hard time telling me.

"All the Nighthawks have them."

"You said it was to remind you to be a warrior always."

"It is. The Nighthawks must be ready to fight against evil spirits at any time. The eagle is the bird of war. He gives us strength, sight, and power."

"Does every Nighthawk do the same thing with their eyes?"

"We can all do something."

"Like?"

He turned, and my hand was left hovering in the air where his shoulder had been. His fingers closed around my wrist, and he placed a kiss at the center of my palm. For just a minute I closed my eyes and let myself feel.

His mouth touched my nose, my cheekbones, my jaw. I bit my lip and tried to be strong, but I wasn't. When he kissed me, I kissed him back.

My palms framed his face, tilted his head so I could explore his mouth. Warm and hot, he tasted of wine and desire, or was that me?

I traced his shoulders, let my thumb rub beneath the sleeves of his T-shirt, learning the contours of his biceps and the smooth trail where his forearm became his elbow. I wanted to put my mouth there, lick his skin, feel his pulse beat against my tongue. Instead, I lifted my head, my hands, and stepped back.

"I can't, Ian. You're married."

"I'm not, Grace. I swear."

Into the silence fell the sound of sudden raindrops—*tink, tink, tink*—against the glass.

"Are you saying that was a lie? You never had a wife?"

"No." He shoved a hand through his hair. "I had a wife."

"And she disappeared?"

"Yes."

"So until you find her and get a divorce or—" I stopped, not wanting to put into words the other scenario, but he had no such problem.

"Until I have a body. Except I do, or I did. Or I would, if there was a body left to have."

"You'd better just tell me what in hell you mean."

"She was one of them."

"Them who?"

"The ones we fight."

"You married an evil spirit?"

"She wasn't evil when I married her; that came later."

"Is this a supernatural variation of 'my wife is an emasculating fiend'?"

His lips twitched, but his expression remained sad. "I loved her, Grace. She was a soft-spoken, sweet woman who lived just for me." I put my hand on his arm, but he pulled away. "It was because of me that she died. Because of what I do. I didn't protect her. They came, they took her, and they . . . infected her."

"Who's they?"

"The Anada' duntaski. The cannibals."

"Cannibals came and took your wife? And they infected her with what? Cannibalitis? You aren't making any sense."

" 'Anada' duntaski' translates to 'cannibals,' but what

they are is—" He broke off and bit his lip as if he suddenly didn't want to tell me.

"You've gone this far," I said. "You think after what I've seen in this town I'm not going to believe you?"

He let his lip go, and a tiny spot of blood bloomed where his teeth had torn the skin. My chest hurt at the pain I saw on his face. He reached for my hand, and I met his halfway.

"What are the Anada' duntaski?"

His eyes met mine. "Vampires."

I opened my mouth, shut it again. Looked away and then looked back. "Cherokee vampires?"

"Every culture has their own version of the vampire and the werewolf myth."

"There's a Cherokee werewolf?"

"In a way. When I was a boy, the old men told me of the war medicine. The ability of certain warriors to change their shape, becoming any animal they wished to triumph over their enemies. Many chose a wolf because he was brave and loyal and fierce."

I nodded. I'd heard about that, too. "And the vampire?"

He glanced down, though he continued to hold my hand. "The Anada' duntaski were called the roasters because they supposedly cooked the flesh of their enemies and ate it."

"Which makes them cannibal and not vampire." Not that either one was all that appealing.

"They began as men who did just that—killed their enemy and ate him. They were the most feared of warriors, even before they discovered that drinking the blood of the living made them live, too. Forever."

Okay, *that* was a vampire.

"The Anada' duntaski are day walkers," he continued.

"The sun doesn't hurt them. They live like any other man, except they must hunt the night. They drink the blood of the innocent, and they multiply."

"How do you kill them?"

"Cut off their heads."

He said it so calmly I got a chill. "You'd better be sure you've got the right man before you try that."

Ian's smile was completely without humor. When he smiled like that he no longer seemed like a healer, but a Nighthawk Keetoowah, scourge of supernatural creatures everywhere.

"What happened?" I asked.

"It was the first time I'd gone after an Anada' duntaski. I was young, foolish, flush with my own power, the secrets I knew that no one else did. I thought I was invincible. I found them; I killed them. But one of them got away, and he made my wife like him."

Which explained why Ian insisted he was no longer married. Undead was as good as a divorce.

"She became a spy," he continued. "Because of her, because of me, we lost a dozen Nighthawks in the next six months."

"That must have been horrible."

His haunted gaze met mine. " 'Horrible' doesn't begin to describe it."

"Do you want to describe it? Would you feel better if you talked about it?"

"I try to forget, as much as I can; otherwise I couldn't go on; I couldn't do my job. And even though I screwed up and people died, the only way to atone for that is to keep destroying the evil ones."

"It wouldn't help anyone for you to quit."

"I won't, but I want you to back off and let me handle this."

I gave one short, sharp bark of laughter. "Yeah, right. You bet."

"I'm serious, Grace. Look what happened last night."

"Another person died. That's as much my fault as yours."

"No." He grabbed me by the elbows and shook me a little. "You could have been killed. That thing threw you against the wall."

"If you think that would kill me, you obviously have a misguided view of me. My brothers did worse than that every day of the week."

His eyes flickered, topaz, then brown, war bird, then furious man. "I want to meet your brothers."

His face, his tone, his eyes—he wanted to do more than meet them; he wanted to beat the crap out of them. I should have been insulted; I wasn't a damsel in distress. Instead I was touched, and that was a more dangerous feeling than just wanting him.

Ian loved his wife; he still wasn't over her. She'd been gentle and sweet and soft-spoken—three more things I could never be.

"I survived," I said. "Being the only girl in a household of men made me stronger. Stronger than you seem to think I am. I'm the sheriff here, Ian. I can't just sit back and do my nails while you save the world. Not even my little corner."

"I can't protect you, Grace," he whispered. "Just like I couldn't protect her."

He moved past me, headed for the door, and I reached out, caught his hand, clung. "I'm not her, Ian. I don't need you to protect me. I don't want you to. I can take care of myself."

"Grace—" He tugged on his hand; I wouldn't let go.

"I know what's out there. I won't be surprised by it.

I'm not going to let this witch win. This is my home; I've protected it before, and I'll do it again."

He opened his mouth to argue, and I kissed him, the one way I knew to shut him up, shut him down.

I took charge, needing to show him my strength, convince him that he shouldn't worry. I was at his side in this, not hiding behind him, getting picked off like a weak link when he wasn't paying attention.

I experienced a moment of unease for thinking of his wife like that, but truth was truth. Ian had been wrong to keep her in the dark, so she hadn't known what she was facing and could then not be prepared for it. However, I couldn't help but think she'd been foolish, allowing some bloodsucking fiend to get the better of her.

That was uncharitable, downright mean. But the way he'd said her name, the way he mourned her, the way he described her, like a saint who'd loved him too much, made my stomach jitter with jealousy. I didn't like the feeling.

But I was here with him now, and from the beat of his erection pressing against my stomach, I was the only one who mattered.

I slipped my hands beneath his shirt, traced my palms across his flat abdomen, dipped my fingers below the waistband of his jeans, under the elastic of his boxers until I brushed his tip. He jerked, and I closed my fingers around him, slowly sliding them up and down in a rhythm to match the pace of my tongue past his lips.

He groaned, the sound vibrating through his mouth, his chest, through me, then grabbed my hips and yanked me against him. I rolled my thumb over him once, then slid a fingernail down his length.

Cursing, he pulled away. My hand came out of his pants. We were both breathing heavily, staring at each other in the silver-shrouded night. I inched sideways, blocking the door.

He reached down, pulling the black T-shirt up, up, up, revealing stomach, then ribs, then chest, his biceps flexing and releasing, the muscles in his belly rippling like water. I was suddenly parched.

I led him to the bed and with a slight shove of my palm against his chest, he went down.

I pressed my mouth to the hard ridge just above his navel, then drew my tongue across his abs and scored his ribs with my teeth. He tasted like the ocean—both salt and the sea—I wanted to savor so much more.

He tugged on my clothes. "I need to feel your skin against mine."

I yanked my shirt, then my bra, off and tossed them away before pressing an openmouthed kiss to the curve of his waist, then suckling hard enough to leave a mark.

His long, beautiful, yet slightly rough fingers ran over my shoulders, my back, then loosened my hair. I mouthed him through the denim, using my teeth at the tip of his erection. He grasped me by the elbows and hauled me up his body, latching onto my mouth, then grinding our hips together until I was rubbing against him as if there weren't four layers of clothing in the way.

He tried to unbutton my jeans; I fumbled with his. Both of us were shaking.

"Screw it." I rolled away so that I could deal with my own fastenings. He did the same. It was a race. Whoever finished first got to be on top.

I lost. I didn't mind. Especially when he covered me with his body and filled me so completely with a single thrust I began to come even before he began to move.

I cried out his name, clenching around him, and he buried his face between my breasts, pulling me more tightly against him, slowing down, drawing it out, until I was poised halfway in between, perched on a second edge. My hips moved of their own accord, taking him more deeply, feeling the tingle start harder, stronger, this time as his lips drew my nipple into his mouth once, twice, the rhythm syncopated—hips, lips, hips, lips.

He nipped me, and I exploded, gasping for breath as he spilled himself into me, body and soul.

When the tremors died, I held on with my legs, my arms. "Stay with me," I whispered. "Stay in me." I didn't want to break the connection. Not yet. Maybe not ever.

He did as I asked, and we kissed languidly, touched gently. I tangled my fingers in his hair, stroking my thumb over his feather as I tumbled toward sleep. He slid away, but I felt him close, our legs tangled, the scent of his skin all over mine.

I awoke in that strange hour between night and day, no moon, no sun, when everything is frighteningly still and just a little creepy.

The rain had stopped, though trickles of water continued to trace the window. The air felt close and hot. At first I thought he was gone. That he'd crept out of bed, gotten dressed, and disappeared, and I sprang up with a gasp. Then I saw him.

He sat on the side of the bed, head in his hands, hair spilling over his wrists, covering his face. He was breathing as if he'd run ten miles in the heat. His back shone slick with sweat, and he was shaking.

"Nightmare?" I asked.

He didn't answer.

I put my palm against his tattoo. He jerked as if he hadn't even known I was there.

"Ian? What's wrong?"

His shoulders raised and lowered several times before he spoke. "I see her sometimes when I wake up, hovering, laughing. Not the woman who loved me so much, but the thing that hated me."

"I'm sorry." I didn't know what that was like. To love someone, to have them love me, to lose them so horribly. I'd lost people, sure, Grandmother, Dad, but it was nothing compared to this. I wasn't sure what to say.

"She's dead," he said.

"I know. The Anada' duntaski killed her."

"No." He turned his head, and his eyes met mine. "I did."

31

"YOU CAN'T KEEP blaming yourself. The Anada' duntaski took her life."

"The first time."

I began to understand why his eyes were always haunted, why they probably always would be.

"The instant I realized the truth, I—" His voice broke.

"You don't have to say it."

He'd cut off her head. He'd made sure she hurt no one else, and even though he knew the body that he'd destroyed had not held the woman he'd loved, what he'd done still tormented him.

"When the body dies and the demon comes," he whispered, "does the soul go to Heaven? She didn't want to become what she did, so why do they say the soul of a vampire is damned?"

He was agonizing over something he could never know the truth of. At least not in this life. What was I supposed to say but the only platitude I had?

"You had to do it. They left you no choice."

"That doesn't make the doing of it any easier." He touched my face. "You love the people in this town very much."

I frowned. "So?"

"I'm going to have to kill one of them."

I straightened, and his hand fell away. I glanced out the window. Dawn hadn't even begun to lighten the horizon, but when it did, we'd go back out and keep searching for the Raven Mocker.

"Or I will," I said.

"Can you? Can you look at the Raven Mocker, perhaps see the face of someone you care about, and do what needs to be done?"

"Yes."

"What if it's Claire, Malachi, Cal, Jordan? What if it's me?"

"You?" I blinked at him. "It isn't."

"It could be anyone, Grace. Anyone at all. Once, it was my wife." He touched my knee. "Let me finish this."

"No." I met his eyes, determined. "We'll do it together. The power of two is greater than the power of one."

His head sank between his shoulders. "I don't know if I can bear it, Grace, if you die because of me."

"Why would I die because of you?"

"If I can't figure this out. If I can't find a way to destroy the witch—"

I put my fingers against his lips. "You will. We will. Good versus evil. Us against them. We can do it, Ian. I know we can."

He just shook his head.

"Come here." I lay back and pulled him with me, flipping the covers over us both. "Hold me awhile," I said.

But it was me who held him for what remained of the night.

∞

I must have dozed, because I came awake with a start when someone knocked on the door. Ian wasn't in bed and for a second I panicked, thinking he'd gone witch-hunting without me. Then I heard water running in the bathroom and relaxed.

I dug my brand-new robe out of a shopping bag and answered the door. Cal stood on the other side, and I got an extreme case of déjà vu.

I nearly asked him how he'd found me, then remembered Jordan.

"Hey, Cal," I greeted. "What's Chuck Norris up to this morning?"

"There's been another death," he said, without sugarcoating it. "Just outside of town. The Browns'."

"But—" I stopped myself before I could blurt that we'd left a protective buzzard feather at the Browns'. Perhaps this death was just a death. I kept hoping.

"Henry or Harriet?" I asked.

"Neither. Their niece was visiting from Chicago."

"Was she sick?"

He shook his head. "She'd come to help them pack and move north to live with their children. According to Harriet, the kid was healthy as a horse and strong as an ox."

Simile city. Sounded like Harriet.

"Then they went to wake her for breakfast this morning and—" He spread his hands. "Dead in her bed."

"Anything strange?"

"Besides a healthy eighteen-year-old woman dying in her sleep?"

"Yeah, besides that."

Cal cut me a glance, but he knew his job. He'd asked questions.

"Strange shrieking in the night, attributed to that weird increase in ravens we've had reported. I think we need to get the DNR in here to blast a few. That noise could scare the life out of a person unfamiliar with mountain living."

"You're saying the Browns' niece got scared to death?" I laughed a little, as if it were a joke, even though I knew damn well it wasn't.

His eyebrows lowered until they nearly met in the middle. "She did look weird, Grace. I pulled the sheet over her face. I couldn't stand to see her."

My hopes that this was an unaided death fizzled. The Raven Mocker was sticking to the new pattern—taking young, healthy people rather than old or ill ones.

"Did you call Doc?"

"I waited until he was on scene before I came here."

I relaxed a little. Doc would know what to do without my having to tell him.

"You could have called me," I said. "You didn't have to track me down."

"This isn't the kind of thing that should be told over the radio or even the phone. What the hell's going on around here, Grace? You've got Doc doing autopsies on citizens who died by natural causes. You're exhuming bodies and doing autopsies on them. We've got people dying for no reason all over the place. Maybe we should call the FBI."

"There isn't a serial killer, Cal. It's—"

"A virus." Ian stood in the bathroom doorway, a towel around his neck, chest bare, pants zipped but un-buttoned.

Cal didn't appreciate the view as much as I did. He scowled first at Ian, then at me. I felt like I'd been caught in the backseat of Daddy's truck with a boy. Not that I ever had been, but I could imagine.

"Is that true?" Cal asked.

"So Doc says." Or would.

"I've had some experience with this." Ian bent and retrieved his shirt from the floor. "Grace called the CDC. Doc's working with them. We need to let the experts do their jobs."

"And in the meantime, people die?"

"I'm afraid so. It's the nature of this beast."

I blinked at the dual meaning to the word but managed to keep my expression concerned when Cal turned to me. "Is it contagious? Is there something in the water? The air?"

"We don't know, Cal."

"Should we evacuate?"

"It's too late for that. If it is contagious, we'd be spreading it across the country."

His face creased in frustration. "How close is Doc to figuring this out?"

"Very close," Ian answered. "Any day now."

God, I hoped so.

"Okay." Cal cracked his big knuckles, something he did when he didn't feel totally in control of things. "What can I do?"

"Keep it quiet," I said. "Don't even tell Jordan. We can't afford a panic."

"Right."

"And if you could continue to handle things at the

office for a few more days, that would free me up to help Doc."

Boy, the more I lied, the easier it got.

"Of course. You can count on me."

I could, which only made me feel like scum for keeping the truth from him. When he left, I sat on the bed with a sigh.

"You couldn't tell him," Ian said, and I glanced up in surprise at how easily he'd read my mind.

The agony he'd revealed during the night was evident in the shadows beneath his eyes, but other than that, he seemed all right—rested, strong, ready to do his job.

Ian smiled. "What you're thinking is all over your face. Your deputy's a good guy, and you wanted to share everything."

"But I can't. He's a good guy who wouldn't understand. Either he'd lock us up for crazy people or his head would spin round and round until it exploded from the stress. I couldn't do that to him."

"You made the right decision. He can take care of the real-world issues, which will leave you free to help me with the out-of-this-world troubles." He paused. "What brought him here? What made him think you need the FBI, which, by the way, would be a waste of a phone call."

"Because?"

"Stuff like this would be routed to the *Jäger-Suchers,* and since you already called them . . ."

"Waste of a phone call. Got it. But don't people become a little suspicious when they call the FBI and get a *Jäger-Sucher*?"

"Not when they get the agent who's also a *Jäger-Sucher.*"

I sighed. "There's an FBI agent who works for Edward?"

"There are agents of Edward all over the place. Saves time."

"Sometimes I think he's as scary as the creatures he's hunting."

"He is," Ian said shortly. "Now, getting back to your deputy—"

"He came to report another death."

"Who?"

"The niece of some residents."

Ian nodded, face intent as he absorbed the information.

"It was at a house we visited." His gaze shot to mine. "One where we'd left a buzzard feather."

"So either the buzzard feather doesn't work against Raven Mockers or it doesn't work against this particular one, which appears to be growing stronger and changing the rules however the hell it wants to."

"I hate it when that happens," I muttered.

Ian coughed. I wasn't sure if he was stifling a laugh, a sob, or maybe both.

"I know of one other method to repel the witch," he continued. "But it's more elaborate. Not as easy to cart around and distribute as a feather." He got down on the ground and pulled his shoes out from under the bed. "I'll need to find some sticks, a sharp knife, pick up my notebook for the spell."

Something tickled in my memory. I tilted my head, waiting for it to tumble free.

"Aren't you going to get dressed?" Ian stood in front of me. "Not that I don't like this robe and what's under it." He untied the sash. "Or rather not under it."

"Shh," I said, and held up my hand.

Ian had the sense to go quiet.

"Sharpened sticks. Set at the corners of a house. Point facing skyward."

"Right." He smiled as if we were sharing a secret. "What we call old tobacco, a sacred blend used only for rituals, smoked just after dusk. Walk around the house, puffing the smoke in every direction, repeating the incantation. When the witch approaches, the stick will shoot into the air and come back down, fatally wounding the creature, be it in human or animal form. How did you know that?"

"I saw it."

His smile faded. "Where?"

"Quatie's."

32

I F SHE KNEW how to repel a Raven Mocker, then she knows there *is* a Raven Mocker."

Ian held on to the dashboard as I took the winding roads to Quatie's place faster than I should have.

"That doesn't mean she knows who it is," I pointed out.

"No. But we can ask."

And maybe we'd get lucky. Although I had to think that if Quatie knew the identity of the evil, shape-shifting witch, she would have told me.

"This is so weird," I said. "Quatie isn't a medicine woman. She doesn't know any of this stuff."

"Some of *this stuff* is common knowledge."

"Well, I didn't know it."

"Grace, I'm sorry to say so, but you don't know much. What was your great-grandmother teaching you all those years?"

I tightened my lips to keep from being defensive. My great-grandmother had tried and I had refused, for the most part, to listen. So we'd made do with what we were both comfortable with.

"She spent time with me," I said. "Talked to me. Walked with me. Showed me her things. Told me about my mother. I didn't have many women in my life." Except for Claire and Joyce, but as much as I loved them, they weren't different, like me.

"She didn't tell you about your heritage?"

"She spoke of the clans, specifically our clan. She showed me a few spells, taught me how to go to the water. She wanted to teach me the medicine, but I kind of got freaked out."

"Why?"

"She was . . ." I glanced at him, then back at the road. "Well, she did some things I couldn't explain."

"Like what?"

I'd never told anyone about this, because I'd known no one would believe me. There were times I'd convinced myself I'd imagined it, that I'd dreamed of Grandmother performing impossible feats, and as time passed I'd come to believe those feats had actually happened. But this was Ian, the man who could change his eyes to an eagle's and back again. He'd believe me.

"She was an old woman, but she never walked like one. She had this gait that reminded me of—" I glanced at him and lifted a shoulder. "A big cat."

His lips curved as he nodded for me to continue.

"Once when we were out walking in the mountains, she tripped over a stone in the path. Instead of falling and breaking a hip, she did some fancy tuck and roll. She bounced back to her feet like a five-year-old. Wasn't a mark on her."

"Spry."

"Very. Another time she saw some root or herb she

needed. She got so excited she leaped onto a boulder. That rock had to have been seven feet high."

In my mind's eye I saw her flying up, up, up, and landing on top. My brain added *Six Million Dollar Man* sound effects.

I smiled now at the memory, but back then I'd insisted we go home, and I hadn't returned for two weeks. Though I knew E-li-si had wanted to talk about it, I'd pretended nothing ever happened.

"She could walk me into the ground any day of the week," I continued. "One Saturday I showed up early and she wasn't there. I waited on the porch and saw her running up the driveway. I'm not slow, but I never would have caught her. I don't think a U.S. track-and-field star could have caught her."

Ian just nodded solemnly, waiting for me to finish.

"But the most interesting thing of all was when we ran into a bear after dusk one night. Usually bears run the other way, but this one had cubs. They ran right up to us. I didn't think, I put my hand on one, and the mother came bellowing out of the trees. Grandma put herself in front of me and—"

"What?" Ian murmured.

"She snarled." I heard again the sound she'd made— feral and furious. It had stopped that bear cold.

"Like a panther?" he asked.

I'd never heard a panther before that day, but after— I'd gone to the library, the Internet. I'd searched and searched until I found a recording; then I'd known the truth.

"Yes," I said. "She snarled like a panther, and the bear and her cubs ran away."

"What did your great-grandmother say about it?"

"Nothing."

"Nothing? She didn't teach you—?"

"I didn't want to hear about it, and by the time I did, she was gone."

"Grace." He shook his head, disappointed.

"I was a kid. My father constantly told me that he'd put an end to my visiting her if I started to act weird. I needed to see her; I couldn't take that chance, so I pretended nothing magical happened, and she let me."

"She could access her other nature like I can. That's a gift not everyone has."

"I certainly don't." My hands clenched on the steering wheel as I turned into Quatie's long, rutted drive.

And I never would, because I'd been too cowardly to fight for what was important, and now it was gone forever.

"Not necessarily," Ian said. "How do you explain the animosity between Elise and you if there isn't a little canine-versus-feline involved?"

"Maybe we just don't like each other. She is kind of a pain."

"And you're not?"

"Hey!"

"You have to admit your social skills could use some work."

I wasn't going to admit anything, even if he was right.

"E-li-si told me we were connected to the panther in a way no one else could ever be."

"She was right."

"But she died without teaching me what to do."

"There might still be a way, if you're interested."

I bounced into Quatie's yard and turned off the motor. "Would your spell work for me?"

My voice shook. I wasn't sure if I wanted it to or not. The thought of losing control of myself, of becoming something else, even partially, scared me.

"No," he said.

I caught my breath in relief, even as my stomach dipped in disappointment.

"I haven't translated all of Rose's papers yet. But if I were your great-grandmother, I'd have left the secret there. You could choose to use it or not, but if she didn't write it down, it's gone forever."

I wondered momentarily if that secret was the reason she'd come over from the Darkening Land. I hadn't seen the wolf in several days, which made me think whatever message she'd brought had been delivered. I just wished I knew for certain what the message had been.

"I didn't know her," Ian continued, "but I can't imagine she'd want such a huge part of your heritage to disappear."

I couldn't, either, but I put aside that problem as the door to Quatie's cabin opened and someone stepped out.

Not Quatie but a much, much younger woman. The great-great-granddaughter whose existence I'd doubted had arrived.

She was maybe an inch taller than Quatie, thinner, though not thin. Anyone lugging around D cups could not lay claim to that. But her waist was trim, and the legs revealed by her knee-length multi-colored skirt were shaped like a runner's.

The voluptuous curves of her body and the way she held herself, as if she knew how to use them, reminded me sharply of Katrine—most likely because I'd seen her last night outside of Ian's clinic. There really was very little that was similar between the two women beyond a huge rack—and even that wasn't the same, since Katrine's was bought and paid for, and this one appeared to be a gift, or perhaps a curse, from God.

Her hair fell long and straight to the middle of her back, framing a wide, attractive face that spoke of very few white ancestors and a whole lot of Cherokee. The type of face one didn't see often around here anymore.

I got out of the car. "Hello. I'm Grace McDaniel."

The woman shaded her eyes against the bright morning sun. "Grace. Grandmother's spoken of you so often I feel like I know you."

I couldn't say the same for her. I hadn't even known Quatie had children until she'd mentioned this relative.

"Is Quatie here?" I asked.

"No. She went—" The young woman waved a hand toward the trees, then shrugged. "You know how she is."

I did. Even though I'd asked her not to wander, I'd known she wouldn't listen. At least there was someone here now who would go searching for the old woman immediately if she didn't come back.

"I'm Dr. Walker." Ian stepped forward, waiting pointedly for her to introduce herself.

I silently thanked him for that. I hadn't wanted to admit to the girl that Quatie had never mentioned her until this week. I'd had enough instances of that in my childhood, when I'd met acquaintances of my father's who'd been very familiar with the names of his sons but had no inkling he had a daughter at all.

She smiled at Ian the way all women must. "I'm Adsila."

" 'Blossom,' " Ian translated.

"Yes."

She did resemble a blossom, all fresh and new. But

she also looked like Quatie around the eyes and the mouth, which made me warm to her right away.

Adsila came down the steps and crossed the grass, holding out her hand. Ian took it and shook, but when he tried to release her, she held on. He glanced into her eyes, startled.

"I have to thank you for helping my grandmother."

"Not a problem. I enjoyed meeting her." He tugged again; she didn't let go. My eyes narrowed. He couldn't be tugging too hard.

"You must be very good," she murmured, her voice low, almost suggestive. "At everything you do."

I wanted to shout, *Hey, I'm right here!* but she obviously didn't care. I was certain this kind of thing happened to Ian all the time. Combine his face, that body, and a medical degree . . . Well, he was kind of asking for it.

"I do my best."

Her smile was definitely suggestive. "I bet your best is amazing."

Ian coughed, or maybe he choked. My warm, friendly feeling cooled. She might just be grateful because he'd helped Quatie feel better; I know I was. But if Adsila thought she was going to show him her gratitude the way that I'd been showing my gratitude . . .

I cleared my throat. They both glanced in my direction, and Ian succeeded in retrieving his hand. Adsila smiled, shrugged as if to say, *You can't blame a girl for trying,* and stepped back.

"I've been having trouble with my neck," she said. "Maybe you could take a look at it?"

"I—uh. Of course."

"Not now," I blurted.

Adsila laughed, the sound bubbly and sweet. Why

couldn't she cackle like an old hen? "Of course not. I'll walk into town sometime this week and come to your clinic."

"That would be fine."

Ian flicked a finger toward the sticks now positioned at the four corners of the house, reminding me why we'd come.

"Do you know what those are for?" I asked.

"Granny Q. said they were for protection. I'm not sure against what."

Ian and I exchanged a glance.

"Is there something wrong, Sheriff? Something I should be worried about?"

I hesitated, but Ian gave a slight shake of his head. Telling Quatie's great-great-granddaughter about a shape-shifting witch would only convince her we were nuts and make her ignore anything else we might say in the future. Quatie had protected the place in the best way she could, the way we would have if she hadn't done it first. They were safer than anyone in this town at the moment, even us.

"Could you have Quatie call—" I stopped. No phone. "I don't suppose you brought a cell phone?"

"She hates them. I know better."

"Do you mind if we wait?" I asked.

Adsila opened her mouth, but Ian spoke first. "We should get back," he said. "I need to finish translating your great-grandmother's papers."

I really wanted to know what Quatie did about the Raven Mocker, but we had sticks to whittle, people to protect.

"Maybe you could bring her to town?"

"No car." Adsila spread her hands. "Sorry."

She *had* said she was going to walk in to see Ian.

"How'd you get here?" I asked.

"My father dropped me off. He had to be in Atlanta for a conference. He'll pick me up on the way back. I figured I could either walk or hitch into Lake Bluff if I needed to." She smiled at Ian.

I couldn't fathom that a young girl would choose to spend any time in the mountains with an old woman and no cell phone, electricity, or Internet connection—although I had. Not that there'd been too many cell phones or Internet connections back then.

"Could you tell her I'll visit again late this afternoon?" I asked. "Make sure she doesn't wander off?"

"I'll do my best," Adsila said.

Ian and I headed for the car. I reached my side first and glanced over to find Adsila staring at Ian's backside. She met my eyes, smirked, then shrugged before disappearing into the house.

Ian opened his door, noticed the direction of my gaze, and paused. "What's the matter?"

"Besides her hitting on you two seconds after we met, she was ogling your ass just now."

He looked at the cabin, then back at me. "I'm a little old for her."

"Ten years? That's nothing."

As he leaned on the top of the truck, his biceps flexed against the sleeves of his black T-shirt, and I did a little ogling of my own. He was so damn pretty.

"I have no interest in anyone but you."

I dragged my gaze from his muscles to his face. He was serious.

"When this is done, if we're both still standing, we're going to have a long, long talk about the future," he said.

With that he got into the vehicle, and I was left to

ponder his words and fight a growing fear. Because he'd said "if" and reminded me that one or both of us could die.

I wasn't afraid of dying, even before the wolf that could be my great-grandmother had come trotting through my life, solidifying my belief in the great beyond. But Ian's words revealed a new wrinkle.

I was downright terrified that he might.

33

I KEPT THAT fear to myself. Ian couldn't stop searching for the Raven Mocker any more than I could.

Driving around the last curve before we reached Lake Bluff, I cast an absent glance toward the trailer park nestled in the shade of a hill. Then I hit the brakes so hard, we skidded on the gravel as I turned into the drive.

"Grace, what the—?" Ian stopped when he saw what I had.

A squad car parked next to a dingy, tiny trailer, a crowd gathering. Cal earnestly speaking to several of the people.

"You think . . . ?" I asked.

"Let's find out."

Together we got out of the truck.

"Who saw her last?" Cal asked as we approached.

"She went to town to see—" The man, whom I identified as Jarvis Trillion, a regular at both the Watering Hole and my jail after he'd been at the Watering Hole, suddenly looked up and pointed. "Him. She went to see that newfangled, fairy doctor."

"Fairy?" Ian murmured, both confused and a little pissed.

"Well, you do wear a feather in your hair," I said. "In certain circles, like this one, you're just asking for it."

Ian's hand lifted, brushing the eagle feather, and Jarvis sneered, "What'd you do with Katrine, asswipe?"

Cal cleared his throat. "No need for that, Jarvis."

Jarvis scowled and muttered, but he knew better than to screw with Cal. Cal ate guys like him for a midnight snack. Or was that Chuck Norris?

I motioned for my deputy to join us away from the others. "Why didn't you call me?" I asked.

"You told me to handle things. That you'd be working with Doc." He scowled at Ian, who stared back non-committally.

"I didn't mean that you shouldn't call me if another dead body showed up."

"Dead?" Cal returned his gaze to me. "Who's dead?"

"Katrine?"

"Where'd you get that?"

"You're here."

"And that leads you to think she's dead? Sheesh, Grace, talk about ghoulish."

"Well, we have had a bit of a problem with dead citizens lately."

He tilted his head. "I guess you're right."

"So?"

"Katrine's missing. Didn't show up to open the Watering Hole this morning, and the regulars got antsy. Came out to roust her." He lifted one shoulder, then lowered it. "She had the only set of keys. When she wasn't here, they called me."

"You checked her trailer?"

"No sign of her. Nothing knocked over. No blood. No note. Her suitcase is in the closet, and so are her clothes, but her car's gone." His gaze switched to Ian and cooled. "Jarvis said she went to see you."

"He was with me, Cal. You know that."

"I know he was there this morning. I don't know anything about last night. He could have killed her, dumped the body, then come to you for an alibi."

"He didn't."

"You got proof of that?"

"He had dinner with me and Claire and Mal. You want to, you can call the mayor for verification."

"And after dinner?"

"I checked into Fosters'. Jordan will confirm that, and he's been with me every minute since."

"That just figgers." Jarvis had crept close enough to hear the end of our conversation. "Two Injuns *stickin'* together."

He made an obscene hand gesture by circling his thumb and forefinger, then pushing his other forefinger through the hole several times fast.

"Is this guy for real?" Ian asked.

Jarvis had been at the head of Dad's list of potential cross burners, though Dad had never been able to prove it. My arresting the man for drunk and disorderly five times a month had not endeared me to him, either.

"Oh yeah," I said. "He's a real Indian lover."

"Bitch," he spit.

Ian's fist caught Jarvis on the jaw. He went down hard. The crowd began to murmur and shift. I recognized quite a few other cross-burning types in the mix. This could get ugly fast.

"Cal," I said.

"I know." He moved in front of me. "Everyone just settle." He rested his hand on his gun and the murmurs faded. I could have done the same, but with these guys that would have only made them crazier. They'd barely been able to tolerate an Indian sheriff; now that the Indian was also a woman, I had all I could do to keep them from foaming at the mouth every time they saw me.

I turned to Jarvis, who shook his head as if he'd been dunked a few times under the water.

I shot Ian an exasperated look. "That was unnecessary."

"No, it was definitely necessary."

"I'm gonna sue your ass!" Jarvis yelled. "I'm gonna kick it, too." He tried to get up but fell on *his* ass with a thud.

Ian moved so fast I didn't have a chance to stop him. Cal tensed, ready to grab him if he needed to. But all Ian did was lean over Jarvis and whisper.

The other man went pale, staring at Ian, transfixed. Then Jarvis slapped his hands over his face and screamed, "His eyes! His eyes!"

Ian straightened and strolled back to us so calm, I half-expected him to start whistling.

"What did you do?" I asked, but I knew, even before he winked.

The crowd murmured some more, this time staring at Jarvis as if he were crazy. Cal did, too. "You been drinking already, Jarvis? You'd better get on to bed."

Cal motioned to two of Jarvis's cronies, and they hauled him away.

"Move along," Cal told the others. "We'll handle things."

Though they mumbled and grumbled, the crowd dispersed, some to the trailers parked in a zigzagging row that disappeared into the trees, others to their pickup trucks. Maybe I should sell mine.

Cal returned. "You say you were with him every minute. You didn't sleep all night?"

"Of course I did. But Jordan was at the desk. I'm sure she would have seen Ian leave."

"There's a back door."

I tightened my lips. Even though Cal was handy in a crisis, right now he was getting on my nerves. "I saw Katrine hanging around outside Ian's clinic last night. We drove past and straight to the Fosters'. She could have gone anywhere. She's probably holed up with—" I stopped.

She could be with anyone, but it didn't seem like a good idea to say so until we knew what had happened. This could end badly, and I didn't want to have spoken ill of the dead.

But I doubted Katrine was a victim of the Raven Mocker. The witch tended to go after people in their own beds, although that didn't mean it had to. Still, if Katrine were dead by Cherokee witch, this would be the first time we had no body and the first time, as far as we knew, that the Raven Mocker had killed so many times in one night. The violence was escalating.

"Start searching for her," I said. "I'm sure she'll turn up."

I only hoped she turned up alive.

⚬⚬⚬

I gave Katrine a buzzard feather, too," Ian said as we drove away.

"When?"

"When I gave her the jar of vitamin solution. I've

been giving a feather to every person who comes into the clinic." He shrugged. "Figured it couldn't hurt."

"It didn't help, either. Where do you think she is?"

"Like you said, she could be anywhere. But for her to have been a victim of the Raven Mocker breaks the pattern again."

He'd noticed that, too. It was so nice to work with someone I didn't have to explain my every thought to. Cal was so literal sometimes he made me want to bang my head against a wall.

"Not that the pattern can't be broken," Ian continued. "We've already seen that. I just wonder why."

Considering the first suspect in Katrine's disappearance had been Ian, I had an idea. If I hadn't been with him, *I'd* have wondered if he were responsible. Which might just be what the Raven Mocker was after. Divide and conquer. Get the man who knew the score and was trying to find a way to even it thrown into jail, and leave the woman who didn't know much alone and floundering.

However, if the Raven Mocker realized we were on to him-her-it, why hadn't the creature just ripped our hearts out of our chests? It would be easier.

My phone rang. I glanced at the caller ID. *Claire.*

"Any news?" she asked.

"You know there was another death?"

"Yes. Same as the others?"

"I assume so, though I haven't heard from Doc yet."

She sighed. "Why is it that since you and I took over, weird stuff keeps happening?"

"Yeah, why is that?"

"You think that weird stuff happened before, but our dads were better at keeping it quiet?"

"Doubtful. More likely our dads figured out a logical solution and rationalized away all the scary stuff."

"I doubt rationalizing did any good. Someone would have had to kill something."

"Maybe last summer wasn't the first time Edward came to town."

"Hadn't thought of that." Claire paused. "Listen, can you come over here?"

"I'm a little busy with a shape-shifting witch and its epidemic of death."

"It'll only take a minute; there are a few things we have to discuss about festival security. Life does go on, Grace. We're going to have hundreds of visitors pouring into Lake Bluff real soon."

We had to have this situation cleared up before then. Last year's Full Moon Festival had brought the town back from the brink of financial ruin. But this year's could destroy us if tourists began to turn up without their hearts.

"Where are you?" I asked.

"The basement of town hall."

"I hate it down there." The place was downright eerie.

"Girl."

"Oh, that always works."

She went silent, remembering the times my dad had used the same insult, which really shouldn't have been an insult.

"Sorry."

"Forget it." I glanced at Ian. "I'll need to bring someone along." I wasn't letting him out of my sight.

"You two are attached at the hip, huh?"

"Pretty much."

"Good. I like him." She hung up.

I found it interesting that Claire liked Ian. She wasn't a man hater, but she wasn't much of a fan, either. She'd had some trouble in the past, and only Malachi had been able to reach through the wall she'd erected between herself and the world. Maybe having a son had helped. It was hard to condemn all males when you had such an adorable specimen at hand.

"I should go to my place and translate the rest of your great-grandmother's papers," Ian said. "We need to know everything she did."

"Fine." I picked up my phone. "I'll tell Claire I can't make it."

"You don't have to. You do your thing; I'll do mine. We'll meet later."

"I don't think that's a good idea."

"It's daytime." He put his hand on my thigh. "The Raven Mocker can't hurt you in the sun."

"I wasn't worried about me."

His eyebrows shot up. "Me?" He paused as if to think about that. "I've never had anyone worry about me before." His fingers tightened; then he slid them higher, stroking the inside of my leg until I shuddered. "I think I like it."

"I don't." He removed his hand, but I caught it and brought it back. "That I like. It's the worrying I don't."

His fingers continued to stroke. I drove down Center Street with his hand between my legs. No one could see, which only made what he was doing all the more exciting.

"You don't have to worry," he said. "As you've told me several times, I can take care of myself. Going after evil spirits is my job, and I'm pretty good at it."

"I don't like being separated. Two are stronger than one, remember?"

"We've got a lot to do and not much time to do it in. Separating in the daytime makes sense."

I parked in front of the clinic. "I know."

Ian got out of the truck, then leaned back in through the open window. "Come back as soon as you're done. Maybe I'll know something by then. We can start pounding sticks into the four corners of houses. Tell people they're squirrel repellents or something."

With a quick grin and then a wave, he disappeared inside. Seconds later he reappeared on the second floor, moving toward his office. My body still hummed from the touch of his. I exited the vehicle. This wouldn't take long.

He'd left the front door open, so I locked it behind me, checked the back door and locked it, too, then climbed the stairs. He turned, surprised, when I came in the room, but when he saw my face, he dropped the papers onto the desk and drew the shade over the window.

I unbuttoned and unzipped my uniform, tossed the bra, lost the gun belt, shoes, underwear, and socks. By the time I was done, so was he. From the appearance of his body, he was as aroused as I was; naked, we met in the center of the room.

Our lips crushed together. I wrapped my legs around his waist, and he walked forward until my back met the wall, then drove home.

I clung to him so my head didn't bang drywall. He was rough; I didn't mind. I'd been on the edge since his finger had first inched from my thigh to my clitoris as I drove through town. He'd been asking for this, begging for it without words, and now I was, too.

The slap of flesh against flesh was loud in the silent room. Our breath harsh, our movements harsher, I began to convulse, to clench around him. He plunged into me once and went still.

"Ian." I arched, pressing against him, and saw stars behind my closed eyelids.

"Grace," he answered. "Look at me."

I opened my eyes, and his were right there, that odd combination of brown, green, and gray. He stared at me with a curious expression, as if seeing me for the very first time.

"Ah, hell," he muttered, then pressed his forehead against mine and laughed.

"What's so funny?"

The shift from rough, intense passion to easy, gentle humor confused me. My body still hovered at the edge of orgasm, and I wanted to go there with him.

"I've gone and fallen in love with you." He rubbed his forehead back and forth, his hair sifting over my cheeks like a waterfall. "Didn't see that coming."

I shoved at his shoulder. "You what?"

He began to move, slowly, surely, softly—in and out as he rained kisses all over my face. My hands clenched on his shoulders, and I rested my head against the wall, limp, oblivious, forgotten.

He tensed, pulsing within me, and I began to pulse, too, the sensation seemingly so much deeper now than it had ever been before. As the tremors faded he gathered me close and whispered, "I'm sorry."

34

W HEN I CAME back to myself and heard what he'd said, I punched him in the shoulder. "What the hell's wrong with you? You don't make a girl come like that and then apologize."

I left out the part about him loving me. I wasn't sure what to say about that.

He kissed my hair and let me go, gathering my clothes and pressing them into my hands without meeting my eyes.

"Ian?" I grabbed his arm. "What is it?"

"They'll come after you now."

I snorted. "Let them try."

"They will. To get back at me. Just like they came after her."

"We've had this talk. I'm not Susan. Whatever comes after me is asking for a very thorough ass kicking. Maybe I should learn how to roundhouse kick."

"What?" His forehead creased. "Why?"

"Jack be nimble. Jack be quick. Jack still can't dodge Chuck Norris's roundhouse kick."

"Are you okay?"

I guess that had been kind of random. "Never mind."

I hadn't realized how those jokes had seeped into my head. Maybe I should make Jordan stop. Then again, I wasn't sure I wanted to start a day in the office without one. What fun would that be?

"What if they make you evil, too?" Ian drew his shirt over his head.

I picked up my shoes. "Then you'll kill me."

He dropped his pants. "No!"

"Yes." I picked them up and handed them to him. "I'll understand, and if the worst happens, I'll want you to."

He just shook his head, looking miserable.

"Let's make a promise. If I'm stupid enough to get infected with the evil virus, you kill me." I held out my hand; he stared at it in horror. "And I'll do the same for you."

His eyes lifted; I met them without flinching. "You would, wouldn't you?" he asked.

"If it comes to that."

Instead of shaking my hand, he pulled me into his arms. "Thank you."

"God, you're weird." My words were muffled against his chest. "Now let me go. I've gotta clean up and get to town hall."

He held on for a few more seconds, then kissed me—gentle and sweet. My stomach turned over.

Aw, hell. I loved him, too.

But now was not the time to tell him. He was already

wigged-out enough. Later, when we'd killed this thing, had a victory under our belts, then I'd let him know. Then we'd decide what, if anything, we'd do about it.

I went down the hall to the bathroom, where I washed up and got dressed, thinking all the while.

What *would* we do about it?

Could I spend my life with a man who was fighting things that existed merely to kill him and anyone else who got in their path? Eventually Ian's luck would run out. Could I go into a relationship knowing he'd leave me, just like everyone else I'd loved in my life had left?

I wanted a family, but I wanted the whole package— husband, kids, a real home. With Ian, I could never have those things in the way that I'd dreamed. But now that I loved him, would having them with anyone else be any closer to that dream?

I'd always wanted to find a man who stayed, but Ian wouldn't, couldn't.

"Hell," I said again.

Before I left, I went in search of Ian and found him at his desk, already engrossed in my great-grandmother's papers. I slid my arms around him and kissed his neck. Absently he patted my arm.

"I'll be back soon," I whispered.

"Mmm."

Why did I find his distraction cute? Whenever my father ignored me, patted me, murmured, or muttered, I'd wanted to lash out with words or kick him in the shin. As a child, I often had. Which might just explain why he'd always done his best to avoid me.

I stepped out of the clinic into the bright sun and heavy heat of a Georgia afternoon. Leaving my pickup where it was, I turned toward town hall and froze at the sight of the wolf on the sidewalk.

I couldn't see the cement through her body. The light summer wind ruffled the beast's fur. The thing appeared pretty corporeal to me. I started to worry that this one was actually a wolf when a pair of tourists walked right through it.

The wolf growled. The couple paused, looked down, frowned, and the woman shivered. "Goose walked over my grave," she said.

I knew what that was like.

They smiled and nodded in my direction but didn't mention seeing any wolf or hearing the disembodied growling. I waited until they were out of earshot before I asked, "What now?"

The wolf promptly turned north, ran a few paces, then stopped and looked back, tongue lolling.

"Trouble again?" I glanced at the clinic. "Ian is trouble? Or is trouble coming? Maybe from the north?"

The animal shimmered and disappeared.

"I hate messenger wolves," I muttered, scuffing my shoe against the cement. "They're too damn vague."

I continued north to town hall, entering the cavernous confines and heading directly to the basement.

When we were kids, Claire had always avoided this place. As I descended the dark, dank cement staircase, I understood why. Back then, the lower level had probably been full of cobwebs and mice.

Someone had cleaned up recently. The only cobwebs occupied a high corner near a ceiling full of old pipes. I listened for the scrambling of rodents, but all I heard was a distant humming.

This area had once been used for storage and maintenance items, but the old cardboard boxes and rusted filing cabinets had disappeared; the dirty brooms, buckets, and mops had all been replaced with shiny new ones.

The lighting was new, too. Fluorescent rectangles glowed above the twisting, turning corridors. I followed the hum toward an old storm cellar with access to the street, since town hall served as the tornado shelter for all of downtown Lake Bluff. There I found Claire in what appeared to be a second office. Desk, tables, telephone, fax.

"What's the deal?" I asked.

She stopped humming and spun around. "Hey. Joyce and I use this place to get work done when it's too nuts upstairs."

"First time the tornado siren goes off, your secret's going to be out."

Her smile faded. "Then we'll have to move." She glanced around. "Too bad, because all the electrical connections are here."

"Yeah, bummer," I said, anxious to get this done and return to Ian. "What was so important I had to come into Dracula's Dungeon?"

As soon as I said the words, I gave a mental cringe. What used to be a joke was now, in the light of Ian's information about his wife, too real to make fun of.

"I cleaned down here," Claire said. "Didn't you notice?"

"Yes. Lovely. Nice job. Get to the point."

"Sheesh, you certainly got up on the wrong side of the bed."

"Being woken up by my deputy with news of another murder usually does that."

"Sorry." Claire rubbed her forehead. "You're right. Let me put these away." She leaned over the table and gathered together the pictures lying there. "I was trying to identify some of these for the show."

Claire had decided to put together an exhibition of

old photographs Joyce had unearthed in the bowels of town hall. The display would open during the Full Moon Festival next month.

"There's one here of your great-grandmother." She pulled a sheet out of the stack. "She's really young. Probably younger than we are now." Claire shoved the photo across the table.

I'd never seen E-li-si like this. I'd been born long after her hair had grayed and her shoulders had stooped. In this grainy black-and-white image she stood tall, slim, and straight, her dark eyes full of mischief, her full, high cheekbones so much like mine, her lips curved as she smiled into the camera.

"That's her, right?" Claire asked.

"Yes." I touched my finger to Grandma's face.

Outside, the wolf began to howl, and I snatched my finger back. "Did you hear that?"

"What?" Claire met my eyes. "You okay?"

Why did everyone keep asking me that?

"Peachy," I answered, returning my gaze to Grandmother.

"I don't know who she's with." Claire tapped the photo. "Do you?"

My phone began to ring, and I held up one hand as I pulled it from my belt, then glanced at the caller ID. *Ian.*

"Hold on," I said to Claire.

The static was so bad I was surprised I'd even received the call down here. "Grace? Can you hear me?"

"Barely. What is it?"

"The sticks. I thought they were meant to keep a witch away."

Snap. Crackle. The sound seemed to explode in my brain.

"The word was 'spirits,' " he said. "Keep away spirits."

"What does that mean? Ghosts?"

Crrrrraack!

"Ian?"

He said something that I couldn't understand.

"Say again."

While I waited for the line to clear, I moved closer to the table, to Claire and the photo of my great-grandmother. My gaze went to the other person in the picture and I stilled.

I knew that face.

I picked up the print, turned it over, but I don't know what I expected to find on the opposite side. "Where'd you get this?"

"In one of the old cabinets with all the others."

"Is this a trick photo?"

"How do you mean?"

"A combination of one image and another."

"No. Why?"

I stared at the woman who stood slightly behind and partially obscured by my great-grandmother. However, I clearly saw her face.

It was Adsila.

But in this picture my great-grandmother was perhaps twenty-five. Adsila's grandmother was a baby. Adsila wouldn't be born yet for over half a century. So how could she be standing next to my great-grandmother in an antique photograph?

All sorts of things fluttered through my head along with the static still coming from the phone.

Time travel. Aliens. Ghosts.

Then, as I continued to look at Adsila's face, all the pieces came together. "Ian—"

"Hold on," he said at the same time. "There's someone here."

Suddenly I could hear him quite clearly, his foot-
steps on the bare floor, thumping down the steps, opening the door.

"Adsila. Hi."

Shit.

"Ian!" I shouted, and Claire jumped. The pile of photos in her hand scattered across the floor.

"Too late, Gracie," a voice whispered over the phone.

I dropped everything and ran.

35

THROUGH THE CORRIDORS, up the stairs, out the front door, and into the light.

Down the street to the clinic, up to the second floor, through every room.

He was gone, as were my great-grandmother's papers. How had Adsila managed that so fast?

I glanced out the window and understood. Where my truck had been was a great big empty. I reached for my cell, but I'd dropped it in the basement, so I went to Ian's phone, but it was dead.

"Nice touch, Adsila." Or should I say "Quatie"?

Someone pounded up the steps and my hand went to my gun, but it was only Claire. She bent at the waist and tried to catch her breath. I snatched her cell phone out of her hand and dialed Cal. "I need everyone on the lookout for my pickup truck," I said the instant he answered.

"Stolen?"

"Yes."

"Any idea who?"

"A young Cherokee woman—five-five or -six, a hundred and twenty-five pounds, long black hair, brown eyes. Her name's Adsila. She'll be traveling with Ian."

Cal cursed. "I knew he couldn't be trusted."

"She kidnapped him."

"Oh."

"Yeah. Get moving."

I disconnected, then pocketed Claire's phone. "I need a car."

Without a word, she reached into her khaki slacks and handed me her keys. "Who's Adsila?"

"Quatie's great-great-granddaughter, or at least that's what she said. But I think she's Quatie, grown younger through the supernatural means of the Raven Mocker."

"And you figured this out how?"

"The picture. The woman next to Grandmother must be Quatie. They were the only full-blood Cherokee women in town then and now. But I met the person in the photo, and her name's Adsila." I started for the stairs and Claire followed. " 'Adsila' means 'blossom' in Cherokee."

"Makes sense," Claire said. "The blossom of youth. The sprout from which the flower grows. Clever."

"I'll be sure and tell her so right before I kill her."

Claire gave me an uneasy glance, but she didn't argue. "How did she grow younger?"

"The legend of the Raven Mocker says the witch steals the lives of the dying, appearing as a crone from the weight of all the years it's stolen. But our Raven Mocker began to kill young people, who had a lot of time left."

"She got younger because she stole more time."

"That's my theory." I remembered the odd flash I'd had when I'd first met Adsila, thinking that her body reminded me of Katrine's, then Katrine turned up missing. I had a bad feeling we were going to find her somewhere minus her cold, cold heart.

"Why did she kidnap Ian?" Claire asked as we exited the clinic and headed at a fast clip toward town hall and her car.

"We must have tipped her off that we were on to her when we went to talk to Quatie about the sticks."

"You went to talk to Quatie about sticks," Claire repeated. "What a fascinating life you lead."

"Crap." I stopped so fast Claire smacked into me from behind. Several passersby looked at me oddly and skirted around us. "We didn't suspect Quatie of being the Raven Mocker because she'd placed sharpened sticks at the four corners of her house, which we thought repelled witches. A spell," I explained at Claire's frown. "But on the phone just now, Ian said the sticks are meant to repel spirits."

"What was Quatie trying to keep away?"

"The messenger wolf." I snapped my fingers. "Which kept trying to tell me she was trouble, and I wasn't getting it."

"What's Quatie going to do with Ian?"

My eyes met Claire's. "I think she's going to kill him."

⚭

It wasn't easy getting out of the parking lot without Claire. She'd insisted on going with me.

The only way to leave her behind was to say, "Oh, Malachi's here."

Then, when she turned, I jumped in her car—actually

her dad's old Ford Focus—locked the doors, and drove off. I'd rather have her mad at me than dead.

Claire's phone rang as I left the parking lot. The caller ID read: *Town Hall.* I ignored it. Claire would only yell at me, and I wasn't in the mood.

Though I doubted Quatie would be stupid enough to go back to her cabin, I checked the place anyway.

Empty, as I'd expected, with no evidence of two people living there, either. Sure there were two sets of clothing, but since Adsila couldn't fit into Quatie's things and vice versa, that was understandable.

But all the clothes, old woman's and sweet young thing's, hung in one closet. Despite there being two bedrooms, only one showed signs of use. There was a single coffee cup, cereal bowl, spoon in the sink, and there wasn't a suitcase, backpack, or overnight bag to be had. Maybe Quatie had taken it with her, but I doubted it.

I ransacked the drawers, the garbage, tore every book off every shelf and shook them out, upended knickknacks trying to find some clue to where she'd taken him, but there was nothing.

I stepped onto the porch and contemplated the sun falling down. I didn't have much time. She'd stolen Ian in the daylight, but she'd kill him in the dark. I knew it as surely as I knew I'd never get over him.

But why had she stolen him now? If she knew we were on to her, that we were working together to end her reign of death, why hadn't she killed us both instead of giving us time to figure out her true identity?

"Grandmother, where are you when I need you?" I whispered.

The wolf didn't come. The last time I'd seen her, the thing had disappeared. Had she gone away forever?

How could I bring her back? I needed Ian, in more ways than one.

I let my eyes wander the tree line, hoping the wolf would appear; then my gaze caught on the sharpened sticks still buried in the ground at the four corners of the cabin, and the light dawned. Even if she *could* hear me, she couldn't come to this place.

I ran down the steps and into the woods, calling for her, but still she didn't arrive. I was at a loss until I saw the glimmer of water nearby. I sprinted for it, losing my clothes as I went. By the time I reached the creek, I was naked, so I jumped right in.

Sun sparkled on the water. I sank in to my neck and recited the only chant I knew. "I stand beneath the moon and feel the power. I will possess the lightning and drink of the rain. The thunder is your song and mine."

Holding my breath, I waited. But nothing came.

I smacked the top of the water. The words said in English were worthless, but I didn't know them in Cherokee.

Frustration clawed at me. I began to jabber every Cherokee word I knew.

"Năkwĭsĭs. A ni sa ho ni. A ni tsi s kwa. A ni wo di." Nothing.

Finally I closed my eyes and shouted, "E-li-si!" I repeated the word seven times, and when I opened my eyes, the wolf stood on the bank of the creek, proving once and for all that the messenger was my great-grandmother.

"Rule of seven," I murmured. I should have known. Every Cherokee ritual involved the sacred number seven.

I climbed out of the water and used my uniform top to dry myself, which left me looking like an entrant in a wet-blouse contest, but I didn't care.

Once dressed, I followed the wolf to the cabin. She wouldn't go near the house but stayed at the edge of the trees. Considering those sharpened sticks were supposed to shoot into the air and kill her if she came too close, that was understandable.

"Which way?" I asked.

The wolf stared north. I stepped in that direction, and she growled, then glanced toward the car. *Woof*.

"I need to drive?"

I didn't wait for an answer—which would only be *woof*—but climbed in and followed Grandmother down the drive to the highway.

Last summer, when we'd had our own wolf problem, I'd done some research. Wolves can run 40 miles per hour. They've been known to travel a hundred miles in a single day. They can chase a herd for five or six miles, then accelerate.

According to my speedometer, at 55 miles per hour Grandma was one fast wolf. Of course she wasn't a real wolf, but I was still impressed.

I hoped we didn't have far to go. The sun seemed to be falling faster than usual. I knew that wasn't true, but I was afraid. Afraid I'd find Ian, but too late. Afraid I'd never find him at all.

My hands clenched on the steering wheel as another thought occurred to me. What if I found him changed into something evil just like Susan had been? I didn't think he could become a Raven Mocker—didn't we need a Thunder Moon for that?—but if Quatie was a witch and she was becoming more and more powerful, who knows what she might be able to accomplish?

Would I be able to kill him as I'd promised? I didn't want to make that choice.

Ian had been forced to kill the body of the woman

he loved, even though he knew the spirit that inhabited it was no longer human. I was struck anew by his courage. Certainly he'd lived with the guilt, thrown himself into his job, probably taken chances that he shouldn't have ever since, but he'd done what had to be done and it had not been easy.

The sun went behind a cloud, throwing shadows across the road, and I panicked, pressing down on the accelerator, trying to get wherever we were going faster. My bumper would have sent the wolf sprawling, if she'd had a butt to bump. As it was, the metal just passed through her tail and she shot me a snarl over her shoulder, so I eased off the gas.

I had to find Ian before Quatie did her worst. If she ate his heart, would she gain his power, too? Considering what she'd gained so far, I had to think so.

Perhaps she'd stolen him more for his magic than his knowledge. To possess the heart of an A ni wo di, a paint clan sorcerer, would make her infinitely more dangerous. If she accomplished it, I had no doubt we were all doomed.

I came around a corner and suddenly knew where we were going.

"Blood Mountain," I whispered.

And the wolf disappeared.

36

THE PEAK OF Blood Mountain loomed over me. Though the sun still shone, the shadow thrown by the massive summit made me shiver. I knew without a doubt that this was where Quatie had brought Ian, even before I saw the flash of red in the trees.

I slammed on the brakes and swung around, unsurprised to find my truck abandoned a few yards down a dirt track. I got out of Claire's car, approaching my own cautiously, gun drawn, but no one was there.

I'd learned how to track at my father's heels. He'd been the best and now I was. Though the past few days of heat and sun had dried the rain from the last storm, I could still find traces of a trail headed upward.

Blood Mountain might not be the highest peak, but it wasn't low, either. Most estimates put the elevation at 4,458 feet. There was no water at the top; countless people had fallen prey to dehydration climbing this mountain.

I hadn't brought a canteen, but it didn't matter. The

sun was falling; I wouldn't reach the top before night-fall, which meant I'd be lucky to reach Ian before the witch killed him. Dehydration was going to be the least of my worries.

As much as I wanted to, I couldn't run. I had to be alert for signs that Ian and the witch were still on the trail or that they might have left it.

About halfway up, I found just that. A tiny scuff of a shoe at the edge of the dirt, then broken twigs and leaves and indentations in the softer ground beneath the canopy of trees. They were headed parallel to the ridge instead of up.

I tried to think about what I'd do when I found them. I had silver bullets in my gun, but I wasn't sure they'd be of any use. I should shoot Quatie in Adsila form—witches could die, couldn't they?—but I wasn't certain I'd be able to. As Adsila, or Quatie, she was a person. As Quatie, she was a person I loved. But if I waited for her to become the Raven Mocker, then she would be damn hard to kill, damn hard to see, too.

The heat made my already-damp shirt damper. Bugs flew into my eyes, stuck to my sweaty face, and all the time I was conscious of the sun tumbling down.

The shadows lengthened. In the distance, thunder rumbled. The scent of rain rode in on the breeze.

I caught sight of a roof ahead and approached cautiously, scooting from tree to tree, just in case Quatie was watching.

The tiny log cabin in the clearing had seen better days. The porch was mostly kindling. The roof had a hole so big I could see it from here, and the windows were nothing more than shards of glass.

I pulled my gun from its holster and hurried across the open space to the rear of the structure. I made it without an outcry or hail of bullets. Maybe they weren't even here.

Peeking into the window, I jerked quickly back. Someone lay on the bed.

Since the shadows of the unlit cabin had combined with the increasing darkness of the coming storm, I couldn't determine if the lump was Ian, Quatie, or someone else entirely.

I slid along the wall, checked the corner, then did the same down the side and the front, until I was at the door. Taking a deep breath, I gave it a shove and went in low.

Nothing moved. No one spoke. Was the body on the bed another corpse?

I inched forward, gun in position, then I tugged the thin blanket with my free hand.

"Ian!"

Someone had beaten the crap out of him. The same someone, I was sure, who'd tied him up. My hand clenched on the edge of the cover until my knuckles went white; then I felt for a pulse, letting out a long, relieved breath when I found one.

He was unconscious. From the amount of blood on his face, he had a head injury. I only hoped it wasn't a serious one.

"Ian," I tried again, got no response. I looked around for water to throw in his face or at least wet his lips. I was out of luck there, too.

As much as I'd like to, I couldn't carry him down the mountain. I checked Claire's cell phone. No service. I hadn't really expected any.

I patted his face, gently, because of the blood. I had no idea where it had come from—head, nose, cheeks, or chin. I didn't want him to awaken in pain.

My eyes burned with tears and before I knew what I meant to do, I leaned over and kissed his big fat lip.

Beneath mine, his mouth moved. I reared back, my own eyes widening when his opened.

"Grace?" His voice was thick, hoarse, confused.

"I'm here."

"How?"

"My father didn't leave me out in the mountains when I was four for nothing."

"He what?" Ian jerked upward, then moaned and fell back.

"Hey, relax. I just meant I know how to find my way around, how to follow someone. She didn't stand a chance."

"It's Adsila."

"I know. She's Quatie."

His face screwed up in confusion, then straightened out as he hissed in pain.

"Killing young, healthy people made her younger and healthier," I explained. "I saw a picture of Quatie when she was about my age. Spitting image of Adsila."

"Interesting."

"Yeah, great stuff," I said impatiently. "Where is she?"

"I don't know. She said she'd be back when the sun died and the thunder was born."

I glanced out the door. The shadows had lengthened, and the storm had begun to swirl old dead leaves across the stubbly grass. "Soon."

He nodded, then cursed.

"What did she do to you?"

"Tied me up and beat me bloody," he said, as if what had happened were nothing more than a normal day's activities. I had to wonder what his life had been like in Oklahoma.

"Why now?" I asked. "She knew I had Grandmother's papers."

"She also knew you couldn't read them until I showed up; then she lit your house on fire."

"How? She could barely walk."

"She could fly."

I recalled the blaze of sparks in the sky as I'd driven from Quatie's place to my own. I guess flying instead of limping, growing younger instead of dying, was some kind of rationalization for why Quatie had decided being evil was better than being herself.

"So she flew to my house and used the sparks flying out of her butt to flame my roof?"

"Or a match."

I guess it didn't really matter how she'd done it. "But the joke was on her because you'd already taken the papers."

"Then we foolishly let her know we still had them."

Whoops.

"Even though she didn't think I knew how to kill her," I said, "it would make sense, in an evil villain sort of way, to kill me, just in case."

"She was fond of you, at least until the Raven Mocker took over completely. The more lives she ate, the less Quatie she became."

"Then why didn't she tear out *your* heart before now?"

"She needed more power. I might not be strong enough to end her, but I had enough juice to keep her from ending me—until today anyway."

"Then why are you still alive?"

Realization spread over his battered face. "Dammit. I'm the bait, Grace. You've got to go. Now. Before she comes back."

"Like hell." I set to work picking at the knotted rope around his ankles.

"She read your great-grandmother's papers. She knows that the only way to kill her is for a sorcerer of greater power to see her in raven form."

"I thought it was great power, and it didn't work. You couldn't see her, even with your eagle eyes."

"The writing's faded. The word was 'greater,' not 'great.'"

"I don't see what that has to do with me."

"I couldn't see her because my power is from the eagle—a great war bird, but a bird just the same. I'm of equal power."

"Okay, still not getting how I can help."

"You're a panther, Grace. Much greater power than a raven."

"I'm not a panther."

"You could be. Remember what you told me about your great-grandmother and the bear? She could access the panther."

"Just because she could doesn't mean I can. I don't know anything about that, Ian."

"She left the spell in her papers. All you have to do is believe." I snorted. "And say the words."

"I have a better idea." The ropes fell away from his ankles. "Let's get the hell out of here."

I reached for the ties that bound his hands, and lightning flashed overhead so brightly I could still see it when I closed my eyes. The thunder that followed shook the mountain. When it faded, another sound drifted in on the wind.

The caw of a raven, the beat of supernatural wings.

"Forget the hands. You can run without them." I

yanked him to his feet, but when I headed for the door, he didn't follow. "Ian, let's go."

He was staring up at the hole in the roof, head tilted, listening. "It's too late, even if I'd planned to run," he lowered his gaze to mine, "which I didn't. I came to kill this witch, and I'm not leaving until she's dead."

"You came because she dragged you here and beat you bloody," I muttered. "And if we stay she's going to send us to the Darkening Land, then feast on the rest of my town."

"Not if you do what I say."

My heart pounded so loudly I couldn't hear the beat of approaching wings anymore, but I felt it. The Raven Mocker was riding in on the storm.

Nervously I kept picking at the knots holding Ian's hands together. "What do I do?"

"The spell's simple. Words and belief. I'll say the Cherokee; you repeat."

"I won't understand what I'm saying."

"Right." I gave an impatient tug on the rope, and it fell away. "Thanks. What we'll be saying is this: 'I feel the power of my past. I walk the path of my people. Give me the knowledge, the strength, the magic of the panther.' Got it?"

I nodded, then flinched as the horrible shrieking commenced from above.

"Repeat after me," he shouted.

He held my gaze as we said the words. I had a hard time concentrating as the wind swirled through the windows, the door, the roof, sweeping past my cheeks like the beat of invisible raven's wings.

The shrieking increased. I wanted to put my hands

over my ears. Then suddenly my chest began to ache as if someone, or something, had punched my solar plexus.

The witch was here.

"Do you see it?" Ian asked.

I shook my head, and the ache turned to sharp, shiny needles of pain. I fell to my knees; I could hear nothing but the thunder from the sky that pounded in my ears like the beat of my dying heart.

A thud drew my attention. Ian lay on his back, eyes wide, face contorted. He groped at his chest. Beneath his palms, beneath the tatters of his shirt, his skin rippled and pulsed as something fought to break free.

"No," I managed. "Take me."

Laughter swirled around the room—both human and birdlike—mocking my foolishness. The Raven Mocker was going to take us both.

My chest on fire, my head threatening to explode from lack of oxygen, I reached for Ian's hand. I was surprised when his squeezed mine.

"Say the words," he whispered. "Believe the magic."

I tilted my face to the night, felt the rain on my fiery skin. I shouted the words in Cherokee into the raging night. I knew what every single one of them meant.

A hum began in the air, electricity all around. Behind my closed eyelids I saw my great-grandmother. I remembered how she'd leaped onto a boulder, how she'd growled at that bear. I knew she'd had magic, and I wanted to be magic, too. I would do anything to keep the witch from hurting the one I loved.

Ian cried out in agony; a snarl came from my lips. Feral fury, the need to defend my mate, a prowling wildness erupted within, and I opened my eyes.

The Raven Mocker hovered in front of me—a huge bird with a wingspan that brushed the walls of the cabin, red glowing eyes in a black beaked face; its shriek shook the mountain. The creature looked nothing like Quatie, not that a resemblance would have stopped me from doing what I had to do.

"Die," I said in a voice that hovered between woman and beast.

Sparks blazed from the wings; lightning flashed above, seeming to spill a celestial glow in a column from the clouds to the earth; thunder rumbled, first loudly, then softer and softer until it blended in with the sound of the rain.

The Raven Mocker screamed one last time before crumpling to the ground, and the pain in my chest eased.

Ian struggled to sit up. I scooted closer, put my arm around him, and together we watched as the raven became Adsila, then her face took on the countenance of everyone she'd killed, ending with Katrine. I wondered if we'd ever find her body.

Last, she became Quatie again and I experienced a moment of sadness for the loss of the woman she'd once been; then she slowly turned to dust and blew away on the remnants of the storm.

"You did it," Ian said. I turned, and he brushed his fingertips along my cheekbones, his expression one of wonder. "You have the power of a panther."

I didn't feel any different, although when I glanced through the open door I could see a lot farther than normal in the total darkness of the mountain beneath a cloud-filled sky. I could hear tiny, furry things rustling in the bushes; I could smell them, too, and my stomach contracted in hunger. I had to fight the urge to run into that darkness and hunt those scrumptious creatures.

"How do I put myself back?" I asked, a little weirded out by the temptation to chase and to kill.

"Close your eyes and say, '*Ahnigi'a.*'"

"Which means?"

"'Leave.'"

I did as he said, and when I opened my eyes again, I couldn't see past the threshold or hear much beyond the whirl of the wind.

"You were amazing," Ian said, and kissed me.

I clung. I'd nearly lost him. Hell, I'd nearly lost me. The remnants of what I'd done made me shaky, but I also felt stronger, better, more myself than I'd felt in my whole life.

"Ow." Ian's hand went to his damaged mouth.

"Sorry."

"*I* kissed *you*. I thought we were dead, Grace."

"You and me both."

"What changed? The first time you said the spell nothing happened."

I looked away, uncertain if I should tell him what I knew. That he was my soul mate, my future, my everything. I wasn't certain I could survive if he left me, too. Not after this.

"I remembered my great-grandmother, how she'd protected me, and—" I stopped, uncertain.

"You did the same."

I shrugged. "Yeah."

"You took care of not only yourself but me, too."

"That's my job."

"Was it?" he asked. "Just your job?"

I hesitated, still afraid to reveal my heart, afraid to have it broken again, this time for good. His job was dangerous; it was only a matter of time until something evil ended him. I wasn't sure I could survive that.

"We should get back." I refused to meet his eyes. "Claire's probably called the Marines by now."

Woof.

I glanced toward the door. Great. The messenger wolf was back.

"What is it?" Ian followed my gaze.

I wasn't sure. The witch was dead; what else did Grandmother have to tell me?

She threw back her head and howled, long, loud, lonely, and I understood her as clearly as if she'd spoken. Better to have some time with Ian than none at all. No matter what happened, at least we'd have love. We'd both nearly lost our lives tonight, and we needed to—

"Seize the day," I said.

"Excuse me?"

"I love you."

"I love you back. What brought that on?"

I glanced at the wolf, but she was gone. I must be headed down the right path.

I returned my gaze to Ian. "Hard to say."

He lifted a brow, but he didn't press for more of an answer than that.

"*Carpe diem,* huh?" Ian brushed loose hair out of my face and smiled. "Seize the day?" I nodded, and he ran his thumb over my lips. "How about we *carpe noctem,* too?"

I grabbed the tip of his thumb between my teeth, then suckled it until his brown eyes flickered topaz. "Would that be 'seize the night'?"

"Yes," he said, and began to unbutton my uniform. "Just be careful of the lip."

37

I WAS RIGHT about Claire calling the Marines.

Or at least one Marine—Cal—who'd brought every cop in town. Luckily, they weren't as good at tracking as I was, and by the time they'd found us, Ian and I were dressed and making our way down the mountain.

We'd gotten our story straight—a garbled tale of jealousy and obsession, starring Adsila. She'd wanted Ian; she'd taken him. I'd taken him back, and she'd taken off. Cal would be occupied trying to find her for days. By the time he realized she was nowhere to be found, there'd be something new to worry about.

Quatie's disappearance could be laid at Adsila's door as well. She'd wanted the land; she'd buried her great-great-grandmother in the forest somewhere. We'd never find Quatie, either. Only Ian and I—and Claire, Mal, and Doc—would know why.

Doc met us at the cars. "Everything all right?" he asked, eyes searching mine.

"Dandy," I said, and he nodded once in understanding. His gaze said he'd expect a complete report when we had time alone. I'd be happy to oblige.

"Claire wants you to come straight to her house," Cal said when Doc had patched Ian up the best he could.

Ian refused to go to the hospital. "I've got better cures at my clinic than any hospital could ever hope for."

Remembering my black eye and how quickly it had faded, I shrugged and drove him home.

"I'll just run to Claire's and fill her in," I said.

"Come back soon." He kissed me, gingerly because of the lip.

"Put some of that gunk on your mouth," I called as he went inside.

Claire ran onto the porch as soon as I pulled up. She didn't wait for me to reach her but flew down the steps and threw herself at me.

"Hey, people will say we're in love," I quipped as she hugged me so tightly I had to fight for breath.

Claire let me go. "Don't ever do that again."

"No problem," I agreed, though I knew if I had to do it over, I'd do exactly the same thing. If we had any other supernatural problems—and considering our track record, I had to think we might—I'd do whatever I had to do to keep the people I loved safe.

I followed Claire inside. The house was quiet; it was just the two of us.

She tossed me a beer; I drank half in one gulp. Then I filled her in on everything that had happened.

"You can make your eyes go panther?" she asked.

"Yeah. It was—" I'd been about to say *weird,* but I changed it to, "Pretty cool."

"Let me see."

"Now?"

"Why not?"

I shrugged. *Yeah, why not?*

I closed my eyes and chanted the spell in Cherokee, felt the power, the magic, the belief, flow through me, and when I opened my eyes again, Claire narrowed hers. "Don't tell Elise or Edward."

"Don't worry," I said, then murmured, *"Ahnigi'a,"* and felt the magic fade. "Elise would want to take me apart and see what made me . . . well, me. Edward would just want to shoot me."

"They're slightly predictable in their reactions to shape-shifters."

"I didn't shape-shift."

"But you might. Considering this was the first time you tried it . . ." She took a sip of her own beer. "There's no telling what you could do with a little practice."

I hadn't thought of that. I wasn't sure I wanted to, despite any childhood dreams to the contrary. There's a difference between seeing like a panther and actually being one.

We worked out our strategy for what we'd say to the people of Lake Bluff to explain all the autopsies and the exhumations. Doc had already laid the groundwork for the virus excuse. Now we'd claim *false alarm* and everyone could go back to their lives. If the medical examiner, the sheriff, and the mayor all agreed, and the news was good, I didn't think we'd have too many people pressing the issue.

I'd learned in my years as an elected official that most citizens didn't want to know the truth.

"We'd better call Elise," Claire said. "Tell her what happened so she can check the Raven Mocker off her list. You know how anal she is."

"You do it. Now that I've actually accessed my inner panther, I doubt she and I will ever get along."

"You weren't ever going to get along anyway," Claire said, and dialed.

I drank the rest of my beer as I waited for Claire to speak. When she didn't, I lowered the can. The expression on her face made me stand. "What is it?"

"No one's answering."

Someone always answered the *Jäger-Sucher* hotline. *Always.* Although the last time I'd called, the place had sounded frantic.

Claire hung up and tried again. She listened, shook her head, and disconnected. "I'll try tomorrow."

I suddenly felt antsy. I wanted to see Ian. Now.

"I'd better go." I set my empty can on the counter. Claire followed me to the door and hugged me again. I let her. Last summer when she'd nearly died by were-wolf, it had taken me a while to get over it.

As I walked to the clinic, the sky cleared and a lopsided moon spilled silver across the rooftops. God, I loved this town.

The front door stood ajar. Shaking my head at Ian's absentmindedness, I slipped in. I followed his voice upstairs to his office where he stood at the window, talking on the phone.

He'd showered and now wore loose cotton pants and nothing else. His hair was wet; the eagle feather lay on the desk next to a jar of balm. Even from the doorway, I could see the bruises on his back and across his ribs. I got angry all over again.

"I think at one time Quatie read about the Raven Mocker in Rose Scott's papers." He paused. "No, she didn't say that, but it makes sense. She read the spell, and when her body began to break down she remembered and performed it."

For several seconds he listened to whoever was on the other end of the line.

"You're sure they're all missing?" Ian cursed. "Okay. Right. I'll be there in the morning." He hung up but didn't turn around. "You heard?"

I nodded, then realized he couldn't see and cleared my throat. "You're leaving me?"

He spun around. "No. Of course not."

"But—"

"Grace," he said softly. "Just because I have to leave doesn't mean I'm leaving you. Didn't you ever wonder why I opened a clinic in this town when I've never stayed more than the time it took me to kill something in any other?"

"Why?"

"I'm tired of wandering. I need a home."

"You're coming back?"

He crossed the room and pulled me against him. "Have so many people left that you don't know they sometimes come back?" I nodded. "I'll come back."

"Unless something kills you."

"I've been doing this for years. Not a scratch on me."

I stared pointedly at his beaten face. He shrugged. "Until tonight."

I walked to the desk, picked up the balm, and screwed off the top; then I spread it gently over his skin just as he'd once done for me.

His gaze remained on mine. "I'd never ask you to quit being a cop. It's part of who you are. But I wish you could—"

I stopped spreading the goo. "What?"

"Come with me."

I considered it. I'd be good at chasing monsters. I'd save more people helping Ian than I did protecting Lake Bluff from the tourists—although there'd been more than tourists here lately. Still—

"I can't."

He smiled and kissed the inside of my wrist. "I know. Lake Bluff is where you belong. It's where I belong now, too. Even if we hadn't found each other . . ." His voice trailed off, and he glanced out the window at the distant hills of blue. "I'd come back here just for them."

I linked my fingers with his. I hadn't known him long, but the bonds we shared—the mountains, our heritage, what we knew about the world that so few others did—gave us a history that went much deeper than mere days.

"When you say you want a home, does that include a family?"

"Don't they go together?"

"Not for everyone."

"For me and for you, too. The way you look at Noah, Grace—" He smiled, and everything I wanted was in his eyes. "I never thought I'd be able to love again. I couldn't take the chance that I'd get someone else killed. But tonight—you were unbelievable—your power, your strength, your courage. I know you'll be safe, and our children, too, because of who you are and what you can do."

Later, much later, when we were all wrapped up together on his bed, I thought to ask, "Who's missing?"

"The *Jäger-Suchers*."

I remembered Elise's phone ringing and ringing and felt a trickle of dread. "All of them?"

"Yes."

"That's impossible."

"So are werewolves, vampires, and witches."

"Very funny." Except I didn't feel at all like laughing.

Without the *Jäger-Suchers* to keep the call of the monsters down to a dull roar, the human race was in big trouble.

"What are you going to do?" I asked.

"Search for them, and take up the slack."

"You're going to be gone for a while."

He shifted so he could see my face. "Probably."

"Okay." I kissed him. "I'll be right here when you get back."

EPİLOGUE

F<small>ROM THE</small> *National Enquirer*

Werewolves Attack Small Town in Northern Maine

Under seige during a terrible blizzard, the residents of Harper's Landing watched their numbers dwindle as the number of werewolves increased.

They were saved when an old man with a heavy German accent walked out of the storm carrying guns and silver ammunition. Within days, every werewolf was dead, and the old gentleman disappeared as mysteriously as he'd arrived.

"Edward," I murmured. I knew he was too tough to die.

I read a lot of stories like those over the next few years. The *Jäger-Suchers* had gone into hiding, popping up here and there, usually in the annals of magazines and newspapers catering to the bizarre. Sometimes I recognized Edward's signature. Sometimes the stories mentioned a gorgeous blonde or a shaggy white wolf and I knew Elise was still alive, too. Other tales told of people I didn't know, but I could recognize the handiwork of a *Jäger-Sucher* anywhere. When there were a lot of ashes left behind, it was kind of obvious.

No one ever got close enough to them to find out just what in hell was going on, why they'd disappeared, how they'd managed to continue their work, but they did.

And because of the *Jäger-Suchers*, the human race not only survived; we thrived.

Read on for an excerpt from
Lori Handeland's upcoming book

MARKED BY THE MOON

COMING SOON FROM ST. MARTIN'S PAPERBACKS

1

She'd been following the man for a week. She'd been after him for a month. Werewolves weren't that easy to find.

They weren't that easy to kill either, but she managed. Once upon a time Alexandra Trevalyn had been a member of an elite special forces monster-hunting unit known as the *Jager-Suchers*. Then they'd gone soft, and she'd gone rogue.

Night had fallen over LA hours ago. Once she might have stared at the sky, dreaming about . . . Well, she really couldn't remember what she'd dreamed. Seeing her father die at fifteen had turned any dreams Alex had ever had into nightmares. Tonight she was just glad the moon was full and soon the guy would shape-shift. Then she'd shoot him.

But, as usual, nothing ever went according to plan.

Suddenly the man appeared before her. Her heart gave one quick, painful thud before she controlled the panic. Werewolves drank the smell of fear like vampires drank blood, gaining both pleasure and sustenance.

"Hey, Jorge," she said. "*Que pasa*?"

His eyes narrowed. "Why you followin' me, *puta*?"

"Nice. You kiss your mother with that mouth?"

"My mother is dead."

"Since you killed her, I guess you'd know."

"You a cop?"

"You wish."

Confusion flickered over his face. "Why would I wish that?"

"Because a cop wouldn't know how to kill a werewolf."

He growled, the sound no longer quite human. But instead of shifting into a wolf, he grabbed her, too intent on pawing her breasts, squeezing them as if he were checking for the best set of melons in the local produce section, to watch her hands.

"Little girls who come looking for the big bad wolf usually find him," he muttered in a voice that hovered between beast and man.

"I always do," she said, and fired the gun she'd slipped from the back of her pants while Jorge was squeezing the melons.

Fire shot from the wound, a common reaction whenever a werewolf met silver. Alex tore herself away from his still-clutching fingers and patted at the flecks of flame dotting her black blouse. Then she emptied the rest of her clip into his body, just to be sure, and watched him burn. It was her favorite part.

Luckily they were in a section of LA where gunshots didn't draw any notice. Jorge had led her here, and she'd followed gladly.

Still, she probably should have waited for the change before she'd shot him. The powers that be wrote off barbequed beast a whole lot easier than barbequed man. However, Jorge hadn't given her much choice. She certainly wasn't going to let him kill her. Or worse.

"You think shooting a dead man more than once will make him anymore dead?"

Alex spun toward the voice, beneath which she could hear the familiar trill of an inhuman growl. A man lounged against the nearest abandoned building as if he'd been there for hours.

Except he hadn't been there a few minutes ago. No one had.

He was big—probably six-three, about two twenty, and dressed in loose black slacks, a black long-sleeved shirt, his hair covered with a dark knit cap. The outfit was a bit warm for the balmy California night, but then so was hers. The better to conceal guns and knives and other shiny things, the easier to slink with the shadows or even disappear into them.

Alex couldn't determine the color of his eyes beneath the moon and the smog-induced shadows, but she thought they might be light like hers, blue perhaps instead of green.

She'd never seen him before; she'd remember, but that didn't mean anything. There were werewolves all over the place.

He strolled toward her as if he had all the time in the world, as if he had no fear of the gun, and that made Alex twitchier than him being here in the first place.

What man didn't fear a gun? What beast didn't fear the silver inside it?

Then in a sudden flash that made her stomach drop and her head lighten, Alex remembered . . .

She'd used every last bullet on Jorge.

She went for a clip, and his arm shot forward, blurring with speed. She braced for the punch that could knock her ten yards. Instead, he touched her with a metal object. She had one thought—*stun gun*—before she fell.

He leaned over her, and she knew she was dead. She waited for the violence, the pain, the blood. Instead, there was a sharp prick; then everything went black.

She awoke to a small room lit by a single bare bulb. She ached everywhere, and her mouth was as dry as an August wind. Her clothes were still on, but she couldn't detect the weight of any weapons—no gun, no ammo, no silver stiletto blade. Without them, Alex felt naked anyway.

Her shoulder-length, light brown hair had come loose from the tight twist she preferred when working and now covered her face. She moved only her eyes as she took stock of the surroundings—four walls, a door, and the man who'd done this to her seated at a rickety wooden table nearby.

Alex was tied to a cot, and though she wanted to yank at the bonds, see how strong they were, instead she lay still, breathing slowly and evenly, in and out. She knew better than to let on that she was awake before she figured out everything she could about where she was.

She studied her kidnapper through the curtain of her hair as he leaned his elbows on the table, staring at something between them. From the sag of his shoulders he seemed sad, almost devastated, but she'd never known a werewolf to feel bad about anything, unless it was missing a kill.

He'd removed the knit cap, and his golden hair shone beneath the light. He'd drawn the length away from his face with a rubber band to reveal sharp angles at cheek and chin, as well as the shadow of a beard across his jaw.

He turned his head. His eyes were the shade of the sky right after the sun has disappeared—cool and blue, dark with vanished warmth. For an instant Alex could have sworn she saw a flash of russet at the center, which made her think of the flames of hell that awaited him just as soon as she got her gun back.

Hey, everyone has their fantasies.

"Alexandra Trevalyn," he murmured, getting slowly to his feet. "I've been waiting for this a long time."

He crossed the short distance between them and pushed her hair out of her face, then grabbed her chin, holding on tightly when she struggled.

"Look at her," he said in a voice that chilled despite the heat in his eyes.

He dangled whatever he'd been looking at in front of her. One glance at the photograph—a woman, pretty and young, blond and laughing—and Alex closed her eyes.

Ah, hell.

"You know her?" His fingers tightened hard enough to bruise.

Alex knew her all right. She'd killed her.

⊙⊙⊙

Julian Barlow could barely stomach putting his hands on the murdering bitch. He was torn between an intense desire to release her and an equally strong urge to crush her face between his fingers, listen to the bones snap, hear her scream. But that would be too easy.

For her.

He had something much better planned.

She tried to jerk from his grasp, but he was too strong, and she only ended up hissing in a sharp, pained breath when he tightened his grip even more.

"Her name was Alana," he said, "and she was my wife."

Alexandra's nose wrinkled in distaste. "She was a werewolf."

"She was a person."

"No." Her eyes met his, and in them he saw her utter conviction. "She wasn't."

Just as all people weren't the same, all werewolves weren't either. Some *were* evil, demonic, out of control beasts. But his wife—

Julian's throat tightened, and he had to struggle against the despair that haunted him. He'd do what he'd come to do; then maybe, just maybe, he'd be able to sleep.

Julian drew in a deep breath and frowned. He didn't smell fear. His eyes narrowed, but all he saw on Alexandra's face was a stoic resignation.

"Get it over with," she said.

"What is it you think I brought you here to do?"

"Die."

"You wish."

Alexandra's teeth ground together as he repeated the words she'd used to Jorge. He released her with a dismissive flick of the wrist. Best to get it over with as she'd said.

Lifting his fingers to the buttons of his shirt, Julian undid them one after the other, then let the dark garment slide to the floor. Her eyes widened, and she let her gaze wander over him. Wherever that gaze touched, goose-flesh rose. He didn't want her looking at him, but he didn't have much choice.

Julian lowered his hands to his trousers, and her eyes followed. But as soon as he unbuttoned the single button, they jerked up to meet his. The sound of the zipper shrieked through the heavy, waiting silence.

She started, paled, and it was then that he at last smelled her fear.

"Dying doesn't scare you," he murmured as he eased his thumb beneath the waistband of the black pants and drew them over his hips. "Let's see what does."

"You're going to have a mighty hard time raping me with that," she sneered, lifting her chin toward his limp member.

"Rape?" He yanked the tie from his ponytail and let his hair swirl loose. "Not my style."

Confusion flickered over her face. "Then what's with the striptease?"

Instead of answering, he threw back his head and howled.

The scent of her fear called to his beast. He'd dreamed of this, of her, planned it, lived for it. He wanted Alexandra Trevalyn to understand what she had done, suffer for it a very long time, and there was only one way that could happen.

Julian's body bowed as his spine altered. Bones crackled, joints popped; his nose and mouth lengthened into a snout. Hands and feet became paws, claws sprouted where finger- and toenails had been. When he fell to the ground on all fours, golden hair shot from every pore. Last but not least, a tail and ears appeared as he became a wolf in every way but two—human eyes in an inhuman face, human intelligence in the guise of an animal.

"No one can shift that fast." He swung his head toward the woman, who stared at him wide-eyed.

Having once been a *Jager-Sucher*, she had to know the basics. To paraphrase Shakespeare: There *were* more things in heaven and earth than could ever be dreamt of.

And Julian was one of them.

He had been born centuries ago, and with age comes not only wisdom but talent, at least to a werewolf. The older Julian got, the faster he changed.

He stalked toward her on stiff legs, ruff standing on end, upper lip pulled back. Her jaw tightened as she tried not to cringe, but her body wouldn't obey her mind's command. His hot breath cascaded over her arm, her neck, her face. She was helpless. He could do anything that he wanted. She knew it, and her fear whirled around him like a mid-summer fog.

Had this been what Alana had felt in the moments before she died? Or hadn't she had a chance to feel anything before this child had shot her with silver, then watched her burn? A growl rumbled in Julian's throat.

The girl tensed and shouted, "Do it!"

So Julian sank his teeth into her shoulder.

◯◯◯

Alex refused to scream even though the pain was worse than anything she'd ever known. Multicolored dots danced before her eyes; then the world wavered, shimmered, and disappeared.

Hours, moments, seconds later, she came awake sputtering. Someone had thrown water into her face.

The werewolf, now in human form—he'd even gotten dressed—leaned over her, empty plastic bottle crunched in his huge hand. "Soon," he murmured, "you'll understand."

Her shoulder on fire, she was weak, dizzy, feverish, but she remembered everything, and the horror of it almost made her retch.

"You bastard!" Alex shouted, pulling at her bonds. "You bit me."

"You told me to," he said.

"I didn't. I'd never—"

"Did you or did you not shout, 'Do it!'"

"I meant tear out my throat. *Kill* me."

If a werewolf *bit* a human, the human become a werewolf. If the ravenous beast ate and/or killed the victim, blessed death was the result.

Her tormentor tilted his head, and his long hair slid across his neck, spreading outward like a golden fan. "You'd rather be dead," he murmured, "than a werewolf."

"Damn straight."

"And my wife would rather have been a werewolf than dead." He shrugged, unconcerned. "I guess you're even."

Frustration and fury welled within her. She yanked on her bonds again, and the cot rattled as she lifted first one side, then the other from the floor. She was already getting stronger.

"Let me go." He did nothing but laugh. "Why are you doing this?"

"I want you to understand what you've done."

"I killed monsters. Evil, demonic creatures that belonged in hell."

"You killed wives and husbands, mothers and fathers, someone's children. You think we don't love? You think we don't mourn?"

"Animals don't feel."

He grabbed her by the chin again. "You're wrong."

Alex should have a huge bruise from when he'd wolfhandled her before. His touch *should* hurt, but it didn't. She was already healing faster than humanly possible.

He let go of her with a flick of his wrist, as if he couldn't bear to have his skin in contact with hers for one second longer than necessary—she knew the feeling—and walked away. Alex had to crane her neck to watch him disappear out the door.

"Hey!" she shouted, then paused. Would she be better or worse off if he left her behind?

The question became moot when he reappeared carrying an inert body, which he placed on the floor.

"Don't worry." He walked to the door again, drawing it closed behind him. "He's a very bad man."

As soon as he was gone, Alex fought to get loose in earnest.

He'd bitten her instead of killing her, then tied her down and left her in a room with a helpless human being. She had to pull free and run, then find a silver . . . anything and kill herself before she changed. Because as soon as she did, she'd need human blood, and there was some right here.

Her struggles only served to make her sweat. The room had no air conditioning, no window. She pulled on the restraints so hard her wrists bled. The scent of blood, of man, made her stomach growl.

Once bitten a human shifted within twenty-four hours. Traditionally werewolves could only change between dusk and dawn—except that first time. Then it didn't matter—day or night, full moon or dark, a new wolf it became. They have no choice.

Suddenly the room vanished, and Alex ran through a dense forest. Warm sun cast dappled shadows through the branches. The cool air seemed to sparkle. The scent of pine surrounded her.

She burst from the trees onto a rolling plain. Here and there patches of snow shone electric white against just-sprung grass threaded with purple wildflowers. In the distance loomed piles of ice that appeared as high as a mountain.

A sense of freedom, of utter joy filled her. She wanted to run across this land forever. It was . . .

Home.

Except Alex had no home. She'd been born in Nebraska—not many mountains there, ice or any other—they were a little short on forests, too. And she hadn't lived in one place for longer than a month since she was five.

She caught the scent of warm blood, of tasty meat, and turned tail—she had one—to return to the forest. Something flashed up ahead, crashing through the brush in terror.

Wham!

Alex fell back into her body, still lying on the cot in the horrendously hot, horribly small room. She wasn't any closer to being released, but from the way her skin felt, too small to contain her, she was much closer to being inhuman.

"Collective consciousness," she muttered. "God."

Once infected, the lycanthropy virus invaded the victim, changing him from human to beast. He began to remember things that had happened to others—the thrill of the chase, the love of the kill, the taste of the blood.

"It's coming," Alex said in a voice that no longer

resembled her own. Deeper, garbled, she'd heard the sound before.

From the mouths of the soon-to-be-furry.

The pain became more of an itch, a need to burst forth. Alex tried to fight that need but couldn't. Her dark jeans and black blouse tore with a rending screech; her boots seemed to explode as her feet turned to paws.

Her nose ached; her teeth were too big for her mouth. Then suddenly that mouth became part of the nose, and those teeth felt just right.

The bonds restraining her popped. She writhed, contorted, snarled, moaned, and when she at last rolled to the floor, she was no longer human but a wolf.

Alex stared at her paws, covered with fur the same shade as her hair; she didn't need a mirror to see that her own green eyes stared out of an animal's face.

The world expanded—sounds sharp as the blade of a knife, smells so intense her mouth watered with desire, she could see every mote of dust tumbling through the air like snowflakes of silver and gold.

Hunger blazed, a pounding pulse in her head. If she didn't eat soon, if she didn't kill something, she thought she might go mad.

Then she saw him—there on the floor, trussed up and still. What was his name?

Oh, yeah. Brunch.

Alex took one step forward, and the door crashed open. The silhouette of a man spread across the floor. She skittered back, startled, growling, then lifted her snout and sniffed. Recognition flickered, just out of reach. She knew him, yet still the hair on her neck lifted as the growl deepened to a snarl.

The urge to attack warred with the clawing hunger in her belly. Her head swung back and forth between the two men as her human intelligence weighed the possibilities.

The bound one could wait; he wasn't going anywhere. Once she took down the newcomer, there'd be twice as much to eat and a lot less to fear.

Her muscles bunched, and she leaped. Before her body began the downward arc that would send her sailing directly into the man in the doorway, a sharp pain bloomed in her chest. Her limbs felt weighted with sand, but strangely her mind cleared, and as she tumbled to the ground, she remembered who he was.

Edward.

Now she was definitely dead.